ROAD TRIPPED

Satan's Devils MC - Utah Chapter #1

COPYRIGHT

Disclaimer

This is a work of fiction. Names, characters, businesses, places, events and incidents are either the products of the author's imagination or used in a fictitious manner. Any resemblance to actual persons, living or dead, or actual events is purely coincidental.

Warning

This book is dark in places and contains content of a sexual, abusive and violent nature. It may not be suitable for persons under the age of 18.

PRODUCTION ACKNOWLEDGMENTS

Cover Design by Wicked Smart Designs

Edited and formatted by Maggie Kern @ Ms.K Edits

Proof reading by Martin Williams

Photographer: Golden Czermak of Furious Fotog

Model: Tyler Bland

SATAN'S DEVILS MC

1

———

*R*oad...

If I was able to, I'd stomp my way across the clubroom as I answer a summons from my prez. Instead, I have to pick my way carefully, concentrating on every step.

"Hey," a sharp voice interrupts. "Where's your fuckin' stick?"

"Don't need it." I round on Peg. "Stay out of my fuckin' business."

He holds up his hands, palms facing outward. "You should use the stick or strap your leg up. You fuckin' fall, you've only yourself to blame. But why should I give a damn about you making it worse and setting yourself back?"

Nothing could make things much worse than they already are. Tossing him a glare, I continue, carefully, trying to walk straight, putting my weight equally on both legs. Which is okay until I step on something and stumble. Luckily, there's a nearby chair that my hand catches hold of to break my fall. Looking down to see what I'd stepped on, I find it's one of the kid's fucking toys. Could be Eli's, Olivia's, Noah's—the list goes on. *Too many fuckin' kids in this clubhouse.* My brothers seem to be breeding like rabbits, but between the club and my sport, I've no time or inclination to find a woman of my own, yet alone a desire to procreate.

Hearing a noise as I catch my breath, I see Peg half out of his seat. I shake my head at him, then righting myself, proceed in the direction I was going with even more care, staring carefully to avoid stepping on half made Lego models or toy motorbikes and cars.

I'm in no better mood when I reach Drummer's office, but why the fuck should I be? A few weeks back, I was all set to take the champion's cup. *Pride comes before a fall*, they say, and my fall had been quite spectacular.

I knock. When Drummer barks out permission to enter, I do and sigh with relief as I make it to the seat he points at without further incident.

That his eyes soften with sympathy really does nothing to improve my mood. "What do you want, Prez?"

Now his gaze changes, hardens, and I'm subjected to his full-on stare. "Should be using the stick," he tells me.

I heft a sigh. "Not you as well. I've just had this from Peg."

"Who knows what he's talking about." He doesn't. Nobody does. Drummer's steel-grey eyes seem to see right down into my soul, then soften as he states, "It was a shame about the championship."

Shame? Something that I've been striving for all my adult life? Is that all it is, a fucking shame? It's a shame when you go to the store and the part you want is out of stock. A shame when you find a stain on your favourite shirt. It's too insignificant a word to use when what you thought impossible a few years back had been so close you could almost touch it, and then to have it snatched out of your grasp. Shame doesn't begin to describe it.

"Have you heard back?"

I don't ask who from. "I'm not allowed to race again."

"This year, or…?"

There's no point lying to Drummer. I tap my head. "Two concussions now. No one wants me to risk a third."

"Then there's your leg."

My anger seeps away, being replaced by a deep sadness. There is, indeed, my leg. The surgeons had done their best to put it back together, but I'm left with a knee that won't always cooperate, the muscles around it being too weak to hold it in place. If I step down on it wrong, it's likely to dislocate. Trial bikes have been developed over the years to handle rough terrain and fast. They are lightweight and are completely stripped of any luxuries or comforts. There's no way in hell I could ride one now.

Drummer nods as though I'd answered a question he hadn't asked. "Wanted to talk to you about your future, Road."

"I can still ride," I spit out, my eyes widening. Drummer can't be talking about throwing me out of the club. No fucking way. I've been on my Harley since my crash, have ridden it with no problem. He's even seen me. Sure, my still-healing leg starts to ache after a while, but I can fulfil the requirements of the club. I can ride.

"Huh," Drummer barks, laughing. "Nothing to stop you still being a member, Road. You've been around this club long enough to know we'd give a man all the time that he needs to come right. Hell, you could lose a limb and we'd wait until you were able to ride again."

"In that case, what do you mean, talk about my future?"

Drummer leans back, linking his hands behind his head. "I can understand what it's like to lose something so important to you, Road. You've been competing in off-road Enduro competitions for years and did fuckin' well. Now, suddenly, you've lost that. I can well understand your frustration. It's turning you into a man I've not seen before. You're on a short fuse, liable to blow if someone looks at you wrong. When you do, it's ugly."

I can't dispute that. Take Peg's observation back in the clubroom and Drummer's opening comment, they'd both been correct. It's easier, and safer walking with a stick, but hell, I could have punched them for just suggesting it, throwing their concern back in their faces. Since I'd returned to the clubhouse after my too long stay in the hospital and rehab, I can't settle. My loss is fucking with my head.

"Brothers, old ladies, even the fuckin' kids are wary of speaking to you, Road."

His pointing it out makes me feel contrite. "I'm sorry. I'll try and do better."

Again his eyes settle on me, and I can't read what he's thinking. *Does he want me to leave, after all?* I know I've become an ogre to live with, but I've got a good excuse. Surely, they'd cut me some slack? Then, perhaps they don't think the loss of everything I ever wanted accounts to much.

Drummer makes me wait until I start fidgeting before he speaks again. "I think you could do with a change of scenery."

What? He is sending me away? "Drum, look, I'm sorry. This has been hard to get my head around, okay? I'll watch what I say, try to keep my temper. Hell if I can't, I'll stay in my room. But please..." I break off, not wanting to beg to my prez, but how else can I plead for him not to send me away? I've gotten used to living at the compound, love my brothers, love the whole damn extended network of old ladies and kids. They're my family. And family should make allowances, shouldn't they?

I suppose I've taken too much for granted—that everyone will have my back when needed. That's unfair, they have had my back. It's more that I've not shown I've appreciated it. That my prez is talking to me this way means I've overextended, stretched their compassion to the limits. Drummer never proposes anything lightly. If he's suggested something, he means it. Maybe the best I can hope for is that if he sends me away, he'll let me come back.

Deliberately, I make my voice less combative and calmer. "Do you mean like Heart?" A few years back, after his wife had been killed, Heart's grief had made him obnoxious and a liability to the club. Drummer had sent him out on the road for six months. He was the proof of such a solution working. He'd used that time to get his head on straight and had returned a changed and better version of himself. In part that might have been down to the woman he'd come back with. Perhaps Drummer thinks he's hit on a winning formula and wants to repeat that experiment.

"No, not like Heart. Nothing of the sort." Unlinking his hands, Drummer now props his elbows on the desk. "I need something sorted, you've got an unease inside you. You need something, a purpose. Am I right?"

I'm not sure where he's going with this, or if the destination is something I'm going to welcome. But I'll play along. "I lost something, Prez. Two things make me get up in the morning. The club, and my racing. Now half of my reason to live has been taken away."

"Can't replace that, Road. Wouldn't know how. But a few weeks off doing work for the club might be just what you need to settle that emptiness inside you."

I can't tell him he's wrong. "What are you thinking, Prez?"

"I've got a problem," he starts, sitting back once again and stroking his beard.

There's not been anything he's raised at church that I can think of. Businesses are running smoothly right now, and there are no known enemies on the horizon. As far as I know, things are relatively quiet. So, I'm intrigued. "What problem?" I prompt.

"Utah."

"Utah?" I scrunch up my face. I know nothing at all about that state, and can't remember it being mentioned.

Drummer strokes his beard, and his eyes narrow. "The Utah chapter to be precise."

My brow furrows further. I don't know much at all about that part of our club. Tucson is the mother chapter of the Satan's Devils MC and Drummer the national president. It's not uncommon that the prezes of the other chapters turn up for official club meetings, hence I've met Utah's prez, Snatcher, and his VP, Thor, on a few occasions and have exchanged pleasantries, but that's about the extent of it. Oh, I also recall they lost a member a year or so back. Utah had been helping the Colorado chapter out and sadly had ridden home without a member called Thumper. He was killed by the mafia, if I recall right. The loss of one of our own, from whatever chapter, is the loss of a brother for any of us, even if we don't know them personally.

Utah doesn't cause trouble and gives support when another club needs it. I have no idea what Drummer's talking about. I ask for clarification. "What's your problem with Utah?"

Drummer rolls his head, then rubs the back of his neck. He looks tired. "I don't know," he replies after a moment. "Gut feel." He gives a quick grin. "Could be an upset stomach, of course."

You don't get to be, and stay, the prez of the mother chapter without having some kind of sixth sense. If Drummer's got an inkling that something is wrong, then he's probably right. I start to run through possibilities.

"Anything like the trouble with San Diego when Dart left to join them? What was it, two, three years ago, now?"

Drummer shakes his head. "More than three. Time flies, doesn't it? Nah, I'm pretty certain it's nothing like that. Snatcher isn't like Snake; he'd never betray the club. He's straight as a die." I don't understand and feel the lines on my brow deepening as Drummer continues, "I can't express it. On the face of it, they're the perfect club. They don't cause trouble, don't seem to go looking for it, and don't hesitate to come to the aid of others. I don't know, Road. Huh, I've a feeling inside me that they're too textbook. They keep themselves to themselves, and I can't get a handle on them. They're doing alright, have money in their coffers, but, fuck. It's hard putting it into words. Something tells me something isn't right." He breaks off, tugs his beard again. "They maybe as flawless as they appear, but I'd sleep better at night if I could be assured of it. I'd like someone to go and check it out."

"You want me to go and set your mind at ease that there's nothing untoward you don't know about?" Seems simple enough. Part of me thinks it's just an excuse to get me away from the club. If Drummer was really worried, wouldn't he send Blade, the enforcer, or Peg the sergeant-at-arms?

He stares at me, contemplating. "Yeah. There's no hurry, Road. It's a long way to ride. Thought perhaps you could take your time, do the journey in easy stages so you don't overdo it and hurt your leg. Stop off, see the sights on the way if you like. Nothing urgent about this."

I'd need to take it slow. My leg plays up if I ride long distances. It sure would be a change of scenery and sounds better than spending the next week or so in the club snapping at everybody. Space and distance might well help me get my head on right, and I can decide what I can do to fill the new gap in my life, or just start to learn how to live with it. Yeah, perhaps it's something I need.

"Sounds like a vacation on the club's dime." I start to grin, feeling the first genuine spark of pleasure for the first time in weeks, and already anticipating the wind on my face. Then I frown. "You sure you're not just getting me out of your hair?"

Drummer snorts a laugh. "Suspicious, ain't ya? No, Road,

I'm not blowing smoke up your ass. I do want to find out how that club ticks. I'll tell you now, I won't be warning Snatcher you're on your way."

My eyes narrow. That's unusual. Sending a brother into the territory of another chapter would normally require a courtesy call, one prez to another. Reading between the lines, Drummer thinks there's something Snatcher might try to cover up. "So I what, just turn up and ask him to show me around?"

Drummer grins. "Yeah. You're just passing and thought you'd be friendly, stop in and say hi."

"You sending me as a nomad?"

He raises his chin toward me. "No official role. Just a brother taking it slow as he heals up. While you're there, you listen, learn and report back."

"Prez," I choose my words carefully. "Are you sure I'm the right person? I know my limitations. Give me a bike and I'll tell you what's wrong with it. Show me a puzzle, and I'll not see what part's out of place. Can you give me a clue as to the kind of shit you want me to look out for?"

His eyes pierce me again. "Don't put yourself down, Road," he snaps. "When you were a bouncer at the strip club, you showed initiative. Wouldn't have made you the manager if you hadn't done that. Since then, you've increased the takings, got the books straight so Dollar has no complaints. You might not have a fancy degree or much schooling, but life has shaped you well. I have no problem sending you out to be my eyes and ears."

I reckon it's more that most other brothers have old ladies and children, and wouldn't want to go. But I'll take his words at face value. Maybe others have already turned him down.

"As to what to look out for, I can't help you there. But you know how this club runs. Just look out for anything different to the ordinary. Sometimes," he shrugs, "it's hard to say. But when I speak to Snatcher, it almost seems too rosy in that part of the woods."

"You think they might be into something illegal?"

Another rise and fall of his shoulders. "I'd say no and feel it's unlikely. But that's for you to find out, and then, for me to know."

This is not just going to be a simple visit to another chapter, such as when I've visited Red's chapter in Vegas, or Demon's in Colorado when I'd ridden up to see Beef. It might be a chance to socialise and have a drink with a new set of brothers, but it looks like my role is more of a spy. Hmm.

"Road?" Drummer gets my attention. "I don't think there's anything to worry about. Snatcher doesn't give me that vibe. Not questioning his loyalty. Not going to forget he lost Thumper in Colorado. I just want something to put my gut at rest. If I thought it was going to be dangerous, I'd not send you on your own."

If he's done nothing else, he's given me something to think about which doesn't revolve around my lost sport. Feeling more lighthearted, I raise my eyebrow. "You sure I can't just get you some Pepto-Bismol?"

Drummer snorts. "Get out of here, Road."

2

———

*R*oad...

The Satan's Devils are loyal supporters of American-built bikes, with the vast majority riding Harleys, though there are a few Indians dotted around the other chapters. Despite my vast experience of riding and having my own trial bike on which I'd already won competitions, they only let me join as a prospect on the condition that I got myself what to them was a proper bike.

Of course, I kept my off-road bike, but bought myself an old Harley. Apart from the difference in weight and that I couldn't ride it on tracks, I soon settled to the relative comfort. It had two wheels, and I wasn't confined like I'd be in a cage, so what was there not to like about it? The benefit was admission to the Satan's Devils MC and the ready-made family I was fast accepted as a part of.

After my prospecting time was done and I'd become a full member, the extra money in my paycheck and no living expenses, as I lived at the club, meant I could trade in my road-legal bike for a real trials model. One for which things like lights and indicators were sacrificed to make it as fast and manoeuvrable as possible. I also, recently, upgraded my Harley to a more reliable and newer version. The seat is soft, padded, and probably to compensate for the discomfort of the trials bike, I'd gone for all the comforts of a tourer. A perfect bike for the five hundred and fifty miles I needed to go.

I've done twenty-four-hour endurance races. An eight-hour ride would normally be nothing to me, but even despite the comfort of the Harley, now riding for long distances with my leg in the same position had muscles screaming after much more than an hour, so I broke up my journey as Drummer had suggested. Being an all-expenses paid trip, I felt no qualms picking places better than the cheapest dump to stay each night, enjoying a different environment, and being in no rush to get anywhere.

Riding only two or three hours each day, it took me three days to reach Utah.

Away from my brothers and their old ladies, all trying unsuccessfully to help in their own way, I'd enjoyed the solitude. My mind was cleared by wind therapy as I rode, my nights spent eating and drinking alone. Being left to my own devices did indeed give me the space I needed to examine the thoughts in my head.

At first my mind was filled with hate and anger, directed solely at the rider who'd taken one chance too many and had ended my riding career. We raced, pushing our bikes to their top speed, our skills using brake, clutch and gears to take that jump, twist or turn and land safely. Our aim to stay shiny side up, and in front of, or at least clear of, other competitors.

Being top class riders, ours was a close-knit community, seeing the same faces at race after race. Decker hadn't been a newcomer, but he did have a reputation as a risk taker. As did we all. You didn't make it to the top without pushing your chances. I don't know what he'd been thinking, he'd been going too fast for the turn ahead. I'd braked in anticipation, he hadn't. He clipped my rear wheel and I'd gone down in the dirt, slid over the edge and into a shallow, *thank fuck*, ravine.

Of course, he'd walked away with only a dented bike and ego, leaving me broken, my bike a wreck wedged on top of me. I'd been knocked unconscious but had seen the pictures. When I got out of the hospital and had saw for myself the twisted metal that had once been my pride possession, I was gutted. Not that it had really mattered, bikes could be replaced, but not, apparently, my riding career and my chance to travel the world and ride in international championships. That first day when I left Tucson in my rearview, all I could think of was how angry I was. Decker was already racing again.

The second day, the sun shone brightly. My eyes were caught by a hawk high up in the cloudless sky. I began to feel some of the ire inside me slip away as, at last, some of the negative feelings eased their grip on me, and I started to find positive ones to focus on instead.

Sure my leg's busted, but it will get stronger and mend. Not as good as before, but I'll soon be walking without the aid of a stick again. Even today I woke up to find it was a little steadier and more able to support my weight. I'm still able to ride, just not competitively. It could have been worse, I could be dead.

As the distance from Tucson increased, I felt lighter, and rather than looking back, looked forward instead.

Still unconvinced this is anything other than Drummer wanting to get me and my bad mood away from the club, I resolve if this is a job he really needs done, I'll do it to the best of my ability. There's a small burn of pride inside me, knowing he's trusting me to go to a different chapter as the representative of the mother chapter prez. Despite my shows of temper, he's trusting me to make a good impression. I hold

Drummer in high respect, so I'll make every endeavour to keep a hold on my temper.

This morning will see me complete the last leg of my journey. I feel refreshed as I wake, ready to take on the world. I settle up at the reception desk of the decent enough hotel I'd found to rest up my leg—I didn't ask for much—cleanliness, a comfortable bed and a place to park my bike—and this place hadn't disappointed.

Heading out to my bike, I buckle on the saddlebags and program the GPS. Kicking down into gear, I turn onto the highway, and follow the route the device on my handlebars suggests.

The miles tick down. I'm riding at a steady speed, the predicted time of arrival doesn't change. As my destination draws closer, twin emotions of expectation and apprehension start to war within me. *What if there's something wrong as Drummer suggested?* Nah, there can't be much, and he didn't have strong suspicions. If he had, he'd have sent someone with me. Still, I can't quite shake this sense of unease.

Two miles to go, one mile. I make the turns indicated by the GPS, and then begin to pull up, rolling the bike to a halt. Damn. While the electronic device had gotten me the majority of the way without leading me wrong, now it seems to have made a mistake. This can't be the Satan's Devils' clubhouse. Without turning off the engine, I look around to see if there's a ramshackle building or auto-shop I might have missed.

Of course, I don't have a clue what I'm looking for. I certainly wasn't expecting an old vacation resort like we've got in Tucson, or even a disused airstrip like in San Diego. Maybe something more akin to the old warehouse in Vegas, or the steel mill in Pueblo. But this? Nah. Can't be it. Through the gates I'm currently sitting in front of, I see a modern steel and glass building on the edge of an industrial estate. *This can't be right. Perhaps where I want is around the back?*

Apart from being in likely looking locations, our other chapters also have large signs announcing we're the Satan's Devils MC. Well, why not? Local law enforcement knows exactly where to find us—no point in hiding. But here there's nothing over the gate to suggest who lives and works here. Live? Well, nothing screams out clubhouse to me.

I check the address once again and take out my phone. My map app agrees this is where I'm meant to be. The road is right, and so is the number. *Has Drummer got this wrong?*

Only one way to find out, go inside and ask. I must be near enough to be given directions. I pull through the unmanned gate and halt outside the door, noticing the parking lot is devoid of bikes. Switching off the engine, I drag my stick from the mount Blade had put on for me. While I practiced walking without it when I vacated the hotel, my leg is cramping from riding, and I can't risk falling flat on my face when faced with strangers. That would make an awkward introduction, or someone might think I was drunk.

Approaching the rotating front door, I know this isn't the right place, but hopeful that as it's a business, someone inside can redirect me to where I need to be. Before I enter the rotating glass door, I notice a holder with a printed card slipped inside and peer closer to read the writing to see what type of business this is. I'm shocked as hell to read *Satan's Devils MC. Utah Chapter.*

I pause, frown, and hastily revise my ideas. Hefting my cut so it sits easier on my shoulders, the colours I only put on when I knew I was back in Satan's Devils territory, I step into one of the quarters. The door begins to move automatically. Walking forward in the semi-circle, I step out into a reception area—the kind you'd expect to find in any office building.

There's even a desk, behind which sits a man. He's wearing

a cut similar to mine, and immediately I feel more relaxed. He looks up as I enter.

"Can I help you?" His eyes move down from my face and fall on my cut. He frowns, stands, and turns to reach under his desk. The back of his cut is revealed as he does. It reads, *Prospect.* I'm not surprised. It would be stranger to find a patched member manning the front desk. I do suspect he's reaching for a weapon. All he knows so far is that I've arrived on a motorcycle and have entered wearing colours. The three patches on my back he hasn't yet seen.

"Roadrunner." I offer my name, and a chin lift. "Satan's Devils MC, Tucson Chapter."

If I thought I'd put him at ease with my introduction, I'm wrong. It would appear I've put him off balance.

"I wasn't told to expect you." His eyes widen, and he seems unclear what to do or say next. I notice he offers no brotherly welcome, but maybe that's because he's not patched in yet.

I don't need to explain anything to a prospect. "Your prez around?"

His face goes blank.

I roll my eyes. "Snatcher, your prez."

"They're all in church." He offers the explanation as though it will dismiss me.

It's Wednesday, and they're in church? *In the middle of a workday?* Of course, it's not unusual to have meetings called at any time when there's a need. I wonder whether something urgent had come up. Could even be something their discussing that Drummer needs to know about. That's exactly what I've been sent to find out, and there's no reason not to do just that. I'm a patched member of the Satan's Devils MC. Visiting members are always invited to sit around our table in Tucson, here shouldn't be any different. Cut one of us, we all bleed Satan's Devils' blood.

There's something about the attitude of this prospect

which annoys me. He's too cocky and too reluctant to offer help. Prospecting's not so far in my rearview that I don't remember having to jump to attention and give a member whatever he wanted, whatever chapter he was from. If I wasn't as obliging as fuck, I wouldn't be getting my patch, had been ingrained in me. This man, though? He doesn't seem to give a damn.

"Where's your meeting room?" I ask, making a snap decision.

He stares at me for a moment. His mouth opens and shuts, and his hands rise, then he lowers them again. He seems flustered as he raises his chin, obviously unable to think of any other course of action. "This way." He pauses halfway down a carpeted corridor and holds out his hand. "Gun, knife and phone."

It's not an odd request. Most chapters don't allow weapons or such devices in church. A habit ingrained from back in the days when disagreements could turn bloody, or conversations not meant for other's ears recorded. It's still the way we do it in Tucson. Well, phones anyway. Heaven forbid if we ever tried to take away Blade's knives. Mouse, our computer expert, is hot on our phones being hacked and there are apps which can be installed which somehow keep microphones live. Sci-fi shit to me.

I do wonder the reason for it here. Utah knows fuck all about tech, hasn't even got an equivalent of Mouse. Maybe they don't trust each other that much here. Thinking nothing of it, it's probable they've never moved on. We've always considered them an old-fashioned club. I pass over my gun and phone. The prospect carefully locks them in a box, then knocks on a door and opens it.

The table is a stretched oval shape, with two definite ends. I look at what I assume is the head of the table, then, when that doesn't reveal the man I would know as soon as I saw him, I move my eyes to the opposite end, words to introduce myself already on my lips as I ready myself to greet Snatcher, President of the Utah Chapter of the Satan's Devils MC.

"I..."

That's all I get out before I realise I don't recognise the man seated at the head of the table at all. The man to his left, though, is Snatcher. *Okay, so different seating arrangements.* It's up to them how they run the club, and who am I to criticise a prez who sits among his men.

I try again. "Prez, sorry to barge in. I was in the area." All eyes are upon me as I speak, but no one leaps to their feet, no hands are outstretched to greet me. Their expressions get me shifting awkwardly and already regretting my hasty decision to walk uninvited into church. If the prospect hadn't annoyed me, I'd have been more circumspect and waited until the meeting had ended before making my presence known.

"I suggest you address yourself to me." When the man at the head of the table makes his demand, my eyes flick back to him automatically.

I don't know him from Adam. I recognise Thor, who's seated opposite Snatcher, and Piston, their road captain who've I've seen a time or two before. But no other face is at all familiar. Not surprising, Utah's a way out from Tucson so not many men would make the trip down there without good reason, and there hasn't been one of those for a while. Not since I became a member. The man missing, Thumper, I'd met and regret his absence. He, I remember, was a friendly, jovial type and who, I believe, would have worn a welcoming smile. But Thumper is dead and no help at all now.

As my eyes scan each face hoping to see something there other than suspicion, I do notice something which strikes me as completely out of place. Halfway down the table seated facing me is a woman.

Ah. Perhaps it's a business meeting. Not church at all. No wonder I shouldn't be here. Club business is one thing, but commercial activity is a different beast entirely.

I turn back to the unknown man at the head of the table, preparing to voice my apology and then back out of the door, when the voice of the stranger I'm now facing barks once more. "Who are you?"

"I'm Roadrunner, Road," I explain. "From the mother chapter in Tucson."

He raises his eyebrows at Snatcher, who gives a sharp up and down nod, clearly confirming my words.

"I'm sorry I interrupted. I'll wait outside." I take a step backward.

"Stay where you are," the stranger's voice snaps loudly.

I don't so much as move another inch in any direction. It's as though he's commanded my feet, making me almost stand at attention. "Why are you here? Did Drummer send you?" His questions are barked out one after the other without drawing breath.

I may be feeling like a naughty schoolboy called in front of the head teacher, but I'm not going to let this stranger have it all his own way. "Prez," I say, letting my gaze land on Snatcher. "Who is this?" I hope Snatcher will understand that I don't necessarily want to talk about club business. Not when there's a stranger in the room, and a bitch at the table. Who are the pair? They're both wearing cuts, but presumably not from this MC. Maybe the bitch is his property?

The tabletop is rapped loudly with a gavel. My eyes go back to the man seated at the head. "You'll address me, not the VP."

VP? My brow creases. Maybe that knock I'd taken on the head was too hard and my memory is muddled. But Thor's VP, isn't he? And Snatcher is the prez. Unless there's been changes which Drummer hadn't known about. Maybe this was the cause of the wrongness he'd felt in his gut. There's been a change in roles or a takeover of the chapter and he's not been informed as the Satan's Devils rules would have it. The switch must have come recently, as Drummer, when I left him, definitely remained under the impression that Snatcher was still at the top of the table.

Now I look closer. The man sitting in Snatcher's old chair has a dirty patch on his cut. Leaning in a bit and squinting so I can read it from my position halfway down the table, I can now see it does say *President*. What's striking is it doesn't look new.

I may have been caught unawares, presented with a situation I know nothing about, but a president deserves respect, if that's what he indeed is. "Apologies, Prez." I raise my chin toward him. "Drummer didn't tell me there had been a change."

"No change," the man who hasn't yet given himself a name, tells me. "I've sat in this seat for years."

Now I can walk short distances, sit on my bike for miles, but standing in one spot? That's a challenge after the distance I've ridden in the last few days. Even balancing with the aid of the cane is making my leg ache. I shift, trying to relieve the soreness in my muscles, only to realise my damn knee has locked. As I move my leg, pain shoots through me making me grab the back of the nearest chair.

The woman almost directly opposite stares and then glances down at a tablet in front of her and recites, "You injured your leg among other things when you crashed halfway around the track on May 8th." As my eyes go wide, she then recites the details of the medical report my doctor had put into laymen's terms for me, which she's obviously got access to and is reading the original notes.

While my mouth drops open, the prez takes pity on me, though his tone is anything but sympathetic, more as though he's identified a weakness instead. "Do you need to sit?"

No. I don't want anyone to make accommodations for me, but the pain in my leg means I have to swallow my pride. "Yes," I respond through gritted teeth.

"Bolt?"

The man who answers to that handle gets up from his chair and pulls one of three spares from against the wall, placing it next to his own.

With a sort of hop-and-drag affair, I get myself into position and sit down with a sigh of relief I can't quite suppress.

Eyes from all around have stayed firmly on me. I resist the urge to squirm like a bug under a microscope.

"Now why are you here?" Prez demands again. "Drummer sent you, I presume?"

"Not exactly." I wasn't supposed to admit the mother chapter prez has concerns, and if I'm honest, wouldn't now that I'm here. With suspicious glances heading my way from all sides, I offer a version of the truth which I hope will work. "If you've got all the info on me, then you know I can't race anymore." I spare a nod to the woman who must be a personal assistant or something, probably here to take notes of the meeting. "Drummer suggested I go away to get my head on straight, and if I passed by a clubhouse, that I'd be made welcome there." I can't help a touch of accusation coming into my voice, that the welcome mat is very much lacking here.

"Drummer didn't warn me you were coming." The prez seems unrelenting.

"I didn't give him my exact plans." I shrug. "To be honest, I wasn't sure how far I could ride, and whether I'd get many miles under my belt."

"You came via Vegas?"

I shake my head. "Headed my bike in this direction. Vegas, is, well, Vegas. Had myself a yearning for somewhere quieter, somewhere I'd not been before."

The brothers here seem to be a different species from any

biker club I've ever met. More disciplined, that's for certain. Apart from the woman's recital about my injuries, the prez is the only man who's spoken. There's no joking around or tomfoolery that I'd become used to, or even raises of chins to request permission to speak. Neither Snatcher, Thor, nor Piston have offered a word of support, apart from confirming I am who I said. There's no sense of brotherhood here, and something warns me it's not just because I've barged in on their sacrosanct meeting.

Had I walked into Red's clubhouse in Vegas, or Demon's in Pueblo, I'd have been greeted with open arms and probably have a beer in my hand by now. The prospect would have grovelled to help me, but here? I could have entered a rival club and not one which shares a brotherhood with ours.

It's unnerving. I can't wait to retrieve my phone if only to hear a friendly voice at the other end. It's not often I yearn for the sound of Drummer's gruff tones. I'll need to update him, this situation is beyond me.

The silence is so complete in the room, I'm hard pressed to tell anyone's breathing. It stretches out until it's their prez who again breaks it.

He's not removed his eyes from me, but now they narrow. "You can ask three questions. Use them wisely."

Three questions?

My eyes must signal my lack of comprehension.

He shrugs and clearly isn't going to revise or clarify his instruction.

It's a test of some sort. I'll have to pass it, but it's hard not knowing the rules. How do I select what I best need answering? Are they measuring my intelligence, perhaps? Drummer should have sent someone different.

Three questions.

Use them wisely.

Christ. It sounds like the genie offering to fulfil three

wishes, and I'm just as lost wondering which to ask first. Talking about mythical creatures, I've certainly popped the cork and let one out of the bottle here. Drummer's gut instinct was right. There is something very wrong in Utah, but I can't pinpoint what, except this is no normal Satan's Devils chapter.

Here is my chance to find out what's going on, but without a clue, I don't know what the most important queries are to shape.

From the way the prez is regarding me, I know he's not joking. I can ask three things, but no more. I'd told Drummer I wasn't the brightest, and I hadn't been wrong. Mouse? Well, he'd know exactly how to frame his quest for information.

Someone coughs, and it's now I notice people fidgeting, but still no one talks, or tells me to hurry up. Their attitude is unnerving.

I don't know where to start, but know I must when the prez simply raises an eyebrow.

I clear my throat. "Who are you, and how long have you been prez?"

He raises both eyebrows now. "Seems that's two questions, but I'll give you one as a freebie. My name is Pip, and I've been sitting in this chair going on almost ten years."

So all those times Snatcher came to Tucson, he was acting out a lie? But, why?

"Why does everyone think Snatcher is prez?" It seems the natural follow-on question to ask.

Pip, at least I know what to call him now, lifts his chin. He's not my prez, so I find it hard to give him that title. "Because I prefer it that way. And your final question?"

An answer which is no real explanation, but I have no idea what to do with it, and I've only one thing left to ask. Pretty sure that's all they'll be responding to, so what information can I get with one more enquiry? And a voice in my head asks, *What happens when I've voiced it?*

I've never felt threatened by men wearing the Satan's Devils' patch before, but here I am in a strange club, unfamiliar in more ways than one. Possible questions run through my head, and I swallow down the one that floats to the top. *Will you let me walk out of here and forget this ever happened?* But already I know too much. I know the Satan's Devils MC Utah Chapter is hiding a secret—a big one—from the mother chapter prez. They could lose their charter for that.

Could I lose my life now I know one of their secrets? A real fear rises like bile from my gut. *How far would they go to hide the truth from Drummer?*

I might have lost the chance of participating in the sport I love, may have a leg that will never properly heal, but I've got the rest of my life ahead of me, and I'm not ready to part with that yet.

They can't kill me. Drummer knows where I'm headed. But he doesn't know I've arrived. I feel like hitting the heel of my hand against my forehead as I hadn't even told him I'd gotten to the clubhouse. I hadn't been certain I was in the right place, then when I found that I was, I'd come straight inside. Last time I called him, I was still miles away. Anything can happen to a lone biker on the road. Oh, Drummer would search for me, but if they're like the rest of us Devils, my body would never be found.

Mouse can track my phone. That's a comforting thought. Except, I'm not in possession of my phone right now. They could do anything with it.

They won't harm me, will they? Surely thoughts of my imminent demise are fanciful? But viewing the men staring at me with nothing resembling sympathy makes me unsure.

Final question. But what do I ask?

I sift through the hundreds floating around in my mind.

"Why is it important that Drummer doesn't know you head up this club?"

Pip sits back in his chair. In a gesture reminiscent of the prez I left just a few days ago, he links his hands behind his head. He seems in no hurry to answer, which gives me a chance to examine him. He's probably in his late fifties, his hair is neatly coiffured, his beard trimmed short without a hair out of place. It's unsurprising I'd initially thought I'd walked in on a meeting with a businessman. Sure, he's wearing a cut, but it's over a button-up shirt. His skin doesn't look weather beaten, and I suspect, were I to see his hands, they'd be carefully manicured. The last thing he resembles is a prez of an outlaw MC, yet that he is, is what he'd have me believe.

"Ah, Roadrunner." At last, he sighs out my name. "Why is the right question to ask, but maybe the one I'm least able to answer, or not right now." He brings his hands down. One disappears under the table but rises again quickly.

Less than one minute later, the door to the meeting room opens, and the prospect I met earlier steps inside. He stands so stiff and straight that I half expect him to salute. Me, he had treated with disdain, his prez though, well he gets respect.

Pip nods to the prospect. "Take our guest to the waiting room and make sure he stays put."

I've got a better suggestion. "If I'm not welcome here, I'll just get on my bike and resume my ride."

Pip's answering smile isn't at all comforting. Nor are his words. "Nice try. You already know too much, Road. But what to do about that is what we've got to decide."

3

———

*S*wift…

Road is an interesting character, good-looking with his long dark hair and piercing eyes. He's well-built and muscular, heavily tattooed, and with probably normally an affable disposition, though today, facing us, he looks anything but happy, instead bemused and totally out of his depth.

When I found out his recent history, I couldn't help but have sympathy for him.

No one knows better than I how just one misstep, just one split second can make the difference to the rest of your life and radically change all your expectations. With him, it had been the misjudgement of another rider, with me, pure chance. But the explosion that fucked up my life had taken more than my hobby away from me. It had taken all my hopes and dreams for my life.

Had he come to Utah to clear his head, as he suggested? Taken at face value, it doesn't sound unreasonable. In my case, it was why I'd made the flight across the Atlantic. To put distance between everything that reminded me what was now missing. Looking at Road, it makes more sense than him being here, as I know Prez suspects, as a spy. I didn't pick up the vibe to suggest any particular mental acuity.

But whatever the reason, he's here now, unannounced and catching the club unawares. It won't go kindly on him.

I watch as Gears leads him away, knowing Road will be in safe hands, well, safe for us anyway. There's no chance of the still-healing man getting away from Gears. Of our three prospects, he's the closest to getting his patch, having almost completed his two years' probation.

Our chapter is the hardest chapter to get into. The first year is the usual grunt work that Road will have been subjected to in Tucson, the second, well, that's when you're expected to develop that particular skillset Utah requires, but still without having access to everything. I know only too well how hard those twenty-four months are. Prospecting is only just in my rearview, having gained my patch only a year ago.

"Well," Pip's voice gets my eyes moving to the head of the table. "It appears we have a problem on our hands."

"We knew this was possible," Snatcher observes, his fingers pinching the bridge of his nose. "If Drummer had warned me—"

"Or if that asshole had waited until we were out of church, we could have switched cuts." Thor sounds angry, as well he might.

And I could have made myself scarce. Fuck knows what Road thought when he saw me.

"We could kill him," Rascal offers in an even tone.

"Kill a brother?" Honor sounds incredulous. "He wears the same fuckin' patch as the one I have on my back. Not sure I'm comfortable with that."

"Could have the opposite effect to the one we're wanting." Duty backs up the man he patched in alongside. "Drummer knew where he was headed. He'd come heavy-handed to give us a much closer look."

"That Drummer sent him here makes me wonder whether the cat's already out of the bag." Snatcher now scratches his nose. "I don't know how I could have fucked up, but maybe I did, Prez."

Pip shakes his head. "Sometimes I think Drummer's got a sixth sense." He sounds more resigned than angry. "Somehow we've slipped up. And now we've got to deal with the fallout."

The man whose gaze Pip's have landed on holds up his hands. "Nothing the fuck to do with me, Brother."

"Did you slip up, Stormy?" I ask. "Could your location have been traced?"

"Knew you shouldn't have played with fire. Two hits. Two Satan's Devils MC chapters. Drummer's nose started to twitch. Something must have made him think the stink came from here." Thor bangs the table.

Stormy stands and kicks over the chair he'd been sitting on. He slams both hands down and leans over. "I did what I was tasked. Removed the scum of the earth. And no, my location was cloaked as you fuckin' well know, Swift. You set it up yourself."

"You fucked with the other chapters, that can't be denied." Pip's face is glowing red. "Now pick up your chair and sit the fuck down."

Stormy does what he's told while murmuring loud enough those closest to him, including me, can hear him. "I fuckin' warned you I didn't play nice."

Pip's hearing is excellent. "Well you better fuckin' learn. You go off half-cocked and now we're at the risk of exposure. We still need to go over what exactly happened in San Diego," he reminds him. "Don't think you're off the hook just because of a stranger turning up and interrupting." He glares at Stormy for a moment, then his eyes roam the table again. "Same question. What do we do now Road's here?"

"Come clean?" Cowboy suggests.

"And risk everything we've built up? We work on secrecy, 'Boy,'" Snatcher retorts. "The more people who know, the more our whole operation is at risk."

"With the timing, we've got to assume what Stormy fuckin' did exposed us." I glare at the man I'm talking about knowing I'm risking another outburst. If he comes at me, he'll end up on the floor with my boot on his neck and him begging for mercy. "Not the hits. The whole 'we can get into Fort Knox' business."

If a man can perfect a smirk while the scowl remains on his face, Stormy manages it. "Well, we can."

"We're the club who don't have any computer experts." Pip wipes a tired hand over his face. "That's how we've managed to stay under the radar. Tucson's got Mouse who's probably the best of the rest. Token is Lost's man, Keys works for Red and Cad for Demon. Not saying you're wrong, Swift. But the suggestion we've got any hacking ability would be laughed out of court."

Snatcher frowns. "The other chapters think we're a joke stuck in the middle of the last century. A myth we perpetuated well. I fuckin' hated having to keep crawling to Tucson pretending we needed help to track someone down."

"But you were the best choice to pull wool over their eyes. You've sat around this table for years and still don't know how to turn a computer on."

Snatcher raises his middle finger toward Piston, and one side of my mouth curves. The road captain only spoke the truth. I don't know how often Snatcher's asked me to do this thingumajig or another, never being able to find the right words. He's a good stand-in for the prez though, looking the part being hardened and battle worn. Thor's cut from the same cloth, and while a whizz at anything mechanical, I suspect someone like Mouse would get frustrated with his lack of tech know-how at times.

Prez knocks his knuckles against the wood. "Whatever. Drummer's sharp as a fuckin' tack, and we shouldn't underestimate the man. Whatever tipped him off, something has. He wouldn't send a man like Road without some cause for suspicion. Now he has, what do we do about it?"

"Road doesn't seem much of a threat," I offer. "Maybe he's exactly what he says he is. A man riding out to give himself time to set his world to rights."

"In that case, I feel sorry for him. His motive might be different, but the result's the same. He's now in possession of information we don't want others knowing." Prez presses his lips together. "I also don't think we should underestimate him. He might not look as though he's got hidden depths, but he could be more than just muscle."

"I vote we can't take the risk and get rid of the problem." Preacher, our sergeant-at-arms raises his hand.

I grimace. It's not that I'm squeamish, but if I'm going to kill a man, I prefer to have good reason. Not just that he showed up at the wrong time. "There's another way," I tell them, waiting until their eyes meet mine. "Bring him on board. Get him to patch over."

"No." Thor's slipped into his enforcer role. "It's not as simple as that, and you fuckin' know it, Swift. There's a thing called fuckin' trust, and that has to be earned."

"He bloody earned it in Tucson." I roll my eyes. "Got his patch, and Drummer's faith in him to prove it."

"But not ours." Though Prez's eyes narrow as though he's considering my suggestion.

Stormy stops sulking enough to say, "We patch him over, that might be just what he wants? If he's here as a plant, he'd agree to a transfer, soak up our operation, then run back to Drummer and Tucson where presumably his loyalties lie. Aren't any of you assholes considering that might be exactly what he was sent here to do?"

Pip's face darkens, suggesting he doesn't much like being referred to as an asshole, but he doesn't comment right now.

"What's Tucson got to offer that we haven't?"

Snatcher snorts before he replies to Rascal. "How about a swimming pool and an all-year riding climate?"

"We got snow. Well, not now, but later in the year." Rascal sinks lower in his chair as eleven expressions of derision shoot his way.

I roll my eyes dismissing Road as a man who has a yearning to build a snowman, and skiing wouldn't appeal either, not with his leg as it is now.

"How about we come clean?" Thor muses aloud. "I agree it's likely that Drummer's suspicious about our chapter, but would he really mind if he knew what we're about? We've discussed bringing other chapters in before. Most recently, San Diego." He tilts his head toward Stormy.

As I expect, Stormy objects. "I didn't trust them."

"*You didn't trust them,*" Pip repeats, emphasising each word, then looking to the ceiling as though praying for strength.

I wonder if he's regretting his decision to call Stormy back to base and strip him of his nomad status. It's not going to be easy with him sat at this table, though preferential to him continuing to go rogue. The way I read it, he's going to do all he can to get sent out alone again. My vote would be that he leaves his patch behind him when he goes.

Snatcher is shaking his head. "If we get too many people involved, Prez, that might fuck up what we do." Snatcher might not know Google from Safari, but he's far from slow. When he speaks, we do pay him mind. "As you said, we operate under the radar. If too many are in the know, we might lose our edge. Keeping to ourselves has worked up to now."

"If Drummer's approached in the right way, he might come around to our way of thinking. Give us sanction to go on as we are without bringing the other chapters in on it," I offer. "We're assuming the worst." I've never met him, there are good reasons for that, but it means I don't know the measure of the man. Snatcher seems to respect him.

Pip drops his head into his hands. When he looks up, he's got that expression which normally means he's made a decision. When he speaks, he doesn't disappoint.

"I'm not happy killing a brother for just being in the wrong place at the wrong time. So that option's off the table except as a last resort. Neither can we send him back to Drummer without explanation, in which case I'd soon be expecting a visit from the mother chapter prez wanting to know what the fuck is going on." He pauses, grimaces, then continues, "I don't see that we've got a choice. We bring Road in on our operation, show him the ropes and then see how the land lies. If he still wants to run back to Drummer, then we'll have to revisit option A."

"What's he got to offer us apart from muscle?" Stormy looks annoyed. "Cleanest way out of this is a bullet to the head."

"What he might be able to bring to the table is for us to discover." Pip's glare at Stormy would have any other man quivering, but Stormy shrugs it off. "And I'd be careful in your fuckin' shoes, Stormy. If I were you, I wouldn't be giving me ideas about bullets to heads."

Pip's words are usually carefully considered, so maybe I was wrong about Stormy keeping his patch. It sounds like if he fucks up again, he could lose much more than the cut off his back.

Stormy is a sniper, an excellent one who hardly ever misses his shot. He's a loner, though, and not a team player. Up to now, he's been useful. His high IQ, his technical skills and the way he can make data jump through hoops, as well as his ability to think outside the box and react to ever-changing situations, makes him ideal to work out in the field on his own without backup. But his intelligence also leads him to becoming easily bored, and the way he'd sort out scenarios were perhaps to cause him amusement, rather than taking the direct route which would work just as well. Having scant regard for other people, he tends to use them as toys. Instead of providing the whole picture, he'd drop clues and then watch them sweat and squirm as they figured them out.

Once, perhaps, he could be forgiven for swooping in and taking the kill that our brothers in Colorado were lusting for when he'd killed Major, their enemy, right in front of their eyes. But then he'd played with the San Diego club, leading them around by their dicks, literally getting his job done for him. Which probably in itself was a good call, he was just one man after all. But then, when the prize of the man the club and he were after was captured, he'd once again taken that fatal shot which meant Alder was dead with questions left unanswered. Lost had been furious, and he and Demon will have compared notes, that's for certain. Drummer would have been fully briefed. What I can't work out was how any trail led to Utah.

Stormy's fuckups were what Pip hadn't forgiven him for, and that's why he's back sat around this table. He's as frustrated as hell and intent on making us all suffer for the instruction that saw him brought home.

Instead of withering under the weight of Pip's threat, Stormy sits back sullenly and folds his arms. "Then make him fuckin' prospect for us."

Pip raises his chin and shows he'll give credit where it's due, whatever direction it's come from. "Stormy's made a suggestion. It's got merit. Has it got legs?"

"Fuck that," Duty says. "I presume he's already done that shit. I can't see him agreeing to that."

I raise my hand. "Road patched in two years back after doing his full prospecting time."

"But only twelve months for Tucson." Duty acknowledges my comment with a nod. "Even so, he won't want to prove himself all over again."

"He's not proved himself, not to our satisfaction," Unusually, Honor offers an alternative view to Duty. "Our prospects work longer and harder."

"Because they need extra skills." Preacher looks down to the opposite end of the table. "Doesn't mean he can't show us what hidden talents he might be able to bring, or if he could be taught shit he doesn't yet know. Why not team him up with Stormy?"

I snort. Loudly.

"We want him to learn skills, not how to piss people off." Thor chortles at his own joke.

Pip raises his hand. "There have been some good points made. Let's break them down. By the time we bring someone to the table, we know their strengths. They've learned how to work with us and can immediately contribute to getting what's needed done. Road is an unknown, we know fuck all about him. He's like Igor, halfway through his first year and just about having learned to ask how high when I say jump. Road will have the basics, but we don't know what else he can bring to the game."

"Probably got damn good riding skills. Could use him for chasing people down."

"If he's physically capable," I jump in, correcting Piston. "We can't judge him on how he can handle a bike while his leg is still healing." Why the hell I'm feeling protective about the man, I don't know.

Bolt raises his hand, then gently lowers it to the table. I thought for a moment he was going to slam his fist down, but I'm glad he didn't. It cost a fucking fortune. He meets my eyes and grins sheepishly, then moves his head in the other direction and looks at Prez. "I don't mind working with him, if you want to partner him up with someone."

"Swift."

Hearing my name, I turn sharply toward Pip, ready to do whatever he wants of me.

"You take Road under your wing."

"Me? What? Why?" My brow furrows. It was the last thing I expected him to suggest and the last thing I bloody well want. "I don't need a partner, Prez."

"Doubt he'll be a partner, more a fuckin' liability." Stormy smirks at me while my eyes narrow and promise him retribution later. He just opens his hands in a gimme gesture, telling me to bring it on. Oh yeah, he'll get it. I've had enough of this. *Later,* I mouth at him, and his lips quirk. Guess both he and I could do with working out our frustration.

"You could do with teaming up with someone, Swift." Pip won't have missed Stormy and my non-verbal communication, but ignores that he's got two members gearing up for a fight. "Like our brother at the end of the table, you like working alone too much."

I bristle at the suggestion I'm not a team player. It's not how I see myself. "I have your backs, Prez."

"Of course, you do." Pip smiles at me. "No one would deny that."

What he leaves unsaid is that in a way I am like Stormy—I don't trust anyone to see things in the same way as myself. It's all the training I've got behind me which they'd never be able to imagine and probably wouldn't survive. But his observation that I'm like the morose man sitting a few seats away from me pulls me up. Is that what I'll end up like? Disgruntled and having no time for anyone else? Never feeling any emotion but anger? Nah, no way, I won't be anything like that.

The thought that they could even think I'm another

version of Stormy forces me to deny it in the only way I know how. "If you want someone to partner up with Road to see what he's made of, then I'm up for it." As soon as the words leave my mouth, I want to grab them back. *What the hell am I thinking?*

I glare at Stormy, *Just one fucking word, you wanker.*

I might not have insulted him out loud, but he gets my meaning. I get his middle finger back.

Pip's eye's go first to Stormy, then back to me. He rolls his eyes. "Okay. Looks like we'll have to move this to the ring later so Swift and Stormy can get their fists on each other."

I see money changing hands between Honor and Duty and wonder which one has my back. Cowboy also hands Duty something. It doesn't take a genius to work out they're betting on the outcome of the upcoming match.

My thoughts are confirmed when Snatcher barks a laugh. "I'll have fifty on Swift."

At least someone is in my corner.

Pip shakes his head and picks up the gavel. "Let's wrap this up. My proposal is that we keep Road close for a few days. Incommunicado, right? No word gets back to Drummer, or only that which is carefully managed." He thinks for a second. "Gears will have his phone and I'll use it to send some texts to keep Drummer off the scent. We'll see what Road is made of, whether he'll fit in or not. If he looks likely, he'll get to work with Swift. Swift, what I want from you is for you to assess whether he can transfer in and keep his patch or come on board and start from the bottom as a prospect, okay?"

I nod.

"If he's not up to muster?" Thor asks.

"Then he'll leave to go back to Tucson," Pip declares. "Unfortunately, he won't make it safely back."

4

—————

*R*oad…

When Pip told the prospect to take me to the waiting room, I half envisaged it was a euphemism such as the term 'storeroom' we use in Tucson. It's a place where activities such as questioning are undertaken, and Blade's allowed to let his dark side out to play, eliciting responses by way of his unique methods of torture.

Relief floods through me when I find the room is exactly what the name would suggest, but not one normally found in a motorcycle club, one percenter or not. There's a two-person couch and several comfortable high-back chairs surrounding a low coffee table. A magazine rack holds an assortment of periodicals and leaning against one wall is a hot drink dispenser. There is also a water cooler. The room's clean, painted in a non-descript cream colour, and there are prints of landscape paintings on the wall.

I help myself to a plastic cup of water, then turn to the prospect. It's not hard to miss he has a gun in a shoulder holster, and from the way he's standing, upright and on guard, I don't doubt his ability to draw and use it should he need to. I dismiss my first impulse to overpower him, run out to my bike and take off for the hills. Having assessed him, in my weakened condition and unarmed state, I doubt I could take him.

I turn and look out of the window instead. There, tauntingly close, just the other side of the glass, I can see my Harley.

What the fuck is going on here? I again look around me, but there's nothing to give any clues.

That woman, she must be some kind of tech expert to have hacked into my medical records so fast. Yet everyone knows Utah doesn't have anyone with such skills. Maybe she's a new employee? Or, perhaps they hide her as no one would want to admit to relying on a woman. It still seems odd she was seated around that table and not dismissed from the room when Pip was asking me questions.

She was pretty enough, enough to draw my attention to her certainly. Not an airhead either, nor afraid to speak up in the roomful of men. There was some edginess to her, and the hardened look on her face makes me wonder if part of her services are provided on her back. If so, I suspect she'd garner a lot of interest. Pip, himself, seemed quite tolerant of her, perhaps she's his? Though, I didn't get that vibe. She's somebody's for certain, or maybe, *hopefully*, general club property. I won't know until I see the patch on the back of her cut.

Let's face it, the whole set up is strange, and I really don't know what to make of it.

I turn back to the prospect. "What's your name?"

For a second, I don't think he's going to answer, then with a shrug, he offers, "Gears."

"You've already got a road name?" Ours aren't usually given until a man's been brought to the table. Though I shouldn't be surprised, I'm also an exception. I joined the Satan's Devils with mine, having been nicknamed Roadrunner as I was so fucking fast on my bike. Not fast enough, I grimace slightly, remembering. If I'd increased my lead by just half a second, I'd have been out of that asshole's way.

Gears looks like he's going to keep his mouth shut, but again, he surprises me. "Got my road name once I passed my initial probation."

Deciding I might lure him into a false sense of security if I appear friendly, I place a smile on my face as I make the one-word a query, "Gears?"

"When I was learning to ride, I'd forget to change them. The brothers kept shouting at me, 'gears' to remind me."

My brow creases. The implication is, he learned to ride here. Men wanting to join an MC usually already come equipped with the ability to ride a Harley, and with said bike as I know only too well.

"You the only prospect?" If I'm held against my will, it will be useful to know what I'm up against for any escape attempt to have a chance of succeeding. I saw eleven men in that meeting room, so how much other manpower have they got? I'm obviously discounting the woman.

"No." But he doesn't elaborate. Not even when I press him, leaving me in ignorance of just how many prospects they've got.

"So, Gears. How long have you been prospecting?"

Trying to get him to open up, I offer some information of my own. "I got my patch two years ago now." I force a chuckle, though I'm not really in the mood. "Prospecting is hard. I remember it well. Man it was tough being run ragged all the time, and not able to touch the club girls. That the same here?"

But he's clammed up. Gone stoic.

Having mentioned club girls reminds me of what I've left behind. Pussy, and Paige and Diva of course. Allie, now with Truck, is rightly not available anymore. But I'd double-teamed with Marvel a time or two before with one of the others. I wonder again whether the woman in the meeting doubles as a sweet butt. I might not have had much chance to examine her, but she had a pretty enough face, short dark hair and dark brown eyes. As my mind conjures up a vision of her, I realise it's best to put her out of my mind. In the event she is club property, I'm unlikely to get a chance to put her through her paces as I'll either be dead, or, and my preferred, but probably optimistic option, I'll be on my way back home and handing this conundrum over to Drummer.

But my thoughts keep circling back to her. Even her voice had been sexy, her accent reminiscent of Sophie, the VP's old lady back in Tucson. The thought sends a pang of homesickness through me. When I left on Drummer's errand, it had seemed simple. Now I admit, there's a chance I won't make it back.

I'd walked into a chapter of the Satan's Devils expecting to receive a warm welcome. Instead, the men who should be my brothers as we wear the same patch are probably discussing how to dispose of me right now.

One thing I know is that you do not lie to the president of the mother chapter, nor hide the truth from him. It seems that they've been stringing Drummer along for quite a while, but for the life of me I can't understand why. Nor why Snatcher is not the prez. He looks the part, and while Drummer had concerns, I'm sure there were none about the man himself. He even told me he thought Snatcher was straight as an arrow.

Pip, now, he would look out of place sitting with Drummer, Lost, Demon and Red. Could it be as simple as Snatcher's face is a better fit, so he sends his VP instead? Surely not, and if so, why all the secrecy, and why not tell me straight? Drummer certainly wouldn't be pleased at having been fooled all this time, but a suitable explanation might sort out this mess. A mess that I'm now stuck right in the thick of.

My leg aches. I limp to the couch and sit on it, draining the last of my water from the cup. I crumple it in one hand, throw it at the trash can and score a direct hit. My lips curve slightly at the small triumph.

How long are they going to take to decide what my future holds, and whether it will be long or short?

Time ticks by. Massaging the muscles on my thigh, I regret not strapping my leg today. A tight binding helps my knee stay in place and my leg better able to hold me up. But it makes my leg rigid and cumbersome and doesn't help the previously torn muscles heal. I need to build up the strength there so they can do their intended work and support my knee by themselves.

Strange how your life can change so fast. Had I not been knocked off my bike, I might not be here now. Drummer would have asked someone else to come, but I can't see them acting any differently than I have. They'd have ended up suffering the same unknown fate as myself.

Maybe they would have approached things differently, not having let the prospect's lack of respect rile them for a start. I never pretended to be clever, proven by my lack of foresight leading to the predicament I'm in.

But if it had turned out the same way for anyone who'd come calling, maybe it is better that I'm here and not one of the brothers with an old lady and kids. At least I have no one who would miss me. There are some benefits to being a free spirit.

Or, on the other hand, not. The thought that I've no family to leave behind and that no one, apart from my Satan's Devils' brothers would notice I wasn't there anymore, is something I don't normally think about. Strange how things come into your head when they're out of your grasp. It's not that I never want an old lady, just hadn't come across someone I saw being a permanent fixture in my life. Now, though, I wonder whether it would be something I'd like to experience. Why now, when I might not get the chance?

My fingers tap on the arm of the chair while Gears stands watching me stoically. Not once has he moved his eyes from me, and I'm starting to feel like an exhibit being stared at in a zoo.

My thoughts churn. My worries deepen as the minutes tick by. It seems like forever until at last the door opens, and another man who I haven't yet seen puts his head around the gap.

"He's to go back in." Having delivered his message, the man turns and I get a sight of the word 'Prospect' on his cut as well. I notice he hadn't acknowledged me.

Feeling slighted, I pull my cane toward me and get awkwardly to my feet, making sure my knee is kept properly aligned. Then, Gears stands back and allows me first out of the door. Not as a mark of respect, I'm certain. No, he's just making sure I don't bolt and run. Or hobble, as is the case right now.

I remember the way and am soon opening the meeting room door.

"Sit." Pip points to the chair I'd used before. I limp over to it and carefully lower myself down, placing my cane beside me on the floor. Once I'm settled, he resumes, "So, Roadrunner. We've been discussing your future."

A humph from a seat close by me makes me look that way fast. A man with his arms folded tightly across his chest looks annoyed and as though he's not in line with the rest.

Pip glares at him. The expression is not quite the same as Drummer's, but piercing all the same. When he thinks the man's got the message, he subjects me to the same look. I shift a little uncomfortably.

"How strong are your ties to Tucson?"

I wasn't expecting that. "The chapter or the location?"

"Club."

Summoning up my thoughts, I let him in on them. "Tucson's always been pretty good to me. Gave me a chance, patched me in. I'm a Devil." I shrug. "Wouldn't have become one if I wasn't prepared to give everything—up to and including sacrificing my life for any one of my brothers." Two things strike me as I say those words; the first being, maybe this is the point where I'm going to have to prove I mean what I say. And while it's true of my brothers I left behind me, I'm not sure I could say the same about those here. They certainly don't seem overly friendly.

Why is the woman still sitting there? She seems to be hanging on my every word.

Pip gives me a measured glance. "Would you be willing to transfer?"

That pulls me up. "What?" I frown. "Here?" At his nod, I swallow down my initial, *Don't be stupid* and try to think how I should play this out. I settle on the truth. "With all due respect, Pip, prospecting works two ways. The club gets to see the measure of the man, and the man gets to know the club." I lean forward, resting my arms on the table. "I've had three brothers transfer out to different clubs. Dart went to San Diego, Paladin and Beef went to the Colorado club. They were given a chance to see how the members melded together and to decide whether they'd be a good fit. All three found things they liked and stayed on when they had the chance. Now you're asking me if I'd consider a transfer, but I know fuck all about this club. I've met Snatcher and Thor before, but only briefly, and Piston in passing." I pause. "As for the rest of you," I let my eyes roam the table, resting on each one momentarily, though skipping over the woman of course, "I've not heard anything from you. I don't know what makes you tick. I got disrespected on my arrival starting with the prospect, Gears. Have I seen anything I like here? Have I learned shit about you to be able to say I'd lay down my life for the club? Like fuck. Right now, I'm feeling the opposite."

Pip looks at me considering, and then he barks a short laugh. "A simple yes or no might have sufficed, Road. But you're right. We are a different club, different in ways you probably can't imagine as yet. How about we shelve the idea of a transfer and put it on the back burner for now? What we," he waves his hand as though encompassing all sitting around the table, "have decided, is to give you a chance to learn about what we are. Stay here for a few days or weeks, however long it takes, then if you're a fit for us and us for you, I'll raise the question again."

I think for a moment. On the face of it, it sounds fair. While I still have suspicions about what happens if I have no inclination to patch over, at least I'll be breathing for now. "I'll have to check with Drummer. He's expecting me back." I'll take the chance to put him on guard, let him know how uneasy I'm feeling. Then, if I disappear, he'll know where to look.

"Ah," says Pip. "The VP will sort Drummer out for you. I'm sure if we explain we need an extra pair of hands then he'll have no objection to you staying on for a while."

I suppose they could square it with Drummer, but I'll be having a few words with him myself and tell him I've been given the opportunity to discover exactly what's going on in the Utah chapter. Because of my injury, I've already been off for weeks, and Marvel's been running the strip club, though I hadn't heard him making many complaints. Well, in the mood I was in before I left Tucson, he'd probably not voice them in my presence, else he'd have gotten my fist in his face. I won't deny I was a bear with a sore paw before I left.

"I'm teaming you up with Swift who will show you the ropes."

It could be useful having someone I could gently pry information out of. As long as Swift isn't the man who's looking like he'd rather kill me than work with me. But, at least before my accident, I was an affable sort, happy to get along with anyone. I'll just have to rely on not pissing whoever the man is off. Idly, I wonder what I'll be doing, they haven't asked about my work experience or skills. But then, if that woman could get into my medical records, finding out I run the strip club having been promoted from bouncer would probably be a cinch.

I glance around the table, but none of the men lift their hands, or indicate in any way that they're this Swift. I wait for the man to introduce himself, or for Pip to point him out.

But neither thing happens. Instead, Pip stands. "Now, I think Swift and Stormy have a score to settle? I suggest we all adjourn to the gym."

Everyone, including the woman, gets up and stands, and they filter out through the doorway. I busy myself getting hold of the cane and getting myself upright once again. By the time I do, I've missed satisfying my idle curiosity to see just what is written on the back of the woman's cut.

Like any man, I'm more than happy to watch a fight. We hold them regularly in Tucson in our own gym. There, I'd know who to place my money on, knowing exactly how each man handles themselves, sometimes using my knowledge of who might not be up to fighting strength having laid one on the night before, or who had put extra training in and might have an edge. Here, where I don't know anyone, seeing how they fight could give me some indications of what I'd be up against if eventually they decide my face doesn't fit. *Do they fight dirty or play by the rules?* How a man faces up to another may give me some clues of what I'm up against. Of course, I'm particularly interested as one of the fighters is the man I'm going to be partnered with.

Thor is hovering, waiting for me to follow the rest,

ensuring I go with them, I expect. I make no outward sign I've realised it's not him being polite, instead he's checking I don't make a break for it and run, or rather limp, to my bike.

Still, this behaviour, more typical of members of an MC, settles me slightly. Especially when I see money changing hands. I open my ears and gather more money's being placed on Swift being the winner rather than the other man, Stormy. At least I'm being paired with someone who can presumably look after themselves. I'll be a liability for a bit where anything physical is concerned. *Hey, can we pause the fight for a moment while I put my knee back in place?* My lips curve slightly as I imagine how that would go down.

The gym is at the rear of the building, reached via a maze of corridors. As soon as I enter, my eyes open wide, noticing some serious equipment here, and lots of it. Peg would be green with envy at some of this shit. And there, in pride of place in the middle, is a full-sized professional looking boxing ring. Three people approach and swing themselves up and through the ropes.

Well, I'll be fucked. The woman, like the others now minus her cut, is in the ring as well. What is she? Some kind of cheerleader or referee? She's also pulled off the long-sleeved top she was wearing and now is just dressed in a sports bra and jeans. I notice her stomach's flat and there's no fat on her at all. She's fit, while I prefer my women to be curvy. But no matter, any port in the storm. If she's a sweet butt and I'm staying on for a while, I wouldn't turn her down.

The man who'd sat with arms crossed looking sulky is also there. He's about my age, and around my height of six foot two. He's ripped off his tee showing a six-pack, or is that eight? The smirk on his face suggests the exposure of his chest was meant to intimidate, confirmed when he puffs it out. He looks a worthy opponent. Is he Swift? I fucking hope not. I've already picked up he doesn't care for me. If he turned nasty, in my weakened state, I'd be no match for him.

The girl, I've decided, must be a sweet butt, though to be fair, she's not flaunting herself. She's just deep in conversation with the other man there. Unlike the others, he's not doing much to get ready, not even taking off his shirt. *If that's Swift, I like his style.* He's acting as if he's confident he can take down the other man with one hand tied behind his back. A bit older than my thirty years, perhaps, shoulder-length brown hair he's not bothering to tie back. A mistake, I would think, as his opponent could get a hold of it. If they fight dirty that is. Yeah, I might have learned a few tricks that I keep up my sleeve.

The more I watch the trio in the ring, the more I hope I've identified the right man as Swift. I wouldn't want to be paired with the one showing off his chest. If I were, I'd need to sleep with one eye open. Or better still, stay wide awake. There's a vibe of fury that's emanating from him. I'd felt it back in the meeting room, as if just by breathing I've upset him. Pip wouldn't be crazy enough to partner me with him, would he?

The man who I'm hoping is Swift beckons the angry man close. All three bow their heads as he speaks to them both. Then, the girl and chesty go to opposite corners, while the man I want to be Swift steps back to the ropes.

I catch my breath and hold it. The long-haired man isn't fighting at all. He's the fucking referee. It's become clear it's the woman who's going to be taking Swift on.

There's no other explanation. The angry man must be this fucking Swift I'm supposed to be partnered with. No wonder the good money was going on him. I suck in air. Jeez. *He's fighting a girl?* Sure, I've seen girls fight before. We've even had the strippers at Angels mud wrestle before to provide entertainment for the customers. But a real fight against a man? No way. And not one in the mood Swift's in.

As Swift waves her forward with a taunt, I look around to

see who's going to step in and stop this. *He's going to fucking kill her.* But everyone's just staring on, their faces eager in anticipation and some are even cheering the pair on.

"This has been a long time coming." Turning fast, I see Pip standing by my shoulder. "Stormy's been well out of line for a while."

But that doesn't mean she should get her face rearranged. I open my mouth to protest, but Pip shakes his head, jerking his chin toward the ring.

"Watch. You don't want to miss this."

I turn back. Swift has launched himself at the woman. She's fast, I'll give her that, dancing under his arm and around him. He's not slow himself. *Fuck, that's going to hurt, he's not pulling his punches...*

Instead of the fist meeting her stomach, there's a blur of movement, almost too fast for my eyes to follow. He goes down with a crash and is on his front, one arm bent painfully behind him, and the woman's pulling his head back with a hard grip around his face.

Swift tries to buck her off, but to no avail. He tries again, but his head's being forced back. Instead of getting free, after a few more abortive attempts... he taps out.

Jeez. If that's my new partner, he just got bested by a woman half his size. Guess I'd be able to take him on after all. My lips start to curve.

Suddenly cries and shouts of, *Swift! Swift! Swift!* go up around me as she jumps to her feet, waving her hands in the air.

Swift?

"What do you think of your new teammate?" Pip asks, laughter in his voice.

I try to compute what he just said. Then I say the first thing that comes to me. "She's a fuckin' *bitch.*"

"I'd advise you not to call her that." He chuckles by my

side. "Not with your weak leg. You'll risk literally leaving yourself without a leg to stand on."

Ignoring what's going on around me, I turn and face him down, feeling personally insulted and hurt, and also conscious of the slur toward Drummer. "Do me the fuckin' courtesy of putting me with one of your members, not with a..." *What is she?* I've got nothing against women, but this is probably a way of keeping me out of the real business of the club. Satan's Devils do not have women members and never have. "If you're teaming me up with anyone, it's got to be someone who's earned a Satan's Devils' patch."

"I have." Where my tone of voice does little to hide the annoyance and slight that I feel, Pip's voice is calm.

"So, you're telling me you're pairing me with a sweet butt as a fuckin' joke?" A twisted one at that.

"Not in the least," he clarifies, then his eyes pierce me like a laser beam. "She is a member. She's patched in. So you treat her with the respect you'd give any brother."

5

____

*S*wift…

I knew I had to get the better of Stormy fast. He's an arrogant asshole who needed to be taken down a peg and having faced him before, I know he's skilled and quick enough that if his hits landed, they'd be hard enough to leave a lasting message. Having previously learned my lesson, I was determined not to draw this out.

Sometimes I'll play the game, put on a show for entertainment's sake, drawing the fight out until I let a brother think he's going to get in a lucky shot and get me on the floor. It's then I'll strike and take them out. Tonight, however, I knew the humiliation would be greater if I took Stormy down before even one of his punches connected.

I'd had no expectation other than Stormy tapping out, so while I'm not surprised at how it ended, I'm still buzzing as I leave the ring. I hadn't broken a sweat so I barely needed the towel that had been thrown at me, but out of habit I wipe my face then settle it around my neck. Grinning, I listen to the group around Stormy.

"Hey, you could have put up a fuckin' fight."

Uh-uh. Someone was crazy enough to bet against me.

"Stormy, what the fuck? You didn't fuckin' last a minute. I wanted a better show than that."

Prez is talking to Road about something serious by the look of it. He catches my eye and crooks his finger summoning me across to join them. Some of my exhilaration fades as I walk over, wondering how Road is going to take the introduction to his new partner. I'm already prepared for the objections. Despite my so recent display of how well I can look after myself, it doesn't hide what appears to be a draw-back for so many men. I've lived with the fact that my geni-tals, or lack of the correct ones, have been the bane of my life. Not that I wanted a dick, no way, no how. I've just learned having the lack of one makes men judge me.

Well, if he doesn't want to be teamed up with me, I'm equally unenthusiastic about being paired with him. As I've just proved, there's no one here who can match my training. Hence, I trust none of them to have my six. I'd spent months learning to rely on no one but myself, and that's the way I much prefer it.

Pip's been tolerant up to now, but it seems I'll no longer be able to get away with being a loner. For the foreseeable future at least, I'm to be paired not only with someone who's far from being my equal, but a man who can barely stand up.

I reach them in time to hear what, for Road, is clearly the punchline.

"Not in the least," Pip says, his eyes no longer on me but on the newcomer. "She is a member. She's patched in. So you treat her with the respect you'd give any brother."

I read the signs that betray Road's reaction to that state-ment. His face goes red, his hands fist at his sides, and the glare thrown at me would make a lesser being want to drop through a hole in the floor. I stand my ground, raising an eyebrow in challenge as I wonder what he's going to say next.

"She can't be." His eyes go from me to Prez. "Satan's Devils don't allow women members."

"Actually," Prez says deceptively calmly, "they don't disallow it."

Prez is right. Before he invited me to prospect for the club, he'd gone over the regulations with a fine-tooth comb. As, it appears, Road is about to find out.

"You're wrong," Road states firmly as though right is on his side. "Satan's Devils do not allow women to join."

Prez grins. "Sure, the regulations only refer to men, and every pronoun is 'he', but there's no regulation actually prohibiting it."

"You're twisting it," Road scoffs. "The intention is clear."

"Maybe I am," Prez agrees, his voice still level and even. "But that happens often enough in many a legal document. What's not emphatically stated allows for loopholes. Men have gotten away with murder on such technicalities before." His face, and his voice, hardens. "Accept it, Road. Swift is a full member of the Utah chapter, and for the time being at least, your partner."

"Drummer's not going to like it."

This time, Prez agrees. "He's not, is he, Road? There are a few things about the way we run this chapter that are different. I'm giving you a chance to see if you think you can accept what we are and what we do. But that's without you running back to Drummer, at least not until you've given us some time. I'm asking you to keep certain things to yourself."

"Can't do that," Road objects. "My loyalty is to my prez."

"There are other ways to make sure certain details don't meet the ears of the mother chapter." Thor, one hundred percent in his enforcer role, has come up behind Road.

Road stiffens, showing he's not stupid. He's clearly aware of the threat.

I sigh.

"Why don't you give us a chance, Road?" I try to defuse the situation. What we do here is too important to be wrecked by one man, and while it wouldn't be my first choice, I do have some sympathy with Thor's view that he wants to make his silence permanent.

It's as though Road's seeing me for the first time when he now turns his full attention on me. Really seeing me, as a person and not as a piece of meat, and not something for his entertainment. I'm all too well aware how women are regarded in other clubs—they are either sweet butts or old ladies, with nothing in between. I can't see there's much difference in either role myself. They're kept women performing on their backs to keep their positions, it's only the number of men that they service which makes the distinction.

I doubt Road's ever come across a woman he needs to see as his equivalent before. He manages a strip club after all.

"Are you into illegal shit? Or drugs?" he asks, his eyes narrowing as he turns back to the prez.

Prez bristles, spitting out, "Nothing of the fuckin' sort."

"You going to come right out and tell me what you're about?"

With a shake of his head, Prez refuses. "I'd rather you took some time to see for yourself."

Road considers him for a moment, then his gaze comes back to me. I wonder if this is where we learn something of the measure of the man. Is this someone who we'd call back in England a 'jobsworth', in that it's more than his job's worth to bend the instructions he'd been given? Which, though he hasn't come out and said it, I'm certain were along the lines of go to Utah and find out what the hell goes on in that chapter. Or is he going to think for himself, and realise we're given him the opportunity of understanding what makes us different, and take the time to discover why we are, instead of just wanting to run back to Drummer and tell him the little he already knows.

I'm starting to suspect Road may not be a man to simply follow orders. The slight gleam in his eyes shows an interest has been sparked.

"Give us a few days," I press, thinking it looks like he's weakening.

He draws in air, lets it out, then jerks his head, indicating the enforcer he's well aware is still standing behind him. "It doesn't look like I've got much choice other than to give you a few days, but I still need to contact Drummer and tell him something. He'll get worried if I go radio silent."

One corner of Pip's mouth turns up. "I've got your phone, Road. Until you know what we're all about, I'm keeping hold of it. I'll text Drummer myself."

Road's face darkens. "Seems lack of trust works both ways. I don't trust any of you assholes here." His eyes shutter, and I can understand what he's feeling. The pause stretches out, then he realises he has no other option. Clearly defeated, he addresses me directly. "What do I fuckin' call you?" His head moves side to side. "Can't call you Brother."

I chuckle. "Swift will do fine."

"You a Brit or Australian or something?"

Rolling my eyes as it's not the first time Americans have muddled up my accent. "I'm from England." It's time to get friendly and defuse the situation. Believing I know just how, I offer, "Hey, you want a beer?" I've noticed some brothers are milling around, unashamedly listening in on our conversation, but others have walked out, and it's not hard to guess where they'll be going. I don't know what Road feels like, but I could do with something to wet my throat. I hadn't exerted much energy taking Stormy down, but the adrenaline I'd had to summon has left me thirsty.

Road closes his eyes, but when he opens them again, they seem to have brightened. "A beer sounds fuckin' good to me."

"I'll leave you two to get acquainted." Prez seems relieved there's going to be no blood spilt in our gym tonight, but he lingers enough to issue a warning. "Just remember, Road. Even if you were at the peak of fitness, you'd not be able to take Swift out."

Road raises his chin toward him, he doesn't bluster or try to contradict. "I've seen that."

At least he admits it. Me taking down Stormy so fast made more than one point tonight. I don't have to give my own warning. Not that I mind taking a man down. I'm used to men thinking they have to challenge my skills and ability, without accepting the evidence of their own eyes telling them they haven't got a chance. Road's casual acceptance scores well in my book.

Getting to know each other works both ways, him the club, and us him. We'll be dancing cautiously around each other for a while yet.

Unlike Stormy, when I'm given a direct instruction, whether I like it or not, if my initial protests fall on deaf ears, I straighten my shoulders and get on with it. I'm partnered with Road, he likes it as little as I do, but we won't move forward unless I make an effort to be friendly.

"Your leg hurting?" I ask, as I lead him back through the corridors and then to the elevator that will take us to the first —*second, must remember I'm in the US now*—floor and up to our clubroom.

"Some," he agrees as I push the call button. He looks around. "This is unlike any clubhouse I've ever seen."

"We like it this way," I tell him. "Purpose-built a few years ago. Before my time."

"Where do the brothers live?"

"On the top floor," I tell him. "Some have places in town." I do myself, but he doesn't need that information. "But there are rooms for all to bunk down here, and some brothers live here permanently."

The elevator arrives and we step inside. I've gotten so used to it, I don't hear the music that's playing softly in the background—the type you'd hear at any mall. Road's brow furrows when he glances up at the speaker, but he doesn't query it. I'm presuming he's clocking it up as just one more of our oddities.

When the elevator jerks to a halt, the mechanical voice announces we've arrived and the doors open. I watch Road's reaction.

His lips start to curve, his cheek muscles pull in and then his expression becomes a full smile. It completely changes his face.

"Feel more at home?" I grin, it's obvious he does.

"Sure do." He takes a step forward, leaning heavily on his stick, his eyes still taking in the room. There's a bar along one side, tables and chairs scattered around, a pool table, a dart board, and a couple of gaming machines.

"Why don't you sit? I'll go get us some beers." I point to an empty table.

For a brief moment I think he's going to protest, but he fights to push down the manly side of him that wants to insist he be the one who gets the drinks. It's an attitude I'm well used to. Being as, if not more, capable than most men, I tend to ignore it. That he doesn't insist is a suggestion his leg must be paining him, I think, as he goes and sits at the table I pointed out. I watch him for a moment as he limps, favouring his busted leg. That ride from Tucson had to be long and draining, however many stops he put in.

"He sticking around?" Rascal asks as I near the bar. He jerks his head toward Road in case I hadn't known who he meant.

I pause to hold two fingers up to Igor and then answer the question. "For now."

"I can't see him staying." Honor shakes his head. "He's got too much loyalty to his chapter."

"Then we'll help him get back home." Rascal moves his finger in a cutting motion across his throat.

Can a man's loyalty be changed, I muse, as the prospect pops the top off two beers. If it can't, Rascal's right and Road might end up six feet under. I'm starting to hope it doesn't come to that. It's one thing to take a man out when you know nothing about him, but what if I find I like him? Worse, become friends with the man I'm working with? Could I stand back and see him executed in cold blood, just to preserve our secrets, however important they might be?

Conveying my thanks via a chin lift to Igor, noting not for the first time how much like a mad scientist the prospect looks, I take the beers and make my way to the table where Road sits, his hand massaging the muscles around his knee. As I see it, I've got two options—stay completely aloof and don't try to get to know the man at all, and keep him on the outside of everything, so I'm unaffected by what happens in the end. Which wouldn't be what Pip wants me to be doing. Pip might come over as a hard man, but I know he'd want Road to have every chance. No, if I keep Road at a distance, it wouldn't help him come to a decision, or not the one that keeps him breathing.

My other option is to invest in him staying. To be totally open, answer all his questions and leave nothing unsaid or hidden. That's a virtual death warrant if I can't convince him Utah is his future. With luck, he'll see it offering him a ticket to something that might replace what he's lost and want to make his life here.

Despite my preference for working alone, I am a team

player. I don't give up on a person with no reason, and it's ingrained in me never to leave a man behind.

By the time I place his beer in front of him, I'm committed to taking the second option.

When Road asks his first question, I'm glad I took that moment to have an internal conversation as I've no hesitation in answering him.

"Tell me, how does a woman end up a member of the Satan's Devils MC?" He lifts his beer and simultaneously raises his eyebrow in question.

"You surprised to know a woman can ride a motorcycle?"

"No, not that." He chuckles. "There are a couple of the ol' ladies in Tucson who ride. Hell, they don't just ride, they both built their own bikes. They're fuckin' good mechanics and put me to shame. Sam, Drummer's ol' lady, she fixes up my trials bikes. Fixed." He grimaces at his own reminder. "Used to ride against female riders in competition as well. I didn't mind racing against either sex." He winks and offers a smile. "I didn't care who I beat."

"Competitive, I see." That's something we've got in common.

"You bet." His eyes close briefly as he remembers that pleasure has now been lost to him.

I decide to counter his question with one of my own. "Why does a man join an MC, Road?"

His eyes snap open and come to mine. Instead of leaping into a response, he gives my question serious consideration. "There are a number of reasons. One is riding beside like-minded people, being part of something. A sense of freedom, of sticking up a finger to citizen's laws."

"And you don't believe a woman might want that as well?"

He regards me carefully. "Not the women I've come across. Look, Swift. I don't know how this chapter works, but Tucson?

Well, we've had a few enemies—rival clubs, the local crime gang. Our women are kept out of that shit. They wouldn't want to be part of it." He picks up his beer again. "I'm not saying women are weak. Darcy, our sergeant-at-arms' ol' lady, she's a fuckin' firefighter. Puts her life on the line every time she goes to work. But I could never see her taking up arms to protect the club." He replaces the bottle on the table. "But maybe Utah is quieter."

Quieter? There are a lot of things Road's going to find out. And Utah being quiet isn't one of them.

"You got men who served, Road?" I know he hasn't himself. I'd seen that on the background check I'd run immediately after he'd entered our meeting room, quickly hacking through Mouse's defences and finding Road's government name of Lucas Winchester, and from there finding out his employment records as well as his medical ones.

"Of course. I haven't myself, but a number of the Tucson club have."

"And they joined the club, why?"

"To replace what they no longer had." His eyes flick to mine, a question in them. "To be part of something again, men around who they could trust to have their six. To be part of a team."

I nod. "I was in the British Army, Road." I watch his eyes widen, but he doesn't know the half of it as yet. "You've heard of the SAS, the Special Air Service?" It appears that he has, but I want to make sure he understands it. "It's the equivalent of your Delta Force."

His eyes narrow. "You were in the SAS?" He sounds disbelieving.

"I applied when they opened it up to females just a few years back," I tell him, not answering his question immediately. "I was selected to be part of an intake of about a hundred and twenty soldiers. It's hard, gruelling, and out of the number initially selected, only ten were expected to make the grade. The odds against succeeding are so high, there's no shame if you don't get through it. But you don't go in expecting to fail, you go in with the thought you're going to be one of the few percent who pass. You go in knowing people have *died* during the hardest training there is. You go in knowing you'll be challenged in ways you could never dream of."

He stares at me as if re-evaluating his opinion of me, but needing more information to complete his new picture. "Tell me more about this training."

As he appears interested, I explain. "First of all, they test physical fitness and your mental stamina. It's tough and demanding, nothing else compares. As a soldier, you're used to superiors barking orders, but during this training you have to make your own decisions. Making a mistake can have dire consequences. As I said, it's not unknown for people to die." My eyes glaze slightly thinking back to my time in the Brecon Beacons, and the long gruelling hikes in difficult, nigh impossible, conditions. But fuck me, I enjoyed the challenge. "The final part of that first stage is a forty-mile hike carrying fifty-five pounds in weight. Not with people beside you encouraging you on, but on your own with no support." He tilts his head, his eyes widening fractionally. "If you don't make the grade at any time, you can be sent back to your unit. It's no disgrace when more than ninety percent don't make it. But if you get through that stage, then they send you to the jungle." I grimace. "There, there an no adequate words to describe the conditions—harsh and testing don't say the half of it. You have to survive behind enemy lines for weeks, living only on your wits and the rations you have with you. You know they want you to fail, because they'd rather you break then, than on a real mission."

My bare descriptions don't really do it justice, living in hell is more like it. "Then the final stage is escape and evasion, which is just what it sounds like. You're held captive and have to get away. Finally..." I pause and sigh. "The last test is learning to withstand interrogation. The methods used are designed to break you. They do everything and anything to you, employ the methods a real enemy might use." By that time you're hanging on by your fingernails, knowing what you can do to make it stop, but determined not to give in as the goal is so close in sight. "If someone's passed all the other stages, this can be where they fail. They pull out every dirty trick in the book, and I mean everything, Road." I shudder slightly. There had been times I wanted to yell out to make it stop. It hadn't been polite, the gloves were off, just as if I'd been taken by the Taliban. Indignity piled on after indignity, the words, the threats, including graphic details of how they'd rape me. In the case of a man, they'd describe exactly what they'd do to the females in his life.

It had been bad, I remember, but I'd rather find out I could withstand it during training, than discover I'd fail when faced with the real thing. In the end, though, it got so you couldn't tell the difference, until, hungry, thirsty, desperate for sleep or for death to take you, mercifully, it stopped.

"Did they?" he asks, a slight catch to his voice. "Did they break you?"

I let him think on it for a moment, then shake my head and grin broadly as I share the proudest achievement of my whole life. "No. They didn't break me. I made it. I was not only one of the few of that intake who were accepted, I was going to be one of the first bloody women in the SAS." I still can't find sufficient words to explain how proud I am of that.

"Was?" He stiffens, catching onto the tense I'd used. He eyes me thoughtfully, while pushing his hair back from his face. "What happened, Swift? You wouldn't throw everything away after going through weeks of that hell. What fuckin' happened?"

"Try months," I correct him. "The training lasted months. And you're right, I wouldn't have." I pause for a moment trying to push thoughts of what I should be doing now out of my head. I should be facing down terrorists, sneaking around behind enemy lines, working for my country. Instead, I'm here in the States.

A pang of what I lost goes through me, and I clench my fists in an effort to stay calm, before continuing. "I was driving along a motorway in England when an accident happened right in front of me. A tanker jackknifed. The driver had fallen asleep at the wheel, one of those split-second naps, you know? He realised he was drifting, corrected too hard, lost control of his rig. He walked away. The man in the car behind that crashed into the tanker, could not."

I stop for a moment to take a breath, viewing the scene dispassionately in my head. "There was smoke, flames. The driver of the car was screaming, so clearly alive, but trapped. I ran to help. I was a soldier in uniform. I told everyone else to step back, and they obeyed as they assumed I knew what I was doing. The passenger side was crushed under the tanker, and the driver's door wouldn't open as it had caved in. But from the outside I had the leverage I needed. I managed to get the car door open and pull him out. He was okay and did what any sensible person should, and ran off. I was following him when the whole damn scene exploded." Automatically, hands go to the back of my head. "He'd just picked up a gas cannister for his barbecue. The valve must have gotten damaged in the collision and the escaping fumes caught fire."

Road sucks in air, eyeing me carefully as though checking for injuries. He won't find them, any visible scars have gone. "How badly were you hurt?"

"The blast knocked me off my feet, dropped me down hard on the tarmac, and metal, from the car, cannister, I don't know what, hit my head. Fire enveloped my back, but luckily a quick-thinking bystander had a fire extinguisher in his car, and managed to put my clothing out before it burned through to the skin. But, the blast, the concussion, well, I've lost most of my hearing."

His brow furrows. "But you're hearing me? You read lips?"

"I should, but I find lip reading hard." Tucking my hair back, I point to what's in my ear. "I depend on hearing aids."

Road stares at me, then lowers his eyes, then moves his head from side to side. He doesn't ask, but he tells me, "Which meant you couldn't be a soldier anymore."

"I was offered an administrative role in my old unit, but it wasn't what I wanted. I wanted the challenge, I wanted..." *The exhilaration. The thrill. The knowledge I was doing what very few could.* I don't try and explain. If captured, all someone would need to do to render me helpless is take my hearing aids away. I shrug. "I took medical retirement and decided to visit the US."

"Where you found your place and stayed."

He's looking at me with a look on his face I'm not able to interpret.

6

———

*R*oad...

    I don't know what to say. I'd watched her face while she was telling me her history. So many emotions had gone across her features. Pride when she told me she'd succeeded in something very few could, especially given her sex. Then sadness when she told me that, like me, she'd suffered the loss of a dream. Though hers puts my minor inconvenience into perspective.

What kind of woman, person, come to that, must she be to have achieved all that she had? No wonder she'd had Stormy on the ground in seconds flat, she'd have to be an expert at unarmed combat. To stand her ground through the types of interrogation techniques I can only imagine, hell, even Blade wouldn't break her. She's so fucking strong, mentally and physically. My first thought when I'd seen her had been that I wouldn't mind getting in her pants. Now I know she's so far out of my league that just me thinking about it seems obscene.

I realise I'm staring, my face blank, as I search for something to say.

"What are you thinking, Road?"

I reply honestly, "I'm thinking you're fuckin' amazing. I'm thinking you're more than qualified to ride in an MC. You put me and most of the men I know to fuckin' shame."

"You?" Her head tilts. "What do you mean?"

I huff. "Look at you. If a man came to the club with half the qualifications you've got, any MC would snap him up. Me?" I gesture toward myself. "I've just about scraped through my GED, I've no qualifications, I haven't even served. I'm nothing but muscle, a grunt." I flex my arm demonstrating that I'm definitely that.

She opens her mouth to respond, when another voice interrupts.

"Well, you haven't killed him yet."

Glancing up at the man who's just placed a beer on the table and is pulling up a spare chair, I see he's grinning.

"Name's Bolt." Automatically, knowing I've already pissed off the men in this club by just breathing, and having heard Swift's story, I'm wondering if they're of the same calibre as her. So, with less confidence than I arrived with, I hold out my hand.

Automatically, he takes mine and shakes it. Something about his feels odd. While his fingers curl around mine with just the right pressure, the skin is ultra-smooth, and cold to the touch. I focus on it, trying to see what's wrong.

"It's prosthetic," he tells me dismissively, eyeing my interest, stating it as though it's of no matter at all. "Left the original in Afghanistan."

"Jeez," I breathe out. "That sucks."

"Nah. I got used to it. Thanks to the club, this is all singing and dancing. And I don't have to worry about getting my fingers trapped in a door."

"Yes you do." Swift's eyes narrow. "We've told you this, Bolt. That thing was bloody expensive. It was a prototype model. You break it, we might not be able to replace it."

"When you shook my hand," I observe, "it was as if you could feel mine."

"I can." He leans forward, picking up the beer bottle unerringly. "It works with my own nerves. Just as you'd grasp anything, your brain computes what pressure to use. The touch sensors in the fingertips tell me when I'm successfully holding something." His eyes meet those of Swift's. "This is a new experimental model, but I can do just about everything I could with my real one."

"Even wank," she puts in, indelicately.

"That too." Bolt grins and winks at her. "But I stayed well away from my apparatus until I was completely certain. Didn't want to squeeze too hard and not be able to open my fingers back up. I waited until I knew I had good control."

I have to bark a strangled laugh at the look on his face. Yeah, being a man I'd be cautious too, wouldn't want to have an artificial hand locked around my junk.

"Was it a long learning process?" I'm interested, then clarify, "I mean the whole using the hand thing, not jerking yourself off."

"Let's just say, I've broken more than my fair share of eggs." Bolt doesn't seem bothered talking about what could be regarded as a disability. But then, he doesn't appear to regard it that way.

"What would worry me," Piston comes over and also pulls a chair up, "is what if the electronics get jammed? There you are, stroking your dick and all of a sudden your hand closes. Squeezes your damn cock right off."

Bolt rolls his eyes. "I can load, fire a pistol, fight. Write with a pen and use a keyboard. But how my prosthetic feels on my cock is all these fuckers ever ask about."

Piston chuckles and slaps his back. "Don't really even think about it anymore, Bolt. You're still the same asshole you were before." He turns to me. "Hey, Road. See you've got yourself a new tourer. How are you finding it?"

In the meeting, Piston hadn't even acknowledged he knew me. But here, sharing beers, it's like being with any other set of brothers. But I can't forget, when I'd seen him in his role as road captain, he perpetuated the lie that Snatcher was their president.

I'm still wondering what that's all about. As I answer his innocuous question, my mind races in the background. Swift may be exceptional, but they've hidden that they've got a female member. Snatcher's not the prez, the stranger, Pip, is. What else is going to turn up if I keep lifting stones to see what's underneath?

Sure, on the surface, companionably drinking and chewing the fat is the same as I'd expect as a visitor to any chapter, but for all intents and purposes, I'm being kept incommunicado and a prisoner. I've got to remain on my guard. I'd told them I'd stay and see where they were at, Which suits my purpose and Drummer's. So for now, I'll go along with that plan.

"Are you really the road captain?" I ask suspiciously, narrowing my eyes.

"Me?" Piston laughs. "Yeah. That's my job."

He gets a bit of ribbing from Bolt about a time he got coordinates muddled up and sent them miles out of their way to the wrong location, while I just sit back, slowly sipping my drink and observing.

The evening proceeds. A few more beers are downed, by them, I'm purposefully limiting myself. I meet Duty and Honor who seem to come as a pair, but whether they're like my brothers Joker and Lady, I have no idea nor care, I wouldn't have any issues one way or another. I also meet Cowboy who seems serious and quiet. A couple of times I try to turn the conversation to how the club brings its money in, but the discussion either gets neatly turned back to bikes or they ask questions of me, about racing or my injuries. In the end, I'm defeated and stop bothering to pry. They are clearly not going to enlighten me, and all I'm doing is wasting my breath.

Swift challenges me to a game of pool, and I manage to best her, though it's not an easy victory. At darts, she wins, but it's no matter, I'm not one of those men who feels they have to prove themselves at games.

"You're good," I tell her, as she tells me the numbers she's aiming for, then watch impressed as her darts landing exactly where she's said. It's as though she's giving them instruction. Me? I'm just lucky if they hit the board.

"I was brought up in an English pub," she tells me. "Played darts from the time I could hold them. Played on the pub team as soon as I was old enough."

"I suspect they were glad you were playing with them and not against them."

She concentrates, throws a dart and hits the bullseye. "Uh-huh. The bar was lined with trophies."

"Your parents run it?"

"They did. But it was a country pub, and as the drink-driving laws got enforced, people stopped driving out to get a drink. Business fell off, and eventually it wasn't profitable anymore. Of course, by then, it couldn't be sold as a going concern as no one wanted it." Pain flicks over her face. "The building was demolished, and a couple of houses were built there instead."

"So your family home was gone?"

She nods. "Seems a waste, but time moves on."

"Your folks still alive?" When she raises her chin, I ask the natural follow-on question. "They mind that you live so far away?"

"I've been independent since I was eighteen, so they kind

of expected they wouldn't see much of me when I grew up. I go back and see them from time to time."

If I had parents, I think I'd visit often, or perhaps, I'd have ended up taking them for granted. Who can say? I was abandoned as a baby, put straight into the system. I'd like to say I was adopted and grew up happy, but that wasn't how things played out. Instead, I first was fostered by a family who wanted a baby. When I started to grow, they decided I wasn't so cute as I was, and gave me up. What followed was a chain of foster homes, some better, some worse, some downright terrible. I was no stranger to bruises and broken bones.

"Did you ever want to try to trace your birth mother?" With that sentence, she reminds me she already knows all the facts about me.

Track down the woman who made my formative years a misery when she left my future to chance? I've thought about it, wondering why she'd given birth to me only to give me up. More than once, there'd been times I'd wished I'd never been born.

"No." I give her the truthful response. Even if I were to find her, what purpose would it serve to hear the sob story that led to my sorry existence? To return, not as the baby she'd given up, but the man who'd lived despite the harsh conditions I'd had to survive. To give her the pleasure of seeing the boy grown up without her having the burden of raising me. In my mind, she didn't deserve a happy reunion. I also didn't deserve to be made to feel worse, to discover in the same way as she hadn't wanted me as a baby, she also might not be impressed with the reminder years down the line. Nah, no reunions happy or otherwise are in my future.

As the evening goes on, glad I've kept sober, I take my chance to watch and learn. I note Swift is treated just like one of the men, which no longer surprises me. Now knowing her background, it's clear to see she fits right in. Her in-depth knowledge of bikes and even my own sport means that after a while I find I'm able to ignore that she's got a decent, if small, pair of tits and other attractive assets, and instead, I'm talking to her as I would any brother back home.

Except there's one question that I don't feel right to ask until Swift excuses herself to visit the bathroom and for a moment I'm left to my own devices. Apart from Swift, I've seen no other women around. No old ladies or sweet butts. Such a masculine environment strikes me as strange and the dynamics are far from what I'm used to. I approach Bolt.

"Do you have sweet butts?"

"Whores? Nah, we're not like other clubs. If you want to get your dick wet, you'll have to go into town, or wait until the weekend when we party. Hangarounds come along, both women and men, depending on your taste." I presume he's talking about Swift, but see him nod toward Duty and Honor which raises my suspicions again.

"Each to their own, but it's pussy all the way for me, man." I'm not comfortable yet calling him or anyone here, *brother*. I rub my leg.

He notices. "Swift taken you to your room, yet?"

"Have I got one?" I raise my eyebrows. "Or is that a euphemism for a cell?"

He slaps me on the back and chuckles. "I like you, man. Your lodgings will be more comfortable than jail, I assure you of that. Hey, Brute, c'mere." His last is directed to a man who's joined the prospect, Igor, as I've discovered his name is, behind the bar. Continuing my reconnaissance, I bank that observation, *there are at least three prospects.*

A big man lumbers over. "Whatcha want, Bolt?"

"Take Road to room eleven. Then get his gear in from his bike." He turns to me. "You want both your saddlebags?"

I nod. "Sure." While answering, I eye up the big man, noticing his nose has been broken a couple of times and not straightened quite right. Reckoning I won't cross the man who looks like he could take on Mike Tyson, I see Swift appearing behind him.

"Oh, I was going to see if you wanted to call it a night. It's okay, Brute. I'll take him to the room, you just get his stuff."

Bolt lifts one eyebrow toward her and smirks. Swift slaps him hard on his shoulder, his bionic hand rubs the sore spot.

They're sharing a joke but I've not heard the punchline.

I ignore them. I'm too old for childish games. In truth, my leg is aching, and I could do with swallowing some painkillers down and getting horizontal to take the pressure off. I pull the cane toward me, push the tip against the floor, and balance myself once I haul my ass out of the chair.

My limp is more pronounced than normal as I try to keep up with Swift's pace. Instead of getting frustrated with myself, I remember I had a long ride today, pushing myself on the final leg of my journey. Then I was forced to stand, sit, stand again. All without the aid of the Tramadol which I usually take because it tends to make me drowsy and dull my senses. In a place like this, I need to be on high alert.

No wonder the damaged muscles and newly healed bones are screaming in agony.

I'm thankful that in this multi-level clubhouse there's no need for stairs, and my grimace when a particularly bad bolt of pain shoots up my leg as I step inside the elevator means I almost miss that instead of pressing a button, Swift presents what resembles a credit card to the keypad inside. The doors shut, and once again the car starts to rise.

I note that access to the level above seems to be security controlled, and once again marvel at the differences in this club. *No tech knowledge be damned.* They aren't living in the stone age, no, they've gone far beyond.

Music is again playing quietly in the elevator, the type that gets on my nerves. That generic nothing played on a constant loop that gets stuck in your brain. Why the fuck they have it, I've no idea.

Leaving my questions about the security access for now, I jerk my head toward the speakers.

"Is that really necessary?"

"What?" She frowns. "Oh, the music."

"Music?"

She chuckles. "Honor's joke. I don't even notice it now."

"Thought an MC would have something more gutsy. Hard rock at least."

Now she eyes me seriously. "You've got a lot to learn."

With that enigmatic statement, it seems we've arrived. When the metallic voice announces the doors are opening, I step out.

The corridor could be that I'd find in any impersonal hotel I've ever stayed in. Doors off to either side, the only thing distinguishing one from the other is the number on the door. Swift stops in front of the one marked '11' and I notice that she turns her back on me as she presents yet another key card to the lock. I have an inward laugh at myself, knowing she's written me off as no threat. But it would be a stupid man that tried to overpower her as I'd earlier witnessed, and also, if I'm to learn anything of benefit to Drummer, she, my partner, would appear to hold all the keys, and I'm not referring only to the one she's holding in her hand.

The light flashes red then green, and Swift presses delicate fingers to the handle, slight but deadly as she's already demonstrated. I suspect she's learned how to pry out a man's eyeballs with them, or twist off his dick without the need for the bionics that Bolt has.

I laugh at myself. The thought of Swift's hand on my cock is one I have to put out of my mind fast. *She's akin to a brother.*

As standing behind her gives me a decent view of her pert

ass, I entertain a niggling thought that that's going to be harder than it should be to remember.

Again, similar to many hotel rooms, the key card slides into a holder by the side of the door and when Swift has done just that, immediately the lights come on.

"Really?" I question again.

"It saves on electricity," she replies. "There's a spare card in the desk so you can leave this one here if you're charging something." I think we both remember at the same time that they'll have left me nothing to charge. She changes tack. "I'll be here in the morning. Zero eight hundred hours suit?"

It suits. Fucking early though for a man who's used to working the late shift at a strip club.

"I'll be ready."

"Oh, here's Brute now." She steps back to let the big man put my bags just inside the door, then her eyes meet mine once again. "Goodnight."

I won't pretend to be surprised that after giving her a moment to walk away, when I reach for the door handle, I find it locked from the outside.

I'm a prisoner. A cursory search of my bags shows my tablet is gone. With Pip in possession of my cell, there is no way for me to reach Drummer.

7

———

*S*wift...

I enter my own room a few doors down from Road's and for a moment lean my back against the door and close my eyes.

My background is no secret from anyone here, but I don't often expose my wounds to the world, preferring to move on rather than look back. Road's first question had challenged me, opened a need in me to explain why a woman with my background fits the bill of someone attracted to joining an MC, even if they don't have a dick swinging between their legs.

I have to admit there aren't too many clubs I could join. A women-only club had never appealed to me, in fact, it wasn't until I'd met Pip that I thought any MC would become my new home. He'd had to convince me to give it a try. But once I saw what this chapter of the Satan's Devils stood for, the tables had turned, and I knew I wanted nothing more than to earn my place to ride beside them.

A woman being able to try out for the SAS is a very big thing, and I treated prospecting for the club no differently. It wasn't that a female had to prove to be equal to the men, we had to be better than the best.

Women are inherently thought of as weak, our size belying our strength. Even though it's the twenty-first century, women are still predominantly seen as homemakers, the ones keeping their men, the main or sole wage earners, happy, and bringing up the kids—especially in the state of Utah with its overriding view of patriarchy. Unless a woman is trained like me, men can use their larger size to keep them in their place with their fists and even without violence, terms still used in everyday vocabulary, like the 'little woman', are used to keep them down. Men tend to be in powerful roles and use their positions to denigrate any woman they see as a threat. A strong woman with a brain is one to be feared and to be kept controlled.

To earn my patch, I had to not only prove I was an equal, but also show the lack of a cock could be an advantage. Sure, I'm a ball-breaker, a woman who takes no shit, but if I have to, I can put away my fatigues and carry off a dress. More than once I have used that talent to make men relax their guard and get taken in.

My disguise is one that comes naturally, a lethal weapon hidden in plain sight. Pip saw the benefits immediately, and on more than one occasion has shamelessly used them.

My Satan's Devils' brothers? Well, they took a little longer to persuade. My credentials had meant nothing until they'd seen what I was capable of for themselves. Then, of course, just like Brute, Gears and Igor were doing right now, I had to prove I was trustworthy.

I passed with flying colours, well, I'd been through that all before when I first joined up and had to prove to the army I was more than a girl.

I gained more than my Satan's Devils' patch. I found my place, my home, and a new family. Would I have been happier in the SAS? Probably. Do I regret saving a life and losing what I hoped for mine instead? No, never that. A man's alive because of me. Do I miss home and my family? Yes, but I can't see me going back, not permanently. Here, I feel, is right where the universe wants me. And, I remind myself, *my world will only stay as it is now if word of my existence, and Pip's, doesn't get back to Drummer. I have to be careful.* Road could be the cause of me once again losing the future I've worked so hard to achieve.

Now pushing away from the door, I take off my cut and fold it reverently. It means something to me, almost as much as the beige beret I was so close to putting on. It's something I've earned and, like any Devil, only death will part it from me. I take off my clothes, throwing most in the laundry basket. Thinking my jeans will do one more day, I put them neatly into a drawer. Then, taking out my sleep attire, I go through my nightly routine.

When I slide into my perfectly made bed, I switch off the lights but know I won't get to sleep for a while yet. When I close my eyes, all I can see is Road.

Fuck, but he'd spent the day perplexed as if he was Alice and had stepped through the looking glass into a world completely different from the reflection he'd thought he would find. Another chapter of the Satan's Devils, but unlike any he could have expected or visited before.

What will he think when he finds out what we're hiding? Will he agree that we might have twisted our tenuous observance of the Satan's Devils by-laws too far? Will he show he has strengths that we've not yet seen? Will he be a bonus or hindrance if he patches over, and if he won't, will it really be curtains for him?

Since we lost Thumper, we are a man down, but won't be if, as expected, Gears soon patches in. We keep our team tight, would there be room for one more?

Playing pool and darts, drinking beside him, I was watching Road the whole time tonight. Even when I offered to keep his glass filled, he restricted himself to only a few beers, was holding himself back and not letting loose, even while the other brothers figuratively let down their hair.

Road's good-looking, I can't deny that. But if I needed a man, I'd do what the brothers do, pick up a likely looking bedfellow for the night in town, or try out a hangaround that comes to our parties. I've no desire to be tied down, not yet anyway. While I'd never say never to the idea of taking a permanent partner, even going the whole shebang and having kids, I don't see that in my future as yet. Maybe ever. How could I, who could best most, if not all, of the men that I know, harness my horses to that wagon?

Children make you weak, not physically, but emotionally. When you have kids, you have something that can be held over your head, and that's not somewhere I would want to go.

Thinking about being weak, I sit up, and do what I should have done when I first came to bed, take out my hearing aids. If I don't, I'll get no sleep. As soon as I roll over, I'll get annoying feedback from one or the other, and the other disadvantage is the build-up of wax.

I hate taking them out, and as usual delay until the very last minute. When I'm wearing them, I feel just like anyone else. Sure, my hearing's not perfect, sometimes I need to ask people to repeat what they've just said. But at least I can forget that I'm all but totally deaf. Without them, I hate the sudden silence that descends. Even after almost four years, I'm not used to it.

Without them, the dark becomes a scary place, even though I have no need to be apprehensive. The brothers have taken care of that. Knowing I can't hear a fire alarm, Duty set it up so my bed vibrates. Likewise, there's a discreet button on the outside of my door that will send a light flashing by my bed if someone comes to wake me.

But still I'm uneasy when I cut the outside world out. It's not peaceful, I hate it. As a soldier, I was taught to be alert at all times. On more than one occasion, a twig snapping or the sound of a gun being cocked literally saved my life. It's not easy coming to terms with the loss of one of your senses. Once my hearing aids come out, I'm no longer the confident Swift. I feel weak and vulnerable.

The first time waking up in the hospital ward and not being able to hear the doctor explain what had happened to me had been the most terrifying experience of my life. Not much had made me afraid up until then. Through the wonders of technology, he'd written out on his tablet that my hearing was unlikely to return, but might improve albeit slightly. I think I knew right then, my life, as I knew it, had significantly changed.

Pushing down the panic that threatens to return when I remember those first bleak days, I lie back down, immersed in complete silence, my fists clenching.

You learn a lot in the army, part of which is training your body to sleep when you can, no matter where you are or whether you're on hard ground or a soft bed. That's a trick I've been determined not to forget. It works now. Tonight, by repeating the mantra I'm safe here and nothing can take me unawares, I stave off the threatening panic. I tell my brain it's time to switch off and know no more until I wake on the dot of zero five hundred hours.

The first thing I do is put in my hearing aids with a feeling of relief, then feeling human again, I check the messages on my phone.

Half an hour later, I'm pounding the streets as I go for my morning run. I've a number of routes that I've measured out each coming in at six miles in length. I try to do each in under an hour. Today I manage it in fifty-five minutes. That I've completed it well within my target time puts a smile on my face.

Once back, I hit the gym. As I approach the weights, Rascal approaches me.

"Want me to spot you?"

I nod my thanks. His eagle eyes watch me, and he helpfully adds an extra five-pound weight to each side of the bar when I ask. When my muscles start warning me I've done enough for now, I replace the bar and slide out from under it.

I'm sweaty, rivulets are running down me. Sniffing under my arms, I pronounce, "Christ, I stink."

"Just what I was thinking," Rascal throws at me, expertly jumping away from my playful fist. "Hey, Swift, I'm always surprised just how fuckin' unladylike you are."

Shrugging off his comment, well, most of my life has been spent with men, I remind him, "I'm no lady, Rascal. Thought you'd know that by now."

He snorts, then changes the subject. "You still mad Prez paired you up with the fuckin' new guy?"

While my preference is to work alone, I've been nursemaid to FNGs before. That doesn't worry me. "Nah, we should give him a chance. Prez knows I won't take any bullshit."

"True." He shakes his head. "Can't see him fitting in, myself. But we can't have him running back to Drummer."

No, we can't. I'm wondering how we can stop that without any bloodshed when Rascal, a lithe but strong and capable man, goes to the leg press and starts his own exercise routine. With a mock salute, I leave the gym.

I've time to take a leisurely shower, grab an energy drink and down it, then, it's time to go and release the man I'm still finding it hard to think of as my new partner.

The word partner suggests an equal, and with Road having to be locked in his room and left with no means of communication with the outside world, he's anything but that. While I've been exercising, I've been going through in my head how to approach today. Strategizing, I'm good at that. First, we'll kick off with a tour of the clubhouse, or at least those parts prospects are allowed to access, which will probably bring up a myriad of questions I'll have to decide how to address.

I wonder whether Road will be rested and ready to take on the day, or will he be in a closed-off mood, once he'd found he'd been locked in last night?

Well, I won't know until I see him. *Here goes nothing,* I think as I knock on the door, then present the key. As the light turns green, I push down on the handle and push the door ajar.

"You decent in there?"

The door's pulled fully open from the other side.

I'm pleased to see Road is, indeed, decent. Delectably so. I have to resist the urge to lick my lips. His hair freshly washed and dried gleams as it falls around his shoulders, his fresh t-shirt clings to his abs, and his bare arms flex bringing my attention to his tattoos. His head is tilted in challenge when my eyes rise to his face.

"You're on time," he comments. Then continues before I can respond, "I expected that."

I shrug. Some habits are hard to kick. Not that this is a bad one. "You ready for me to show you around?"

His head shakes, and his eyes widen slightly as he leans his forearm against the door jamb. "Only if that tour starts in the fuckin' kitchen. Not sure if you noticed, Swift, but I've been locked in this room for eight hours and there's nothing the fuck to eat here."

Mentally I backtrack, realising he's right. Sometimes the sociable niceties of snacking or eating at other than set times pass me by. "Sure."

Standing back, I let him precede me out of the room.

"Elevator?" he asks.

"Yup. Our kitchen is on the ground floor."

"Ground… First. Got it."

"Road," I growl, warningly as he presses the button to call the elevator. He'll need no card to activate it for a downward journey, nor to let him out on the right floor. I'm conscious he might be planning to try to incapacitate me and attempt an escape. It wouldn't work, and I don't want to hurt him.

He turns, fast, his large body crowding me as I stand my ground. "Fuckin' said I'd stay, didn't I? Fuckin' great team we're going to make if you don't trust me at all. How's this going to work, Swift, if you're always watching out for me trying to run?"

He's right, but… "I don't know you."

He sighs. "I get that, Swift. But Pip asked me to give you a chance. And how the fuck would I do that if I walked out right now?"

Prez had also suggested Road might be leaving in a box if he didn't decide to patch over, or, if he couldn't bring anything to the table that we haven't already got. That, alone, would get a sensible man running for the hills.

As if he can read my mind, Road shakes his head again, his hair moving around his shoulders. "I'm no fool, Swift. I know what's waiting for me if I don't like what I find. But," he raises his eyes to look over my head as if wondering whether to tell me. "I love my Tucson brothers, never think other than that. My club lifted me out of the role of bouncer and put me in fuckin' charge at Angels. Never thought I'd make manager of anything, but that said, running a strip club, well…" His voice trails off. "Let's just say, keeping the strippers from tearing each other's hair out, and the customers hands away from things they shouldn't touch wasn't my life's ambition."

"Which was to ride in the World Championship?"

His shoulders rise and fall. "To take part in the qualifying races at least. Huh," he snorts. "I even applied for and got a passport. I was supposed to go to your part of the world next year." He shrugs again. "Now everything I thought I'd have to look forward to has been taken away. What's left is…"

"Boring?"

"I dunno. Maybe I need a new challenge."

He's surprised me. "You're saying you're ready to move on from Tucson?"

"Maybe I am." He's still talking at the wall over my head. "The club is all about family, which is as it should be, brothers united against the world. In Tucson, it *is* family. Most brothers have ol' ladies, and most now have kids of their own."

"You want your own ol' lady?"

"What would I do with an ol' lady—no, don't answer that." He grins and looks down at me, in doing so, his face grows serious again. "Kids? What the fuck do I know about them? I know nothing about having a happy home. Doubt I'd be a good role model."

That's about how I feel about being a mum. What could I do? Show my kids how to strip down, put back together and shoot a gun or kill a man using only their hands to do it?

I stand back and gesture toward the elevator. "Come on. Let's get you fed."

His eyebrow raises slightly as I allow him to precede me inside the car, giving him ample opportunity to shove me back as the doors close. He'd be on his own with a clear route to freedom unless Igor or whoever's on reception duty today had the gumption to stop him. If he walked out like he owned the place, they might let him pass. Everyone knows I've got responsibility for him, and I never lose a man I'm guarding.

But we're partners. Trust has got to start somewhere. I have the notion Utah might have the something Road is searching for—a new purpose, a new reason for living. Fuck knows, I can understand that. It had been that way for me.

Road's loyal to his prez, as he should be. But maybe his spying mission is turning into personal exploration, something to fill that hole inside him.

As he moves to the back of the elevator making space for me to join him, I start to think I might not be mistaken. Finding an escape route isn't the top of Road's agenda, or not at this moment. His raised eyebrow and his look of expectation shows he's intrigued.

Perhaps Pip was right to pair us together. Someone else might not have seen that Road, it appears, is interested in giving us a chance. If not for our sakes, for his.

Or maybe he's cleverer than we've given him credit for and has spying skills we don't expect. It could be he's scoping us out to flesh out a report for Drummer. I frown. I mustn't forget that possibility.

8

———

*R*oad...

I'd woken feeling groggy as though I had a hangover, the slow-to-clear fog in my head being a result of the painkillers washed down with the beer I'd found in the convenient mini-bar in the room.

The first order of business is to put myself under the shower, letting the cascading water wash some of the cobwebs away. A little more refreshed, I dry myself, then take a clean t-shirt from my saddlebags and dress.

Clicking on the television bolted to the wall, I mute it, but notice the time, glad I had an hour or so to kill before Swift was due to come and release me, using it to start my brain working once again.

I've never been arrested, never been trapped somewhere I couldn't get out, so my eyes keep going to the door, focusing on the lock. While at first, the sixty minutes seemed useful, they soon began to drag. *How dare they cage me like a fucking animal.*

I'm on edge and want to pace, but my leg's feeling easier after a good night's sleep, and unless I want to lean heavily on the cane, keeping my weight off of it will keep my muscles from being strained. The acknowledgement of my limitations do not add positively to my mood. I do some exercises that the physical therapist had shown me. Each day there are small improvements. Today, I'll leave my stick in the room and try to do without it.

My stomach rumbles.

I've already searched what hospitality there is on offer, but it's not much. The bar contains drinks but no food. So not only am I locked away, it seems they intend to starve me. *Nah, don't be stupid.* There are far easier ways of killing me.

I've never felt claustrophobic before, never really had need to. But that must be what I'm feeling now as part of my brain insists they've forgotten all about me. This room may resemble a hotel, but I doubt housekeeping calls regularly. What if I'm left here, no way out, no sustenance, and all they find when they eventually remember me is my dead body?

Don't be fucking stupid and melodramatic. I find I'm lecturing myself again.

Swift told me she'd come get me at eight o'clock, and her army background suggests she'll be punctual and won't keep me waiting.

I take deep breaths, forcing myself to think rationally.

Weird doesn't begin to describe this strange Satan's Devils' chapter I've come to. To say things are not what they seem is an understatement. First, they appear to have technical knowledge which no one thought they had, and access to shit I never expected. That hand of Bolt's is incredible for a start. The prez isn't the prez and the VP is not who I thought either. As for what business they're in, I've still no idea.

Could there be something for me here? Would I find a purpose to replace my lost dreams? I won't know until I give them a chance to show me what they are about, and how they earn their money.

If I wanted to, is there a way I could escape, get to my bike and ride off, find some means of contacting Drummer? Hell, even slip away and find a phone to use here. But as it stands now, I've no way of alerting my prez.

If I bolt, I lose my chance to find out what's going on, and whether I'd like to be part of it.

If I stay, I've a good excuse to stay quiet. I don't have a way to update anyone, and I'll be gaining more information for when the time comes that I can.

But to learn as much as I can, I'll have to earn the trust of the members here. To do that means letting go of my anger at the way they're treating me. If I go on the verbal attack when Swift finally appears, that's not going to win her confidence.

Anger I can push down with justifications of why it's not the correct emotion right now, the gnawing of my stomach is a physical fact far harder for me to deal with. I'm a big man, I can't live on air.

So when Swift appears and starts going on about a tour she wants to take me on, I've only one thought in my mind. Hunger.

My question about breakfast seemed to take her by surprise. Suspicion dripped off her when we arrived at the elevator. It hadn't actually crossed my mind that I could push her aside, descend to the first floor and head out to my bike, the key for which is still in my cut. I'd already decided if I ran with my tail between my legs, I'd have no info for Drummer other than that the wool has been pulled over his eyes with regard to the structure here, oh, and for the existence of Swift herself.

I'd been taken aback, so I called her out on it, and found myself admitting something that wasn't just an excuse to make her think I was buying into transferring to Utah. It was the truth that maybe staying in Tucson wasn't where I wanted to be for the rest of my life.

My arrival in the Arizona city had been by accident. I'd stayed in Washington where I'd had my last foster home, and knew I was sliding downhill. At the age of eighteen, I'd been too old for the system, but no one offered me a home. There weren't many who'd take me in. I'd had nowhere to go other than to accept the offer of bunking down on a sofa with one of the old school friends I'd remained in contact with. I managed to get a job stacking shelves in a grocery store, my friend, well, I didn't quite know how he was coming by his money.

If I'm honest, I didn't want to know, just as long as he didn't drag me down into his business. One of the homes where I'd been placed, the man had a drug habit, and the money they got from fostering fed that rather than the children they brought home. It was there I'd learned the damage drugs could do. I'd witnessed his mood swings, learned how to evade his fists, seen him climbing the walls when he needed his fix. I'd seen enough to steer well clear of anything to do with that scene.

But it wasn't drugs my friend was into, or not directly. When confronted, he'd assured me of that. He was, however, part of a gang. A gang who were into any shady dealings which brought in money without them having to do hard work. Even then I'd had bulk which made me look threatening, and I'd begun to get approaches of the type it was getting harder to refuse. It culminated in them wanting me to get them into the store where I worked so they could rob the tills one night.

They weren't the type you refused easily. I could either start a criminal career or find my time on earth limited. I had to get out but had no idea where to go. Desperate, I took all my available cash that I'd saved and got myself to the bus station. I got on the first Greyhound headed south and rode that as far as the money I'd spent on the ticket would take me, and that ended up getting off that bus in Tucson.

It was warm as I'd hoped, so sleeping rough wasn't a problem. As I hadn't aided or abetted a robbery and without me being there to open up, none had yet taken place, I got a decent enough reference from my old employer and was able to pick up more work. Mostly lifting and moving shit, as my main attribute was brawn. I stayed in Tucson at first as it was convenient, then I answered an ad for a bouncer's job at a strip club. Hey, don't judge me, I was a young man and the thought of spending all my time among naked and half-naked women sounded right up my street.

The job, however, wasn't what I expected. Instead of watching the ladies strut their wares on the stage, I was stuck at the door weeding out undesirables and flexing my muscles to show others what they'd be in for if they caused trouble inside. When I did get close to the show, it was to persuade someone who'd had too much to drink or had got far too touchy-feely with the girls that it was in their best interests to leave. Sometimes I needed to eject them physically.

Before and after the shifts I'd meet the girls, by then dressed in their street clothes. I became friendly, got to know their circumstances and they became women with histories to me, and not objects for my eyes to leer over.

The Satan's Devils were good to work for, and when a chance to prospect for them came up, I jumped at it. Well, as soon as I could afford to buy the Harley, my trials bike didn't impress them. Until we had to bury twenty bodies, and they had the idea to make me a practice track up in the forest behind the compound.

It still makes me smile to remember it. It was just after I'd taken a bullet trying to prevent Sam being kidnapped. Unable to ride myself, I'd been terrified when Peg commandeered my precious baby, my competition bike—I couldn't object, I was still a prospect then. They all took turns riding it, while I hardly dared watch. In the end, it had been Sam, who by then had become Drummer's old lady, who had beaten everyone. It had ended up a fun day, and surprisingly both my bike and my sanity had survived it.

The track, known as Road's, was still in use when I left Tucson. It's been extended for its original purpose a time or two, but I didn't complain. It was a great practice track, and what bother was a few more skeletons buried under it?

But I no longer needed it.

I need the Devils, I know that. I loved the camaraderie from the first moment I stepped foot onto the compound. But Tucson? That's the thing, I don't know. Apart from my brothers, I've no ties to it. Maybe it would be better to move on, to find new interests and challenges. In Utah?

The suggestion might have me thinking about moving, and staying a Devil is a given. But there are other chapters which might suit better. Here, I've hardly been welcomed—I've been threatened, coerced and imprisoned.

I need respect from the brothers I ride alongside, and the confidence to respect them in return. That being missing, I could never transfer, and neither if they were into drugs or dealing. Those are my hard limits.

So yeah, maybe I'm at the right place for a change. Admitting to Swift that Tucson perhaps isn't the be-all and end-all for me any more seemed to change how she viewed me. When the elevator doors opened, she waved me on inside. I could easily have pushed her clear so I could escape, and I half expected her to be holding a gun on me. But no, instead, she'd decided to show a little trust in me.

Partners. That's what Pip said we'd be. Okay, so partners don't lock each other in a bedroom, but I'll just have to move on from that today and put it behind me. Carrying a grudge won't help me discover the secrets of this chapter.

We exit on the first floor, which surprises me. I'd expected the kitchen to be on the same level as the clubroom, close by in case brothers want snacks. Swift directs me along a hallway in the opposite direction to the gym, and soon I'm entering what looks like it could be any work cafeteria. There are empty Formica-topped tables, even fucking napkins in holders scattered around, as well as tidy assortments of various condiments laid out.

The counter and display cabinets are empty. It looks like the place is closed, although tempting odours are wafting our way.

Led by my empty stomach, I follow Swift as she makes a path around the tables, and pushes open a swing door by the side of the counter.

A man, crouched down, speaks from his position on the ground. "What d'ya want?"

"Road's hungry," Swift announces, glancing around.

"Well, he should have fuckin' come down on time. Kitchen's closed now."

I open my mouth to say I would have done if I'd been able to, when Swift goes to a large industrial-sized fridge and speaks on my behalf. "My fault, 'Boy. I didn't think."

Ah, yes. This is Cowboy. I recognise him as he stands. The checked shirt he's wearing makes him look like he just rode in off the range. All he needs is a ten-gallon hat to complete the look.

Cowboy tosses a glare at Swift. "I'm not cooking for him."

"It's okay, I'll do it," she casually replies.

The cowboy-come-biker rolls his eyes. "I didn't hear Pip telling you to kill him." Then he turns my way, and frowns. "You cook, Road?"

"I get by."

His shoulders pull back a little. "Been in a professional kitchen before?"

"Been in one, yes, many times. The Angels cooked up fries and snacks, and Tucson runs the Wheel Inn, our restaurant. Used one? No."

Swift snorts. "Doubt if Road's the person you're looking for to help you out. Not from the sound of it. Look, Road, there's some bacon and eggs. 'Boy's right. If I cook it, you'll end up with food poisoning, so here you are."

She places them down on the counter. I eye them dubiously. Not that I'm a stranger to pots and pans, it's just I wouldn't know where to start with the monstrosity of a cooker that's facing me.

A sigh, then Cowboy takes the food Swift pulled out. He presses a few buttons on the digital stove, then points a spatula toward me. "Breakfast is seven to eight. Eight-thirty on Sundays. You want to eat in the future, you'd best remember that."

"So," I hop up onto a counter, then immediately jump down seeing his glare. "So, you're the cook then?"

This time Swift's snort is strangled with a laugh.

"Chef. I'm the *chef*," he clarifies, waving a spatula threateningly and holding my eye until I give a sharp nod.

"He was a Navy chef," Swift informs me, picking up an apple and taking a large bite. Once she's swallowed she continues, "Used to cook gourmet food for the admirals."

"Yeah, well…" Cowboy looks somewhat mollified. "That's as well as feeding a crew of two thousand or more."

"How did you end up here?" I ask, genuinely interested.

"Well, I did my time, got out. Had dreams to open my own restaurant." His face darkens as though a cloud has passed over it, then he visibly shakes himself. "That didn't pan out. One thing and another led here."

"Satan's Devils put you to work?" It's clear he's in charge of the kitchen, another difference from back home. There the old ladies feed anyone who doesn't want to cook in their own home, or lives on the compound in the suites used by single brothers.

Cowboy looks amused now. "Not at first. They used to take turns. Seemed easier to take it on myself, then risk death by salmonella. Fuck, but at times I was more scared than facing an enemy." His eyes widen slightly as he recalls those days. "So, while I thought I'd put my chef's whites behind me, I donned them again. Well," he glances down at himself, "figuratively."

The wonderful smell of bacon fills my nostrils, and I watch him expertly crack eggs into a pan. As they sizzle, he adds a few herbs and spices. It's not long before he places two loaded biscuits in front of me.

Dubious about the extras, I reach for the ketchup and apply my normal amount, then raise the biscuit to my mouth.

Christ. If this is a sample of the way they eat here, maybe transferring would be a good idea. Even Ma's breakfast recipes from the book she left us when she died can't match up to this. I don't speak, don't ask questions, just carry on eating until not even crumbs are left on my plate. Then I raise my fingers to my mouth and lick them.

"Good?" Swift's mouth quirks.

I nod, still trying to savour the final moments of flavour.

"Wash it down with this." Cowboy places a coffee pot in front of me, and pushes creamer and sugar my way.

It's good stuff, some special blend or something. I eye Swift. "You're not having any?"

"Huh." Cowboy scoffs as he cleans up the kitchen, clearly for the second time today. "She's a fuckin' heathen. Only drinks English breakfast tea." My eyes follow him as he carefully wipes everything down.

Swift grins but doesn't apologise for the error of her ways.

"You done?" she says when my cup is empty.

I find I am indeed done. My stomach feels full, and my

body has been re-caffeinated sufficiently for now. "Is this where you tell me what's going on?"

"I'm going to show you," she says. "Come."

"Lunch at noon, dinner at eighteen hundred hours," Cowboy calls after us as we leave the kitchen.

"You really have set mealtimes?" In Tucson it was usually when the food was ready, or heated up leftovers at any time.

"Cowboy hasn't got the patience for anything else. He's got better things to do with his time. Or course, when shit hits the fan, he adapts. When it's quiet, as it is now, he likes to serve us all at once."

I don't know of any MCs with a top chef in residence, so I can't compare, and I'm definitely not going to put in any complaints. From the haunted look in Cowboy's eyes, I've a feeling there's an unhappy story as to why the chef isn't running his own top restaurant. Jury's out as to whether he'd win any Michelin stars, though that breakfast comes close to suggesting he might be worthy.

9

———————

*R*oad...

We head out through the cafeteria again, and this time Swift uses her key card at another door. I expect it to lead into an office, instead I'm presented with a room which Mouse would probably offer to sell his soul to the Devil in exchange to be allowed inside to play. One wall is completely taken up by a range of monitors, all flat screen. A couple are showing the outside of the compound, and others are currently dark, clearly switched off.

"The receptionist gets the same view," Swift explains, when she sees where my eyes are fixed. She nods at Duty and Honor who have keyboards in front of them. There are half a dozen work stations in all. In addition to the wall mounted monitors, each work station has its own screen. There's a low hum of computers whirring in the background as fans keep them cool. In the corner, his back turned toward the rest, sits Stormy. I notice he doesn't greet me. I also find I don't care.

"Okay, question time." I look down at Swift. "Why do Drummer and all the other chapters think Utah's got no technical capacity? And no computer experts?" It gets worse, I recall. "Why the fuck do you call on Mouse's help when you need information? Or," I wave my hand, "is this all for show?"

"There," Honor's voice interrupts, pointing to his screen.

"Got it," Duty replies. His hands fly over his keyboard. "Tickets sorted." He then sits back and fist bumps his, what? Partner? Colleague? Lover?

"And," I add to my list of questions, "what are you doing here?"

Swift nods her head toward Honor. "Part of it is what these two are working on. We sometimes provide aid to a pipeline to help women, and men, escape from abusive partners. They're currently tracking the progress of a woman and her kid, making sure they get to the next stage of their journey. Duty's just hacked into the Greyhound database to ensure tickets are waiting for them when they arrive at the terminal. That moves them on safely, with no trace back to them."

It sounds impressive and far more worthwhile than anything I was thinking. "What else?"

"This is the hub of our operation. If, when, you go out on a case, you'll be connected back to here. Where possible, camera feed from our body cams will show on these monitors, and you'll be given the information you need to know."

"What operations?" I ask, then backtrack. "No, go back to my original question. Why the fuck make Mouse, Cad, Token, and Keys jump through hoops when you're set up better than they are?"

She purses her lips and gives a slight grimace. "We're good at what we do, Road. We run a tight ship, as 'Boy would say. Sure, we can, and do, help other chapters, even when they don't know. But we can't have our facilities used for every little enquiry that Mouse needs help with. If they knew what we could do, they'd want to use us and our capability, and at times we're almost too stretched to help ourselves."

Mouse has got his own expert hacker on speed dial—a woman who's married to an Arab prince of all things. I doubt he'd be calling on Utah. My lips thin. But that's beside the point. Surely chapters should want to help each other out?

But she's intimated they do, just not openly. Wheels whir in my mind as I try to dredge something up. Something I remember hearing about sat around the table back in Tucson. *It couldn't be, could it?*

It adds up. With a touch of anger, I try my idea out. "San Diego? Were you the fuckin' dicks leading Token around by the nose? Telling Lost his old lady needed protection without explaining why? Giving Token the key to decipher the information?" It might not have happened in our chapter, but Drummer wanted us all to know. None of us like a mystery. "You were the ones who fuckin' sent up the drone?" That my words have struck home is shown by the way Swift's lips have thinned. I don't need the slight raise of her chin to confirm it.

"Goddamn it." I smash my hand down on the back of a chair.

"That would have been Stormy." Swift's tone suggests she didn't approve. *That he helped? Or the way he did it?*

There's more. Could Stormy have…? Suddenly I find myself taking a step toward him. "Did you take out that fuckin' bastard Lost deserved to have his time with?"

Stormy waves a dismissive hand above his shoulder, but doesn't turn around. "The fucker's dead. What more did they want?"

Revenge. And, if I recall rightly, answers about why Alder was so intent on finding Lost's old lady.

"You motherfucker," I roar. Everyone in San Diego and Tucson had been running themselves ragged looking for answers, when they were to be found in Utah all along.

Stormy stands and looms menacingly. "You want to

fuckin' take—" His voice abruptly stops and his eyes goes wide as he looks toward his screen.

All the bodies around me have frozen, then as fast defrost. As if summoned by an invisible deity, Honor and Duty stand, then, with Stormy rudely brushing past me, knocking into my shoulder and almost putting me off balance, they head toward the door.

"Come on," Swift says, her voice as urgent as their actions had been. "This way."

I hold my hands out in a *what the fuck* gesture, but then do as she says. Again I have to let her lead the way, this time into a room I do recognise. It's their meeting room where they hold church. Every man is present. *Don't they have regular jobs?* To get here so fast, they must all have been hanging around the clubhouse. Bolt and Rascal look sweaty as though they've come straight from the gym. Thor too, he's wiping his face with a towel as he walks in, and if I'm not mistaken, his t-shirt has been put on inside out.

A spare chair is to Swift's left. I suppose that's for me, so I take it.

Unlike in Tucson, there's no friendly banter, and the expressions on everyone's faces is various versions of seriousness, curiosity and preparedness. There are a couple of murmured conversations which I can make little sense of. *Fuelled and ready,* is one answer supplied.

But it's total silence when Pip and Snatcher walk in, and all eyes go to the head of the table.

"Kidnap." Pip doesn't waste time waiting until his ass hits the seat before talking business. He lets that one word sink in as though it's supposed to mean something, then continues, "Thirteen-year-old girl snatched off the street on her way home from a friend's."

"Planned?" This is from Honor.

Pip dips and raises his chin. "Pretty sure her movements were tracked."

What does it all mean, and why are the Satan's Devils involved in it?

"Ransom demand?"

Pip nods at Thor. "A cool five million."

"Note or phone call?" Bolt asks.

"Call."

I think my mouth has fallen open. These men seem elevated from MC brothers discussing business. They seem to speak in a language I'm finding hard to follow, picking up information from short questions and one-word answers. One thing that can't be denied, they're professionals.

"Send me the details," Duty requests.

"How fast were we involved?"

Snatcher takes over from Pip, and answers Piston. "Kid was due home at twenty-hundred hours last night. When she didn't arrive, they tried all the normal shit, contacting friends, tracing her journey."

"Cops involved?"

"Nah." Snatcher continues, this time looking Thor's way, "The kidnappers didn't give them much of a chance. By twenty-one hundred they got in touch."

Thor raises an eyebrow. "With a 'go to the cops' and you'll never see your daughter again', I suppose."

"You got it," Snatcher confirms.

I'm trying to translate what's going on but admit to having difficulty keeping up. Case in point, the twenty-four clock might be as natural as breathing to these military men, but I'm getting lost. I remember Peg once telling me you just needed to subtract twelve to translate it to normal time. My head must look like someone following a tennis match as it whips back and forth trying to keep track as comments come from all sides about things that make sense to all but one of the members seated around this table. The odd one out being me.

"And they only called us this morning?" Swift's rolling her eyes.

My head swings back Pip's way as he nods. "Probably trying to work out if they could get the cash together."

"They probably can. The kidnappers would make sure any request could be fulfilled," Honor remarks.

"Where?" Preacher's got his hands clasped on the table, and his sharp eyes view his prez.

"Santa Barbara," Pip replies.

Preacher raises his head, closes his eyes, then opens them and looks back down. "I can have boots on the ground in four hours."

How? I might be able to ride a motorcycle fast, not that fast, nor the stamina to maintain the necessary high speed for so long. But that begs the question, what's this all about? What the fuck is going on? And what are the Satan's Devils supposed to do about a kid getting kidnapped, sad however much that is.

"Swift, I want you in on this one." When the woman beside me offers a chin lift as though she's been expecting it, Pip glances around. "Piston, Rascal, Thor and Honor. You go with Snatcher."

"What about me?"

"You stay here, Stormy." The words *where I can keep an eye on you* are unspoken, but nevertheless, come through loud and clear, even to me a stranger.

The face of the man in question goes bright red.

There's a family in California missing a thirteen-year-old child. Apart from the parents' anguish, she must be scared out of her mind. Never mind these aren't my brothers, and I don't have a clue how an MC could help, I raise my hand, getting Pip's attention, remembering I'm supposed to be partnering with Swift. I know my limitations though. If *boots on the ground* can be interpreted as the members named are heading out to California, there's no way in hell I'll currently be able to ride along. Nevertheless, with roles being handed out, I'm not comfortable being locked in my room and forgotten while shit's going down.

Which drives me to ask, "What do you want me to do?"

Pip looks around the table, seemingly ignoring my question. "Duty, Bolt, Stormy and Cowboy. I've sent you everything we've got so far. Go start digging." The men in question get up from the table and leave with chin lifts towards their prez. When they're gone, Pip looks down the table at me. "Can you handle yourself, Road?"

"I was a bouncer, seen my share of roughhousing. I can handle a gun." I might also have taken a few knife-throwing lessons from Mouse, but I don't bother to mention that.

"You a man who runs from danger?" he continues to probe.

"Nah," I tell him. "Can't say I'd run toward it, but if one of my brothers is in danger, I'd have their back." I have had to more than once.

It's Snatcher who asks the next question. "That patch you wear is the same as ours. You going to be able to count us as your brothers?"

I stare at him for a second, incredulous he has to ask. "I can't pretend I know what you're doing, or how or why you're involved. But from what I've heard, there's a thirteen-year-old kid in danger and fuckin' terrified by now. I take it you're mounting some sort of rescue. Well, if you're offering me a part of that, I'll be right there alongside you."

"What about your leg?" Swift asks, from beside me. "That going to hold you back?"

I turn to her and reply honestly, "If we're riding all the way to California, then yeah, I might have a problem." Darn thing will seize long before we get there. "If I can stay local, strapping it up keeps it in place."

"You get that knee bound, you hear me?" Pip instructs in a tone that Drummer would have used, meaning it's useless to argue. "And you won't be riding more than a couple of miles." His eyes find mine. "Know you've got lots of questions, Road, but now's not the time. Not sure about throwing you into the thick of things, but it gives you a chance to see how we do what we have to get done." He wipes his hand over his clean-shaven face. "Need your word, Road. Need you to stay away from contacting Drummer. When you return from California, I'll fill in any gaps in your knowledge." Now he moves his attention away from me. "Now you lot get gone. Go and do what you're paid for."

The men who haven't already left the room, get to their feet. Swift eyes me carefully. "You stick with me, okay, Road?"

I'll stick with her like fucking glue. What choice have I got? I don't know a thing about where we're going, or what I'm supposed to do.

After a visit to my room to collect my stick I tried to do without today, I decide to take it. I don't need it right now, I just don't know what's ahead of me and want to be prepared. I also pause to wrap my knee tightly as Pip had instructed, hating the effect of being unable to bend it properly, but realising that's better than it popping out. Then once again, I trail in Swift's wake down to the first floor. When we exit into the fresh air, I breathe it in deep, my hand resting gently on the saddle of my bike, greeting it like an old friend I feared I'd never be seeing again.

"Wait here," Swift instructs. "Our bikes are out back."

As she walks off, I realise she's not leaving me unguarded, as the sound of engines already meet my ears, and Snatcher and Preacher appear from around the corner. They pull their bikes up next to mine, and nod as I stow my stick on the bike, then swing my leg carefully over the saddle. The strapping on my knee providing sufficient support that I'm not as awkward as I am without it. I do grimace though, finding the bandage restrictive, but trying it out, I know it won't stop me changing gears. I wonder why Preacher is here. Pip hadn't named him. Still, it's of no consequence, must have been a last-minute addition.

Like back in Tucson, Utah's laws do not require helmets to be worn, so while we're waiting, I take a band out of my cut and tie my hair out of the way. Then I start the engine and let it idle for the few seconds it takes for Swift, Piston, Thor, Honor and Rascal to come join us.

Snatcher takes his place at the front, behind him are Thor and Preacher, then Rascal and Honor. Swift slides into a spot behind them, beckoning me to join her. Piston, as road captain, takes up the rear.

I take note of my surroundings. On the way here, I was so intent on following the GPS instructions that I hadn't taken much in. But then, I didn't realise I had to, nor that I might need to plan an escape route.

"Where are we going?" I call over to Swift when we are stopped by a red light. She ignores me. But before I can take umbrage, the light turns green and we're off again.

I'm intrigued that instead of heading toward the city, we take the main road for a couple of miles until we're out into the country, then turn onto a paved track. After riding for another minute or so, the land around flattens out completely, and I notice we've come to a private airfield, a single runway heading off into the distance.

I count three small hangars, and we pull up beside the furthest one. I back my bike into the parking spot next to Swift's, then following the examples around me, cut my engine and dismount. Swift fiddles with something behind her ear, then copies my action.

A stranger appears. He's dressed as a mechanic. Preacher's the man he approaches first, greeting him as he would a blood brother.

When they stop their back slapping and pull apart, the man nods at the sergeant-at-arms. "Flight plan's filed. She's gassed up and ready for you."

I already kind of guessed we'd be flying else why would we have come here?

"Thanks, man," Preacher replies to him. "You sort that engine glitch out?"

My eyes widen slightly. I've flown before, but can't say I enjoyed it, preferring to keep my feet on terra firma. Faults with engines you rely on to keep you in the air and alive are not what I want to hear about.

"I think so," the man replies to Preacher. "Let me know if you have any problems."

Any problems? Visions of the small plane we're walking toward crashing to the ground would probably be the result of any problem, major or minor. My unease begins to grow. "Is this thing safe to fly, Preach?"

Preacher turns with a face-splitting grin. "Guess we're about to find out."

At least I'm not the only one having concerns. Piston looks about as reassured as I feel. Looking ahead, I focus on the transport we're approaching. The plane, I notice, is white and devoid of any logo except for the identification number printed on the side. When I've flown before, it's been commercial, but this is clearly a private plane. I've heard about those from the Tucson brothers, but so far have never been in one.

As Preacher finishes up his conversation with the still unidentified man, I think about what I was told. Before I patched in, a sheikh sent a private plane to take Drummer and most of the patched members to be guests at his wedding in

Amahad, the Arab country of which he was a ruler. Apparently, that had been the very definition of luxury, gourmet food, and comfortable seating miles up in the sky. I'd been jealous that as a prospect, I hadn't gotten to go. Then, again, I sat out the journey to Colombia to rescue Mouse's old lady. That plane had apparently been military transport with no frills. I wonder which this will turn out to be, but I'm not hopeful of luxury. It's small with twin propellers.

"Whose plane is this?" I ask Swift.

"Ours."

10

———

*R*oad...

This day just keeps piling on surprises. *Satan's Devils own a plane?* But I'm not given long to question how they can afford it, or why they've got one in the first place as Preacher calls out.

"Time to board."

As we walk to the steps, I pass by Preacher who's got his head bowed, and I see his mouth moving, but any words seem directed at the ground.

"What the fuck is he doing?" I get out, directing my question toward Swift again.

But it's Snatcher who answers me, his lips curving. "He's praying that the plane stays in the air, lands where we want to, and then flies us back home again. He always prays before a flight, it's how he picked up his name."

My sympathies go out to the man who clearly likes flying as little as I do, though I doubt having faith in a deity I can neither see nor touch would do much to keep me safe.

Reaching the top of the steps, I'm pleasantly surprised to see the inside is better than I expected—rows of seats in a formation of two on one side, one on the other, and an aisle between them. I quickly add them, it looks like it could seat around twenty.

"I don't want to waste time," Preacher warns us. "Get in and buckle up."

Why's he instructing us?

When Preacher disappears through a door at the front, I start to get a bad feeling. "Who's the pilot?" I ask Swift, my voice laden with concern.

She startles as though I should have already guessed, but tells me anyway, "Preacher."

The man who was just praying for a safe journey?

I don't know the man. So far he's done nothing in partic-ular to impress me, and now I'm putting my life in his hands.

"Does he know what he's fuckin' doing?" I hiss, easing over Swift to seat myself in the vacant seat next to her.

Rascal, taking the single seat on our row, chuckles. "He's ex-air force, so yes. Preacher cut his teeth on jet fighters, so yeah, if it's got wings he can probably fly it. Anyway, there are parachutes if we need them. All modern conveniences here."

The thought of parachutes chills me more.

"If you're not belted and seated, then get your ass sat down now." Preacher's voice booms through the loudspeaker as the plane starts to move. "Ready for take-off."

My gut feel is to make a run for door and make a swift exit, but the small plane quickly picks up speed. I wasn't aware that I'd squeezed my eyes tightly shut, but I obviously had as my first indication that we're airborne is the change of sensation when the bumping over rough ground becomes a smooth feeling, and the engine makes a deafening roar. Then my stomach drops as the plane loops around, heading off in what I take is the right direction.

I risk opening one eye, seeing objects on the ground

receding, and close it again, fisting my hands and just hoping that I'll get to feel my feet on firm ground again.

"Cruising altitude," Preacher's disembodied voice informs.

There's a clicking of seat belts unfastening.

"Road?" Swift taps my tightly fisted hand. "Snatcher's going to want a meeting."

I open my eyes to see men around me standing and stretching. Honor belches loudly.

"Okay." Snatcher leans over one of the front seats. "Rascal, you're on equipment. Make sure it's all handed out and that all cuts are off and stowed securely." He waits for Rascal's nod.

I finger my cut. I hadn't been sure whether it was a similar crime to wear one on a plane as it is in a cage, but as others had left them on, I had as well. But it seems I won't long be wearing it. I hate being parted with the leather bearing the patch that had cost blood and guts to earn.

"Okay," Snatcher continues. "Update from Duty—he's got all the info and is sifting through. He should be able to get a rough location for the origin of the call demanding the ransom using triangulation. That's where we'll be heading to once we've landed. He's got transportation set up. We'll be in two SUVs. Any further updates come in, I'll let you know."

He moves down the aisle and stops next to us. "Swift." That's all he says, just her name.

"Snatch?"

"Time to go quiet," he tells her in a gentle voice, his eyes softening. "Else you'll be no fuckin' good to us when we land."

"But I was going to brief Road." I notice Swift's voice sounds pained.

Snatcher shakes his head. "I can do that." He walks off down the plane.

It's the look in her eyes when she turns to me that does something strange—it brings my protective instincts to the fore. "What is it, Swift?"

"The noise," she confides. "I, er, I gotta turn my hearing aids down." The engine noise isn't overly loud, but it drones on. As Swift's fingers go behind her ear, she explains to me. "Loud noises fuck with my hearing aids. I get a migraine if I leave them at normal levels." She looks like she's apologising for being weak.

I hold up one finger asking for a moment. "The bike's engine sound?"

She nods, then tilts her head in query. I shake mine, and she turns her hearing aids down, now clearly no longer able to hear me.

The penny drops. She hadn't been ignoring me at the traffic lights and I'd thought her rude for ignoring my question. When riding her bike she must turn her aids down then too.

Swift's turned her head and is staring past me out of the window, and sympathy floods through me. She'd told me she was deaf, but as she seemed to be able to hear well enough, I didn't give much thought to how it would affect her life. Someone like her, so in control all the time, must hate to give that up, and being unable to hear, must make her vulnerable. At least here, she's with people she can trust.

I tap her gently, then indicate the aisle. She eases back to allow me out of my seat, then moves to take the one by the window I'd just vacated.

"Here, Road." Rascal is waving at me, and I go down the narrow walkway to meet him. "Cut." He holds out his hand. When I slide the leather off my shoulders, he places it carefully on a growing pile. Then he eyes me up. "I think you're Bolt's size, here, try this on."

I'm no stranger to Kevlar vests, and the one he passes me is certainly large enough to fit me. He eyes me carefully. "You with us, Road?"

"You got doubts?" I nod, understanding them. "Yeah, I'm

with you for this. Whether or not I transfer, I'm along for this ride. You can depend on me."

"I hope so. Pip's usually a good judge of character." He sighs, as if he hasn't got the same reading of me that his prez has, then unlocks a cupboard.

Once again, I'm dumbfounded. There's an armoury inside —enough weapons to outfit a small army.

"Handgun or rifle?"

I point to a Glock, knowing my limitations, and that I'm no sniper. He passes it to me.

"Knife?"

I nod. *Oh yeah.* "Two?" I request optimistically. He hands me the number I'd requested, one in a handy ankle sheath.

Again armed, I feel more like myself. It's a sign they're treating me as part of a team, and not an add-on or someone they're going to need to carry. But as much as they don't know what I'm capable of, I'm conscious I haven't yet got the measure of them.

Hearing shuffling behind me, I twist to see the others are forming a line, clearly waiting to be assigned their equipment. I turn sideways to squeeze past, making my way down the narrow aisle to the front again where I'm confronted by a sight I didn't want to see—Preacher drinking a cup of coffee.

"What the fuck? Who's flying the plane?"

Snatcher and Preacher burst out laughing, and it's the latter who informs me, "Autopilot. Hey, want to come see upfront?"

I kind of do and don't. But when will I next get the chance to be in the cockpit of a plane? When Preacher jerks his head, I look past him and take in the array of instrument displays in front of me. Immediately I'm impressed that Preacher knows what any of them do. Thank fuck I've only got to contend with a speedometer and rev counter on my bike.

Preacher stands behind me and starts pointing some of

them out, describing what they do. It's intriguing as fuck seeing it all. I stay with him while he points out the weather radar, the altimeter and navigation system, even the ground proximity warning which seems useful to have. He loses me when he talks about something called TACAS, until he translates that it's a traffic awareness and collision avoidance system.

"The club had the plane long?" I ask.

"For the past ten years, yeah."

That coincides with when Pip came along and stepped into Snatcher's chair.

Preacher retakes the pilot's seat and checks some settings. I watch on. It's a different view from up here. Instead of just seeing out of one side or another, the world stretches out in a panoramic view. It's almost mesmerizing.

"How high are we flying?"

"Seven thousand metres, or about twenty-three thousand feet. That's near our max cruising height. We'll be starting our descent shortly."

That sounds high. Even a quick calculation of five thousand feet to a mile means we're over four miles high.

The warning it won't be long until we begin coming into land and seeing Preacher start competently flicking switches makes me turn to go back to the cabin. As I reach the seating area, I catch Snatcher's eye, indicate the empty seat next to him and at his raised chin, sit down.

I lean forward, clasping my hands between my legs. "Why did you step back as the prez?"

He offers a half-smile. "Pip thought you would ask. There's a long story behind it, but it's not all mine to tell. Let's just leave it that the club decided to move in a different direction, and Pip was the man for that."

"But why not be straight with Drummer?" I narrow my eyes. "Surely he'd accept a club vote?"

Snatcher's eyes fill with mirth. "Drummer's the prez of the mother chapter and would have wanted to have his input."

"Pip seems alright," I comment, not understanding. "You clearly trust him, and from what little I've seen, everyone else does. I can't see anything Drummer would raise objections about. An ex-criminal wouldn't be disqualified, unless he was dragging the club into things Drummer wouldn't put his name to." Suddenly I frown. "He's not law enforcement, is he?"

Now the ex-prez barks a loud laugh. "No, he is not. Nah, there's not much that Drummer would object to, except for one thing."

He turns to look out the window. My eyes follow his line of sight, and I notice objects on the ground becoming clearer and guess it won't be long before we land. As for his last comment, he appears content to leave me hanging.

"And that one thing is?" I prompt.

Snatcher shakes his head and chuckles. "Fucker can't ride a bike, doesn't own one, and has no inclination in that direction."

What the fuck? The prez of an MC, the man who wears our cut, can't ride? Snatcher's right. That would definitely disqualify him from being prez, fuck, from being a member at all. It also explains why Snatcher takes back the title whenever Utah rides out to meet the other chapters.

"Regulations mean he can't be a Devil." I almost spit the words out through gritted teeth, feeling it's a personal insult that Pip wears the Satan's Devils MC cut.

Snatcher turns around, his eyes cold. "Don't like your tone, Road. Man's due respect even if he doesn't ride. For reasons you're yet to discover."

"But you must see—"

"No. You give him a fuckin' chance. All will become clear in time."

Christ. This is explosive information if I get it back to

Drummer. Fuck, he'll disband the Utah chapter altogether for their blatant disrespect of everything we live for. I'll never transfer now, not when the so-called prez of the chapter isn't qualified to even prospect for the club.

I wasn't allowed to join, despite that I already had a bike, because I didn't ride one that was American built. I've heard whispers around the table that that might come to change, as Heart's wife, Marcia, had built her own rat bike which beat any of ours—a subject that when mentioned causes steam to come out of our sergeant-at-arms, Peg's, ears. The ability for speed and manoeuvring might change our priorities on what we want from our rides, but never, ever, has it been discussed that a man could join the club without any bike at all. I can't put it any plainer, our regulations clearly specify that if someone can't ride, they don't have a hope in hell of becoming a Satan's Devil.

"Take your seats for landing." The speaker makes Preacher's voice sound tinny.

"Go make sure Swift's seat belt is fastened." Snatcher jerks his head toward the woman who's sitting a couple of rows behind.

I've been given information which I need to process and see if I could ever find a way to accept it. No wonder the options given to me are to throw in my lot with Utah and keep my mouth shut, or never go back to the real MC led by a bike riding prez. I do know that if I voice my objections in terms that I want to, I risk landing on the ground a lot sooner than this plane will, and without the aid of a parachute.

The suggestion that Swift may need my assistance, coupled with the necessity of, for now, keeping my mouth shut, gets me rising. Whether or not to fight a battle is not the only consideration, it's also important to consider timing.

I'm armed, but outnumbered.

11

―――――

*S*wift...

A soldier needs to be aware of their situation at any given time. The last thing you needed was insurgents creeping up on you. I had been taught to use my ears, my eyes, and even on occasion, my nose would come in useful to detect a waft of perfume in the air or the approach of an unwashed body.

To have one of those senses taken away was crippling.

Bolt had lost his hand, but that had been replaced by a bionic one. While he probably doesn't sleep in it, he wouldn't need to take it off during a flight. He's also got his real one that he can use to scratch any itch if need be.

Despite the best endeavours of my audiologist, my hearing aids don't completely restore what I've lost. I can hear, but not normally. Sound is converted into a digital signal which is then amplified and directed into each of my ears. Mine are some of the best on the market, small and neat, and work well enough that I'm able to have functioning conversations in most environments, adjusting for ambient noise automatically, or with the aid of my app I have on my smartphone. But even they have limitations due to my type of hearing loss. A constant drone, of an engine particularly, seems to reverberate in my head and I have to turn them down. Once I do that, I lose one of the senses I rely on. I cease to feel normal and become vulnerable.

No, I don't, I rebuke myself firmly.

It had been Pip who'd forced me to become part of the deaf community. As a condition of prospecting, he'd made me reach out to others with the same disability. Yes, it is disabling to be unable to hear properly, but it didn't lessen the contribution I could make in the world or the enjoyment I, myself, get out of life. Learning to appreciate things differently was all part of the process I had to go through.

At first I had found the world a frightening place, my hearing aids amplifying not just speech, but ambient sound. Too many people talking at once made it hard to follow a conversation. But switching down or removing my hearing aids left me feeling isolated and excluded. My audiologist had worked with me so we'd found the best match we could, and now, with aids in, a lot of issues had been resolved.

At first, I'd rebelled against using sign language or trying to lip read as I refused to acknowledge what had happened. Then, when I tried, I felt like a kindergarten kid just starting school, or even a baby learning their first words. Lip reading I haven't conquered just yet, but sign language I have got under my belt. It helped that signing is a way that soldiers communicate, so to me it was an enhancement, not a step back.

Pip suggested the brothers learn to sign as well, and to my surprise, some of them had done just that, acknowledging being able to communicate without words would be helpful on missions. They'd also become more circumspect about their contributions in meetings, trying to control themselves so no one talked over the other, or at a signal from Pip, would slow down. Music in the clubhouse is kept to a reasonable volume.

While I appreciate what those around me do to give me a near-normal life, I hate that they had to make adjustments. I'm Swift, one of the strongest and most badass females in the world. but without my hearing aids, I no longer feel like her anymore.

I hate the silence that removes me from the world, but Snatcher was right. I've had debilitating headaches before, so going quiet, as he put it, on a plane journey was best all around. I need to be in tip-top condition when I re-enter normal life and perform my duties as a soldier once more.

I didn't want to read or stare at the clouds out the window, so I'd dozed throughout the journey. Not fully asleep, the pressure in my ears and sinuses signal the change in altitude telling me we're coming into land. I open my eyes and find Road settling in beside me. He makes some gesture with his hands, miming a plane going down.

"I can see that." I grin at him, jerking my head toward the window, but I appreciate his efforts.

Thor leans over the seat in front of us, and signs, *Wheels down in ten.*

I give him a thumbs up.

Road touches my arm lightly to get my attention on him. He points at my hands, then at himself, his gestures followed by a questioning rise of his eyebrow.

"You want to learn?"

He shrugs, then nods.

Maybe this partner thing might work, if we can communicate even when my aids are off. I start to feel more optimistic about working alongside Road. He could have dismissed me when he discovered my weakness, but instead it appears he wants to find ways around it.

Ten minutes later, we do indeed touch down, Preacher

bringing the plane in smoothly, with only a slight jerk as the wheels meet the ground. As I turn my hearing aids back up, Road's face fills with visible relief as we taxi along the runway and finally come to a halt in front of a hangar, not much different to the one we'd left only a few hours before.

"It's another private airfield," I tell Road, seeing him looking around curiously.

"You've used it before?"

While I'm unbuckling my seat belt, I reply, "No, but Duty will have set it all up for us. He's great at logistics and seems to have contacts everywhere. Finding a discreet airfield for us to use near Santa Barbara would have been easy for him."

"You avoid the big airports?"

I nod. "When we can. We'd rather not draw attention to ourselves."

"So, what's the plan?"

"Snatch didn't fill you in?" The question is redundant, I can tell from the look on his face. "Duty will have arranged accommodations for us, and I suspect we'll head there. Then we wait for more info to come through. Hopefully it will be a clean in and out—we'll rescue the kid and go home."

Road looks disbelieving. "That's how it works?"

I shrug. "That's what we hope for, but often it's not like that. We'll plan for every eventuality and be ready to change course based on information those back at base feed us."

"You rescue kids a lot?"

"Kids, men, women," I confirm. "We do what we can when a call comes in, Road. Look, Pip will explain what you need to know. For now, our focus is the mission on hand."

He looks at me, then nods sharply. "What about the kid's parents? Will we make contact with them?"

I have to remember Road is completely ignorant of how we work. "The parents have been told not to contact the cops, and they've decided to follow those instructions. There's a risk the kidnappers might have eyes on them, and if so, they'll be suspicious of any stranger visiting their home. A tradesman, or salesman, for example, entering at this time would be risky. The kidnappers might think it was an undercover cop. We stay well away so nothing looks out of the ordinary. One wrong move, and we could cause the death of a child."

That brings the seriousness home to Road. A stare, another of his chin lifts, then he follows my lead as we exit the plane. Road is carrying his stick, some of us hefting the duffel bags Rascal hands out over our shoulders once we're outside. He'll have packed them with all the equipment we could need to rescue the little girl. As always, I offer up a plea to whichever deity might be listening that we get to her fast and before she becomes too traumatised, or worse, abused at the hands of the men who've taken her. It's not been unknown for photos to arrive showing things being done to which no parent would ever want their daughter subjected, or a severed finger is used to hurry the payout along. Speed, as always, is of the essence.

As we'd been told, two SUVs are waiting, and we separate four of us to each. Road is with me, obviously, and Snatcher is driving, while Piston, after laying his burden down carefully behind the rear seats, goes to the front passenger door and sits beside him.

As we drive, a call comes in. Snatcher answers and puts it on speaker.

"Duty. Whatcha got?"

Duty's voice comes through. "I've narrowed it down as best I can. The call came from a residential area where there are a dozen houses or so. I've gone through the records, most have been owned for a year or more, some rented out. The newest tenant was six months back. There's one that's supposedly vacant at present."

"Sounds like it could be our target," Snatcher replies. "Or

the one rented most recently if they've been planning this for a while."

"You might be able to tell more from an external look."

"Any utility usage in the vacant property?" Piston asks.

There's a pause, then, "Utilities are connected. Hold on, just getting into the electricity feed… Bingo! Yes, you could be right, Piston. Some electricity being used. Not a lot. Lights at least."

"Could be security lighting, to make it look like someone's home," Snatcher observes. "But we'll check it out, Duty. Text the address."

The call is ended when it appears Duty's got no more. Hopefully it's enough. Piston's got out his tablet and is calling up Google Earth. "We need to send up the drone," he tells Snatcher. "Fuckin' place is surrounded by high fences and trees."

Snatcher takes his eyes off the road for a split second to look at the photo Piston's holding on his lap. "Neighbours?"

"Houses are spread out, VP," Piston replies, not sounding particularly happy.

"Okay. Tell Preacher where we're headed, and we'll go straight there. Get the drone in the air and go from there."

Piston takes out his phone and puts a call through to the sergeant-at-arms driving the SUV behind.

"How can you be sure that's even where they've got the girl?" Road breaks his self-imposed silence and speaks. "Surely they'd know their phone call could be traced?"

"We don't," Snatcher answers him. "But the parents were told not to go to the cops. Without their help, the kidnappers will hopefully assume they haven't got the capability to trace a call. The number was a burner phone, so maybe they think they are safe as long as there's no police sniffing around the parents' home, or BOLOs put out for any sightings of the missing girl."

"It's worth checking out." I supplement the VP's observations. "Sure, to us, it's obvious, but we don't know who we're up against. We suspect it was planned, that the kid's routine was known, but it could still be opportunistic. It could be they're not too experienced nor used to covering all bases. What's obvious to us is still worth checking out."

"Swift's right. And back in Utah, they'll still be looking for other leads. It's up to us to get confirmation this is either the place or a bust for the purposes of elimination."

"We're not dealing with experts." Snatcher takes over again when Piston finishes. "When we landed, I got more information. They've asked for too much. Stormy's run the parents' financials. Professional criminals would know to ask for less, where the parents have assets that can be liquidated immediately, or loans taken out. Whoever has taken the kid hasn't done their research, or doesn't know how this works. There's no way in hell the parents can raise that amount."

"On the other hand, they might know that," Piston interjects. "They might have a vendetta against the parents and want them to suffer mental torture."

"Which again means they could be new to the kidnapping lark, if it's not the money they're after but about causing distress." I pause, then my voice hardens. "If they know they can't afford to pay up, chances are the kid won't see her parents again unless we get to her fast."

Road stiffens as I spell out the consequences that failure of our mission could entail.

"We move quickly," Snatcher agrees. "Because while I hate to admit it, Swift could have a good point."

"Where the fuck do we start?" Road asks.

"We need more information. Like how many people are there, what their firepower is. If this is the right location, where precisely they are holding the girl. Finding where they've got her is one thing, getting her safely out, another.

We don't want to bust in all guns blazing to find she's directly in the line of fire. The drone should give us some info. Hopefully, someone conveniently shows their face so we can identify them and start making sense of why she was taken."

"Can I see?" Road leans over and gestures to the tablet Piston is holding.

Piston passes it over, and Road studies the house intently, then uses Google Earth to examine the area. "It's not going to be easy, is it? There's a garage where vehicles could be hidden and overhanging trees blocking the line of sight to the windows."

"It's all we've got, Road. We may need to get closer to have better visuals. The drone will show us the best way to approach."

Another call comes in. Again it's put on speaker. Duty's been working hard and found us a place to park from where we can launch the drone. That's where we head, after again updating Preacher. Soon the two SUVs are pulling off the road.

This is far from our first rodeo. Piston quickly has the drone out of the back of the SUV, taken out of its covering, launched and flying. Within moments, it's hovering over the target location. It's military grade, able to send decent pictures back but fly high enough to evade detection. Like a lot of our methods, totally illegal.

We gather around Piston who's got the app that controls it called up on his tablet, and the pictures are coming in clearly. For a while we watch as it sends back images from different angles, but there's nothing to be seen, nothing to show whether the house is occupied or not.

Suddenly Preacher points to the screen. "What's that?"

When Piston zooms in, we all see what he's noticed—the back door which would be hidden from the road is open. We stare down, watching, hoping to see movement. *Had it been open all along and we missed it earlier?*

"There!" Rascal points out, but we've already all seen it. A garbage sack appears and is placed outside the door.

All we've seen is a disembodied hand, but it's enough.

"It's occupied," Snatcher confirms, unnecessarily.

We find that out, but not much more. As Road had already noted, the overhanging trees prevent us from seeing inside. Yet, a house with someone in it which should be empty suggests we've come to the right place.

Road's brow is furrowed. "What happens now? How would you want this to go?"

I remind myself this is all new to him. "We need to get access to the house, but how, that's what we've got to work out. If we could get inside, we could place a bug to get more information about what's going on in there." That's the ideal, but it would seem impossible to do. Not with the little we have to go on.

"I've got Duty getting the house plans," Snatcher informs us.

I raise my chin. Hopefully that will help.

"Why not just walk up to the front door?" Road asks, seeming serious.

Piston snorts loudly. "Yeah? You reckon? Walk up and ask if we can borrow a cup of sugar or some shit? If the kidnappers are in there, they're likely to shoot first. They won't invite a stranger inside." Piston's one of those who can sign, and he uses it now to ask me, *Is this guy for real?*

I'm wondering that myself.

But Road doesn't back down. "What about someone in need of assistance?"

I glance at Road, his face is set, his jaw clenched. Perhaps we were wrong to so quickly dismiss him. It looks like he might be thinking of something. "Difficult," I tell him, letting him down gently. "Remember, they'll be ultra-cautious and suspicious as hell. Someone in need of help because their car just happened to break down outside would set off their alarm bells."

Road raises his chin in acknowledgement, but continues, "Can you get me some running gear?"

It's Snatcher's turn to snort incredulously, while I shake my head wondering what planet Road has disappeared to.

"Like you could run anywhere with your bad leg," Piston scoffs.

"I can run far enough," Road tells him. "And my knee can give out right outside that house."

Everyone goes silent, still trying to interpret Road's words. The penny drops in my head. "You can pop it out?"

It's Road's turn to chuckle. "If I take the binding off, keeping it in is harder. Sure, yeah. All I need do is put my weight on it wrongly, and out it will pop."

"They might not help," I warn him.

"But then we'll know for sure whoever is inside has got something to hide," Snatcher responds, his voice animated. "Road will be in fuckin' agony, and anyone with an ounce of compassion should help."

"It could be dangerous," I warn him. "They'll be suspicious." I think for a moment. "I'll come with you."

"No." Road shakes his head adamantly. "One person they might help, two and they'd wonder why you weren't calling an ambulance or something."

"Road's right." Snatcher waves at Preacher. "You stay here and wait. We'll get Road equipped. You wait here and update Duty as to what's going on."

Again, Snatcher, Piston, Road and I take our seats in the SUV. Piston programs the GPS and Snatcher puts it into drive and moves off. It's not long before he starts indicating and pulling off outside a Walmart.

When he parks, Road gets out and walks off to the store. Piston accompanies him as hey, they have phones in there, and Road could buy one and sneak a call to Drummer. He might have come up with a plan that appears workable, but we still don't trust him.

It's not long before Road reappears. He's wearing running shorts, a tank top framing his muscles and tats very nicely indeed—not that I should be noticing—and has on a baseball cap and sunglasses. On his feet are brand new sneakers, which he takes a moment to cover in dirt and scuff by dragging them against the ground.

"Do you run?" I ask, interested in possibly having my new partner as a running mate too.

He gives me an incredulous look. "Like fuck."

We return to where Preacher, Thor, Rascal and Honor are still standing outside their SUV.

"Here." Honor passes Road a tiny earpiece. "This will allow you to hear us, and for us to hear anything that goes on in the house."

Road nods and takes the box from him. "What about bugs you want me to place?"

Honor nods and passes something else to him. "Doubt you'll get a chance to place more than one. This is one of the smallest listening devices on the market."

That one Road extracts from the box and puts into the pocket of his shorts.

"Don't let them catch you, Road," I warn. My worry is only my concern about his lack of experience.

"Here." Snatcher has written something on a slip of paper. "Put that in your wallet. Ask to use their phone, and Swift will swing by and pick you up. Calling a girlfriend will be less suspicious than one of us putting in an appearance."

"And Swift can give him a bit sloppy kiss to add to the illusion."

Preacher gets my middle finger for that suggestion. But for a second I wonder what it would be like to kiss Road's full lips, and whether they'd be as soft as they appear to be. I shake my head trying to unthink what just went through my head.

"How about I'm his sister?"

"Long as you don't open your mouth."

Yeah, sometimes I forget that I've got an accent which sticks out a mile.

"We'll have the drone up, Road, so if they refuse you help or won't let you call, we'll spot you and pick you up."

"And know if you don't come out." It bothers me that he's going in alone. "Don't be a hero, Road. We want info, not for you to try to rescue the girl on your own."

We hang around no longer than necessary. With a quick salute toward Preacher, Snatcher puts the SUV into drive, and off we go again. It's not far until we're at the end of the road where we can drop Road off without being seen.

"He'll be okay," Snatcher tells me, looking at me in the rearview mirror as we drive away leaving Road all alone.

I hope so.

"I just hope he knows what he's fuckin' doing and doesn't give the game away," Piston complains.

I, on the other hand, am fully convinced Road understands a girl's life is at stake. He'll stick to the script and won't go, as we say in England, *off piste.*

Road's microphone is transmitting, and I realise he wasn't lying when he said he doesn't run. His breathing sounds laboured after only a short time. The drone is hovering high above the house we're suspicious about, and it picks him up well enough to see when he's almost outside. I get the visual of him crashing to the ground, as well as hear the screech of pain that is one hundred percent genuine.

I wince.

12

———

*R*oad…

I don't run for pleasure, as I'd told Swift, but Peg had had me on the elliptical as part of the exercise regime trying to strengthen the muscles in my bad leg, so the action wasn't entirely unfamiliar.

What I'm most in danger of is stumbling and putting my knee out before I reach the house that I'm aiming for.

I put to the back of my mind that this is going to hurt like a bitch. Normally my knee dislocates, and it's agony while it's out of place, but once it's righted, the relief is immediate. This time I'll have to suffer until Swift picks me up. My teeth are already gritted in anticipation.

I don't expect I'll learn anything to make it worth my while lingering in the house, if they let me in, that is. I'm conscious I mustn't do anything to put the kid in any more danger than she is already. The most I hope for is to get inside, use a phone, and drop the bug somewhere unseen. The listening device is currently burning a hole in my pocket.

It's small and flat and doesn't show, but I'm overly conscious of having it. If the men are suspicious and search me, well, with five million at stake or for whatever other reason they kidnapped the kid, I don't have any illusions about my future.

If I get hold of a phone, I could call Drummer.

But that thought only fleetingly passes through my mind before being dismissed. It's become a matter of honour that I play my part and help rescue the girl. Preacher can fly, Swift's the most impressive woman I've ever met. Duty, Honor and Stormy are tech experts, and I've no doubt the others have skills I've yet to see. I've got nothing to offer, except my ability to ride at speed. Something makes me want to leave my mark on them, even if that's only to show they can trust me to get a job done right. That translates to only calling one number, Swift's, and leaving the update to my prez for later.

Okay, here we go. I start to run faster, but still carefully, picking each place to plant my feet, concentrating hard on not stepping on a stone or loose pavement that would cause my leg to twist. It's a few hundred yards that I need to cover, so I run on. My breathing starts to labour at the unaccustomed exercise, especially in this heat. Sweat starts pouring off me, which is all to the good. I should look like I've been running a fair distance to throw them off the scent.

I'm almost at the house now. It's the closest one to me, the nearest neighbour's I'd passed about fifty yards back. I take a deep breath and lean my weight to the side and… *Shit! Motherfucking hell that hurts! Shit! Fuck! Motherfucker.*

I drop to the ground. I rock, holding my leg to me, genuine tears streaming down my cheeks while I fast look at my surroundings. The front door of the target house is about sixty feet up a driveway. It could be sixty miles right now, as I know there's no way I can get to my feet. Trying to hop would just send more pain shooting through me.

Gritting my teeth, I put both my palms to the ground, and

crab-like, dragging my ruined leg behind me, I crawl up the path.

Why had I worried about sweating? My face burns red, and rivulets run down my face mingling with my tears. If no one's home, I'll have to put my knee back in, and hope that I didn't cause more damage by not doing so sooner.

I eye the front door, and the doorbell up high. As I reach out my hand to grab hold of the frame and pull myself up, the door opens.

"Who the fuck are you?"

"I-I..." I'm not exaggerating the difficulty getting words out. I'm in genuine fucking agony. "Running." I huff, then take a breath, feeling like I'm going to vomit and swallowing hard. "My knee's popped, man. Please, I need to use a phone?"

He doesn't immediately agree, but neither does he tell me to get lost. His eyes travel over me, settling where my leg is contorted dramatically and I see him wince and pale.

"Who's there, Tub?"

"Runner. Fucked up his leg."

Another man appears and pushes Tub to one side, subjecting me to the same examination.

Swift and Snatcher had been right, they're as suspicious as hell, but my leg's at such an awkward angle, it's clear to see I'm not putting it on.

"Fuck," the second man says, as he gets a good look.

"Can... can I use a phone, and man..." I grit my teeth, even speaking hurts.

"He needs a fuckin' ambulance."

The look the two men give each other is enough for me to know we've got the right house. They're clearly concerned about bringing any type of authority here.

"My... girlfriend... she'll pick me up. Just need to call her. Had enough of hospitals, man. She'll take me to a doctor I use."

"Don't you have your own fuckin' phone?"

"Some fucker stole it. Yesterday," I explain, not having to lie as I give them the truth, the bite in my voice fuelled by the memory of Pip hanging on to it.

"You want to call your girlfriend," the second man repeats, but not as a question, but as though he'd trying my suggestion out. "She live far away?"

"Down by the coast." I don't know the area, so I hope they don't ask me for more. But then I hear a reassuring voice straight into my ear, and I'm immediately able to name a street. "She'll be here in..." I pause, grimacing with real pain, but giving time for Piston to give me an ETA and complete my statement with, "ten minutes."

"Tub get your phone."

"Can I come in? I could really do with a glass of water?" I hope I'm not laying it on too thick, but that's what an injured man would ask, isn't it? And he'd want to get comfortable rather than lying on a concrete porch under the burning sun.

"Christ," the second man says. "Oh for fuck's sake, yes." He even holds out his hand to help pull me to my feet.

I'm not a small man, so it takes his other hand as well, and then I'm leaning on his shoulder and hopping into the room, taking the opportunity to slip the listening device into his pocket when my hand grasps his hip for support. He leads me to a sofa. I flop awkwardly on the seat, my sharp exclamation of pain not an act in any way. Not thinking, I tuck back my hair.

"What's that in your ear?" he suddenly asks, suspiciously.

"Hearing aid," I tell him, pointing to the scarring on my leg. "Fucked up my ears when I was knocked off my bike. I had a bad concussion." Isn't it always best to stick as close as possible to the truth?

"Take it out," the man instructs. I do. When he speaks

again, I act like Swift had done on the plane, and lean in, focusing on his face.

"Is that what it is?" Tub looks concerned.

"Fuck, how would I know?"

I shake my head. "I can't lip read yet," I explain. "Are you talking to me?" In truth, I'm holding my breath, but he examines the device that stays silent in his hand.

"You really deaf?"

I let my face stay blank.

With another look toward Tub, he hands it over to me and I put it back in, remembering the look on Swift's face when she'd done the same thing, letting my face relax as though I'm relieved.

"Thank you, being deaf, well, it sucks, man."

I seem to have convinced him. "Neat little thing," he tells me.

"Best I could afford," I agree.

"Here's the phone." Tub extracts his own from his pocket. "Faster you call, the faster you can get out of here."

I grimace, not having to pretend I'm in pain. Nodding, I take out my wallet, and extract Snatcher's handwritten note.

I've raised their suspicions again. "You don't know your fuckin' girlfriend's number?"

"Do you?" I challenge. "It was stored on my phone." It's a safe bet. No one knows numbers by heart anymore. Or not many, unless you're in an MC and need to be able to call any of the brothers from a burner phone.

I close my eyes briefly as another wave of pain goes through me. Tub disappears and returns within seconds with a glass of water. I wasn't lying, I need it, and drink it greedily. Then without wasting more time, I tap the numbers on the screen. It's only then I realise I don't know her first name.

"Hey, babe... My knee's gone... Yeah, I'm at...?" I look up questioningly, and the man who's clearly in charge gives me the address. "Sure... Yeah, thanks babe... I know, you were right..." I roll my eyes. "I know, I pushed it too soon... Love you too, baby."

"She's on her way," I inform the men watching me, passing the phone back to Tub.

Then, I rest my head back as though I'm exhausted, but really I'm listening for any cries of help, or anything to suggest a kid is here. But apart from the whirr of the air conditioning, there's no sound at all. I don't ask questions like, *how long have you lived here?* Or make observations like, *nice place.* I'm the epitome of a man in pain who's lost in his own head. Cracking my eyes open, I see Tub and the other man starting to relax.

The minutes tick by. When, at last, I hear a car driving over gravel, I sit up. "I'm really grateful, thank you. Tub, and?"

"Weaver," Tub helpfully supplies.

Weaver gives him a look as though Tub's going to feel his wrath when I've gone.

Which shouldn't take long. The doorbell rings. Tub glances through the peephole, satisfies himself it's to him a harmless-looking woman, then lets Swift in. She brushes past the man by the door, ignoring both him and his companion. Her eyes focus on me conveniently situated directly in her straight line of sight.

"Oh, darling. What on earth have you done? I warned you, didn't I? I said it was far too soon to start running again. Hey, have you got your hearing aid switched on?"

I suppose I hadn't been listening to her words, more intent on what Tub and Weaver had been doing in case they decide to keep us both here.

"Yeah, sorry, babe. I'm just in pain."

"She's got a fuckin' hearing aid as well," Tub remarks.

She turns and gives them the kind of smile I wish she'd give to me. "That's how we met. Lucas lost his hearing and was being fitted for his first hearing aid. I'd gone to have mine checked. Strange how things work out. It was love at first sight. I invited—"

"Don't want your whole fuckin' life story," Weaver interrupts.

"Babe, I'm in pain," I add, not wanting to wear out our welcome. "Please, I need to see the doc."

Tub goes to help me up, but Swift waves him off, helping me to my feet expertly as though she's done it a hundred times before. Then, as soon as we're out the door, it slams shut.

"Thank you for coming to get me," I tell her in case they're still listening.

"Come on, lover. Let's get you sorted."

I pucker my lips as though for a kiss, but she ignores me as she opens the door of the SUV.

"Babe," I tell her, tapping my mouth.

"I'm going to get you back for this," she hisses, as I settle into the seat, and she loops her hand around my neck, and puts her lips against mine. My arms entrap her, pulling her close. My mouth moves over hers and my tongue presses against the seam. She allows it, but only for a second, then presses her fingernails painfully into my neck. But she's smiling as I release her.

"All for show," I murmur, as she gets into the driver's seat. "They could be watching."

"Damn you, Road," she says as she does a U-turn and drives out onto the street. "Don't you ever do that again."

I reach down and stretch my leg, putting the right pressure on the right places, and then let out a heartfelt sigh of relief as at last I can pop it back into place. I can start breathing normally again.

"Didn't you like it?" I ask her, knowing she'd deny it. "I did."

"I'd quit now while you're ahead," a voice full of laughter says in my ear. "I think you've seen what Swift can do."

I have. I take the hint and close my mouth. Doesn't stop me grinning however, nor remembering the touch of her lips on mine.

"Where are we headed?" I ask, seeing her following the GPS.

"Duty got us an Airbnb that's quite close," she explains, her eyes fixed firmly on the road. "We're going to regroup there, examine the footage the drone sent back, and that bug is transmitting loud and clear by the way. We can hear everything they're saying. Good job, Road."

"I didn't hear any sounds from the house." I lean my head back, while simultaneously massaging my knee. It aches, but at least that sickening pain has faded away.

"I've got Bolt and Stormy trying to dig into who Tub and Weaver might be." The words sound into my ear. "How far away are you, Swift?"

"Five minutes."

She's right. Five minutes later after a journey completed in silence as I'm mindful of the people listening to everything we say, we draw up to a pleasant enough house not far from the beach.

"Careful," Swift warns me as I go to get out of the SUV.

I make sure I am careful. I pick my steps once again as I head into the house. I remove the ear bud when I get feedback howling at me.

"Come in." Snatcher who's opened the door hurries us in. "Duty's come back to us. Those names were useful, thanks, Road." He raises his chin my way. "Tub could have been anyone, but paired with Weaver's name, Duty's managed to track them down. They've just come out of jail after doing a stretch for larceny."

"Could have gotten the idea for kidnapping inside," Thor

yells over. "One of the inmates they were particularly tight with was in for a kidnapping gone wrong. In his case, he got life as the kid died."

"Murder?" Swift asks, snatching a sandwich off of the table. Before she unwraps her own, she throws another at me. I catch it one handed.

"Second degree. Young lad, left alone with a gag in his mouth, he asphyxiated. Fucker was more concerned about the loss of his payout than the death of the kid."

"So Weaver and Tub got the idea from him?" Or that's what it sounds like to me.

Thor presses his lips together. "Probably got quite the education inside."

Hopefully not to leave the kid with a gag in her mouth, but I have my doubts. "House was quiet," I tell them.

"What are they up to now?" Snatcher asks Preacher who's sitting with a headset on.

"They're discussing Road, and whether they did right to let him in. Hate to say it Swift, but Weaver's just observed that if you were feds, you wouldn't have kissed so passionately. Apparently, it was quite an impressive show. Good job."

"Something we should know?" Rascal asks with a grin.

"No," both Swift and I say at once. But I have to stop my hand reaching up to touch my lips. My arm wants to reach out and wrap around her, pulling her into my side. But not only would I probably be the recipient of a hard kick in the balls if I tried, I need to remember she's the same as any of my brothers, both here and in Tucson, and I'd show disrespect if I treated her any differently to them. I'll have to act as though she's not missing a piece of equipment between her legs.

That kiss had been a mistake. It had started me looking at her differently. *I'm lying to myself.* I started thinking about her in the wrong way when I noticed her ass last night. Maybe even before that. I thought she was an attractive bitch when

I'd first seen her sitting around the table. Then, the way she'd taken down Stormy, that had been as sexy as fuck.

"Getting something." Preacher takes off his headset and presses some keys. As the voices of Tub and Weaver fill the room, all other conversations cease.

"I still don't like coincidences. Maybe we should move the kid and leave."

There's the sound of footsteps echoing off wood, as though someone is pacing.

"How long are you giving the parents?" That's Tub.

After a short pause, Weaver responds, "Let's get a photo of her all tied up to hurry them along. As far as they know, the sooner they get the money to us, the sooner her suffering will end."

"Or begin." Tub's chuckling. "You still got that buyer lined up?"

"Yeah. And he wants her unmarked." Weaver's voice carries a warning. "So you keep your hands to yourself, Tub."

"Shame. I'd have enjoyed breaking her in."

"You're sick, man. You know that?" The sound of footsteps are heard again.

"Why are we waiting? It's a risk keeping her here. We could just sell her and pretend to the parents we've still got her."

"Proof of life, that's what they'll ask for. You know, her holding up the newspaper of the day."

"Haven't you heard of Photoshop man? Learned that shit inside."

"Jesus, Tub. Why are you just reminding me now? Great fuckin' idea. We'll take the pics tonight, then alter the photographs as we need to. Get her moved on as soon as we can, then all we need do is sit back and wait for the money to drop into our hands."

"Don't even have to stay here." Tub's voice sounds gleeful.

Snatcher waves at the laptop Preacher has open. "I'm not happy with this. They're making too much fuckin' sense. We've got to make our move tonight."

"How do you want to play this?"

"Road? Any idea where they could be hiding the girl?"

I frown. "Place isn't big, one of the bedrooms is my bet. I should have asked to use the bathroom or something, but I—"

"You couldn't walk." Swift comes to my defence.

"Three bedrooms," Honor says. "That's what was on the plans. One floor only."

"Hold up." Preacher raises a hand.

"Kid's fuckin' crying again. Man, it's doing my head in," a new voice sounds.

"Tub, get back in there and watch her."

"That's three," Preacher observes.

Eight against three. The odds are still in our favour. But, a thought occurs to me. "They're going to be desperate, right? We get this wrong, that kid could get caught in the crossfire."

Snatcher's eyes meet mine as he nods. "Or they'll use her as a human fuckin' shield. Might even kill her themselves."

Preacher's eyes are narrowed. "We've got to get into that house, but the backyard has little shelter."

"Not going to be easy sneaking in from the front either," Swift observes.

A plan is formulating in my head. I smirk, suspecting how my suggestion will be received. "So I walk up to the front door."

"Nah, Brother." I take a second to note it's the first time I've been called that by anyone from this chapter. "That's not how this shit works. And you'll be staying back this time. You've done your share."

"No, I haven't." I grin. "Listen. Swift drives me back. I take a bottle of whisky or something as a thank you for helping me out. We distract them at the front, giving you a chance to creep in the back and dispose of the third man presumably guarding the girl."

Swift's looking at me carefully, but it's Snatcher she addresses. "It could work. Preacher is listening. He can tell us who's in the main room, hopefully both will come to the door. We'll need to fool them—"

Snatcher interrupts her, suddenly changing his mind and now onboard with the plan. "You, Swift. You're the one who wanted to come back and thank them for taking care of your man. It's more the type of shit a woman would think of."

Swift rolls her eyes, but nods. "I can do that."

"Body armour," Rascal warns. "You're both to wear it. They've got five million plus riding on this. They might prefer to just shoot you and have done with it."

"There's the third man. One of them might be staying with the kid to make sure she doesn't choke on the gag. He's the unknown risk." Snatcher is frowning. "He could hurt the kid, or try to escape, taking her with him."

"Unless," I butt in again interrupting Snatcher, "we get Tub to call him out. A dead body at his feet and a gun to his head can be pretty persuasive."

"You know?" Swift says, a quirk to her mouth. "I kind of like the way Road thinks."

13

———

Swift...

When Pip had first suggested partnering me with Road, I had several problems with the idea. First off, it wasn't the man himself, but that I didn't want to work with anyone at all. Then, I was prejudiced against the man from the Tucson club. What had he to offer except for his muscle? Couple that with the fact he wasn't fighting fit right now, even that wasn't going to be much help.

But he's been the ideas man today. First, getting the bug planted in the house which had supplied vital information had been all down to him. Now he's come up with a suggestion that would at least provide the opportunity for a distraction. I have to admit to being impressed, and maybe a little wary that we've become set in our ways. Sure, our normal formula gets results, but there's something to be said for thinking outside the box. Maybe it is time to bring someone new on board to bring something else to the party. Of course, he's the only one able to fake an impressive injury, but that thought about going back with a thank you gift? That's not the way we normally operate.

I'll admit to wanting to slap his face after he'd kissed me, but even that had been a good idea, as I'd heard with my own ears. Feds do not enthusiastically kiss their partners, but then, neither do Satan's Devils. Then there is the tiny issue that I had enjoyed it. Which is strange as normally I don't kiss.

I've never had the inclination to want a relationship. At school I'd seen girls go googly eyed when certain boys looked their way. As my teenage years passed, my friends had changed completely. Plans were dropped if a boy claimed their time instead. My best friend through primary then secondary school had been a great example of that. No longer the tomboy wanting to play football, she'd spent her days either over the moon when the flavour of the month had set his eyes on her or moping when his head turned a different way. What was worse, she'd dress and do her hair in the style her current boyfriend preferred.

My head had spun with the different personalities she adopted to keep a boy in tow. He wanted someone submissive? She could be that. Someone who was decisive? She'd make all the decisions.

Her degeneration into being someone another person wanted wasn't restricted only to her. I saw examples to a greater or lesser degree all around me. I'd made up my mind I was who I am, and I wouldn't change me for anything, particularly for a member of the male sex, or one of the female persuasion. I definitely don't swing that way.

The problem being, or benefit as I saw it, was that I had a strong personality. You took me as I was or not at all. I was never interested in dressing up. I played football, darts and was a black belt in martial arts. I didn't need a man to be my protector, neither did I want a weak man I had to look after.

Not having a relationship might have been my choice, but neither was I the type to interest the boys. They'd tended to steer clear of me.

Sex? Well, yes, of course I have needs like everyone else, but I don't need a ring on my finger or any type of promise to get my needs met. If there's a man I find sexually attractive, I go after what I want. We scratch our mutual itches, then part ways. Variety is the spice of life, I always tell myself. There have been times when my chosen bed partner hasn't seen it in quite the same way, and I've had to discourage repeat performances. Extricating myself from something when I've no desire for anything more than a one-night hookup has made me overly cautious about who I choose to scratch my itch.

One idea I've never entertained is jumping into bed with any team member, knowing it would complicate matters going forward. Soldiers or MC members have a protective streak a mile wide. Something they can't seem to turn off and being with them sexually would signal a weakness I otherwise try to ignore. I'm a woman, and while I'm their equal in all other ways, there's one thing I'm missing—I don't have a cock.

That I find Road someone I'd fuck were he anyone other than my assigned partner is inconvenient to put it mildly. While I tell myself I shouldn't even be thinking about it, I find my eyes wandering his way, noticing things that I'd normally use to select someone to take to my bed for the night.

His hair. I've always had a weakness for hair long enough to wrap my hand around while a man's going down on me. Something to use to direct him to the exact right spot. Soldiers have short hair, nothing to hold on to there, so he would be completely different. His eyes, hmm, so expressive. His large hands are matched by the bulge in his jeans which offers so much promise. His muscles, thick, he's not going to break when I ride him. And his tats, he's not fully covered, but just enough to be interesting. His ass? Well, I might have caught myself checking him out a little too often. Luckily no one appears to have noticed.

He's tall, standing taller than myself. I'm probably four inches shorter. At five foot ten, I'm a good size for a girl.

I know what manwhores they are in MCs and expect Road's no different. Perhaps he too would be happy with just one night so I could use him to get rid of this inconvenient attraction?

Perhaps if Road fails to make the grade as a member, Prez would think about bringing him on board as a male sweet butt?

The thought makes me snort. I try to cover it up with a cough, but am not totally successful.

"Why are you grinning?"

"What?" Fuck it. I also blush. I can feel my cheeks burning. "Well, if I was, I was thinking about rescuing that girl and getting her back to her parents." I'm proud at how quickly I come up with that.

But Road, fuck him, *oh yes, I'd love to,* is smirking the bastard. *He can't read minds, can he?*

It seems he can't. "We'll have to pretend to be all lovey-dovey again. I mean, you'll have to show you like me by cuddling up, else our line about you being so grateful won't stack up."

Piston's just been dispatched to buy a suitable gift for us to deliver, so we've got a few moments to kill. I just wish we could get going. Sitting around waiting, though the bane of a soldier's life, isn't something I relish. Especially now as my brain seems stuck in only one gear.

"What's your first name?" Road asks, tightening the binding he's just applied to keep his knee in place. He adds, perfectly reasonably, "It would look odd if I call you Swift."

"You called me babe before," I remind him.

"Yeah but knowing your name would help." He stands, grimacing slightly when he puts the weight on his leg, but it seems to hold him up.

"No, it wouldn't." Swinging around, I present my back to him, but he touches my shoulder and makes me turn back.

"Hmm," he says, thoughtfully, "Shall I guess? You don't look like a Tami, or a Mary. Ann seems too plain. Savannah? Nah, too fancy, perhaps."

"Stick to babe," I suggest again.

Overhearing, Rascal snorts. "Keep guessing," he calls out to Road.

I start worrying he'll hit on it by accident.

"Paris? London? Chelsea?"

"I'm not fuckin' named after a place or football club," I sneer.

Road shakes his head. "You know my name. You know everything about me. So what's the harm in me knowing yours. Unless you're keeping your real one secret for a reason. Don't fuckin' like that. It's not as if I'm not putting myself in a world of hurt to help you out."

"No need to keep names secret. I'm Sawyer Young. Pleased to meet ya." Honor waves his hand toward Road, then raises a challenging eyebrow at me.

I press my lips tightly closed.

"Oh, for fuck's sake." Snatcher comes over, knocking against my shoulder. "Her given name's Karen. Karen Swift. Swift seemed good enough as a road name, and as she already came with it, there was no reason for a change."

I growl deep in my throat. "No jokes, Road. No fuckin' jokes."

"Jokes?" To his credit, he looks completely bemused.

While Honor just can't help himself, he comes up to my other side and puts a friendly arm around my shoulders. "Yeah, we've got our very own *Karen*."

He gets my fist in his stomach and I didn't pull the punch. Bastard was ready for me though.

"Wanker," I snarl at him.

He makes a gesture imitating jerking himself off.

"I don't understand," Road says quietly.

"Karen's been hijacked to refer to a privileged white woman," I explain, keeping my voice equally low and maintaining one careful eye on Honor. "There are tons of jokes and memes on the internet."

"That's not fuckin' fair." Road too, now glares at Honor. "It's your fuckin' name, you're entitled to use it without anyone saying anything about it."

As Honor opens his mouth, Snatcher interrupts. "Jesus. Kids. Just fuckin' leave it. And you, Honor, not one more word." As the VP wipes his hand over his face, clearly exasperated, the front door opens and Piston, thankfully, walks in carrying a bottle.

"Okay, then." Snatcher seems to gain in stature as he straightens. "Let's get this show on the road. You and Road head out, we'll follow behind."

I raise my chin knowing exactly the role I'm going to play. Though it might stick in my claw, I'm to simper and be Road's girlfriend. Until the guns come out, that is, and then I'll be showing my true colours.

I'm driving again, well, we've already pretended it's my car, both of us wearing our headphone/mic earpieces, and in my other ear, my normal hearing aid. I'm glad to see Road's all seriousness now, sitting beside me, completely still. I had expected he might display some nervous energy, want to make small talk, or bounce his good leg to betray his nerves, but instead he appears one hundred percent focused. It's a stance I can admire.

We're coming up the road and turn into the driveway.

"Stay in your seat until I come around," Road says.

I want to protest, but this is all part of the plan, so I patiently wait for Road to come around, heavily leaning on his stick.

"We're in position," Snatcher says into my ear.

Game on.

"I still don't think—" Road starts, his voice strong and clear.

"Darlin'," I go up on tiptoe, taking advantage of my position to tangle my hands into his hair, taking the opportunity to find it's just as silky as it looks. "I want to say thank you."

I'm not the only one taking advantage. He lowers his head, brushes his lips against mine, then cradles his hand around the back of my neck, pulling me in tight. I resist the urge to raise my knee to his balls as his mouth presses on mine and his tongue sweeps inside. Instead, I bite his lip.

"Bitch," he says under his breath, his eyes twinkling with mirth as he pulls back.

"What the fuck are you doing here?" an annoyed Weaver asks, the front door having been opened. I've not been unaware, I'd noticed out of the corner of my eye.

"Oh." I grab hold of Road's hand, pulling him forward. "I just had to come back and say thank you. You were so good earlier today helping my boyfriend out. A good deed can't go unrecognised."

Weaver seems taken aback. His face signals how much he wants us to leave, but he doesn't want to arouse suspicions by being rude. Put in a quandary, he hesitates, then attempts a smile. "It was no problem. You okay now? At least you're standing."

Road taps his thigh. "It's painful, but back in place."

"And Lucas won't be running anywhere for a while. Will you, sweetheart?"

"Of course not, babe." Road smiles down at me, the heat in his eyes making my insides clench and for a split second I wish it were real. Then his gaze moves to Weaver. "Thank Tub for letting me use his phone, will you? Oh, and we bought you this." He passes over the bottle of spirit.

I highly suspect Tub is standing behind the door. Either him or the other man. I doubt Weaver would have opened it on his own. But as Weaver does what any man would, holds out his dominant hand to take the gift, I draw my gun fast and have it pointing at him before he can react.

Using his good leg, Road kicks at the door and it flies back. As I predicted, there's an oomph from the man standing behind it, but Road's past Weaver with his own gun drawn. A muffled pop and Weaver's knocked sideways by the body of his sidekick.

"Call him out now," I hiss, jerking my head toward the doorway I assume leads to the bedrooms.

"You've got the wrong house." Weaver tries to bluster, and whines, "Why d'you have to kill Tub?"

He's not doing a good job of convincing me. I put a shot through his leg.

Yeah, a startled scream works just as well as a shout, as the sound of a door opens and footsteps sound. "What the fuck's happened, Weav—"

As last words, it's not much. Working as efficiently as any one of us, Road's crossed the room impressively fast seeing as he needs the stick right now. The third man walks straight into the gun and takes a shot through the mouth. The walls behind him are splattered as blood and brain matter shoot out.

"No, no..." The man at my feet starts backing away, limping heavily on his injured leg.

Weaver's kidnapped a kid, didn't have a thought about reuniting her with her parents, was going to put her through shit then sell her into a life where she'd pray every day for death. I feel nothing but relief when I'm responsible for a neat hole appearing in the middle of his forehead.

"All clear," I say. "Three men down and out."

"You get all the fun, Swift. You left nothing for us." Piston, emerging from the rear of the house, still carries his pistol down by his side. Cautiously, he comes to inspect the dead bodies, but with the neat, or actually, big round and glaringly obvious kill shots to their foreheads, or in Road's case, the guy with the back of his skull blown out, there's no need to be cautious or to check for a pulse.

Snatcher's voice comes from where Piston had appeared. "Need you back here, Swift."

Our mission has been completed with surgical precision. While I can take pride in that, it wasn't as clean as it could have been. When the third man had emerged from the bedroom where he'd been keeping an eye on the kid, presumably so she didn't snuff it like their comrade in the pen's kidnapped victim had, he'd left the door wide open. The result being, Road had shot a man's brains out in clear view of a frantic, gagged and bound thirteen-year-old child.

As I move in that direction, I can see Snatcher trying to approach her, gently, as though coaxing an injured wild animal to trust him, but it's obvious she's gone into complete panic mode. I assess the situation immediately. While I normally keep my feminine side suppressed, this is one of those occasions when my sex is definitely a benefit.

"Hey, sweetheart. It's Mona, isn't it?" I've already holstered my weapon, trusting my team to have my back should an unknown threat exist. I approach slowly, cautiously, my voice as soft as I can make it. "You're safe now, Mona. We're going to get you home to your mom and dad." While she's eyeing me warily, I inch closer to her. "I'm going to get you loose now, okay?"

Fuck, but she's a tiny thing, small for her age, still with some growing to do is my bet. Her eyes are red raw with crying. I suspect her tears will have been flowing for nearly twenty-four hours. The cloth tied around her mouth looks soggy with saliva, and she's twitching as her body reacts to her fear.

"Let me get that horrible thing out of your mouth," I suggest, moving another fraction nearer. "And we'll get those hands freed."

I wouldn't have said I've much of a natural maternal instinct, but I don't think you need to be female, just human, to want to reach out and hug Mona close, to reassure her the bad men are gone, and won't be able to do any more to hurt her.

Pausing my movement, I wait until her eyes fix on mine, me trying to telegraph that she's safe now.

"Let me help?" It's important to me that she gives consent. Whatever's been done to her so far has been without her agreement. Now she needs to have control given back, especially anything involving a stranger touching her.

She shudders, then gives me a small nod. It's enough. I move closer. The knot on the rag is soaking wet. I've no desire to waste time trying to undo it, so instead, I carefully move behind her and take out one of my knives, and the gag falls away.

Snatcher passes me something, and I take it. It's a clean tissue, so I use it to quickly wipe away the excess saliva that's pooled around her mouth.

"Better?"

She's still too scared, too cautious to speak, but with a small jerky movement, her head bobs up then down.

"Here, Swift."

Turning I raise my hand, catching the item Snatcher's thrown to me. It's a universal handcuff key and will work to undo those cuffs fastening her to the bed. After I do, Mona flexes her arms which I notice have sore red rings around her wrists. I swallow back down the rage that rises.

Mona rubs her sore eyes, and brushes the back of her hand

against her runny nose. I pass another of Snatcher's tissues to her, and she noisily blows it.

Then, finally, in between sobs and in a hoarse voice, she speaks. "I want my mommy."

"Sure you do, sweetheart. And we're taking you to her right now, okay?" I hold out my arms and she throws herself into them.

For a moment, I just hold her, knowing she'll relish the human touch given with kindness. She'll have been through hell the last twenty-four hours. I'm just grateful we hadn't taken any longer.

I've been in her situation. In my case, I was restrained as part of my torture that was preparing me for service in the SAS. The ordeal had provided me with the tools to know I'd be able to mentally survive should I ever be held against my will in a real situation.

But poor Mona had no idea what was coming or how to mentally prepare, how to somehow divorce her mind from the discomfort and stay positive. She'd had no tricks to sustain her, and no hope that rescue would ever appear.

She'll need therapy, and will maybe have nightmares for ever.

But she's been given back her future. She's going home to her family, and that's down to our team.

14

R oad...

Like most of the men, I stay well in the background while Swift comforts the kid. Christ knows what she's been through since she was taken when, probably without a care in the world, she walked home from her friend's house last night. I can't help but feel a sense of pride that along with these men, we've set her world back to rights. Or, as right as it can be now she's seen some of the worst of human behaviour. We'd saved her from the ultimate fate, but who knows how these men have verbally taunted her?

With therapy and support, I hope she'll come right, if her parents are good to her. The signs are there that they are, calling on us to save her. That right there reminds me I've a number of questions I need answering, like how the parents knew to contact the Satan's Devils and ask for their help. But that can wait until later. Being a Devil myself, I know there's a more pressing issue which needs to be addressed. Like the three dead men out in the living area.

I step beside Snatcher and ask quietly, "What do we do about cleanup?"

In answer, Snatcher jerks his head indicating I should follow him. In the main room, Thor and Preacher are slipping on latex gloves, just as Honor walks in through the front door carrying a bottle and a roll of paper towel.

Thor looks my way. "What did you do when you were here, Road? When you came in with your busted knee?"

I point. "Sat there. Didn't touch anything except the arm of the sofa." I watch as Honor carefully cleans anything my hand might have landed on. "Oh, and I had a drink of water."

"Already got the dishwasher running with all the glassware in there," Preacher confirms.

"When you take the girl out, I'll clean anything in the bedroom, strip the bed and throw the sheets," the enforcer informs the VP.

"Best do the bathroom, too, Thor."

The enforcer raises his chin, showing that's in his plan.

To me, Snatcher explains, "We're leaving the bodies here, weapons too. The guns are untraceable unless Preacher hadn't been doing his job properly." Overhearing, Preacher raises his middle finger at his VP.

"We're leaving them here for the cops to find? What will they think?"

"Home invasion or a fight among themselves." He looks at me and smirks. "They're not exactly upstanding citizens and I doubt the cops will waste much time trying to find who's responsible. We'll have removed all signs that we've been here."

"No cameras or security systems," Piston confirms, after carefully examining the door.

It goes against the grain leaving bodies where they can be found, but they seem to know what they're doing. I'm looking around, wondering if there's anything they, or I had missed, when I hear the sound of a back door slamming shut. It makes me jump.

"That will be Swift taking the girl out the back way. She doesn't need to see what's in here." Snatcher looks down at Weaver, his face tight. "Fuckin' assholes got off too lightly for the damage they've done to that kid."

It seems he and I agree entirely.

"All done here, VP." Thor casts a careful eye around the room.

"Right, you're with us, Road. Piston, go with Swift and drop the kid back home. We'll go back to the Airbnb."

"We're not going straight to the airport?"

"It's already late, Road." Preacher appears. "I need someone on the ground back home to guide us in. That's best done in daylight."

I suppose that makes sense.

After everyone's done a final check around, I follow Snatcher out the front door, not sorry to be leaving this house of kidnap and death. As I sit in one of the rear seats of the seven-seater SUV, I rest back my head, thinking about the whirlwind day I've had. First the flight, then purposefully putting my knee out, and yeah, there's still a residual ache. Then killing two men while Swift took out Weaver and seeing that poor kid rescued. I couldn't feel any sympathy or remorse for the lives I ended, just the remnants of exhilaration that I'd been part of the team. One wrong righted in the world. I'd do it again in an instant.

What I knew I'd miss most about racing was the adrenaline rush. If this is the kind of shit the Utah chapter routinely does, maybe they do have something to offer that can replace what I'd lost.

How they sprang into action, that the plane was on standby and not mothballed led me to believe this is nothing out of the ordinary for them. They aren't law enforcement or have connections with them, I'm certain of that. The evidence being that they have left bodies in the house and didn't call on the local cops for backup or help.

If this type of work is what they're offering me to be part of, would I want to sign up? Managing a strip club in Tucson doesn't really come close, though I suppose there is danger involved when one of the dancers swears her diamanté thong has been stolen by another stripper. There have been too many times I've broken up fights between two clawing and spitting women.

"Come on." A prod on my arm makes me start and I realise I must have dropped off. With a yawn, I unfold my body and slide out of the seat. Once standing, I stretch.

"Pizzas are on their way. Didn't know if you had any particular preference as you were asleep."

"Yeah, you looked so peaceful, mouth open, snoring…" Rascal's laughing, the jerk.

"Could hardly hear myself ordering," Preacher joins in.

In an adult manner, I show them my finger, but you know what it means when people yank your chain? It means you're accepted. I enter the house wearing a grin.

We'd left in such a rush, I hadn't packed fresh clothes, but that's okay, I don't need any to sleep and what I'm wearing will be fine until I get back tomorrow. But my mouth feels like it could do with freshening up. I'm half wondering whether I should ask if anyone knows if there's somewhere nearby where I can buy a toothbrush, when Rascal starts chucking packages at each of us. Automatically catching it, I realise it's exactly what I was thinking of—a small kit containing a toothbrush, toothpaste and a disposable razor. Well, the latter I really don't need. How prepared they are again makes me realise that nothing about this is new to any of them.

"Hey, Snatcher. I think I'll go freshen up."

"Sure, Road. Your bed's upstairs, first on the right. Bathroom's adjacent." I give him a nod then go up to check on my lodgings for the night. Bed looks comfy enough, but hell, I just fell asleep in the back of an SUV, doubt if much will keep me awake tonight. After a quick peek in, I brush the fur off my teeth, then go back downstairs to find I'm just in time for the pizza delivery, which coincides with the return of Piston and Swift.

"Girl get home okay?" I ask, concern still remaining about the kid.

"Nah, I left her at Disneyland instead." Piston rightfully rolls his eyes at the suggestion she wouldn't. "We watched until she was inside, then drove away."

"You speak to her parents?"

He shakes his head. "Not our way, Road. The fewer people who have eyes on us the better."

"Kid saw you," I point out.

"That kid was a mess," Swift tells me. "She probably won't remember any details at all. If she were older, we'd have worn masks, but those would only have frightened her more."

They seem to have all the bases covered. I suppose they're right, kids her age do not make particularly reliable witnesses.

It appears it's not just me who's suffering the aftereffects of an adrenaline rush. After stuffing our faces with food—I'm easy and there's not much I dislike so I'm happy with the selection they got—someone flicks on the television and breaks out the beers, but it's a fairly quiet night.

My leg's really aching again now, maybe running earlier wasn't the best idea in the world, so I pat my pockets to make sure the bottle of Tramadol I always carry with me is still there, then make my excuses and go to turn in for the night.

I piss, splash my face, use the toothbrush again, then strip off my clothes with the exception of my boxers and slide into the bed.

The day's activities, the rescue, the overuse of my leg and

the tablet I've taken mean I don't toss and turn, just go out like a light.

It feels I've only been asleep seconds when movement causes me to wake. At first I'm groggy, then I realise there's someone in my room.

"Who's there?" I call out.

I do so at the same time as someone knocks into something. "Shit. Sorry, Road. Didn't mean to wake you. Thought I'd do okay without putting on a light. Shit, that hurt."

"What did you do?"

"Stubbed my fuckin' toe."

I flick on the bedside light. "What are you doing in here, Swift?"

Her brow creases. "Coming to bed."

"But this is my room."

"Sorry, princess, but there are only four bedrooms so we've all got to double up." She starts undoing her blouse and throwing it down on a chair. Then her hands move to the button on her fly.

"Jeez." I start to throw off the sheet, then remember I've stripped down to my underwear. I lean over the bed, reaching for my t-shirt. "I'll go sleep on the couch."

"What the fuck, Road? You worried I won't be able to keep my hands to myself?"

No, I'm more worried about me keeping mine where they should be. I shouldn't have the hots for Swift. Not only is she my partner, but she's also not the type of woman I normally go for. I like mine soft, feminine, with curves. Long hair which I can wrap my hand around when she's sucking my cock is a definite plus. Swift is lean, muscular, and I have no doubt every inch of her is firm, and her hair is cut into a short bob, not much to hang onto there. Her breasts are small, not the bouncy pillows I normally prefer. Her hips, well, they're slender more like a man's.

Nothing to get my cock showing interest, except, for some reason it does. I should do the gentlemanly thing and avert my eyes as business-like she undoes her functional sports bra—her breasts, so firm I notice, barely drop—and then she reaches for a t-shirt and covers herself back up.

The brief glimpse of her white cotton panties, hell, that had been as hot as any pair of lacy underwear. It was what was hidden from view that made my mouth water.

I'm a man who works with women constantly in a near or completely naked state. I should be immune to the female figure. When it comes to Swift though, I find I'm not. So yeah, I'm worried where my hands might roam while I'm asleep.

I shift further over to my side of the bed as she lifts the sheet.

"Switch the light off, will you?"

I do. Then roll onto my back, throwing my arm up over my head. *Christ.* My cock is rock hard and throbbing. Normally after taking Tramadol it puts my whole body to sleep, but Swift seems to have an effect on me even medication can't prevent. This is as awkward as fuck. *Why didn't Pip partner me with Rascal?* There'd be no attraction there.

Maybe it's not her that's causing my dick to swell. Perhaps it's just the adrenaline rush not quite worn off.

"I apologise if I snore," I warn her, knowing that I often do.

"Road, I won't hear you. And I've slept in a room full of men often enough before. There's nothing you can do which I won't have already experienced."

You've never known the feel of my cock in your pussy... And, she never will. Fuck, one move toward her and she'd probably slice my dick off.

She fidgets. The bed moves as she turns over, then with a quiet *fuck*, she sits back up, then lies back down.

This mattress is obviously cheap and well-used. There's a dip in the middle and I work hard to prevent myself rolling over. I lie still, willing my cock to settle down, turning my thoughts to maintenance on my bike, anything to take my mind off the nearly naked woman lying by my side.

Every movement she makes, I feel. It's when the bed starts to gently vibrate, that my eyes snap open again.

Oh hell. She can't be rubbing one out, can she?

Fuck. *If she is, maybe I can. Maybe that would allow me to sleep.*

Fuck it. I may not have been a gentleman when I ogled her while she was undressing, but there's no way on this earth I can put my hands on my dick while she's lying next to me in the bed. Not when she's doing *that*.

The vibration continues.

Fuck this. That couch downstairs sounds pretty inviting right now. At least it would give me some privacy to take care of my own needs while she can carry on taking care of hers.

Not wanting to disturb her, I curl my abs and start to sit up. It's when I swing my legs off the bed, I hear her voice.

"Road?"

Assuming she's asking where I'm going, I explain, a little tersely. "I can't sleep." It's an honest reply, but I don't want her to be embarrassed by pointing out the reason why.

"Road?" She reaches out her hand. When her fingers curl around my arm, strongly enough to hold me back, I feel her shaking.

Her hand is shaking?

I flick the switch in the bedside light. It's pale glow illuminates something I didn't anticipate. I'd expected to see her face flushed with pleasure, instead, her eyes are open wide, and her skin is pale. "What's the matter?" I ask. Conscious of others sleeping around us, I've kept my voice low.

Her eyes are staring intently at the lower part of my face, then her eyes raise to meet mine. "My hearing aids, I can't use them when I sleep. I can't hear you, Road." She bites her lip, looking for her, surprisingly helpless. "Unless you speak very clearly into my left ear."

She can't hear what I say unless she puts her hearing aids back in, and I can't sign. There is one quick solution.

I lean right over her. "Change places." I'm lying on the right-hand side of the bed. My words had been falling literally on her totally deaf ear.

A small smile appears, then a nod. I get out of bed, pulling my t-shirt down over my boner, and getting back in the other side once she's shifted across.

"Is this better?" I ask, enunciating each word clearly and directly into her ear. She raises and dips her head. "When you're wearing your hearing aids, I don't think of you as deaf."

"With them, I'm not. Oh, it's not perfect. If someone mumbles, if there's too much background noise, I sometimes can't catch things. But the team knows and makes allowances."

"You compensate," I tell her. "Adjust. You've overcome your disability, Swift. You haven't let it hold you back. I'm fuckin' impressed." I can't be sure she's hearing every word, but she's heard enough.

"Before this happened, I was never scared. Cautious, wary, of course. But a soldier turns fear into adrenaline, otherwise they'd run from danger, not into it. I trained, I can handle situations that most others can't. I'm not bragging, it's fact."

I lie back down, listening to her speak, wanting to pull her into my arms, but I value my balls too much. At least talking is relaxing her, the shivering that had disturbed me so much is receding, her trembles becoming weaker.

"You need to know my weakness, Road. I can't sleep with hearing aids in. For a start, they cause feedback if I lie on my side, and guess what? That's the position I navigate to once I close my eyes. Also, if I kept them in all the time, that leads to a problem with wax. But when I take them out, I'm helpless."

She pauses, but there's no point in me saying anything. Instead, I reach for her hand, to offer tactile reassurance, but realise my mistake before I make contact.

"Unless I'm lying on my right-hand side, if a fire alarm goes off, I probably wouldn't hear it, and depending on the frequency, I might not even hear that. Low sounds I can't pick up at all, so if an intruder entered, I wouldn't wake. I feel so darn helpless. Back at the compound I've got technical aids—the bed shakes, or lights flash if the door opens or an alarm goes off. But away from home?"

She's helpless.

It would be frightening for anybody, but she's highly trained. She can handle herself in every situation. I might not have served myself, but I've gotten close to men who have. Someone like Peg, for example, always wants to be in control. He'll always sit with his back to the wall and face any point of entry. Always vigilant, always on the lookout. Swift's training is more advanced than anyone I've ever met, so this will have hit her badly.

If I'm going to be her partner, she's right to open up to me. If we're going to work together, we need to know each other's strengths, and where we're not so strong. She's seen my weakness, a fuckin' leg which will hopefully improve in time, though never come right completely. Now she's admitted hers, and I fucking hate it on her behalf.

"At home," she expands, "I feel safe. Here, I'm exposed." She takes a breath. "I've got PTSD, Road. And I shouldn't fuckin' have that. I wasn't injured in action."

I pull myself up and lean on my elbow to speak into her not-so-deaf ear again. "Swift, you were fuckin' injured saving a man's life. Your training and quick thinking meant he's alive today. What was that if not action?"

She goes so quiet I wonder whether I've spoken too fast, whether she's picked up on anything that I've said.

"I hate it, Road. Hate that I can be strong during the day. Hate that it's only those aids which make me that way. Hate that I rely on them so completely that when I take them out I feel so fuckin' vulnerable that I uncontrollably shake. And I hate that for some fucking reason, I'm talking to you this way." She glances up at me and shakes her head. "I don't know why I'm telling you all this."

I don't know why she is either. I hadn't expected her to open up with such honesty. "I'm glad you are," I swallow back the 'babe' that comes to my lips automatically, "because I didn't think it was PTSD, I thought you were taking a personal moment."

Her brow creases, then her eyes widen. After a couple more seconds a startled snort comes from her. Then she starts to chuckle, followed by an outright laugh. When Swift bumps her fist to your arm, I find you know all about it. Immediately after, I'm massaging where she hit.

"I can't believe you thought I was having a frig." She snorts again.

I lay back against the pillow, feeling a bit proud that despite the seriousness of our conversation and her admission of weakness, I've managed to put a smile on her face.

15

Swift...

I hate admitting I'm weak.

I hate that my vulnerability affects me in ways I can't control. That being in an unfamiliar environment with none of the technology that I normally depend can cause a panic attack to come up as if from nowhere and make me physically shake. I can't help myself, can't control the fear that comes over me. I can sleep on a plane, in a chair, but put me in a bed, when my PTSD hits, the ability to drop off evades me.

It's the silence, so acute. I can hear things like a voice very close to me, or noises like a gunshot, loud enough to penetrate my deafness, but I always know if I close my eyes an enemy might sneak up, unheard and unseen.

Talking with Road, I'd picked up enough to satisfy his questions, but when he was speaking fast, I could only make out the odd word.

Snatcher knows I get PTSD, and his solution is ensuring I don't sleep alone and that without my technical aids, I have working ears in the room with me. I should have expected he'd team me up with Road, but I didn't think. I suspected it would be Rascal or Piston.

I'm a soldier. I've never asked for, or expected, to be treated differently from a man. Of course, when I served, separate bedrooms and bathrooms were available for the different sexes on base. But out in the field it was a case of make do where and when. Here, with the Devils, it's more important than ever to pretend I'm the same as them.

When we walk into a situation such as how we rescued Mona today, we receive information in bits and pieces. So we tend to set out en masse, even if only a few of us end up taking part in a mission. It's better to be overmanned than under, and better still to get to where we need to be fast, even before we know what we'll be walking into.

Duty is good at finding us places to stay but were we to insist on the right number of bedrooms, it would cause him a headache. It's not unknown for eight of us to be faced with just two rooms.

Unless I was going to act like a prima donna and insist on my own room, I would have to suck it up and sleep with however many brothers needed to share. I was never worried about anyone making a pass at me, but I knew from the start I risked exposing my PTSD.

My hope that I could keep it hidden was defeated early on, and it soon became clear that something happens to me when the lights are turned out.

Luckily, I was with men who knew how debilitating PSTD can be. My Satan's Devils' brothers' reaction had, to a man, been supportive. We're a family first, and they went out of their way not to make me feel excluded or different, my deafness just an obstacle to be overcome. The solution was obvious. When I didn't have my technology around me, I'd have human ears sleeping near me. That was why I'd been scared when I'd felt the bed move and thought Road was going to leave.

Usually a human presence is enough to reassure me, but sometimes I'll still get panic attacks at night, in whatever form they might take. Sometimes, I freeze, lie awake, and just wait in hope that the attack will pass and I'll either sleep or day will break. Sometimes I whimper in my sleep. Sometimes, apparently, I call out.

Other times I uncontrollably shake. I should be embarrassed for the explanation that Road had jumped to, but it's so ludicrous it had made me laugh. Never, ever, before had I been accused of rubbing one out.

There was no reason not to explain to Road, and there's some comfort in him knowing now. Now he knows, he won't leave me alone. With that assurance, I should be able to go to sleep now.

But I still can't. And now it's not my PTSD plaguing me, talking to Road had pushed that back into its box. It's Road himself. It's knowing how close he is. It's the effect he's having on me. Once we're back in Utah, maybe I should try him out, get him out of my system once and for all.

What message would that send though? I've deliberately avoided going anywhere near my brothers, knowing that if I gave it up to any of them, I could end up being treated like a sweet butt. That wouldn't be bad in itself, I'd often welcome the chance for a release, and most of them probably wouldn't disappoint. But some of them wouldn't turn me on at all, and feelings would be hurt if I turned anyone down. I'd always thought it much easier to say no to everyone and retain the strict boundaries between us.

If Road's going to transfer, my exclusions have to include Road.

Damn it.

I roll over and beat the pillow into submission, then rest my head back down.

You're safe, I remind myself.

But Road's closeness, the sweet smell of his breath, the warmth extruding from his skin which I can feel even though our bodies don't touch, taunts me. *Why do I find him so darn sexy?* To my dismay, I'm having to concentrate to stop my hand moving down and taking care of myself. For real this time.

Think of something different. Mona's face, when we found her. *Think over the mission.* What had gone well, what we could do different next time. How we only knew what was happening in the house through Road's bravery and his quick thinking.

Damn. Stop thinking of the man.

Bikes. Mine could do with an oil change. Yes, think about that.

Eventually, I manage to get my mind off the man who's probably snoring beside me. My mind quiets, and I drop off.

I'm woken when the mattress dips and then rises. Opening my eyes, I see Road standing, but looking back over his shoulder at me. He mimes washing his face.

"I'll be fine." I start sitting up, reaching for my hearing aids, and out of the corner of my eye, catch him bending to pick his jeans up off the floor. When he straightens, I get the glimpse of some impressive looking morning wood.

Mm mmm.

Then I mentally slap myself. *Didn't I just explain to myself what a bad idea sampling Road's wood would be?*

I thought I had, but it hadn't worked. A girl can dream though. It wouldn't hurt Road if he didn't know I was using the thought of him while enjoying myself later with my vibrator.

By the time Road's back, I'm dressed and ready to hit the

bathroom myself. I give him a rise of my chin, then disappear to do what's necessary. After that, I meet him downstairs with the others, then get caught up in the flurry of morning activity as we get ready to hit the road.

Breakfast is a quick pit stop at a convenience store, then we arrive at the airfield. Preacher goes to do his pre-flight checks on the plane.

I always find flying home anti-climactic. Heading out on a mission, we're full of anticipation, knowing we're walking into the unknown. However much information those left back at base will feed us, there's always a chance something will go wrong. Always a chance of not all of us making it back. All our affairs are in order, Pip insists on that, though on my part it was just a formality and a matter of updating what was already there. Soldiers have to be ready for anything, and I hadn't lost that habit.

Returning is always to the known, to the familiar. Welcome at first, then I begin to get an itch inside me, willing the time to pass before we're sent out again.

I live for these missions, and love that, despite my disability, I've found a way to make my mark on the world, albeit anonymously. Then that's not much different to if I had joined the SAS, where no credit is given, and participants aren't named.

As normal, I turn down my hearing aids and zone out on the plane until I feel it start to descend and the vibration of the engine changing. I open my eyes and watch until the wheels touch down. Then I turn my hearing aids back up and join the world again.

We wait while Preacher talks to the man who makes sure our plane's able to fly, giving him some kind of report about how the plane handled and what it might need, then, when he's ready, we go to our bikes.

Hearing aids again turned down, I ride alongside Road,

enjoying the feeling of fresh air on my face. I notice how competent he is at handling a bike, but that shouldn't surprise me. What does, is how in tune we are, leaning and straightening perfectly in unison. Maybe soon we can go for a longer ride, and not just the couple of miles back to the clubhouse.

When we pull in through the gates and ride around to the parking lot, I'm not surprised to see Pip out the back of our clubhouse with a coffee in his hand. He'll have known the second we touched down.

"Church?" Snatcher needlessly asks.

"Yeah. We'll debrief now." Taking his coffee with him, Pip walks back inside.

One by one we drop our duffel bags off with Igor. Preacher will trust him to sort everything out. The guns which were fired had been left behind, but those unused and the spare ammunition will need to be put back into our stockpile.

Pip's already seated by the time I walk in. Copying the brothers, I first approach the coffee machine and select the setting for hot water. I drop a tea bag into the cup and drown it, then add a dash of milk. I turn around to see Road grinning widely at me.

"Reminds me of back home," he says as he gets himself a coffee. "Sophie prefers her tea."

"Yorkshire tea," I tell him. "My mum sends it to me."

"When you've finished your discussion on beverages..." Pip's voice sounds more amused than angry.

"Fuckin' foreigners," Stormy mumbles.

"Wanker." I purposefully insult him in my form of English again as I walk past, enhancing my comment with a swipe to his skull to add injury.

"Stormy!" Pip barks and points his finger in challenge. "Don't say the words I know are about to come out of your mouth as it would be boring to see Swift humiliate you again."

"Why's he such an ass?" Road asks me quietly out of the corner of his mouth.

I shrug. He is. That's all I know.

"Right." Pip bangs the gavel. "Mission completed successfully. Two happy parents and one little girl back where she belongs."

"They pay up?" Rascal asks, then nods in satisfaction when Prez gives a confirmatory raise of his chin.

"Road," Prez begins. "Hear it was down to you that it all went off so smoothly. How's your leg?"

I've never liked being singled out, for praise or a stripping down, and the way Road shifts awkwardly before replying suggests he's much the same.

"My leg's fine."

I glance at him, concerned. I saw him favouring it earlier and could see that's far from the truth. But I don't have the chance to say anything as there's a snort from the end of the table.

"So his talent is pretending to be a fuckin' cripple. Don't know how many times that will come in useful."

"His talent," Snatcher roars at Stormy from his seat beside Pip, "is thinking with his fuckin' brain and coming up with something out of left field."

"We can all fuckin' do that," Stormy retorts.

Pip slams his fist on the table. "Yeah? Road's quick thinking cut the mission time in half. Everything he suggested was right. We still haven't dissected all the fuckin' mistakes you made in Pueblo and San Diego."

"Didn't make fuckin' mistakes," Stormy says stonily.

Prez glares at him. "Don't think that's fuckin' been brushed under the carpet. But your failings will be discussed once I've decided on a suitable punishment." He pauses to let that sink in. Stormy's face is as black as thunder, but soon Prez looks away from him and toward

Duty. "Have the cops found the bodies in Santa Barbara yet?"

As he gets back to the case in hand, the man he's addressing shakes his head. "Nah. Looks like they were keeping themselves to themselves. It could be some time before anyone goes to the house. It's been empty for a while. I dug into it. Owners are abroad for an extended time."

"Hopefully they've got an agent keeping an eye on the place. Great welcome home from a vacation to find bodies rotting in their living room."

Not a great homecoming, I silently agree with Thor.

"The third man was called Rice," Duty continues. "He got out shortly after Tub and Weaver. Guess they planned all this together when they were inside."

"Anyone reported them missing?"

"Not so far. I'll keep my ear to the ground."

Prez leans back on his chair looking well satisfied. "Another job well done. Great work, team."

I hear Road clearing his throat by my side and am not surprised when he starts to speak. "I've got questions, Pip. Even more now that you allowed me to tag along to rescue the girl. You've captured my interest, I'll say that, but I still don't know why you say you're Satan's Devils, yet are unlike any other chapter we have. You wear cuts, ride motorcycles, but that's where the resemblance ends. And I still want to know why you're sitting in that chair. Snatcher ran the show down in California, and I had no problem answering to him. So I have to wonder, what do you bring to the table?"

My cheeks hollow as I suck in a sharp breath. Road's got balls to put it so frankly. I notice even Stormy's raised an eyebrow as though he's impressed. Glancing the other way, I wonder how Prez is going to take the challenge.

"Yeah." Prez presses his lips together, then smooths his hands over his shortly shorn hair. "I can see why you're wondering. I promised you information, Road. The opportunity came up for you to see us in action. A physical demonstration is often better than words."

"Words is what I'm after." Road puts his fingertips against the edge of the table and taps them. "Going to California raised more questions than gave me answers. Look, I don't know what's going on. You're asking me to transfer into something I know nothing about, and," he raises his chin toward Stormy, "your brother there has a good point. I don't know what I can offer that no one else has got. I can't fly a plane like Preacher, and I can't squeeze information out of a computer beyond asking Google what I want." He now nods toward Duty. "As for Swift?" He turns and offers me a grin, "Well, I'm not just not in her league, I'm not even on the same planet."

He's so wrong. I want to tell him not to put himself down. I want him to see that although we'd have rescued the girl anyway, his quick thinking, his putting himself through pain just to move the mission along, had her home and back with her parents probably a day sooner than we would have done. With those three men, another twenty-four hours was a fucking long time.

But I say none of that. I sit stoic and quiet. Road's nothing to me, so why should I feel this need to console him, to make him see he has something to contribute if he decides to stay?

Because if I keep my mouth shut, he'll leave.

Which would definitely be for the best. Then I won't think about him every minute of the day or wonder just what he can do with the morning wood I'd seen earlier.

Road's not transferred yet. He's not one of my brothers. Maybe I wouldn't be breaking my rules if I jumped in the sack with him. Perhaps putting him through his paces for a couple of hours would get rid of this inconvenient urge. It's possible he wouldn't even take that long, and he'd be a disappointment.

But he might have hidden talents, and that would compound my mistake.

What the fuck's wrong with me? I never look at other brothers this way. What is it about Road that makes me feel feminine? I could break him in two with one hand tied behind my back.

I don't understand why he affects me. I almost hate him for making me feel things I shouldn't.

I watch him out of the corner of my eye. He's still looking around him, as if analysing what everyone can offer which he can't. After a moment, he shrugs, looks straight at Prez and asks, "So yeah, I've got questions. Are you going to answer them?"

<h1 style="text-align:center">16</h1>

oad...

I want to laugh. It's so blatantly obvious I have no place here. No one had leapt to my defence telling me I was wrong when I told them I had nothing to offer. Swift had just sat silent beside me, no word of support or comment about how well I'd done.

Though Snatcher had defended me earlier, he doesn't remind them now, and in the scheme of things the ability for me to easily dislocate my knee isn't a particularly useful talent, just one which had worked yesterday. Its ability to normally pop out when I least want it to is normally decidedly inconvenient.

If I press Pip for answers and hear him say there's no place for a grunt like me here, maybe I could be on my bike and headed home later today.

Carefully though, extremely carefully, I'm not ignoring the threats.

They think Drummer would shut down their operation or take their Satan's Devils' charter away if the mother chapter prez learns exactly how far Utah has stretched the club's rules. In that, they are probably right. What I don't understand is why that's so important to them. With or without that label, they'd still be a close-knit team, a family, a brotherhood. With the exception of Stormy, they seem to be loyal to each other and disciplined. And not people, I suspect, who'd end a man with no good reason. So they must have a fucking good motive for wanting the Satan's Devils' patch on their backs to remain. A purpose that might see them execute a man who's sat around the table with them, broken bread with them, and, yesterday, supported them.

I had been part of getting that little girl back to her parents. No one had faulted my performance. I've got new respect for Snatcher, for Preacher who seems to have no limit to his talents; for Thor, Rascal, Piston and Honor who I was happy enough to work alongside. Swift, hell. Maybe one good reason to leave is that I want her but would never be able to have her.

Her competency, her skills, her confidence and control. Even if I had a chance, would I even be able to keep up sexually? If I did, what then? I'm not in the market to have an old lady, or to be an old man, and I don't know what she'd expect from me. Would she be happy with my time and body for a couple of hours, or would she want more?

Hell, last night was the first time I slept beside a woman in a very long time. My last experience had soured me. The last time I'd stayed the night, I'd fallen asleep after pleasurable, but not spectacular sex. It hadn't been my intention, nor had I thought it was a signal I wanted more. But phone calls and even visits to the strip club where I worked had followed. She'd been insistent that we should have a repeat. Lesson learned, it was much cleaner to have sex, then leave and go home to my own bed.

Why am I sitting here thinking about Swift naked beneath, or hell, on top of me, either way I wouldn't care, when there are far more important things that should be on my mind right now?

Reluctantly, I make myself push the thought of Swift out of my head and get my mind focused.

If I don't have anything to offer, the decision of whether I stay or not would be taken out of my hands. Hell, prospects here have to work twice as hard to join the ranks of the members. Had yesterday been a test? Had I passed or failed it?

If I'm not a suitable match for their club, but they don't want me to betray them, for me to agree to leave with their secrets intact, they need to give me something worth lying to my prez. An explanation I can accept for pulling the wool over Drummer's eyes.

An acceptable reason why it's Pip at the top of the table when he doesn't even ride a motorcycle, why there's a woman member, and why they've lied to all the other chapters. Could a sufficient reason exist that I could accept? I really can't see it. But I'll give them a chance.

I shrug, look straight at Pip and ask, "So yeah, I've got questions. Are you going to answer them?"

Pip looks at me in a calculated way, then raises his chin. "It's time, so yes. You stay, Snatcher, you too. The rest of you can leave."

"Want me here?" Cowboy asks, sounding reluctant. He seems a strange person to offer, so I look toward him sharply, in time to see relief cross his face when Pip shakes his head. Cowboy, still looking tense, gets up to follow the rest of the men—and woman—out.

Pip stands and goes to a cabinet I hadn't paid much attention to. He opens it, pulls out a bottle of whisky—a quality single malt, I notice—and three glasses. Coming back to the table, he pours three shots, pushing one toward me, the second toward Snatcher, and takes the other for himself.

He stares into the smoky depths for a moment, then raises

his eyes toward me. "Some of this isn't my story to tell, some of it is. But Cowboy didn't want the pain of telling it, so it's been left to me."

Snatcher raises his fingers from the table. "Perhaps, as it's a Devil we're speaking to, the story goes back further than that?"

Pip tilts his head slightly as he thinks. Then he dips his chin. "Perhaps it does."

Snatcher nods, then takes over. "It was fifteen years or so back, I was in my current spot. VP to the old prez. Butler and I worked well together. Some of the members we had then, we still got. Thor, Piston, Rascal. Thumper was here as well. It was before Honor and Duty's time, and the others who sit around the table now." He pauses to take a sip of his whisky. "There were another half-dozen members. We were Satan's Devils then too, patched over in Drummer's father, Bastard's day. You heard about how Bastard ran his club?"

I nod, my teeth grinding together. Drummer doesn't have much good to say about his dad, and the shit he got the club into. Drug and gun running, prostitution as well. His dirty dealings had ended with a police raid which had decimated the club. Members jailed or, in the case of Bastard and several more, killed outright. Drummer stepped into the hot seat and cleaned up the club.

"Drummer was fairly new to his role; I suppose hiding shit started there. Butler and I were quite happy making money the easy way. We'd go to meetings with the mother chapter, said our ayes and nays in all the right places, then came back and did what the fuck we wanted. Oh, we'd learned lessons from what happened to Bastard, but didn't take them to heart well enough. Thought we had, but we were wrong. What we did do was make sure our dealings were watertight, concentrating on keeping beneath the radar of the cops. Thought if we kept the law off our backs, everything else would stay in place." He shakes his head. "Thought we could be cleverer than Bastard."

He seems to grind to a halt, so Pip encourages him. "Tell him the rest."

"It wasn't the law that came for us, but the mafia crew. See? We'd gotten into a lucrative gun trade without realising our supplier was ripping them off. We thought we were the big boys, hell, we weren't anywhere close. They didn't mess around. Butler led the run making a delivery, and they were all taken out. We lost our prez and darn near half the club in one fell swoop."

"That's when you stepped up?" I prompt.

"Yeah. I didn't have much choice. We took a club vote and decided maybe Tucson did have it right after all. But how do you go legit and put food in men's bellies, when they've been drug and gun running all their lives? We couldn't even continue our prostitution business—the mafia stole that from us too. With so little manpower left, we couldn't defend ourselves."

"You could have asked Drummer for help."

"Not our way, Brother. We'd fucked up, we had to make it right. Just was a struggle trying to find some way to do it. Grinch, Mystic and Goofy worked their asses off building up an auto-shop. Thor turned his hand to mechanics and backed them up. We were on the bread line, only just surviving. Continued that way for three years. We had no choice, the mafia was always in the background, watching in case we stepped on their toes again." He nods at Pip.

"I'll pitch in now." Pip raises his chin at Snatcher. "I was with the CIA, one of their top hostage negotiators. Yeah, I'll say it myself. I worked with embassies all over the world when there were international kidnappings. I was the one they wanted when they needed to get hostages released. My last mission though was a bust. It was a setup, and I never had a chance of success. The mistake was on the clown who called me in. I should never have been involved." He sighs heavily and picks up his whisky. After a large sip, he replaces the glass on the table. "The kidnapping was staged to cover a premeditated murder of someone a powerful senator wanted out. There was never a chance of a rescue, and I quickly figured it out." His face reddens and his fist hits the wooden tabletop. "I was taken for a fuckin' fool, but fool I certainly was not. I saw it for what it was and sent the message up the chain. Another message came back down." He takes a deep breath. "I was terminated from that day, my recommendations and observations disavowed, as was I myself. After a career hunting the bad guys, I was a wanted man myself."

I hadn't expected that. I cock an eyebrow at him. "So you had to hide? What the fuck brought you to the Satan's Devils?"

"It's a longer story than that. Goes back to that final kidnapping." A wave of visible pain washes over Pip's face. "You had any dealings with Cowboy while you've been here?"

I shrug. "Only enough to know he was a Navy chef who was going to open his own place when he'd done his time. It was strange to discover he's cooking for an MC instead."

Pip nods, acknowledging my point. "As one of the Navy's top chefs, he not only provided meals for the sailors on the ship, he also was personally responsible for providing gourmet food for admirals and visiting dignitaries. A senator brought along his assistant to one of those dinners. The food was excellent, I'm led to believe, and the senator wanted to pay his compliments to the chef. His assistant was pretty, and she caught Cowboy's eye. Well, the attraction was mutual, and phone numbers were exchanged. Cowboy caught up with her when he had shore leave, and things progressed quite fast. They married, and shortly after, a daughter was born."

Pip pauses to take another sip of his whisky, while my

brain puts things together. What he's going to say next won't be good hearing. Cowboy made no reference to a family he clearly once had.

Pip replaces his glass on the table and resumes. "Cowboy obviously had to conduct a long-distance relationship, spending long periods apart. He'd decided to end his time with the Navy, and he and Gianetta had plans. She was going to give up her job and they'd open a restaurant together. She'd do the admin, and Cowboy would concentrate on creating the delicacies he was famed for. But it didn't work out. The senator went out on a trip to Paris. It was there, Gianetta was kidnapped, along with her little girl."

"Your last case?" I put two and two together. "Not a genuine kidnapping, but someone wanted her out of the way? Why had she taken her daughter along?"

"She always did when she could if she travelled. She didn't like leaving her at home, and Cowboy was doing his last tour. France is safe. Cowboy thought she wanted to show her the sights like the Eiffel Tower." Pip raises his chin then dips it. "As his assistant, she had access to the senator's paperwork, often being called into meetings to take notes. She was an intelligent woman, too many brains as it turned out. She got to know too much about things the senator didn't want getting back to the States, in particular a large payoff from the Russians."

When Pip pauses and takes another large sip of his whisky, I know we're getting down to the details now.

He picks the story up again. "It was made to look legit—they were kidnapped, snatched from her apartment, ransom demands came in. As a coincidence, I was close by, having just completed another mission. I was called in as negotiator. I was taken in by the senator's crocodile tears for a while, then things began to smell off. But I was an agent, and he was a politician." Pip shrugs. "Clearly, he was being protected by powerful people who also didn't want her info to circle back this side of the Atlantic, and by people who didn't appreciate me sticking my nose in."

"Cowboy's wife and kid were killed." I don't ask, I make the obvious statement.

Pip doesn't bother to confirm it. "I'd been dealing with Cowboy, liked the man. He'd been given leave as his woman was missing. He was a frantic, desperate man, while we were waiting. When their bodies were found, he was devastated. To this day, he's never gotten over it. He wanted revenge, especially as he'd put the situation together the same way as I had, and he had the benefit of knowing that woman of his. He told me if she knew something, something so important it could bring the senator down, she'd have backed that up. He found it, gave it to me. I told him..." Pip wipes a hand over his face. "I told him I'd deal with it. Instead, I was kicked out and had to go underground. But I stayed in contact with Cowboy. I knew there was only one thing that would help him. Justice."

"What happened?"

Pip's eyes meet mine. "The senator returned stateside. I followed him. Found I wasn't the only man on his trail. We ended up working together as a team, and the senator met with a fortunate accident. That man..." he pauses, and looks directly into my eyes, making me feel the next piece of information is going to be significant. "That man went, still goes, by the handle, Devil."

That name rings a fucking loud bell. But surely, it can't be? "He have a jagged scar down his face?"

Pip smirks. "I thought you'd know him. Jason Deville is his proper handle. Of course it was long before he met Drummer in Tucson. When that business blew up with Sam, it was me who recommended he contact Drummer head-on."

"I thought it was because Drummer had met Devil's business partner at the sheikh's wedding." I press my lips together.

"That was the useful thing. He had. But we'd been monitoring the sex slave traffickers. We were the ones to find out Sam was being targeted, and Devil was already on that case." His eyes meet mine. "You've already seen what we're capable of. Devil is just one of the people who use our skills."

Skills that shouldn't exist in Utah. But I don't comment about that, instead I think of what I know of Devil. He's a partner in a security company based in the UK. He works for the feds as a consultant from time to time. If he hadn't have appeared when he had, Drummer wouldn't have known Sam was at risk. I know Drummer remains suspicious of his motives, but then he's that way about everyone who doesn't wear our patch.

"Getting back on track, the senator was dead, and Devil was already investigating one of the people Gianetta's information had named. We pooled our resources. I'd taken Cowboy under my wing. He was anchorless and needed to exact revenge. Well, let it just be said that another man who didn't deserve to live is now gone. As I'd proved useful to Devil, he offered me a job with Grade A Security, but I didn't want to work for anyone anymore, whoever they were and whatever their resources. And Devil himself? Well, it wasn't just his surname that earned him that handle. He's straddled the line between good and evil for so long, I'm not certain he knows which side he's standing at any one time."

Much like Drummer's assessment of the man. Devil hadn't led us wrong and seemed to be on the right side. He'd helped us rescue Mariana from Colombia, but it had suited his purpose to take her evil father out. If we hadn't been treading the same path, would he have gone to the same lengths he had? It's impossible to know.

17

_R_oad...

"It must have destroyed Cowboy. I can understand that. But I don't see where the link is between you and the Satan's Devils MC."

Pip slowly raises his head and dips it again as though I've asked something intelligent.

"Cowboy was a man who had no dreams, and nothing left to live for. He'd planned to go home to Texas, but that was when his family was alive. He couldn't even stomach the thought of returning alone. He needed a fresh start. To be honest, we'd struck up a friendship, and I was worried what would happen to him on his own. I decided to stick with him. We basically stuck a pin in the map and headed here, to Utah."

Snatcher glances at Pip, who raises his chin toward him, and he takes over again. "Our club had been decimated, our businesses taken away from us. The auto-shop was turning a profit, but again, the mafia started fuckin' with us, and wanted to use our skills to adapt their vehicles so they could transport weapons and drugs. None of us remaining members wanted to work with them pulling our strings. One night, we were out drowning our sorrows and chucking ideas around, when Pip and Cowboy appeared." Snatcher chuckles. "Well, it's fair to say Preacher threw his beer over Pip—quite accidentally—but Pip, well, for a moment I wasn't sure how he'd react to that. He was a man who could handle himself, and for a moment I worried that we might be carrying Preacher out in a box. So I stepped up, apologised, and invited him and his companion to join us."

Pip sighs. "Cowboy and I had just arrived in Utah. If we wanted to stay, we had to blend in, and that meant getting on the right side of the locals. So there was I, in a borrowed t-shirt, sitting down with the remnants of an MC. As they talked, it was clear they were a club with a problem and Cowboy and I needed a home."

"Surprisingly they fit in." Snatcher takes over again. "Well, Pip is the master of that, and Cowboy, he rode a motorcycle and knew all the right terms. When we found they'd just arrived, we took them back to the clubhouse to give them a bed for the night."

"Mystic had had too much to drink. In his drunken ramblings, he let slip that the Devils had a mafia problem. Just so happens I quickly came up with a plan for sorting that out." Pip grins, showing his teeth.

Snatcher barks a laugh. "Suddenly, all the truck's carrying drugs and guns were being stopped by the police. Pip's plan was so clever, the mafia suspected, but couldn't prove shit, and Pip was more than a match for them when they came and threatened us."

"Devil helped," Pip acknowledges. "The mafia got the message and stopped using the shop. At last the Utah chapter was free. Devil, though, wanted a reward."

"And in paying his price, we started doing some of his work. Then branched out, taking on most of what we do alone. Sometimes we still help Devil out, but we're not beholden to him. It's been both satisfying and lucrative." Snatcher grins.

"We left Grinch, Mystic and Goofy to continue to run our shop and we moved in here." Pip nods at his VP.

They keep mentioning the names of men I haven't met. Presuming they've moved on, I don't bother asking about them. "This clubhouse," I focus on what had bothered me from the start, "it's more like an office block."

"That's what it is," Pip says. "It's a front. We still have the old one, that's where we have our parties, and that's where the locals think we live. But this is where we do business."

"And your business is finding and rescuing kidnapped kids?"

"Partly," Pip says. "We track down bad guys. Some we deal with ourselves, sometimes we help point people in the right direction. We keep our ears to the ground. It's right to say, information is our business."

"San Diego and Colorado," I state, recalling again how angry Drummer had been. "You didn't just pass on information. You took the fuckin' kills."

Pip's face goes dark. "Stormy can't follow fuckin' orders. He likes to show off. Look, Road, I know it was wrong. Fuck, if I were Lost or Demon I'd be out for blood as well. That's why I've pulled Stormy in."

Pip's ire is palpable. At least he acknowledges they'd fucked up. "Why you?" I ask the other burning question. "I can follow that you joined the club because you gave them a direction to go in, but Snatcher was the prez."

Snatcher takes up the story. "Sure, I was the prez, but Pip was the ideas man. If someone wants their daughter returned safe and sound, he's clean-cut and shaven and can pass for a respectable man." He grins at Pip who shows him his finger, and it's my first real glimpse of how this partnership works. "Pip became the front for our business. When he started to issue orders, no one objected. Came so I asked myself why the fuck I was sitting at the top of the table, repeating what Pip had said first." He glances at me, but I stay quiet. "We brought in new members. Not only did they want to join an MC, but we picked them for their skills. They automatically looked to Pip as a leader." He raises and lowers his shoulders. "I didn't care. After all the hassle with the mafia, losing our members as we did, I was happy to step back and abdicate responsibility."

"We work well together." Pip sends his second-in-command a sharp look. "Don't read Snatcher wrong, Road. He's the outward face of the MC, while I'm the person who brings in the business. When someone turns up to ask for our help, they enter a modern, clean environment and are greeted by a receptionist. Hell, they have a meal in our cafeteria. They find exactly what they're expecting and have confidence we can do what they want."

"They enter the Satan's Devils MC." I narrow my eyes. "I saw the nameplate."

"You saw a card which can be replaced with whatever we want when we're expecting company. SD Consulting, or something appropriate to the situation. When we invite someone back here, we put on a front that they are most comfortable with."

Except when I'd turned up and caught them off-guard.

"But why keep this from Drummer?" That's what I can't understand.

"I don't ride a bike and have no desire too," Pip starts to explain. "That would exclude me from leading the MC, publicly or privately. And what about Swift? I may not have broken the regulations as they don't specifically exclude women members, but Drummer's assumption is that we all have dicks."

Apart from being totally unable to understand why Pip

won't ride a motorcycle, I suppose I've been told everything I need to know. It's one hell of a backstory, but one which is credible. Perhaps if I hadn't previously met Devil, I'd have found it harder to believe. What I don't know, is, "Where does this leave me?"

"Pip and I have had some discussion, Road. A suggestion was already made that you patch over, and we want you to seriously consider it. We'd like you to join us."

I snort. "You just don't want me running back to Drummer and let him in on your game."

Snatcher looks annoyed. "There's that, but there's more to it. We think you've got something to offer."

For the second time I snort, then scoff. "Yeah, right. I can see I'm a good fit—"

"Road, I don't think you realise what you can bring to the table," Pip interrupts. "Snatch has told me that your ideas yesterday shaved a day off us rescuing that kid." He taps his brain. "Sometimes it's not about schooling, certificates or having a trade. Sometimes what's needed is good old-fashioned common sense. You've got to be quick-witted to be able to ride as you do—"

"Did." My turn to break into his speech.

"Did, do, will, won't. That's beside the fuckin' point." At that moment I see what Snatcher had seen all those years ago in the bar. This is a man who'll take no prisoners and who I should stay on the right side of. His appearance of respectability is an illusion.

"We won't even make you prospect." Snatcher relieves the building tension with a quick grin.

That was an option? "What if I say no?"

Snatcher mimes cutting his throat which makes Pip roll his eyes. He picks up the bottle and waves at my glass. When I nod, he tops it up.

"Depends whether we can trust you, Road. This operation we run has saved hundreds of lives."

"I get that," I tell him, raising my glass and breathing in the fumes before taking a sip. This is the type of whisky you savour. "But say Drummer wanted to close this chapter down. You've got everything you need to go it alone, start your own club. I don't understand what's so important about staying Satan's Devils."

"Satan's Devils are known. They've got a charter from the dominant club, the Wretched Soulz. It's not just a cover for us, being Devils is our way of life."

"I understand that from you, Snatcher, but Pip doesn't ride a bike."

Suddenly Pip lurches forward. "I also don't have tats or a beard. Want me to grow one so I look like I fit? I run this club. I look after the members. I run this business. You want me to give that all up because I don't want to ride a fuckin' bike?"

"You want to, Pip." Snatcher nudges him.

"Whether I want to or not is moot. I don't have… How the hell did we get on to this? I was asking Road if we could trust him." Pip's face has gone red.

"You sound like you're giving me a choice, but what choice is it? Whether I transfer or return to Tucson, I wouldn't be able to avoid lying to my prez. You're asking me to fabricate some story about what you get up to in Utah." My eyes meet Pip's. "He's not stupid, Pip. Don't underestimate him. He'll not be satisfied with an 'everything's fine'. He'll want to know all the details, how you're making your money for a start."

"Then stay. Don't go back."

"Just as bad, Pip. I don't return and Drummer will come looking for me. He won't consider a transfer request without seeing me face-to-face. You were right when I first arrived. Drummer asked me to check your chapter out. Sure, I can tell him you don't run drugs or deal in guns and have nothing to do with prostitution, but that will lead him to ask how you do make the dollars you earn. I don't want to lie." If I do, eventually it will come out, it's hard to keep anything from Drummer. If I stay in Utah, I won't want to feel exiled from Tucson. I'll want to go back to visit my brothers, their old ladies, and hell, I'll even miss Grunt the dog, Allie's fuckin' cat, and, goddamn it, the kids.

Snatcher looks at me, then moves his eyes to Pip. "Seems we're at an impasse. Road can't stay, and he can't go."

Pip grimaces, then a sad expression comes over his face. "Why the hell did you have to come here, Road? Why the fuck didn't you head a different way?"

Silence sounds loud after those final words, the ramifications hanging in the air. I'm no fool. If they want to keep what they're doing secret, then I'm a liability they can't afford to leave alive.

Is this it? I'm unarmed, and even if I were, it's two against one. Is this the point where Pip takes out his gun and shoots me?

Do I plead? Beg for my life? Tell them I'll stay then go behind their backs and speak to Drummer? But I won't be reduced to falling onto my knees and pleading with them to keep me alive. And I won't live a lie. While inside there's a myriad of questions going through my brain, *Will it hurt, will Pip choose my head or my heart, and will that first shot take me out?* I force myself to remain outwardly calm. Challenging the man with my eyes. *If you're going to do it, do it now.*

Instead, I'm offered a reprieve. "Would more time help you change your mind?"

I could say yes. At least have a chance to say a proper goodbye to Swift. If I'm honest, she's the one piece of unfinished business I'm going to regret most. Though I doubt I'd have gotten anywhere with her, I was never able to give it a try. I could say it would, but... "I can't change my mind, Pip.

Whether I transfer or return to Tucson, I need to speak to Drummer, and I won't be part of a lie."

He sighs heavily, exchanges a glance with Snatcher, then his hand moves toward his cut. I try to brace myself, but how does a man prepare for his imminent death?

He's not going to string this out. I'm about to meet my maker. But then, why prolong the torture any longer than necessary? It would be crueller to make me wait.

I take a deep breath, wondering if it's the last I'll ever take, or whether I'll have time to fill my lungs again. In slow motion, Pip's hand disappears, then reappears and I fight to keep my eyes open.

It's a battle I win, thankfully. It's not a gun Pip's taken out, not even a knife. It's my phone.

I try not to collapse back into my seat as relief floods through me, then I grow tense again when I realise this could simply be a stay of execution and not an acquittal. When Pip slides the phone closer to me, I view it like a snake.

The corners of Pip's mouth turn up fractionally. He dips his chin toward the device. "Call Drummer."

"And say what?" That instruction, I didn't expect.

"The VP and I have been talking. Your coming here has set things in motion, and we've got to see how this plays out. Thing is Road, we really do want you here. Your answers today have showed you're a man of integrity, and you're a man we'd be proud to have on our team. If you want to return to Tucson, I won't stand in your way, but I'm not going to have you tattling to Drummer. If he's going to find out, I want it to be my way."

My gaze is going between him and the phone. I shake my head. "I'm not certain what you want me to say."

"At some point, he's going to need to come here. I want him to see our operation, and to understand what we do, and why. I want to face him man-to-man, prez-to-prez. Up to you whether that time has come."

"And if things don't play out how you want them to?"

Pip looks at Snatcher. "Then we'll rebrand ourselves. Every man and woman in this club, Road, is fully committed to what we do. Sure, not being Devils will hurt, but it will hurt the Devils too."

"We ride to support the other chapters," Snatcher reminds me. "Losing Thumper in Colorado was fuckin' hard, but that's the commitment we made. We keep our ears to the ground for anything which affects our brothers in other states. We knew Alder was alive and likely to give our brother's brother-in-law, Connor, a hard time were he to find he was alive. So we were watching out for signs he knew where he'd gone. Of course, as it turned out, the target was wrong, but if Stormy hadn't been watching out for them, Beth's mother could well be dead, and Connor put in a grave where it was sure he'd stay this time."

"We've given pointers to Mouse a couple of times, untraceable of course," Pip interjects.

Snatcher acknowledges the observation with a raise of his chin. "Mouse is clever, so's Cad and Token. So in their cases, it's leaving a trail for them to join the dots themselves rather than dropping outright clues in their laps."

"That's the other thing I don't understand," I tell them. "Your chapter is a joke in that no one here knows how to turn a computer on."

"I don't." Snatcher laughs at himself. "Well, barely. But can't you see that keeps us safe? Our operation is watertight when everyone thinks we live in the stone age."

Pip grinds his teeth and nods at my phone again. "Which is all now going to change. Go on, Road." He pushes it closer to me.

Is this some sort of reverse psychology? I place my hand over the device which isn't normally far from me, and which I've been lost without over the past couple of days. But I don't pick it up immediately. There's no doubt they do good work here. I, myself, have seen that. But should that be kept hidden from Drummer? Drummer isn't just my prez, he's the prez of the mother chapter. What if I keep quiet, and something else blows their deception wide open? What if I transfer and someone else from Tucson comes visiting?

Christ. Why has this been put on me? I'm just a grunt, what do I know about anything? A flash from yesterday goes through my mind—the girl, those bastards who had her and what they intended to do with her. I was part of rescuing her from the fate they had planned.

I used to think winning a race was the pinnacle of my achievement, but Pip had given me something to top that. The exhilaration of the rescue topping any trophy I could bring home, even though it wouldn't lead to fame and fortune or even recognition.

But I respect Drummer. How can I lie to a man who's given me so much?

Under the watchful eyes of Pip and Snatcher, I pick up the phone and call up the first number on speed dial.

It's anti-climactic. The ring tone sounds and sounds, then it cuts out and voicemail answers. I end the call without leaving a message and put the phone back down. I cock an eyebrow toward Pip and start pushing the phone his way again. I doubt he'll want me to make the call in private, he'll want to be forewarned of what I've told Drum.

But before he can take it, the phone vibrates. The action so unexpected, I think all three of us jump, then look sheepishly toward each other.

The phone clearly shows it's a call from Prez. Looking again resigned, Pip nods. I answer.

"Road."

"Got a missed call from you. I was riding, just pulled over to call you back. What d'ya need, Brother? Kind of getting a bit worried about you being out of touch."

"I texted you." I apparently had.

He snorts, but I can't quite work out why until he adds, "Man of few words, aren't you? 'I'm here.' 'All OK.' What the hell was I going to make of that?"

Pip must have read my other texts. With my large fingers I don't write much. "Well, I'm talking to you now, aren't I?"

"So what have you found, Road?"

I take a deep breath. "It's a completely different chapter." *And ain't that the truth?* "I'm still getting my head around it. Feeling my way with the brothers here."

"Anything I should worry about?"

"Worry?" I think I can honestly answer that. "Not that I've seen. Tell you the truth, Prez, the change of scenery is doing me some good. Getting me out of my head for a while." That's no lie. I haven't felt the need to strike out or even snap at anyone since I've arrived. My anger replaced by a sense of bemusement.

I hear his chuckle. "Something needed to. Been less walking on eggshells since you've been gone. You intend staying on for a bit?"

"If that's okay with you, Prez."

"Yeah. Take your time, Road. But keep in touch, yeah?"

Prez ends the call which is like him. Why waste time saying goodbyes when they can be taken for granted.

I bow my head as I replace my phone on the table.

I've never lied to my Prez before, and it feels like I've gone against the patch on my back. He trusted me, and I've betrayed him. I had my chance, and I've blown it. Whatever happens from here on out, Prez will know I misled him.

I go to slide my phone back to Pip who shakes his head. "Keep it." He wipes a hand over his relieved looking face.

"Drummer's not found out for ten years, Road. And hell, *Brother,* I'm grateful for you keeping us a secret."

"You're using this club as a cover," I remind him.

"We *are* Satan's Devils," Pip throws back.

"Think we ought to show Road that." A grin comes over Snatcher's face. "Give him another incentive to join us."

Pip's mouth starts to curve up as he turns to his VP. "You could have a good idea there."

18

―――――

*S*wift...

"You alright?" I rest my hand on Cowboy's back as we walk out of church.

"No," he replies honestly. "I know it's ancient history now, Gianetta's been gone twelve years now." His eyes glaze slightly. "Annie would have been fifteen. It kills me to think about that, how she never had a chance to grow." Glancing down at me, he shakes his head. "I've no choice but to go on, but hell, Swift, sometimes it's so fuckin' hard. Losing Gianetta was bad enough, but why the fuck did they have to rob a little girl of her life? That's what will haunt me forever."

He knows why, as do I. It was to throw up a smokescreen. Instead of taking out one target, it had been made to look like the panicked action of amateur kidnappers. The truth, Pip had said, wasn't hard to find. Annie's death had been for nothing.

"I think about them every day." Cowboy's eyes are still staring into the distance. "Sometimes I can focus on the joy they brought to my life. Other times, well, I know Pip's telling

Road my story now. It brings it all back up as if it happened yesterday."

There's nothing I can say. Cowboy had had all his hopes and dreams wrenched away from him. I knew joining the MC, helping to build the business we're in now, has given him a new lease of life, while he can stop others having to suffer the same grief as he had. He's got a reason to keep breathing.

"Well, I better start getting the food prepared for tonight." Cowboy flicks his imaginary hat, and strides off leaving me staring after him. I suspect we're in for a culinary treat later. 'Boy can lose himself in his trade, using it to focus his mind and push his darkest thoughts down. Though we know that grief is the reason he cooks and sadly, when a gourmet meal appears, it's because he's feeling particularly blue.

I wonder whether he'll ever find happiness again—a new woman to help ease the hurt of losing his wife. Then I want to slap myself for my feminine thought. Why should a relationship be the answer to someone's woes? Man probably just needs a good fuck with none of the messy commitments.

As I make my way to the comms room, I can't help but think about Road. I know Pip's going to persuade him to stay. I, and the team with me, had been taken by surprise when Road had impressed us with his quick thinking in California. Sure, we've all got skills. Me, I tend to look at a problem in tactical ways, working out the logistics of getting in and getting back out. Stormy's a sniper known for his long-distance shots. Rascal is our money man. Thor and Piston are mechanics, geniuses at fixing or modifying anything. Honor and Duty are tech experts—though we all keep our hands in to help them out. Bolt, well, he's bilingual, able to speak Spanish fluently.

But there's a place for someone like Road, a man who looks at a problem from a different angle, without being fixated on a particular approach.

Opening the door to our technical hub, I nod at Duty who looks up and catches my eye. He's got his headphones on, so I don't speak. I rest my hand on Honor's shoulder in passing.

"Anything interesting?"

"Nah. Chatter's quiet."

"Are you still following up on anything about Alder? Any noise about him being taken out?" I pull up a chair and sit down.

"Border patrol closed the tunnel down." So far, Honor's only telling me what I already know. "It seems that Alder kept all his cards to himself. His mafia contacts are more interested in finding new ways to get their drugs into the States, and the rest of his operation seems in disarray, more concerned with lying low and keeping out of the way of the law. There's zero mention of retaliation for the death of their boss. I'll keep an ear out, but I think Lost's woman is safe. It could be that what he wanted with her was personal, something to do with her ex, perhaps."

That's what we'd hoped, but there was always a chance he had a second-in-command who'd step in and fill the void, and that Patsy was still in danger.

"There'll be someone else," Honor says, shaking his head. "Someone who's trading in human flesh, views money as more important than life."

"We'll never stop it," I sympathise. "But at least we can throw a spanner in the works from time to time."

"Wrench," Honor corrects automatically, to which I roll my eyes.

I spin my chair on its wheels and roll over to a free work-station, then log on using the complicated authentication routine that Duty insists we use. Then I pull up the list of names I need to research.

I'm following a trail leading me deeper and deeper into the

dark web when the door opens and Road walks in. I can't read the expression on his face.

"Anything wrong?" My eyes narrow as he approaches.

"I'm feeling like shit right now," he admits, and then explains, "I called my prez and lied."

A feeling of elation goes through me, which I suppress immediately. It shouldn't matter a damn to me whether he stays or goes. But still I'm driven to ask, "Are you patching over?"

Road grimaces, then picks at his fingernails before he replies, "Pip's just asked me to stay on for a while, so officially, no, the decision's not made as yet. In the end, though, I might not have any choice. Drummer's not a man whose back you go behind. When the truth comes out, he'll never trust me again, Swift. That fuckin' hurts." After giving a sad shake of his head, he continues, "I always thought I was known for my integrity, but I've not so much set fire to my boats, I've blown them out of the water."

"Patching over, joining us, wouldn't be so hard, would it?"

His eyes meet mine. "I lied to my prez in front of Pip and Snatcher. Pip will always be watching me, he'll never completely trust me. If I turned my back on Drummer, I could turn it on him too."

I suppose he's got a point, but Pip wouldn't have invited him to join us if he didn't have faith in him. "Thing is, Road, you could have betrayed our trust, yet you didn't. It took guts to hide things from Drummer, and Prez and the VP would have appreciated that."

Road doesn't seem cheered up.

"Look, why don't I show you what I'm working on?"

He raises his chin. "Can't say I'm good with computers and shit. I have got questions though."

"You don't need to have those skills." I click a few keys,

closing down what I was working on. "Go ahead, ask what you want to know."

"How did Mona's parents know how to contact you?"

"That's a good question, Road." I call up another program. "This is an algorithm we use. We look into a number of factors of how likely it is someone is going to be a kidnapping target."

"What factors?" He looks brighter now, as though I've caught his interest.

"Wealth being one, no one is going to kidnap anyone when the payout isn't worth it, or the perceived payout as in Mona's case. Sometimes what looks like money is just on paper, but still, opportunist kidnappers may not factor that in. We also look into whether they have children or other family they wouldn't want to lose. Then we look at existing security. If someone's already got protection arranged, we leave that alone. We end up with a database of targets on the basis of probability, then, Prez starts working through the most-likely candidates."

"What do you mean?"

"Pip is an MC prez, but as you know, Snatcher's the outward face of the MC. One reason being, it allows Pip to stay in the background. He's a master at blending in, probably from his CIA days. We get him into embassy functions and exclusive parties—Duty works his magic, and hey, Pip's on the invitation list. He gets talking to people we suspect could be targeted and gives them a number to call should the worse happen to them."

Road looks perplexed. "He tells them what he does?"

"No. He doesn't admit that it's him. He'll approach them with something like a story of a friend whose daughter was kidnapped, and as concerned parents with kids of their own to protect, they'll want to know the details. Pip knows his trade. He usually ends up being asked for a contact they can have 'just in case'."

"He tells them not to go to the cops?"

"No. That's up to them. If they call in the feds, sometimes we just work in the background and make sure they're heading the right way. We can feed information into their databases for them to find."

"So that's how you get your business?"

I shake my head. "Not all the time, no. We also watch out for human traffickers. Duty and Honor spend a lot of time on the web. Right now, we're keeping a check on names which have come to our attention, people like Alder for example."

"You used San Diego to take him down."

"An ambassador's daughter was stolen. We knew Alder was responsible, and knew he'd be heading down to the border. What we didn't know was his routes, or where the girl was in the USA. We heard talk that he had a crossing point in San Diego, so Stormy was directed there to try to flush him out. Lost came up with the coded information. Once it was decoded, we had the location of the tunnel. From there, it was sussing out the likely date and arrival of the transport. The girl was one of the women Lost and his members freed and dropped off at the hospital, and the authorities contacted her folks."

"From what I heard, it was lucky Alder was there that night."

"There was a high chance he would be. The girl was too valuable to him. Not only was she young, pretty and would attract a nice sum on her own, the cartel wanted to send a message to the ambassador, her father, who'd crossed them. So it was important to Alder that she crossed the border safely. Stormy had listened into the MC's communications that night—well," I glance at him sheepishly, "we all had. That's how he knew the girl was safe, and then he waited to take Alder out. Those were not his instructions," I add hastily. "But he had a clear shot and couldn't resist."

"Lost was spitting mad. He's not going to let it drop," he warns me.

"He'll never find out it was us," I assure him.

"Why the fuck didn't Stormy just sit back and let things play out? The girl was safe, that was his concern, not Alder."

I half defend him. "The world's a better place without someone like Alder in it."

Road's not appeased in the least. "It was Lost's call how Alder was dispatched."

I agree. "Stormy's got trust issues. I don't think he even trusts us."

To get off the subject and onto something else, I show Road a little more of our capabilities, then notice the time. "You hungry?"

Road's face lights up. Seems that he is.

As I expected, Cowboy has excelled himself with a three-course dinner for anyone who wanted to partake. There was an asparagus delicacy with some kind of cheese sauce to start with, filet mignon for the entrée, and key lime pie for dessert. Road's eyes just about bulged out of his face as he ate.

"Christ," he told me, as he cut into his steak, "this is like eating out at the Wheel Inn. That's our restaurant in Tucson. You eat like this all the time?"

I grimace. "We do alright, but when Cowboy's having a bad day, he goes to town."

Road grimaces as he processes what I've said. He doesn't ask questions, and I know it's because Cowboy's sad story has been shared.

At last all the knives, forks and spoons are put down. Igor and Brute start collecting the dirty plates, and Snatcher stands.

"Heading out now," he announces.

"Heading out, where?" Road asks, as he follows my lead and gets to his feet.

I grin. "The old clubhouse."

Once again that deer in the headlights look appears on Road's face, but he asks no verbal questions, just hoists his cut more comfortably on his shoulders and joins the rest of us as we leave the premises.

It's just a mile ride to the clubhouse that Road will find more to his liking, or at least, somewhat more familiar. Leaving the new one under the eye of Gears in the comms room and our civilian caretaker for the night, we leave and travel back to the old warehouse on the outskirts of town.

It's a rundown building hunched behind the large sign that denotes it as the Satan's Devils Utah clubhouse, far different from the slip of card used to identify our new one, and which can be switched out to denote any business we want to be taken for at any time.

When we draw up and park in a line out front, Road is again wearing that expression that I see most on his face. He cocks an eyebrow as if to ask, *really?* But he backs his bike into its parking spot, switches off the engine and carefully dismounts.

"Your leg okay after yesterday?"

"I've strapped it up," he replies, dismissively.

"This him?" Grinch stubs out a cigarette, grinding it into the ground with his boot. He eyes Road carefully, his expression unreadable. But I reckon they'll get on like a house on fire, Road's more old school than the rest of us.

I do the introductions. "Road, meet Grinch. Grinch, Road, Roadrunner."

Road eyes the worn leather which rests on the older man's shoulders. "Patched member?" He looks puzzled again and taps at his chin. "Pip mentioned your name, I assumed you were no longer with the MC. You weren't in church."

Grinch grins. "Nah, can't be bothered with that shit, not unless it directly concerns us. We'll attend if we're needed."

"Grinch, Goofy and Mystic keep up the pretence of the club," I tell Road. "They're fuckin' good mechanics, but don't get involved in our main business. They live here to maintain a presence. This is what the citizens see, and we deliver exactly what they expect of an MC."

A look of enlightenment crosses Road's face as if I've answered one of his questions.

"And what's your trade?" Grinch queries.

"He rides bikes. Fast," I answer for Road.

"Enduro racing," Road explains.

Grinch's eyes light up. "*That* Roadrunner?" When Road gives a self-deprecating shrug, Grinch holds out his hand and shake's Road's vigorously. "Fuckin' impressive riding man. Shame you were taken out before lifting that trophy." He raises his chin by means of salute. "Pleased as fuck to meet you. Hey, I might just fuckin' have something right up your alley." He nods my way. "Got a sweet deal the other day. Man wanted to swap it out for a tricked-up Harley."

"Ah, yes," I say, remembering. "The Kawasaki ZX14R." The previous owner had scared himself on it and wanted something that didn't have so much power.

"Yeah?" Road's eyes light up.

"Yours if you need speed," Grinch offers. "Take it for a spin sometime if you want."

"Oh, I want," Road tells him, his eyes sparkling. "One of the fastest fuckin' bikes on the road. Riding position would suit a man of my size."

I get the impression if I leave them together they'd be out here for hours. "Come on." I nod toward the doorway. "I want a beer."

Those seem to be magic words as Road raises his chin to

Grinch, then wastes no time following me inside. Again he comes to a dead halt, pausing to take it all in.

As an MC clubhouse this place screams it's the real deal. Christ knows when it last had a makeover. The interior is dark and dingy, not helped at all by the nicotine-stained ceiling and walls. Rock music is playing at a tolerable background level. Those who arrived before us, or who had not tarried outside, are already standing with beers in their hands, or queuing at the bar, shouting at Igor to get a fucking move on.

I frown as a group of giggling girls, regulars in from the city, immediately look over to see who's entered, and their eyes, ignoring me, focus on Road, recognising him as fresh meat. One pushes past her companions and if I'm not mistaken, is already making a beeline directly toward him.

Forcing myself not to watch her progress, I work hard to suppress my irrational jealous instinct. Road will probably end up fucking one of them tonight, and he's a free man so what should that matter? I've made no play for him, he's shown no interest in me. He can get his rocks off where he likes.

Fuck, but that thought hurts. It's a pain I can honestly say I've never felt before. *Indigestion. That must be it. Too much good food this evening.*

Hastily, I look around to see if the men who sometimes hang around the club hoping to have a chance to become a member might have turned up. If Road's going to pair up, maybe I should find something, or someone, to take my mind off the thought. There are a couple talking to Goofy, but I'll be damned if they come close to being my type. They hold no candle, not even a match, to the man at my side. *Maybe I should make a trip into town later, visit a bar.*

"This is more like it." Road rolls his shoulders, breathes the stale air in deeply, then glances at me and grins. "So this is where you all let down your hair. Not now, sweetheart."

The last is said to the woman wearing a tight leather tank top and tight leather shorts which only just cover her ass. She's had the audacity to put her hand on my... Road's arm, but he's firmly lifted it off.

"Later, perhaps?" she simpers, fluttering her eyelashes.

"Not tonight," he replies in a tone that doesn't encourage further overtures.

Immediately my mood lifts. I continue as though we hadn't been interrupted. "Yes, we have parties here every week on Fridays and Saturdays. This is what the locals know of us, a club who lives for riding their bikes and partying hard."

"The girls are hangarounds?"

I nod. "We get men too, men who like discussing bikes. That pair with Goofy? He did some work pimping their rides. We get the odd one wanting to join up as well."

"Any get in?"

"Only if their background fits the club, or we see something in particular we like."

"So you really are living your cover," he says with an appreciative nod toward Snatcher who's already got his arm around one of the girls.

"This is us, Road. Two sides of the same coin."

He looks thoughtful at my reply.

"Road! Good to actually meet you, when you're not looking like you're going to throw up."

Road spins around. "I know you." He points his finger at Mystic. "You were at the airfield. And I can't fuckin' help it if I prefer my feet on the ground." His words are offered with a good-natured grin.

"Yeah, I can understand that. I maintain the plane, keep it airworthy. Doesn't mean I like to go up in it," Mystic agrees, the two men seeming to bond over their fear of flying. "Goofy over there keeps the auto-shop busy with work." He points the other member out.

We reach the bar, take a couple of beers, and Road downs half of his fast as though he needs it. When Grinch comes back inside and approaches Road, asking him about racing, I wander off, not wanting to monopolise my partner, and giving him a chance to make new friends. I've a feeling the three who live here are men more like the members Road left back in Tucson.

As in our more modern clubhouse, there's also a pool table and gaming machines here, though admittedly they're more battle-scarred, and I prevent myself thinking exactly what that pool table's probably been used for. For a while I get lost in a shoot 'em up battle, and then Bolt challenges me to a game of pool. I drink another beer, but that's my limit. I learned long ago not to let my guard down. It's not that I don't trust my brothers, more that I don't trust myself, especially with someone as tempting as Road around.

It's been a while since I scored, and a long time, if ever, that I've felt such a pull toward a man. Losing my inhibitions might lead me to make a mistake I'd regret. Now Snatcher and Pip have asked Road to patch over, it could mean he'll soon be a member of my club, and I don't fuck on my own doorstep. I learned that lesson when I was in my first squad.

I have no problem having sex without emotion. But when I did let temptation overrule my head, it was unfortunately with a man who could not. In the end, I had to transfer to a different unit when he started watching my back to the extent of not watching others. I'd felt guilty, having left a man heartbroken which had never been my intent, but it wasn't my fault he'd wanted more than I had to offer.

Since then I've been careful, and I'm only too well aware, seen through the bottom of too many bottles of beer, that most of the men around me, in desperation, I wouldn't turn down. Restricting my alcohol intake is far safer.

I keep my eye on Road, just to make sure he's enjoying himself and settling in. As I'd predicted, he seems to be getting on great with Grinch. Grinch is exactly what you'd think of if you tried to picture a biker. A long grey beard, a bald head, and a beer paunch hanging over the top of his jeans and an encyclopaedic knowledge of two-wheeled machines.

I'm not disappointed when I look around and spy Brenda, an older woman who sports a head of curly grey hair. As normal, Grinch is sneaking sideways glances at her. Why the hell they don't get together, I'll never know. For some reason they think they're being discreet, but no one will be surprised when Grinch navigates her way sooner or later, then, both will disappear.

There must be a dozen girls and women who've turned up, all happy to spend the night or just a few hours in the bed of a biker. I don't have it in myself to blame them—sex with no strings and no recriminations—what could be better? Snatcher's already disappeared with the one he targeted earlier, and my pool partner is chatting another up. Thor and Preacher are moving in, and ah, yes. There goes Grinch, heading Brenda's way now, Road going with him.

Has Road got his eye on the girl who's barely wearing any clothes standing next to Brenda? I wouldn't be surprised. She couldn't really make her assets more obvious.

I notice Road stumbles slightly on his way over and realise he's tipsy, not surprising. Everyone's been making sure he's felt welcome by ensuring he's had a drink in his hand all night. Even drunk sex, I suspect, with Road wouldn't disappoint.

I'd like to fuck him and find out.

19

Swift...

But I can't.

I can't afford to make what would be a colossal mistake.

It does surprise me how much it would hurt if he were to show an interest in somebody else, and admit my earlier thought was wrong. I'm not suffering from Cowboy's excellent cooking. Which is crazy. I have no grounds to be possessive. I've given him no clues I might be interested in him myself. Looking at it coldly, Road would just be one more dick. I'd hopefully have a good time, and then move on after. Certainly not worth staking a claim over.

I'm not interested. He's likely to become a brother.

Sure, he's pretty... *Uh-uh. Is that another bitch heading his way?* I pull myself up when I realise I'm taking a step which would put me right in her path and block her approach.

This is crazy. Maybe I am ill or something. Road can do what he likes, and who am I to prevent someone from having a good time with somebody else if I'm not making myself available?

I don't give a damn who's bed Road ends up in tonight.

I'm lying to myself. I want him in mine.

When I turn my back, knowing it's safer for all concerned if I don't watch, I can't understand myself. I do not get jealous. When a man leaves my bed, he's free to move on, and I don't give him a second thought afterwards. Why do I have a feeling it would be different with Road, and that even if he weren't my teammate, any liaison between us would be dangerous?

Unless he totally sucked in bed, I'd want to go back.

I sneak a peek behind me. A circle of girls has surrounded him now. *I can't take this.* I can't handle this burning feeling inside me. I turn away and walk over to the bar, asking Igor for a soda. Anything to keep my hands occupied and my mind focused elsewhere. I can't bear to think of the lucky woman who soon will have Road's hands all over her.

I hate myself for caring. Maybe I should leave and go home?

I might have a room back at the clubhouse but after I got my patch, I invested in a small property in town. It's got all the features a deaf woman needs, just like I have at the club. It's my home, my sanctuary, and there's no reason not to feel safe there.

"Hey, washa doing on your own?"

"Road?" I spin around. My relief he's here with me and not the scantily clad girl is immense.

It shouldn't be.

His unsteady hand reaches out and touches my hair. As it's short, he also ends up massaging my scalp. "So soft," he murmurs appreciatively. "Why don't yous and Is get to know each other, besher, babe?"

He's playing with fire using the 'babe' word on me. Especially as I find I actually like it coming out of his mouth and my scalp is tingling where his fingers touched it.

"I don't think that's a good idea, Road." I move his hand away.

"Awh, com'on. How about a kissh?"

I hear a loud intake of breath from behind the bar, and glancing that way, see Igor standing stiffly, poised as though ready to witness a fight.

"Not a good idea," I repeat, softly. Road's drunk, otherwise he'd never be coming on to me. "There are the hangarounds who'd love to give you some attention, Road."

"Nah, I want the prettieessh girl in the room." Again his hand reaches out to touch my face, and I prevent it reaching its destination.

"Not going to happen, Road," I tell him, firmly.

"Awh, babe." Swaying, he leans in perilously close and gives an exaggerated wink, pausing a little too long to open his eye again. I want to laugh as he's actually adorable. "I can showsh you a good time, babe." He tries to put his arm around me.

"Christ, he's got some balls. Surprised you're leaving them where they are." Catching my eye, Thor winks at me.

I've surprised myself, too, that I'm not emasculating him for his overt advances and tell myself it's because he's drunk that I've got sympathy for him. But a circle of brothers is forming, and I narrow my eyes, suspecting soon they'll be making bets on exactly how this is going to play out.

Abruptly, I step away, causing Road to crash against the bar, needing it to support him. I have to extricate myself from this situation and fast.

"No, Road," I tell him, firmly. "It's not going to happen. Igor?" I say to the very interested onlooker. "I'm off home. Tell Snatcher and Pip where I've gone, will you?"

Igor's answering grin is a mile wide. "Sure… *babe.*"

I start to move but Preacher is there, holding me back, but it's the prospect he addresses. "You show fuckin' disrespect and you can kiss your fuckin' future patch goodbye."

Igor raises his hands, his grin disappearing fast and his face going taut. "It was a joke. And *he* said it first."

"*He's* a patched member," Preacher reminds him. "Who—" He breaks off as Road slides to the floor, his legs outstretched in front of him. He's chuckling quietly to himself, oh, and then belches loudly, which sets him off laughing again. The sergeant-at-arms shakes his head, then continues, "Who's fuckin' had too much to drink. Come on." Preacher releases me, then stretches out a muscular arm to help Road to his feet. "Let's find somewhere for you to crash for the night."

"You clean my bike with your fuckin' toothbrush tomorrow." I glare at Igor. "Then you can use it to scrub the heads."

"Ma'am." He salutes me.

Glaring at him, I grin when my back is now turned toward the prospect. Guess fun times are ahead when… if, Igor patches in. I'll enjoy taking time to teach him some manners.

At least Road seems to be an affable drunk, that's one thing going for him. I wonder if he'll remember making a pass at me when he wakes up?

I hope he doesn't. It will be embarrassing if I have to brush an apology off. At least I don't have to worry about him going off with one of the girls tonight. Tipsy? Sure, he'd still get it up. Passed out drunk? Different matter entirely. My mind can be at ease tonight.

"You off?"

The voice coming from the shadows off to my left doesn't startle me. Years of training have my senses always on the alert, and I'd seen the man there long before he'd started speaking.

"Yeah." I raise my chin toward Rascal. "I'm heading to my place tonight."

"Need some peace and quiet?"

At that moment, the music inside is turned up, and I grimace and nod. Yeah, Rascal's right. Despite them keeping the jukebox at a respectable volume while I'd been around, just the sheer level of noise from people talking louder the more they had to drink and bottles and glasses clinking was starting to get too much for me, and a headache is beginning to kick off.

"See you tomorrow," I call out as I step toward my bike.

"Pip wants to meet at eleven."

I raise my hand in a half-wave, half-salute. "I'll be there."

Turning my hearing aids down with one hand, I switch on the engine with the other, then kick down into first and head out across town. It's a nice clear summer night, warm and peaceful after the din of the clubhouse. Half of me wants to keep on riding, but the rest of me is tired and sleepy, so I head straight home and turn into my driveway. I point the remote, and the garage door opens. Soon, my bike is parked next to the jeep which I use in winter.

Home is a small single-storey house with just two beds and one-and-a-half baths, just the right size for a single person like me. It's quite quaint looking with shutters on the windows, and I'd fallen in love immediately after I'd seen it. It's on the edge of the city with daylight views out across the farmland toward the distant mountains beyond.

While I was in the army, I'd lived mostly in barracks and was used to having people around. When I lost my hearing, I also lost living among others at the time I needed them most. One of the carrots Pip had held out when he wanted me to join the MC had been living in the clubhouse where I wasn't alone.

From the moment I joined as a prospect, I could relax at night, confident that someone would wake me should there be an intruder or a fire. But I was also aware that I was an adult and needed to learn to cope with what I had lost. Being weak isn't in my nature, and I was determined not to let fear rule my life, so I pulled up my big girl pants and bought myself a house.

At first, I'd felt uneasy living here on my own, and stayed

infrequently. During the daytime it's no problem, but at night I'd lie awake, worried I was going to be taken unawares, every one of my soldiering instinct telling me I had to be conscious of my surroundings at all times.

The MC stepped in once again. Without asking, Honor and Duty had scoped out some equipment and helped me to install the security system an ant would have difficulty getting in without my tactile alarms waking me. A fire? Again, I'd be jolted awake and lights would also flash to warn me. Should the main electricity fail, I had a backup generator to make sure all my systems continued functioning normally.

Looking around now, a smile comes to my face. I had had to stop Honor's technical skill being combined with Thor's mechanical genius to make the ejector bed that I hadn't been one hundred percent certain they'd been joking about. I wanted to be woken, I'd objected, not shot up into the air. I grin at the memory that enters my head. *It had been a joke, surely?*

Each time I stay it's with less trepidation. Having the confidence to live alone is like becoming an adult all over again. My vulnerability no longer defining me. I'm proud at what I've achieved, and how I don't let my PTSD beat me.

I'm safe here. It's my sanctuary. This is my space, my home. As I enter the living room, I glance around and smile at the photographs I have on display—the ones of my mum and dad in the pub where I grew up. I remember those times so fondly. I really need to take some time off and go visit them. It would be good to see them again, and I know they'd love to see me. I don't regret making my new life so far away, but at times, I do get homesick. Like any kid, grown or not, I miss my mum's cooking.

Leaving my keys in the dish on the table by the door that I've placed there for that purpose, I grab a bottle of water and take it into my bedroom and place it beside my neatly made bed. Old habits die hard, and I still make it exactly the same way that I had to in the army. In fact, my whole house is clean and tidy. I can't abide mess.

All my dirty clothes go straight into my laundry basket, and I shower, then find a tank top and sleep shorts I wear to bed. As I do, thoughts of Road come into my head. Why do I find him so attractive? What is it about him that gets to me the way it does? Why did I feel so jealous tonight? Why should I care who he takes to his bed? That's so unlike me. As Thor had reminded me, if any other man hadn't taken my first no as a response, drunk or not, he'd have felt my knee in a place he definitely wouldn't like.

I admit, the main reason I came home tonight was I didn't trust myself. Had I remained in the clubhouse, I have the sneaking suspicion I might have gone to his room. Maybe I'd have used the excuse he was too drunk to sleep alone. Whatever, he pulls me to him like metal toward a magnet. I had to put distance between us.

I bet he's good in the sack.

Huh, I'll never find out. If he stays, he'll be part of the MC and unavailable to me. If he decides to go back to Tucson, hmm. Maybe, before he goes…

Mentally, I slap myself, get into my bed and beat my pillow into submission, making a concerted effort to get the disturbing man out of my head. Then I take a deep breath and complete my preparation to sleep and remove my hearing aids. The hum of the air conditioning disappears as complete silence descends, and I try to suppress the feeling of panic.

I'm fine. I'm alright.

Nothing and no one can get to me. I might not have my ears, but there's a vibrating alarm under my pillow which will warn me a smoke alarm is going off, or if there's someone on the perimeter. As a backup, the security system will send signals to my watch which will continue to pulse until I turn it off. Lights will flash and disturb me. Someone will be monitoring all our security in the comms room back at the clubhouse, and that will include my house as long as Igor gives Pip and Snatcher the message. And if he wants his patch, he won't fail me.

I should have brought Road back here to sleep his drunken stupor off.

Crazy idea. But it would have meant I wasn't alone.

As my body starts to tremble, I focus on running through everything I've got to keep me safe, knowing my PTSD is creeping up on me. I breathe deeply, reminding myself all the gadgets I have are at the leading edge of technology. The prospects test that the backup generator works once a week, and they were here yesterday, I believe.

Breathe in, breathe out. Mentally, I try to still my body and push the bile rising in my throat back down. Gradually, the violent shaking wracking me slows as my relaxation techniques begin to kick in and work.

Remembering, I smile to myself when I recall what Road had diagnosed my uncontrollable trembling to be. Well, he's right in that it's one way I can relax enough to totally switch off and sleep. And if it's Road's face and muscular body I think about as my hand moves down and begins to massage my clit, that's not going to hurt anyone. It's also far safer than having the real thing in my bed.

20

———————

*R*oad...

The old clubhouse is a place where I definitely feel more at home. In no way does it feel like an upmarket hotel which makes me think I should be on my best behaviour, no, it's a place where men can be men, fart and scratch their asses if they get the urge. Earlier, Snatcher had passed a key card to me with the explanation this would get me into the new clubhouse and into my room, but I'd already decided not to use it tonight when I was told a place to crash here was available. This is my type of place.

And the three old timers, Grinch, Goofy and Mystic are more my kind of men—men who talk my language, and not of missions and rescuing kidnapped people. But then, as the night draws on and the talk turns to motorcycles, other members approach our table and join in. I start to see a different side of men like Bolt, Piston and Rascal. Like me, they love bikes and want to live free.

As far as I'm aware, there's nothing in our written regulations that stipulates the Satan's Devils have to ride American-built bikes, but unwritten ones mean any that Peg would call plastic-built crap are heavily discouraged. I, myself, had fallen foul of that when I'd had to pick up a cheap Harley to gain entry into the Tucson club. Here, in Utah, while the majority of men are faithful to Indians or Harleys, the speed and handling of Japanese or European bikes were discussed, not dismissively, but with admiration. I found it a refreshing change.

The Kawasaki model Grinch had spoken about is one of the fastest street legal bikes, and to be honest, I couldn't wait to put it through its paces. I started riding trials bikes, then progressed to off-road Enduro. Trials require the skills of controlling the bike when you're going slowly, a question of throttle and clutch control and maintaining your balance. Enduro is that, but with the additional requirement of high speed and the ability to cover long distances. A bike such as the Kawasaki ZX14R has the ability for fast cornering as well as high miles per hour on the straights. I couldn't wait to try it out, having never ridden such a fast bike on the road. The main thing to take into account is unlike most fast bikes where my leg would need to be bent up around my ears— something difficult after my injury—this bike doesn't require the riding position where I'd be hunched over, but still provides enough speed and manoeuvring to satisfy me.

Whether it's because I'm a new face and everyone seems to want to find out more about me, or put some story to the facts that Swift had managed to dig up, one by one all the brothers come to speak to me, and each one brings me a beer or a shot. I don't want to appear rude, so I drink them. I know I pass my limit early, but my guard is down. I don't get the impression anyone wants to hurt me. But after numerous beers and chasers I start to think, even if they did, I'm so drunk, I wouldn't care.

The girls here, well, they're eyeing me like a prize to be won, but none get my head turned their way. There's only one woman I want, and she's the one who won't give me the time of day. Or, at least, not in the way I want her to. Even when I've been deep in conversation, my eyes have been following her. I watched her ass flex as she played that games machine, and darn near got a chubby when she bent over the pool table. I'd quickly looked away before my mind could conjure too much up, like ideas of ramming my cock deep inside her.

The girls who've come to the party are pretty enough, but Swift has them beat in every department.

I know how to party, and can normally control myself better, but after the number of drinks that I have had, even I know I'm drunk off my ass. When I see her at the bar, I stumble my way across the room, my inebriated self having decided it's a great idea and the perfect time to approach her.

I don't remember much more. But I don't recall getting a knee to my junk for which I'm grateful. I struggle for consciousness, not sure where I am or how I got here. There's an external sound competing loudly with the heavy thumping of my head. It takes me a moment to place it. When I do, it's the sound of a fucking fire alarm ringing loudly.

Shit. This place is on fire. I've got to get out of here.

Rolling out of yet another unfamiliar bed—clean sheets but the room is shabby as hell—I switch on the light, blinking in the sudden brightness, then pull on my t-shirt and cut which seem to be the only items of clothing I removed last night. Sliding my feet into my boots, I put my hand to my head.

Fucking shut up with that screeching sound. It's not a constant ringing, just a few short blasts, and then it repeats.

Opening my door, I sniff, but can smell no smoke. I do hear loud voices and follow the direction they're coming from.

"What do we know?" Pip snaps as I enter the clubroom.

"Not a lot. After the power was cut, not one damn camera was working."

I have no idea what they're talking about, and why we are all hanging around if there's a fire? Just as I'm thinking that, the alarm thankfully shuts off.

"Backup generator?"

"That's out too."

"Fuck. Anything else?"

"That's all we know so far."

I shake my head trying to clear the vestiges of the hangover fogging my brain. *Ah, it's probably a new case we'll be working on.* Hoping I won't have to damage my knee again this time, I listen out for what duties I'll be assigned. Another hope is that we won't be using the plane. *I fucking hate flying.*

Pip bows his head, his fingers pinching the brow of his nose. It's only a few seconds before he raises his eyes again and starts barking his orders out.

"I don't like this. I don't like it one bit. Snatcher, Stormy, Thor, Preacher and Road. You get over there and check the place out. Keep your eye out for any fuckin' thing. You know your jobs, report back anything you find. The rest of us will get back to base and start digging around. Hopefully it will all be for nothing, but it's too much of a fuckin' coincidence that all the electronics were taken out."

I don't know what part I'm supposed to play, but I'm sure someone will tell me. I glance around for my partner, but Swift isn't around. *Did she say she was going home, last night?* My memory isn't clear, but I think that she had. If so, maybe she's been contacted and is on her way now.

"Anything for us to do, Prez?"

"Nah, Grinch. Just keep things here going for now. I'll let you know if there's anything I need."

Snatcher starts making a move to the door. Bleary-eyed, I go to follow him out, wishing I'd taken the time for a piss before leaving, but I'd feel like a kid were I to have to ask permission. They're in a hurry to get wherever we're going. I just hope it's not too far.

Preacher pushes a gun into my hand as I go past him. "Not sure what we're heading into, Brother. Need you tooled up."

I start to sober. Whatever's going on, it's serious.

"Could be a fuckin' trap," Stormy murmurs, walking past.

"So I want you set up. Duty tell you the vantage point?" Snatcher's surprisingly patient.

"Yeah. And I'm equipped." Stormy taps his ear for some reason, and I notice he's got some kind of device in it.

As far as I'm aware, he's not deaf, so it must be a communication device.

I could ask what this is all about, but it seems I was late to the party and everyone else knows. So a bit sheepish that I appear to be the only one under the weather, I just follow them out, hoping it won't be too long until I can relieve my bladder.

My tongue licks my teeth as I ride. They feel furry as hell. But having seen the brothers with hair uncombed, something's so urgent there's no time for us even to go through the briefest of morning routines. For one, I'm in desperate need of a shower. Last night's beer seems to be seeping through my pores.

Glad it appears to be somewhere local as we're not heading out toward the airfield and the plane, I just tag behind the other four men who seem to know where they have to go. *Pip said her.* But is it a woman or child we'll be rescuing, and shouldn't we have discussed a plan?

Although my hangover headache still throbs, my adrenaline has started to rise. *I'm part of a team and we've got a job to do.* The feeling is similar to that which I used to get when I was poised on the starting line.

After about a mile or so, Stormy peels off, but not having

been issued with any other instruction, I follow Snatcher and the rest of the pack.

We come to a house on the outskirts of town. It's small, the yard looks in good order, and the building itself is full of charm. But one thing it doesn't shout is money. If someone's been kidnapped from here, I can't think that there are dollars behind any motivation. Unless, of course, there's a rich relative somewhere in the wings. *Hey, look at me, I'm starting to think like the Utah members.*

Snatcher leads us straight onto a driveway, parking right outside the house. I note we're not trying to be discreet and wonder why the difference. In Santa Barbara, we never met the family involved.

Bracing myself to find distraught parents who've lost a child or a husband beside himself missing a wife, or even a woman in tears if her man is missing, I cut my engine at the same time as the others and dismount.

"Careful!" Snatcher holds up his hands. "Thor, Preacher. Fan out. You're searching outside and be fuckin' careful. Someone could be setting us up. Road, you're with me." He puts a hand to his ear. "You getting this, Stormy?" He listens for a moment, then turns to us. "He's got a good line of sight. He'll let me know if we're likely to have visitors."

I notice the front door is wide open. I start to approach when Snatcher pulls me back. "There could be booby traps. We go in carefully. And wear these." He hands me a pair of latex gloves.

My eyes go wide as I turn to him, sliding the gloves over my hands. "What are we doing here, Snatcher? Is this another kidnapping? Whose house is this?"

"You don't fuckin' know?" His eyes are wide.

Sheepishly I tell him, "Not a clue, man. I got to the meeting late."

"Fuck." His lips narrow. "It's Swift's house. Her security system's gone dead."

"Swift?" I feel frozen to the spot. "She's in there?"

"Hopefully we'll find her fast asleep in bed with not a clue anything's wrong." But from Snatcher's face, he doubts it.

I try to push past him, and he holds me back. "Careful," he growls. "Keep your fuckin' eyes open. We don't know what's happened here. Could be a home invasion."

And Swift wouldn't have heard a fucking thing, not with her security system taken out.

My hangover now pushed far back in my mind, holding my gun in front of me, I swing right and left, searching for any fucking thing. Snatcher waves me to the kitchen area, but there's nothing there, and no sign of Swift. Having cleared the main room, even checking behind curtains, making sure no one's hanging around, I follow the direction where Snatcher had gone. This hallway leads to a bathroom and two bedrooms. The door is open to one. It's obviously a guest room, minimal furniture in here. Snatcher's in the next. He holds out his hand to prevent me entering, but looking around his head, all I can see is an empty bed. For a brief second, I'm relieved not to see Swift's dead body lying there.

"Looks like a struggle." Snatcher points to the sheets tangled on the floor. "And she's fuckin' gone."

Gone? Swift? How the fuck? And how could anyone get the better of her? "She's a fuckin' expert in self-defence. She wrote the fuckin' book. No one could get the drop on her."

"They could," he answers, while smoothing his hand around the doorframe. "She's deaf, remember?"

"Not with her hearing aids." *But she takes them out at night,* I remember, and easing to stand alongside him, I notice them on the bedside table. *Shit and double shit.* But still, I can't see how anyone could get the drop on her. "Her room at the clubhouse, she told me that was all set up with warnings which vibrate or lights which flash." But she wasn't in the clubhouse. A chilling thought occurs to me. "You let her live off compound in a home that was unprotected?"

Snatcher's face is dark as he abandons his check on the door and rounds on me. "Did you not hear a word Pip had said? What do you fuckin' take us for? Swift had every piece of equipment it was possible to procure and install to keep her safe." He flicks the switch beside the door, and points to the overhead light which remained dead. "Every electronic fuckin' device."

Comprehension dawns on me. "The electricity was cut off."

"We'd catered for that too. Whoever did this, knew not only how to get to the mains, but to cripple her backup generator as well."

"But why take Swift?" I try to focus on that, not to think of the woman who, expert she might be at defending herself, is terrified and vulnerable when her ability to remain alert is taken away. I try not to imagine how scared she must have been when intruders broke in and stole her away. I hit on a better solution. "Maybe something happened, and she's gone somewhere."

"I would love to think that, Road. But someone knew how to take her electronics out. They knew what they were doing." He puts his hand to his ear and shakes his head. "Her jeep and bike are in the garage. She wouldn't have walked anywhere, not this time of night. And not without taking those." He points to the hearing aids I noticed before.

"Who?" My question is terse. This is too much for me to process. That Swift, so strong and self-reliant, has been taken seems unbelievable. The thought I might never see her again, unbearable.

"That's what Pip and the others are trying to find out.

Come on, let's look for clues. But tread carefully. This place could be a fuckin' death trap."

"You think someone wants to take us out?" I glance around. My eyes, while not trained in the same way as the others, are still perfectly capable of looking for trip wires. I inch forward, my feet gingerly touching the floorboards, checking in case one might be loose.

"Could be." Snatcher's proceeding with equal care. "They know we'll come to the scene of the crime, so yeah, if they wanted to take a bunch of us out, this place could be primed to blow."

"Have you been here before?" I wonder if he knows the layout.

"Yeah. When we installed the equipment."

"You think it's anything to do with a case?"

For a reply, Snatcher makes the motion of zipping his mouth.

I take the hint. As well as taking Swift, whoever's got her may have left something behind—a camera or a bug.

Slowly, too fucking slowly, we search the room where Swift sleeps. My eyes keep being drawn to Swift's hearing aids left by the side of the bed. *Christ.* I'm not sure why, but seeing Snatcher is ignoring them, I pocket the small devices and put them into the pocket of my jeans. I'm determined we'll find her, and when we do, they'll be the first things she'll want. She's strong, capable of resisting the most severe torture methods, but even so, it must be terrifying not to be able to hear. It's her literal nightmare come true.

Why did I get so drunk last night? As I watch Snatcher expertly searching for any small clue, I feel guilt settle on me that maybe I had chased her from the clubhouse last night. I vaguely recall people making comments about my idiotic approaches to her. Had she removed herself from the situation, rather than disabling me? Had I not come on to her, she might have stayed surrounded by people who'd keep her safe.

Something on the floor catches my eye. "I got blood." Once again, I feel chilled.

"Yeah, man, you on your way? We got blood." Snatcher's touching his ear again and speaking to someone who's not in the room.

"More here." I notice what looks like a bloody smear on the door.

"Two samples. Yeah. See you soon."

He sees my raised eyebrow and explains, "Honor's on his way. He can collect blood samples and dust for prints."

"He can?"

"Yeah, he's an ex-cop. Both he and Duty got out a few years back. Got fed up with all the crap they saw going on. You didn't know that?"

I shake my head. "Why isn't one of them here now?" It seems like we're wasting time.

"Honor went back to collect his shit. He'll be here soon, and Duty's best used behind a computer. Whoever did this, it was carefully planned, and may have left some kind of digital footprint. We're here to look for any message left—something to give us a clue who they could be or why they've taken her."

There's clearly so much I don't know about how they do things. I glance around again, looking for anything obvious or not that might help us find Swift. There's nothing that jumps out. I turn around, trying to see if I've missed something, but notice Snatcher looking equally puzzled.

"Would you expect to find something?" I query, feeling out of my depth. Knowing part of my helplessness is that this isn't some stranger whose disappearance we're investigating, this is Swift. A woman who seems to mean more to me than I care to admit, and which I hadn't allowed myself to acknowledge until she went missing.

He shakes his head. "No, but the fact we haven't suggests this was planned and carried out by people who know what they're doing. All we've got are those splotches of blood, and they could have come from Swift herself."

That's what's worrying me. Is she hurt? I'm assuming she is, so the real question should be, how bad? *Is she even alive?* My heart speeds up, then I tell myself, *If they've killed her, why take her body?* Surely if that's their purpose, they'd have left her here for us to find. Next, I wonder whether the people who've taken her know who she is. If they don't, then it's them I should be worrying about.

"If she's not incapacitated, they won't know what's hit them," I tell him, a little more confidently than I feel.

His sharp eyes find mine. "You like her, Road? I mean, *really* like her? Last night you were coming on to her strong."

"I was drunk." But I'm not going to deny it. "But hey, drunk or sober, she's a fuckin' attractive woman. Strong as steel on the outside, but with a soft core."

His eyebrows rise. "Nothing about Swift is soft. She'd bust your balls."

But I'm not so certain. Though one thing I am sure of, I'll be doing her no favours when she returns for her to have become the victim of jokes about me mooning over her. "You know her better than I. But hey, last night I was drunk. Sober, I'd steer clear as I value my junk too much. I'll use a hangaround if I want to get my dick wet." Speaking of which… "Any problem if I use her bathroom?"

"Nah, I checked it out."

I take a long much-needed piss, immediately feeling infinitely better, then wash my hands. While I'm certain Snatcher will have already searched, I open the cabinet above the sink, noting its contents. There's a box of condoms, which under the circumstances I should ignore, but instead my dick perks up as I think of sinking into her depths. I bang the heel of my hand against my head. *Focus.* It was unlikely before that I'd ever fuck her, but now she's gone, I might never see her again. That thought is far more painful than I expect.

Resting my hands on the edge of the sink, I bow my head for a moment, vowing silently that while I don't have a clue about how I'm going to do it, I'll do my part to bring her home. Then, maybe, I'll take my chance with her sober. Christ knows whether she'll give a grunt like me a second look, but she's gotten to me in the very short time I've known her. I've never met anyone like her.

I take the opportunity of splashing cold water on my face, then putting some toothpaste on my finger, do an inadequate job of cleaning my teeth.

"You taking a shit or something?"

"Be right out," I reply. But before I do, I stare into the mirror, not seeing my face, but hers instead. *I'll move heaven and earth to find you, Swift. Might not have a clue how to do it, will have to be guided by your brothers, but I'll do my best. Just hold on. We're coming to get you.*

*S*wift...
I'm deaf.

I'm alone. But I'm not in my home. There's a cuff around my hand that's fastened to a chain about six feet in length, and that, in turn, is fixed to an iron ring cemented in the wall. I give it an experimental tug. It holds fast.

I've been taken. But where and by whom or why, I don't know. I rise to a sitting position, putting my hand to my head. I feel dizzy, my head throbs and I'm nauseous. I can't remember anything after going to bed and falling asleep.

I add the few clues together. My physical symptoms suggest I've been subjected to chloroform or some drug to render me unconscious, I must have fought as there's a bruise and graze on my arm, but I can't remember. How had it happened and why the hell hadn't my security system worked? The technology I'd put so much faith in hadn't alerted me that someone had invaded my home. While I wish this was a nightmare, I'm very much awake and aware I've been kidnapped.

My hearing aids? Well, they are the first things I look for, but whoever took me, hadn't brought them, or if they have, they've not left them out for me.

A wave of panic rises inside me. *I can't hear anything.*

I can see and touch. I taste a sour flavour in my mouth, and smell a stale odour but it's not enough. I can't hear voices that might give me clues as to what's happening, nor footsteps that could warn me of someone's approach, or even a rattling to show the door's being opened. *I'm helpless.*

No. I can't think that way. As I feel the onset of a panic attack—the ones that can overtake me ever since I woke up and found my hearing impaired—I consciously try to slow down my breathing, trying to stave off the weakness that would ensue should I give into the urge. I'm Swift. I'd reached the rank of corporal in the army before passing the selection process for the SAS. Part of the training involved kidnap and negotiation training. I know the advice I'd give someone who could potentially be kidnapped, and the words I'd use to negotiate their freedom.

I just never expected to be on this side of a kidnapping, to be the kidnapee. I'd more likely be the kidnapper. I hadn't expected to feel so helpless and out of control, which definitely are alien feelings for me. I breathe in through my mouth and out through my nose, then I do it again.

Think Swift. Use your head. Rule one for someone who's been kidnapped, keep your eyes and ears open for anything that might help, either to free yourself or to bring the kidnappers to justice once you're released.

Is this what it's like to feel terrified? I don't think I've felt real fear before, apprehension of course, when we were waiting for the order to proceed, but it was the adrenaline as with my comrades we prepared to head into what the intelligence reports had told us of the unknown. Our advances strategically planned, our weapons at the ready, while always knowing that the best laid plans could fall apart in an instant.

Reacting to minute details changing in a situation was something I'd learned. But I was always in control, the adrenaline fuelling my actions.

Now that useless hormone is threatening to overwhelm me as I've no one standing in front of me to fight, and the chain prevents me moving very far. It's a stimulant which I could do without, pumping my body up, preparing it for action without being able to flee or fight.

I try to push it down, make my heart rate slow, and tell myself there's no enemy to engage right now. Promising myself when my kidnapper puts in an appearance, he'll soon wish he'd picked on somebody else.

Another rule. Don't antagonise your kidnapper. Hmm. So maybe kicking him in the privates just for the sake of it isn't the way to go. Not while I'm still chained to the wall and sitting on an iron bed which seems to be bolted to the floor.

But free me, and all bets are off.

Forcing myself not to think of everything I can't hear, I try to think of the positives and use the senses I do still possess, I look around me. There are no windows, the room lit by a single bulb hanging from the ceiling. That musty smell suggests I'm in some kind of cellar or basement. There's a bed, a bucket, presumably placed conveniently close by should I wish to answer a call of nature, and a single wooden chair.

Weapons? The bed's an iron frame. Lifting the thin mattress I see it has springs, but none that look loose or which, without a tool, could be taken out. There's no handy screwdriver or other implement which would help me. The floor is dirty and dusty, but with cleaner areas which suggest things have been removed. *They've prepared for me.*

For me? Or for anyone? Was I a deliberate target?

No one knew I was going home last night. I'd only decided on the spur of the moment so I didn't give in to my impulse to go with Road. Maybe fucking Road would have been the lesser of two evils. *I could still be in his bed…*

Think, I admonish myself.

My electricity was taken out. Sure, it's easy enough to cut a power line, but the generator would have kicked in, and that's set to warn me if the power has failed. That it hadn't means that was disabled too. To know I had the backup in place means it wasn't just a random home invasion. It was premeditated and planned for. That my appearance in my house wasn't on my agenda last night, whoever is responsible for bringing me here had to have staked the place out, waiting for me to make one of my rare visits to my home. Which means I was the target, me. And taking me was important enough to make all the necessary preparations.

My hands are slick with sweat, my heart's beating too fast. I feel lightheaded and while I try to put it down on whatever sedative was used on me, I know I'm hiding the truth. *I'm panicking.* Me, Swift. One of the first women to be selected for the SAS, and here I am, shaking and scared.

I hate this deadly silence. Hate not knowing what's going on or why. Why does anyone want me?

I can still fight. Being deaf has only taken my hearing from me.

But I have to be free to go on the offensive. While I search for something useful within reach, I keep glancing toward the door, only too well aware that someone could creep up on me. I'd never hear a key turn in the lock, nor the door opening. Or someone's voice.

I tackle the chain, unable to undo the cuff around my wrist. The chain itself is too sturdy to break. *Maybe I can pull the ring out of the wall?* But while I'm strong, I don't have sufficient weight or leverage to loosen it at all. *If someone comes too close to me, the chain is a weapon all in itself.* My mind goes through options of how it could be used. Options I begin to look forward to.

I don't know who's holding me, how many there are, and whether they also are trained. I don't know whether they're expecting *me*, or a weak helpless female. Is there something in my past that would make someone target me? I can't think of anything, and my parents, while not poor, couldn't put much of a ransom together. My activities with the club? Again, unlikely. We keep our heads down low for that very reason, so no one knows who we are or what we do. A random kidnapping? Why go to all that trouble? I know sex traffickers often target people who fit someone's particular tastes, could that be what's happened to me? I wouldn't call myself pretty, or the shape that a typical female would have. I'm hard and muscular, not soft and curvy. Is it possible that's what someone would like, someone who wants to break me?

Do they know who I am? Or more importantly, what? I'm less human being than weapon.

I grin to myself. I've got a chance if I've been kidnapped because I'm a particular type of woman, who matches someone's desires. In that instance, they could be unaware of what skills I have.

On the other hand, if they do, they'll be prepared. And I'll be fucked, and not in a way I'd like.

Considering my options, I see that if I stand on the bed I could karate kick out the light, but I'm unwilling to give up on any remaining senses I have, and I'm not sure what advantage it would give me when I need to find out what I'm up against. I need to ask questions.

I can ask, but I won't be able to hear any answers unless someone speaks very slowly and loudly into my left ear. Even then they'd have to enunciate clearly. Would they do that?

Damn, and fucking damn.

After scrabbling at the iron ring in the wall until my

fingernails are broken and bleeding, I have to acknowledge the cement around it doesn't loosen at all and concede for now, I'm at the mercy of whoever's kidnapped me.

Settling into wait, I let myself slip into the mindset that I had during those long periods I spent on sentry duty, staying motionless for hours while remaining vigilant. Summoning up my inner soldier, patient but alert, my eyes, almost unblinking, stay focused on the door. I have no way of knowing how much time passes before I see the knob start to turn.

Game on.

I've decided to play it like a scared woman, hiding for now my abilities and skills. If they don't know what I am, I'll keep them in the dark. If I show I'm no threat, maybe they'll unchain me from the wall.

The door opens and a man appears. His lips move and his mouth turns up in an approximation of a smile. I've seen more welcoming ones on a corpse.

His eyes narrow and his lips move again.

I remain impassive, as clearly, I can't hear a word he says.

His face darkens, he comes closer. His lips move again and this time his body vibrates. In my left ear I hear an indistinguishable rumbling sound. His increasing anger shows he doesn't know I'm deaf. That gives me hope he doesn't know much else about me.

Forcing myself to back away and up the bed when all I want is to strangle him with this chain, I open my mouth. "I'm deaf." I hear the words only as a dull echo in my mind.

He pauses, tilts his head to one side, then his smile broadens, and his body moves in a way that makes me think he's laughing. Then he shakes his head, moves to the door and leans around it.

I read the clues. *He's talking to someone else.* I suspected he wouldn't be alone.

I'm right. It's not long before another man appears. This one, I feel is more dangerous. Unlike the first one, he doesn't come close. He mouths something very slowly, and I wish I'd taken more time to learn how to lip read, but I can't make what he's saying out.

"I'm deaf," I repeat.

He taps his lips.

This time I hazard a guess what he's asking. "I can't read lips, but I sign. And read. I've a little hearing in my left ear if you speak loudly and clearly up close." Perhaps if I get them in the habit of getting near, I'll have them where I want them when I make my move. "Wh-who are you and why am I here?" I try to put a quiver in my voice. The last thing I want them to guess is that I was so nearly a member of one of the world's most revered and feared army units.

He rolls his eyes and shakes his head. Whether he's refusing to tell me even if I could hear his response, I don't know. He doesn't approach so I have a chance to hear. He might not know I'm an ex-soldier, but he's still taking no chances with that chain.

"Please, let me go. I don't know why I'm here." I tap my left ear, a plea for him to speak so I can understand.

His lips move out of habit, but it's no good. The two men glance at each other, their shoulders shake once more, then with twisted smiles, they leave. Once again, I'm alone.

The bastards like that I'm deaf. There are ways they could have addressed my questions in a manner I could have understood, but they prefer the additional torture of leaving me in ignorance.

My hands curl into fists, my short nails cutting into my palms. I'm kidnapped, I don't know why or who by, and even if he had been explaining, I couldn't understand.

Instead of focusing on what I don't know, I try to consider what I do. I'm not sure of the time, when they took me or when it is now, but Pip will know something's wrong as my systems failing would have raised an alert in the clubhouse, and maybe by now will have realised I'm missing. I know my brothers will leave no stone unturned to find me. Every one of them will play their part, bringing their particular skills into play. My house will be forensically examined by Honor and/or maybe Duty. Stormy and Piston will be scouring the deep web for clues and Snatcher will assemble a team to follow up on anything they find. I've just got to hang on, be patient and wait.

I can do patient. I can do any fucking thing I put my mind to. It's not like I've not been in a similar situation before, it's just, last time, I had my hearing.

Being deaf is inconvenient at the best of times and especially right now. I need to pee, desperately. It's not using the bucket that I have a problem with, though I do find the concept that after I'll have to sit here smelling my body's waste unpleasant. My problem is, I feel vulnerable enough as it is, without being able to hear means I'll have to chance my captors walking in unheard, catching me with my pants literally down. But needs must. I do the necessary as fast as I can, feeling better once my bladder is relieved.

Then I go back to doing the only thing I can to help myself escape. I attack the ring the chain is attached to again.

Positioning myself so I keep one eye on the door, I pull, wriggle and kick the iron loop trying to see if it will loosen. My activity is an outlet for my frustration, but whatever I do, that damn ring holds firm, with not even a crack in the concrete.

Fuck. In disgust I look down at the cuff around my wrist, it's too tight to get my hand through. I try, but even when I've rubbed the base of my hand raw, the blood doesn't help ease it off. *I could break my thumb.* I could, though that doesn't guarantee my success, and it could incapacitate me. On balance, I'll wait until that's the only option that remains to me.

A bobby pin would come in handy right now. But all I'm wearing is my tank and shorts that I went to bed in, not even a zipper that I could use as a makeshift screwdriver. I flop down on the bed, frustrated as hell, angry that someone got the jump on me.

Think, woman. Think.

There must be something I can do.

The door starts to open. I sit up again. It's the first man returning. He throws something at me. Automatically, I reach up my hand to catch it. It's a paper sack containing takeout. *At least they aren't going to starve me.*

He's also carrying a cup, and I get a whiff of the contents and shake my head rapidly. "Water." Then belatedly I add, "Please?" Why do all Americans think everyone likes coffee? I can't even stand the smell, so I'm pleased when he takes the cup back out.

Ignoring the thought that the food may be drugged—my body needs fuel—I unwrap the cold unappetising burger in its bun. I've eaten worse. The fries are also far from warm, but it's something to keep me going. Shortly after, he returns, tossing a plastic bottle of water onto the bed, then leaves again. I couldn't say if he'd said a single word.

More time passes and I'm still left alone. I refuse to be beaten or cowed. I'm more annoyed that this is such a waste of my time. I allow anger to grow inside me, it's better than panic or fear.

Having eaten and drunk the water I feel a bit better, as I again work through my options. While I know Pip and the MC will be doing what they can to find me and get me free, I need to do what I can to help myself.

Lulling them into a false sense of security is a good start. If they think I'm just weak and helpless, they'll start to take risks. Then, when one of them lets down his guard and comes closer, I'll choke him with the chain, or my bare hands, either will work. Then, if he has the key, unlock the cuff, or, if he hasn't, take his gun and shoot out that concrete and loosen that ring.

Armed and free, I'll be able to make my escape. I'm confident anyone else in this house will be dispatched to meet Satan. When I'm no longer restrained, they won't stand a fucking chance. All I have to do is bide my time and wait for the right moment.

It's boring as hell, but I'm used to that. A lot of a soldier's life is hanging around waiting for the moment to jump into action. I doze as I've done so often before, allowing my body to relax while remaining partially alert, ready to leap into action.

My instinct is to protest and fight. Acting timid and scared is so unlike me.

How would a woman who's kidnapped behave?

She would be angry, beg, she'd cry… I can do the former well but not the latter. A soldier doesn't show weakness, and they don't shed tears. Well, not in my book anyway.

22

––––––

*R*oad...

I'm worried as hell as I follow Snatcher straight into the meeting room. My hangover is a thing of the past, concern has pushed it right out of my head. Pip's already there, his eyes perusing papers in front of him. He glances up as we walk in, then lowers his head.

Gradually the room fills, the only person missing is Honor. He's still back at the house going over everything with a fine-tooth comb. I sit in the seat next to Swift's empty chair, filled with emotion and regret. *Will I ever see her again? Why had I gotten drunk yesterday? Would she have stayed in the safety of the clubhouse had I stayed sober?*

Why hadn't she just punched me in the balls and told me to get lost? I'd prefer an aching groin to the mental anguish I'm going through now.

I tell myself I'd feel the same were it any one of the men here missing. Never mind they're not the same brothers I've ridden beside since I patched in, but they wear the same patch. We're all Satan's Devils. It's not anyone else though, it's Swift, and that knowledge darn near renders me helpless knowing she's gone, and that I might have made it easy for someone to take her.

When all the seats are filled bar the one next to me and the one used by Honor, Pip tidies his paperwork and puts it aside.

"What are we going to fuckin' do?" Stormy blazes from the end of the table, impatient to get the meeting started. "It's one of our own, Prez."

My eyes widen slightly. Stormy's an asshole of the highest order, yet he's the one who's spoken up first. I hadn't expected him to be so concerned.

"I'm fuckin' aware of that!" Pip thunders. "We're going to get her back. Update." His eyes go to Snatcher.

"They knew what they were doing. Generator was disabled first, then the power line was cut. None of her electronic warning systems would have worked." As Snatcher goes on to list what we found when we visited her house, I'm still blaming myself that she was there. "No sign of a struggle in that no furniture was overturned, though there was blood, but not enough to be worried about. My guess is that she was drugged." Snatcher finishes up.

I concur with that. If Swift had been conscious, she wouldn't have gone easily. But any blood is worrying.

"It's been dry lately." Thor takes over. "There were tyre tracks, but it's doubtful we'll get much from them. Footprints, but nothing distinguishable. Multiple people though, two at least, maybe three or four."

"A big load of nothing," Stormy comments again, his frustration coming over clearly.

"Until Honor gets back, we won't know more from her house," Pip sums up. "Let's talk about reasons. Duty, have you turned up any motive why she should be taken?"

Duty takes a breath and pulls his tablet toward him. "I've been going through everything we know, Prez. I started with recent cases she's worked on, but they've all been in and out, and unlike her kidnappers, we don't leave footprints."

"Digital ones? Could she have been traced back to us?"

"Nah. Our systems are watertight, you know that, Prez. We might," he spares a glance toward Stormy, "be able to get into Fort Knox, but I'd stake my life that no one can break into ours. We've got systems constantly tracking external access."

"And no one knows we exist." Preacher's word supports his brother. "If they knew what we do, they could have come after any of us."

"She may have been targeted because she's a woman?" Rascal suggests, his brow furrowed. "They could think she's the weak link?"

"Huh," Stormy scoffs, rubbing his jaw. "If they do, they'll soon realise their mistake."

Pip taps the paperwork. "I can't see it's anything to do with any of our assignments. As you say, Duty, we've kept our involvement under wraps. Nothing to link what we've done back to the Satan's Devils MC."

"I've started looking into her past," Duty resumes. "Her service record is clean. Of course it was harder to get into the information about her SAS training, but I managed to break in at last. It seemed quite standard. Worth noting she got top scores on everything."

She would, that doesn't surprise me.

"Was she ever used for a kill or something that a person might want retribution for?"

Duty grimaces. "I wish I could say it was as easy as that, but she's clean as a whistle. She never took up her post in the SAS, so wasn't involved in any of their activities. Of course," he glares at Stormy before he can ask more, "I'll keep digging as something could turn up. If in her service career she pulled the trigger at the wrong time, there could have been a coverup. But there'll be a trail, somewhere."

"On the face of it, there's nothing to suggest why she was taken." Pip rubs at his clean-shaven chin. "Therefore, nothing to suggest who."

"Should we contact her parents?" I ask.

"Her parents? Why the fuck worry them?" Stormy rolls his eyes.

"Because," I turn to him with more than a hint of anger in my voice, "if there's going to be a ransom demand, it's likely to go to them."

"Road's got a good point," Pip states firmly. "We need to discuss it. Far as I know, Swift's on good terms with her parents, had mentioned taking a trip back soon to the UK."

Duty's tapping on his tablet calling up some information. "Her dad's retired with a small private pension, and the mortgage on their house is all but paid up. But it's not a mansion and they live comfortably, not extravagantly. If someone wanted to shake them down, this is an international operation which has to be expensive. I can't see they've got the money or contacts for a payout that would make it worth it."

"In which case for now, let's keep it quiet," Pip decides. "I don't want to worry the parents unnecessarily. They know where Swift is. If they get a demand out of the blue then they'll contact us, if only to confirm she's missing."

On balance, I suppose he's right. No point getting her parents involved when they'd be concerned as hell and couldn't help. An unwelcome thought occurs to me. "Could it be sex trafficking?" I wonder aloud. "That there's nothing in her past, just the fact she's female?"

"Who'd want to traffic Swift?" Piston's eyes open wide.

"I know she's female, but..." Rascal opens his hands wide as if the prospect is unthinkable.

"She's a mighty fine woman," I snap. Though I have to be pleased that no one here seems to view her sexually.

"Well you made it plain what you'd like to do with her last night." Preacher gives a quick grin, then grows serious again. "Road might have a point. She might be athletic and muscular, and she doesn't flaunt her feminine assets, except when they're needed on a job, but she could be a type someone is after. There are some twisted fucks out there with particular tastes."

Pip nods. "We can't rule it out. Duty—"

"Already got searches going, Prez. If someone is looking for a woman matching her characteristics, hopefully their request will turn up on the dark web."

"Christ." Bolt's shaking his head. "I almost pity the motherfucker."

Cowboy raises his hand. "Could it be opportunistic? Someone broke into her house thinking it was empty and found her?"

"It's got to be premeditated and researched. Else they'd have missed the generator or not disabled that first."

Thor looks distraught. "She had top-of-the-line security. Maybe someone saw that and thought she was protecting money, jewellery or something else worth stealing?"

Snatcher looks across at the enforcer. "We found blood," he repeats. "Not a lot, but it's possible you're right. If that's what went down, and they found her there unexpectedly, then we could be looking for a dead body."

I'd been hanging onto the idea she'd been taken, not that she'd been killed and her body dumped. If she hadn't heard anyone enter, she could have been hit over the head hard enough to knock her out, so there might not have been much blood. Or strangled, choked... My gut churns at the thought. *Not Swift. No.*

"Check the morgues, police reports—"

"On it already, Prez. Hospitals too. So far we've drawn blanks."

Pip looks around the table. "Let's concentrate on the positives for now. Without a body, we'll work on the assumption she's alive. Getting back to what we know. I hate to say it, but I think Road might be on to something. We know there are kinky bastards out there. The fact she's deaf might make her attractive.

"She's not mute, though." The way Preacher puts it causes a quick chuckle to go around, but the moment of mirth is short-lived. It's as though he's reminded us all that there's someone who should be sitting around this table who isn't.

"I'm worried. She'll be lost without her hearing aids. She won't know what the fuck's going on." I drop my head into my hands and massage my temples.

An incredulous bark comes from Thor. "I'd be more worried about the people who've taken her. She can look after herself." The enforcer looks down the table. "We have to remember, Swift is probably better equipped to handle this situation than anyone else here. Don't forget, she was trained for being in a kidnapping situation."

"If they took me without my hand, I'd survive." Bolt stares across the table at me.

I think he's trying to be reassuring. But Swift's got a vulnerability that she'd shown me in the dark of the night. A fear of exactly what seems to have happened to her—someone creeping up on her unawares. It will be as though she's in a perpetual nightmare. During her training, she'd had all her senses available to her. I know how crippling PTSD can be. If that kicks in, she might not be as competent as Thor is painting her.

While I'm thinking that and growing more worried, the door opens and Honor walks in. He kicks out his seat then takes it. He gives only a brief questioning gaze toward Pip. Receiving a nod in return, he gets straight on to his report.

"I've left Igor there to continue to search, but I think we've got everything we're going to. Two patches of blood as we know already. Brute biked them over to my contact at the lab. One's type O neg which we know Swift is. That's rare enough for me to stick my neck out and say that it's hers. The other is O positive."

"How much blood?" Thor asks.

"The O neg patch, not much. Looked to me like she might have knocked her hand or arm against the door and grazed it. The O positive just a smear."

"DNA?"

"Will take longer, but I told him the hurry and he's going to try and rush it along." Honor looks up. "We've got access to lots of databases, but unless he's already known to cops or has investigated his ancestry, it might not tell us a lot."

I don't bother questioning how they can access DNA databases as everyone else just accepts it. I'm beginning to realise their boast about Fort Knox was probably genuine.

"What I did find," Honor continues, a frown appearing on his face, "was surveillance equipment hidden in her house. It was behind the ventilation grid in her bedroom."

"Camera?"

Honor nods. "They could see and hear everything."

Pip growls. "When did we last sweep the private homes for bugs?"

"Kind of leave that to everyone to keep their own places clean," Snatcher reminds him.

I grimace. "Swift wasn't expecting to go back there last night."

Preacher's watching me carefully. "What's on your mind, Road?"

I slam my hand on the table. "It's my fault. I pissed her off, made her uncomfortable so she left the clubhouse."

Pip snorts, loudly. "Heard you made a pass at her, Brother. Do you think you're the only one to have done that?" His eyes land on Cowboy who shrugs, and then Stormy who grins widely. My eyes narrow at that. *Had any of them been successful?* Pip carries on, "She's an expert at turning men down, and not very lightly. They're usually walking bow-legged the next day and not for any pleasurable reason."

"Swift got the hots for Road?"

"If she has," Honor raises his chin toward Duty, "it might have confused her. Especially if Road's sticking around and becoming part of the team."

I'm getting uncomfortable with this discussion, not thinking any attraction between Swift and myself is a suitable topic for church, but I suppose anything is fair game, including my sensibilities, if we're going to get her back.

"Why she went home yesterday, and why she didn't do a sweep for bugs are questions for later not now!" Pip bellows. "That the bug was there means someone was targeting *her*, waiting for her to go back, and that it wasn't a random pick up."

"Still could be sex trafficking," Piston remarks.

Preacher shrugs. "Some run fairly sophisticated operations. Especially when targeting specific types. It's a lucrative business. A woman living alone might have been seen as an easy target."

"Anyone notice anything out of place? Strangers hanging around when Swift was about?"

"I'll get Gears to examine the surveillance footage around both clubhouses and see if anything shows up." Honor makes a note on his tablet. "Just to recap, apart from the bug and the blood, that was all I could get from the house. I dusted for prints, but apart from Swift's, I couldn't find any."

Snatcher and I had worn gloves, it seems so too did the kidnappers.

"I still wonder if it's anything in Swift's past," Pip observes, tapping his fingers on the table. "We don't want to focus on one assumption and then find we were wrong. I'll contact Devil and see whether she was ever deployed on work for MI5 or MI6."

"I'd find that," Duty scoffs.

Pip gives a half-grin. "Not doubting you, Duty. Doesn't hurt to double-check though." He pauses, then raps the table. "Okay. Honor, Duty and Stormy, the three of you keep digging. Let me know immediately if the DNA turns anything up. Everyone else, stay close and ready to move out as soon as we've got a location for her."

"Mystic's already got the plane fuelled and ready," Preacher informs us. "Just in case she's already been moved out of state or over the border."

"Everyone check your bikes. If your tyres need changing or oil topped off, bring them into the shop now." Thor glances at each of us in turn. When he receives nods from each of us, he turns to me. "You want to take that ZX14R for a spin, Road? See how it handles?"

I do. But it would be fun, and doing anything fun right now feels completely wrong. I shrug.

"We might need someone to get somewhere fast," Pip observes, his eyes viewing me critically. Not for the first time, I suspect he's got an uncanny capability for seeing inside a person right down to their soul.

That puts a different spin on it. I give a sharp nod. As soon as we know where Swift is being held, I'll waste no time rushing to her.

The brothers here might all be desperate to find her, but I doubt anyone has such a driving urge to be the one who first reaches her.

For the first time, I understand why Mouse was so distraught when Mariana was taken, or Blade when Tash disappeared. What's harder to comprehend is why I feel like a part of me is missing when I barely know her.

Or why I want to shout to the room that we have to find her because she's mine.

Mine? In my head only. Swift will never belong to me or anyone.

23

———

Swift...

    I think a night has passed, but I can't be sure. All I know is I was thrown another hamburger what feels like hours ago, and a breakfast wrap was delivered just now.

At least my time in the army had trained me for accepting my time as a kidnapee. During the stage of my SAS training while I was fending for myself, I had to eke out my meagre rations, surviving at times on energy bars which tasted just like cardboard. A cold egg and bacon sandwich was actually a step up, and the protein and calories were such that I couldn't be fussy or pass it up.

Ignoring my body's complaints have become ingrained as my way of life. Being on sentry duty meant retaining the same position for hours which could lead to cramps, as could trekking forty-odd miles carrying a fifty-five pound pack.

I'm tired though. I can't relax and sleep as I wouldn't hear anyone creep up on me. I refuse to close my eyes, and keeping them focused on the door–the only way I'd be warned of someone approaching–is exhausting. I'm slowly being driven crazy by the silence. Usually, as soon as I wake, I switch on my hearing aids and the world becomes as close to normal again as I'll ever have it.

My fear, which I'm trying to manage, continuously bubbles under the surface. *What future have they got planned for me? Will I ever hear again, or will my future just be silent?* That scares me more than anything.

During what I expect was the long lonely night, I'd gone over and over again why they could have kidnapped me. It was planned, I've become even more certain of that. Possibly I've been watched, but as I hadn't been aware of anything or anybody wrong, they're not amateurs. But why take me?

I'm a woman, and while I keep shying away from giving it serious consideration, the only thing I circle back to is they've kidnapped me to be sold, just like so many people I've helped rescue with the Utah Satan's Devils. I've tried to think of something else, why I'm important to them in any other way, but I was never able to wear my beige beret and take up a position as part of the SAS. I've been involved in no intrigue, have upset nobody's plans.

I've got hands, feet, and if it comes to it, teeth. My arm can wrap around someone's neck and choke out their life in an instant, and my legs can kick theirs from under them. Helpless is not a word which applies to me, unless I'm drugged, overpowered or, left tied up and chained to a wall.

I know people are into kinky shit, and if that's my planned future, doubt if I'd be given a safeword. I wouldn't go anywhere or do anything willingly, and I'm not helpless. If someone tried to rape me here chained up as I am, I'd use my hips and attempt to break off their fucking dick. I can't evade a bullet, I know that, but death would be on my terms and not theirs.

What petrifies me isn't the thought of anyone getting physical with me, it's being left in this world of silence to rot. *Would I ever be able to sleep again?* I think not. It hasn't escaped me that I might have been taken for some sick fuck who'd get off on the thought he could hurl insults and threats at me when without hearing them, I couldn't retort back.

No. No. No and no. As my heart starts to race, I yank at the chain again and again, hoping if I keep this up, a link might break or the concrete loosen enough for me to pull the ring out. I've got plans for this chain whether or not I can escape from the cuff. I'd revisited my thought about breaking the thumb, but having studied it, I'd have to break more than that to get free. There's not enough play in the metal surrounding my wrist.

I'm angry. *How dare they?* How dare they take a woman from her home, wrest her away from everything she knows, from a life that she loves. *From the man she'd like to get to know better.*

Road. Yeah, well he's been in my head a little more than he should have. What would it be like to have him submit to me, or, heaven help me, a little part of me wants to know what it would feel like submitting to him? Rather than me taking the lead as I normally do in any sexual encounters I have, I think I might trust him enough to let him use my body as he wants to. A shiver goes down my spine, and this time it's not fear causing it. It leaves me wondering, would one night be enough?

Would one night be too much? If Road's going to be part of the team, would it change the working dynamic between us? Yes, of course it would. We'd either both end up dealing with sexual frustration, or more likely, just one of us would while the other had gotten it out of their system. The utterly alien thought strikes me, I can't say for certain that in Road's case, it would be him left wanting.

But I never go back. I always find it easy moving on. Surely, Road hasn't got something that's able to smash down the walls I've carefully built up around my life?

What do I see in my future? A long road stretching off into the distance ridden alone, or somewhere along the way, would I want someone beside me?

I'm still young…ish. Thirty-three isn't old, is it?

While still yanking on the chain and keeping one eye on the door, I allow myself to think, and of things I don't normally let myself consider. Like where I'll be in ten, twenty, thirty years' time. A vision of me as a female version of Grinch comes into my mind. Someone whose whole life revolves around the club and motorcycles, no old lady, no children, no legacy for him to leave for the future. When he dies, the club will remember him, and maybe Brenda will too. But memories fade. *Do I want to end up like that?* In time, he'd be just a faded photograph on a wall.

Do I want loneliness like that? Or do I want to find a partner?

It's always been a shadowy thought for my future. I haven't seen me fading away all alone, but nor have I viewed the years laid out in front of me with any particular man by my side. But now, here in this cellar or wherever this is, when my future has possibly been taken out of my hands, how I'd like it to be shaped becomes clearer.

I can't say the man at my side would be Road, it's far too early for that. We might be incompatible in or out of bed. But if it wasn't just the drink talking the night before last, maybe I'll take Road up on his offer. At least I'll hopefully get an orgasm or two out of it. It might be a mistake, but hell, I think I'd enjoy it.

For the first time since I awoke from my drug-enforced sleep, my lips curve. Then I redouble my efforts to get free. I'll not have a chance of anything if I don't get out of this predicament I'm in.

My eyes catch the movement of the door opening, and I

swing around, ready for anything, wanting nothing more than someone to produce the handcuff key.

The first man, who seems to be the leader, enters. This time he has a gun trained on me. He gestures to the man beside him, who comes closer, looking at me warily, making sure I understand the unspoken threat of the gun, then dives for the bucket. His expression of disgust is clear to read and I don't need more than his body language to scream what he's thinking. Well, I've must have been held captive for more than a day, and it's the first time they've bothered to empty it. Me? Well, I've gotten used to the smell now, and it would take far more than that for me to be squeamish.

Gingerly, he carries the bucket out the door. Then the man with the gun stands aside, and a third hitherto unseen man comes through the door. He's a bloody giant of a man, enormous, twice my size and looks like he's been hitting the steroids. *Brawn, not muscle,* I tell myself, confidently. I can take him with one hand chained. I couldn't beat the bullet firing from the gun though.

They wouldn't go to the bother of kidnapping me, only to shoot me.

Why's this man here? To rape me? I'm not naïve. Christ, I've seen enough on the dark web, I know there's a market for snuff movies, let alone forced intercourse. But there's no camera equipment, and none that I could see planted in the room.

I could seriously injure him before he touches me. At least, render him incapable.

But I'll still be chained and unable to get free, so where would that leave me?

Another new man enters, he also looks strong. *What the hell is going on?* Despite my confidence I can do serious damage, I start to fear they might really rape me.

The man with the gun moves closer to me, his gun

pointing not at my head, but at my knee. *He's making it plain he can shoot and injure me.* I've seen a shattered kneecap before, and it's not pretty. Incapacitating, with a long recovery and that's if I'm given medical treatment quickly.

I will my muscles to relax. Whatever they intend to do, they mean to do it. It's probably worth more for me to maintain my weak female persona than show my hidden strengths. There's more chance then of them releasing me if they think I'm no threat, and with them being totally unsuspecting of what I'm capable of. Whatever plan he has, I'll endure it. For now.

"What's going on?" I ask, but he doesn't bother to reply.

Then, strong man two pulls me around, sits on my legs and the giant gets behind me. His arms encircle my body, my arms pressed tight against my sides. I haven't the angle to break free, even if I tried. I'm in a position no one wants to be in. Trapped.

The man who'd gone out with the bucket returns, this time carrying something which he hands to the man with the gun. That weapon is passed over.

The leader grabs my right hand and pulls it upward, my upper arm still trapped by the giant behind me.

My eyes widen in horror as I see he holds pruning shears in his hand.

"No." I flinch back, trying to pull my hand away, but I've got no leverage. A soldier might stay silent, a woman picked up off the street would not. "No!" I say again. "No, please! No, please no, no. *No!"* I don't try to hold back my screams.

But he could be as deaf as I am as he ignores my pleas. Instead, he holds my hand tightly, and seconds, and a sharp pain later, my little finger is in his hand and no longer attached to mine.

He signals to the other men and I'm released, cradling my

bloody hand to me, saying, "No, why? What have you done?" I don't have to force the sob, I just don't suppress it.

Next, he throws a roll of bandage and a Band-Aid to me.

Then, they're gone.

Knowing I don't want to bleed to death, I wrap my throbbing hand, using the Band-Aid to fasten the bandage securely. The white becomes red almost immediately.

I think I must be in shock, I hadn't expected that to happen.

A few minutes ago I had ten fingers, now I have nine.

Fuck, my hand's throbbing. I rock to-and-fro. But why did they do that? I still as I force myself to think through this new development rationally. If I was taken to be sold, they'd want me undamaged and whole. The reason why kidnappers take pieces of their victim is to show they mean business, and it usually accompanies a ransom demand.

But who? Who would pay a ransom to get me back?

Or, it's to prove they can hurt someone's loved one, and who cares about me enough they'd worry about keeping me alive? My parents? But they've got no money. While I'm worth the world to them, it would be impossible for them to get any sizeable sum together. The only other people are my club.

While motorcycle clubs aren't everyone's favourite groups, they're not usually the victims of a kidnapping scam. Any enemy would hit us head-on. But it could be that, someone we've crossed in our line of business and they want to make the club hurt for revenge.

The club has funds, I suppose, a private plane for a start. But would the Satan's Devils give up everything they own just to get me back? Maybe they would. Maybe this would soon be over, and I'll be released with the only damage a loss of a finger.

But that theory is full of holes. I've seen their faces.

If the kidnappers know anything about our club, they'll

know we've got the resources to track them down and take them out of existence.

They won't leave me alive.

Damn it. If they know I'm a member of the MC, they may know all about me, and I've been hiding my skills for nothing. *I should have fought. Should have taken them out.* Even if my corpse was left with theirs to rot in this basement, I shouldn't have played it by the book.

The door opens again, and they come back in. This time, one's carrying a tripod. A smartphone is fastened to it, and it's focused on me on the bed.

The leader stands behind it. His lips are moving, and he's using a mic. If I'm not mistaken that little box connected to it will change the tone of his voice. He's staring at me, but obviously not speaking to me. I conclude he's dictating something for the tape.

While he does so, mindful I'm playing to more than just this audience, I'm wiping my eyes, hard enough to make them water and the skin red, as if I'm the expected weak female crying in pain, fear and confusion. I don't have to try too hard. My eyes are watering as my wounded hand is smarting.

"Please let me go," I start to beg. "Please. My hand hurts. Please." I try to inject a sob, but unpractised, and unable to properly hear the result, am not sure if it worked. But then I conjure up the possibility of never seeing Road again, and the sob becomes real. How and why he's become important to me, I have no idea. Maybe when I'm out of here, I'll find it's just a fantasy brought on by being locked in this world where I can watch but not hear. Maybe the real man will be a disappointment, but heaven help me, I'm going to do what I can to get back to him and find out.

After he's finished his spiel, he motions one of the other men forward. Before he approaches me, he covers his face with a mask. I flinch back, giving a good imitation that I'm afraid of what he's about to do. When he draws close enough, he holds up a tablet.

The instructions at the top are clear. Read these words.

They move the smartphone on its tripod a little closer. I start to wring my hands, raising the damaged one, showing the bandage stained by my blood. There's no reason to protect anyone's sensibilities. Any information I can get out might help. This message, *I'm not injured elsewhere.* While to the people in this room, I look scared, the actions of my hands aren't due to any fear. I'm doing what I can to give some limited signs which will mean something to the people for whom this video's being made. As for the bandage, that probably needs no explanation. There's good reason to suspect, the person or persons seeing this footage will also be in receipt of the appendage that used to be affixed to my right hand.

The man in charge frowns and his lips move, followed by a circling gesture of his hand. It's not in any recognised sign language manual, but it's clearly a signal for me to hurry up and get this done.

"You are a man of honour," I read, scanning ahead seeing clues slip into place. "They have taken me your club girl." I gulp before reading the next words, as any girl would, "Your whore. You have received a package to show they are serious." It's hard to inject emotion when you can't properly hear the tone of your own voice. But I try to sound horrified, stumbling over the next words. "I will be raped... and hurt, then returned to you... piece by piece... if you do not surrender yourself. If you do, I will be released with no further harm."

Four men. One big. I've seen faces. I sign as discreetly as possible, and as well as I can with one hand bandaged.

Not much, but enough to let them know it's a lie, and I'll never be let free with breath in my body.

24

-----

*R*oad…

"She's in pieces." Rascal's eyes widen as he watches the screen. "Fuck, I hate seeing her like that."

"No, she isn't." Once again, it's Stormy who's come to her defence. "They think she's a fuckin' club girl. They have no idea of what they've taken into their lair. She's being as clever as I expected and is doing what she has to—she's acting a part."

"And giving us a message. Play it again, Duty," Pip instructs. "So far we've made out what she's signing. We've got four men, one a large fucker, and that she's seen their faces so they've no intention of letting her go. Anyone picked up anything else?"

Dutifully we watch it again. Those who can sign, concentrating on her fingers. Me, who can't, well, I'm watching her face, trying to read everything written on it, the main message shown in the tightening of her eyes. As expected, she's in pain. It must hurt like a bitch to lose your finger. They wouldn't have used anaesthetic.

Last night I hadn't been able to sleep, tossing and turning, worrying about Swift and what the fuck she was going through. Breakfast had been subdued, none of us wanting to go through the bother of eating, but doing it anyway, just to keep our bodies fuelled. Then it was back to the meeting room to put our heads together again.

A summons for Pip had him leaving. When he'd returned, what he'd brought with him had my breakfast threatening to make a reappearance.

Now it's been half an hour since Pip received the horrendous package containing what at first we could only suspect to be Swift's finger, quickly confirmed once we'd viewed the footage that was on the USB stick which arrived with it, and had seen her hand injured and bleeding. Thirty minutes when I've had to digest that the woman I want back in one piece is already missing part of her body and is obviously hurt. She looks just how a club girl would, scared. But her eyes, along with pain, show an expression that I've seen before—the one she bestows on Stormy. She's fucking angry.

I've witnessed just what she's capable of, so while we view the footage for the fifth time, I force my eyes away from Swift, and view her surroundings and how she's secured instead. She appears to have a cuff around her left wrist, and that attaches to a chain which in turn is fastened to a wall. Swift will have tried to escape already, but is clearly biding her time, or has found it impossible.

"So now we know it's you they want, are we any closer to finding her?" Snatcher asks, directing his question to Pip.

"It's my past," Pip confirms, his face darkening. "It has to be. When I was with the agency, I worked on many cases. I was with them twenty years. We put people inside, killed, broke up families. I don't know where to begin to start identifying anyone who'd want me. There would be too many. But I went by the name of Mr Black in those days—nothing to connect him with me."

"Unless someone broke into the CIA database," Duty observes.

"Philip Hound didn't exist back then," Pip states, his hand wiping down his face. "My real name is Lawson Kraft. In the CIA, my cover, as I said, was as the anonymous Mr Black. I had sufficient connections, when I... left... my new identity was constructed up carefully. I'm a wanted man."

"You had plastic surgery as well," Cowboy reminds everyone, viewing us one by one as he makes his statement.

"You didn't," Pip tells the man who brought him to the club. "It's possible someone located me via you, but I'm inclined to rule it out. Twelve years is a long fucking time to wait for vengeance."

"So, could it have been something while you've been with the Devils? A job you've worked on?" I might be able to string a sentence together, but inside I'm seething, wondering what kind of people kidnap, torture and from what Swift signed, would kill the innocent girl that they believe she is, just to get even.

"Unlikely. The MC performs well as a front for our work, but as you're aware, Road, we get in and out without leaving a calling card, such as we did in Colorado and California. When we get in close and personal, we leave no one alive."

"What about Mona, and people like her? What about the ones you rescue?" There must be something. My hands clench in frustration.

"We minimise contact." He's thoughtful for a moment. "Can't rule it out, I suppose. Duty—"

"Check into all our cases where we could be identified," Duty finishes for him. "I'll focus on the ones where you were in the field."

"Have we got time?" I slam my hand down on the table. "How long until they take another finger from her?"

"We haven't time." Pip turns eyes on me which look so cold

I almost shiver. "What I picked up from that video is that they're cruel fuckers and don't care how much they hurt her. We risk her losing more fingers, or what next, her whole fuckin' hand? So, no, you're right. We've got to get into the driver's seat on this. Only one option, I give myself up."

"No." Snatcher's voice is firm. "Not having you do that Pip, it's too fuckin' dangerous. And it won't help Swift, you'll only be bringing her death warrant forward. Once they've got you, they've no use for her."

"Kill her?" Stormy says. "The first man who tries to touch her will lose his hand and his dick."

I look his way, and for a second see a hint of sympathy in his eyes, and wonder whether his comment was to help me. Or maybe it's the truth. But for Swift to observe one of the men was large, it's something to be concerned about. Someone had had to hold her down to take that digit off. She wouldn't have sacrificed it voluntarily.

I'm not the only one to believe she's got limitations. "She couldn't dodge a bullet, Stormy. She's not fuckin' super-woman," Rascal scoffs.

I sit, feeling blood drain from my face. I think it's only just catching up with me just how much danger Swift is in.

"She wouldn't want you to do that anyway, Pip," Thor puts in. "She's a fuckin' soldier."

"My life's worth more than hers?" Pip snarls. "Fuck that, Thor. And fuck any of you assholes who think that."

"You go in," Preacher says firmly, "they'll kill both of you. Won't help her." Pip narrows his lips, as the sergeant-at-arms continues, "He disguised his voice." Preacher points to the screen with his finger. "And he stays behind the camera. That suggests you could recognise him, or something about him could ring a bell. If he was short, perhaps, or exceptionally tall."

Pip rubs his chin, at least Preacher's got him back to thinking. "If there was anything like that, Swift would have told us. But if you're right about the voice, that suggests I would know it. Which narrows the field as I normally stay out of sight."

"Have you, as Swift would say, thrown a spanner into anybody's works?" Bolt asks.

Pip's gaze rises. "Do we ever do anything else?"

Bolt shrugs.

Having calmed the rushing of blood through my ears, I try to think objectively. "What would be big to Swift? Why did she comment on it?" I'm thinking of the only description she's given.

"Large, big, huge," Pip expands. "Her signs were restricted as she didn't want to let them know she was communicating. But for her to make that observation, he's probably a giant of a man, and one who might be able to overpower her."

"She can take a man twice her size down without breaking a sweat." My eyebrows draw down. "So this means his size is significant."

"They were all white," Cowboy puts in. "Else she'd have mentioned it. One large, one black, that sort of thing." It's a good point looking at what she didn't say.

"Lot of white men around." Snatcher pointedly looks around the all-white table. "Doesn't mean fuck."

"But isn't it something to think about? Sure, Brute is black, and we all know the history of the club when skin colour was important." No longer, thank fuck. "We're clutching at straws here. Somehow these clues must add up." I find myself tugging at my fingers in the way I've so often watched Drummer do. "One, you might be able to recognise a voice, two, there's a man who's obviously so strikingly large that Swift commented on it, three, they think she's a club whore and don't know she's a member—"

"And have no suspicions about her background," Snatcher

butts in. "Else they'd have secured her better. They're not data experts."

I raise my chin at him. "Which also supports the view that they could be white supremacists. Women are no threat to them."

"The talk about raping her adds into that," Stormy says. "That's the kind of threat they'd make. Their sort tend to control women with sex. I find myself agreeing with Road." His tone suggests, reluctantly.

Duty starts tapping on his laptop. I notice Pip staring off into space.

"We been up against any white supremacists?" Snatcher asks him, as his own brow creases.

Honor suddenly whistles loudly. "My man at the lab came through with a match on the DNA."

"Name?"

"Christian McGregor." Honor looks at the man by his side. "Birthdate, June 10, 1990."

"Kincaid," Pip says out of the blue. "But he's dead."

Duty's eyes narrow and he looks at Pip, then back at his laptop.

"Did you pull that name out of the air, or was it triggered by McGregor?" Thor asks, which is what I was wondering as well.

Pip shakes his head as though to clear it. "McGregor rang no bells. But Kincaid fits the profile."

"Any known connection?"

"I'm searching." Duty glares at Honor. "Give me a moment."

"Kincaid," Snatcher repeats, as though a brainwave has struck. "And the mark wasn't black, but Hispanic. Ivan Dengra. It was his daughter. We got her back. Well, you did. It was one of those times Thor and I were visiting the mother chapter."

"Yeah, that's him. She'd been taken to make a point."

"She returned home pregnant."

I take a breath. "She'd been fuckin' raped."

"That's where it gets complicated." Pip sifts through some of the paperwork in front of him and finds what he's looking for. "She was groomed by Kincaid. He, as you suggested, all white." He slides a photo toward me.

"Christ, she's a kid."

"Fifteen. She was 'in love'." Snatcher uses air quotes. "She thought she was special and running away, they'd completely fooled her. Ivan Dengra was loaded, started with nothing, ended up with a chain of furniture stores. Kincaid didn't think an immigrant, legal or not, deserved to have made a success of his life, while he had nothing. Or, no jobs that he wanted to work. He set out to destroy him."

Pip nods. "So he groomed the daughter, turned her against her father, then encouraged her to run away with him. Her head was turned by attracting the attention of someone who was much older."

"He asked for a ransom?"

Duty's tapping his chin. "He did."

Pip again raises and dips his head. "Snatcher, as he said, was away, so I led the team myself. It was me who shot Kincaid, unfortunately in front of the kid. I really thought I was getting somewhere, talking him down. But suddenly he produced a gun and pointed it at her." He looks up. "Sure, he'd hate my guts. But he's dead. He was the only person there at the time. He didn't need anyone else, as the girl trusted him. I think we're on the wrong track. All we've got is a tremulous link with white supremacy. Keep digging into other cases, Duty."

Bolt purses his lips, clearly remaining on the Kincaid topic. "Dengra's kid's reaction wasn't what we'd expected. Instead of being pleased at being rescued, we'd killed the love of her young life. She went crazy. Hadn't calmed down by the time we returned her to her father."

"Do you know what happened?" I prompt. "Did she continue the pregnancy?"

"Baby born six months later." Duty nods. "I checked up. Would be getting on for a year old now. Oh, fuckin' shit."

"What?" Pip sits forward.

"Kid died a few weeks back—cause of death, heart failure. Looks like he was born with problems. Hang on a minute… Fuck, you're not going to believe this, Prez. Kincaid had a brother who was one of the mourners at the funeral." A raft of questions are thrown at Duty, but he holds up his hand, then looks up, shaking his head. "Kincaid's brother was his twin."

"Shit. The kid died?" Pip takes a moment to let that sink in, then shakes his head. "And his father's twin brother was at the funeral? How the fuck did Dengra allow him to get close?" he asks, without expecting an answer. "Something's off about this. It might be a red herring, but it's worth getting our net out. Keep digging, Duty, concentrate on Kincaid for now. Honor and Stormy, you sift through everything else." Abruptly he stands. "I've got a fuckin' phone call to make." He leaves without another word.

"I'm going to get some food on." Cowboy also rises to his feet. "An army marches on its stomach."

Honor signals at Duty and jerks his head toward Stormy. "Come on, let's go get our shovels out."

I wait to see what everyone else is going to be doing, but Snatcher indicates that Piston should start the video rolling again. I hate watching it, but can't pull my eyes away from the woman on the screen, trying to see any clues that we might have missed.

"What's that?" Bolt stands. Taking over the control from Piston, he winds it back a few seconds, then starts it playing again and pauses. "Is that a tattoo?"

So many of us crowd toward the screen it takes a moment for each of us to get a good look. When I get there, I'm slapped on my back by Thor. "You were fuckin' right, Road. That's part of a swastika on his wrist." The he, in this instance, is the man holding the tablet that Swift is reading from.

A thought occurs to me. "With all this super-duper technology around, have you ever thought about tracking devices?

"She didn't have her phone with her."

"Nah, I mean one implanted."

Piston barks a laugh. "A GPS tracker? Doesn't exist yet, Road. When it does, we'll be the first to know. Make our jobs a fuckin' lot easier."

"Yeah, get our clients to chip their kids like they do their dogs."

I feel a bit stupid. "I thought I heard—"

"Myths, Brother." Snatcher shakes his head. "It's all about battery power and how to recharge it."

"You can have a microchip, but that only stores information." Thor waits until I confirm I understand with a dip of my chin. "We'd be all over that shit if it existed. And we do have tracking devices, on our bikes, of course, and we can use them set in pins if we think we need to use them, or Swift could have worn one on a necklace. But seriously, I don't think we thought there was much danger of something like this."

"You ever thought you'd be kidnapped as you were a Satan's Devil, Road?" Snatcher asks.

When I'm about to reply, of course I didn't, I realise he's got a point. And Swift, in particular, would believe she was invincible.

There's a knock at the door. When it's opened, Igor appears.

"I've found something on the security feed. I sent it through to here." He nods at the remote still in Bolt's hand.

"What we looking at, Prospect?" Preacher asks, his face lined. He waves for Igor to stay.

"Wait a sec. Watch here." Clearly used to the devices in here, Igor uses a laser pointer, aiming it onto a taller building a couple of streets over. "Keep looking here. There it is, see?"

There was a definite glint from the roof. Someone using binoculars, perhaps?

"Brute's gone to check it out," Igor says. "It was from last week, so unlikely he'll find much."

"Good thinking, checking it out. But that's how they could have seen Swift coming in and out, and assumed she was a club whore not a member."

It's at that point when Pip re-enters the room. He asks Igor to round everyone up again. When they arrive, things finally start coming together.

Pip kicks it off. "Okay. So I've spoken to Dengra. When the baby was born, Saul Kincaid turned up. Dengra wouldn't let him near the kid at first. Obviously he was suspicious as hell, but Saul vowed he had no connection to his brother, that they'd parted ways some years before. But he'd somehow heard he'd fathered a boy shortly before he'd died. As he had no remaining family and seemed to have a good job and no connection to crime, he allowed Saul to see the baby. From then he became a doting uncle. He showed no inappropriate moves toward his daughter, and to be honest, reading between the lines, she blamed him, her father, for getting the man she loved killed. I think it's fair to say that Saul Kincaid befriended her as he wanted revenge. He was a regular visitor to their house, then just disappeared. They haven't seen him for a few weeks which is unusual."

"How would he have found you, Prez?" Snatcher asks.

Pip's face darkens but shakes his head.

Duty takes over. "Been looking into Saul Kincaid. He wasn't the angel he led Dengra to believe. All the background information he provided had been fake. He hadn't been an upstanding citizen working a decent job, he'd been in the pen. But somehow was able to fake evidence to show otherwise. Someone created a history for him which I managed to find. It was quite impressive. On a first look, it would have fooled anyone."

"So," Pip resumes as things start falling into place. "He either has skills himself, or has a friend who can work with data. Dengra did say he was pretty interested in the story of how the girl had been rescued. When I asked him outright, he said he saw no reason for not giving the details of how they contacted us. Said Saul genuinely seemed unsurprised his brother had met a bad end, and that he was grateful he'd been stopped before the kid had disappeared. I presume that's how he traced us. The daughter knew what I looked like and had reason to hate me. Whoever works with data might have searched for my image."

"And he thought as we were in the business of rescuing women, the best way to get your attention was to threaten a 'club girl'." Snatcher growls.

"I looked into Christian McGregor, the man who's DNA we found. He was in the pen at the same time as Saul Kincaid." Stormy gives that snippet of information.

"Keep looking, Stormy. See who else was in there, who was in cahoots with the pair."

I notice Pip looks tired and know he must be feeling responsible. But being closer to naming a culprit, doesn't mean we're closer to finding Swift. "Now we think we know who," I ask, "how do we go about rescuing Swift?"

"Ain't that the million-dollar question," Stormy grumbles. "Road's right, that's our focus. What have you dug up, Duty?"

"Fuck all at present. We've found where he was, which was Washington, but there's no trail from there."

"He's local now," I tell them, pinching the brow of my nose.

"I hate to say this, but that finger was fresh, couldn't have been taken off long or been brought far."

"Courier collected it from the bus station," Snatcher confirms. "So Road's right, he's holding her locally."

Duty raises his chin. "Gears is searching for recent rentals. He might turn something up."

"Look for something with a basement or cellar," I offer. "That will narrow it down a lot."

"If I offer myself in exchange, there's no guarantee that they'll direct me to where they're holding Swift." Pip seems to be pondering what to do. "This isn't like last time when Kincaid was able to subdue one young girl by himself. This time there are four men, and they could split up."

"There's no benefit to you giving yourself up, Pip. I agree, you might be sent elsewhere and they'll simply kill Swift. Give us some time to work the Kincaid angle. We can rethink if that doesn't work." Snatcher is talking sense. I want Swift back, but don't see how Pip sacrificing himself would achieve that.

I sit, listening, thinking, all the while worried about Swift and what she's going through. *Is she having panic attacks because she can't hear anything?* They all seem to think she's strong, that nothing will faze her, but I've seen her in the dead of the night. I know about PTSD and how debilitating it can be. Not being able to hear what's being said, not being able to relax and sleep because someone might sneak up on her is going to be terrifying, however capable she is of fighting anyone off.

"Got him," Stormy suddenly announces, looking up from his laptop. "The big guy? It's a fella called Weston Hughes. He was released from the pen shortly before Kincaid. He was in for aggravated assault. He's a heavyweight boxer, or was." He turns his laptop around. On it is the photo of a fucker I wouldn't want to come across in a dark alley at night. Or daylight for that matter. No wonder Swift pointed him out.

"You sure it's him?"

"Can't be certain. But it's a coincidence. He's also missed his last appointment with his probation officer."

It's Duty's turn now to point to his screen. He reads something, then states, "Okay, Gears has found there have been six rentals in the past two weeks with basements or cellars."

"Let's go check them out."

"Not so fast, Road." Pip's eyes narrow. "Where are they, Duty? Can you narrow it down at all?"

Duty presses a few keys and the big screen on the wall lights up behind him. "This is the first. Rented by a Ms Masterson."

It's a smart little two-storey house halfway down a residential road, it looks old. More modern houses are close by.

"Swift didn't say she'd seen a woman." Thor is shaking his head dismissively. "And the neighbours would be too close. Too many people to notice comings and goings."

"Risky, I agree. Next one, Duty." Pip waves his hand.

The next one is a farmhouse along a dirt track. A bit rundown, the sort of place that would be an ideal setting for a horror movie. Just the sight of it makes us all sit up straighter.

"That looks hopeful. Who rented it?"

"Father and son, a Max Haven Senior and Junior. Mind you, that's a stretch." Duty pulls up two pictures. "Here are their drivers' license photos." He puts up a photo showing a man in his sixties.

"Senior," Bolt states.

Ignoring the comment, Duty puts up the next photo. It's a man two decades older, and makes a comment of his own. "This is Max Haven Senior."

While others sigh or shake their heads, Pip observes, "It could still be a front."

"Worth sending the drone up," Stormy suggests. "See who's really there."

I tap the table with my fingers. "We're dealing with white supremacists. I hate to say it, but they're just the type. Could be they're providing cover for Kincaid."

"Any links or connections?"

"Working on it, Prez." Duty frowns.

"I still say the drone could get information. Numbers of cars for a start."

"Drone won't see fuck if they're holed up with Swift. If they need supplies, one of the Havens could go get them. And look at the barns. If there are extra cars, they'll be hidden away and hard to spot."

"I think it's worth paying a visit with the drone and then going inside if necessary." Prez accepts Duty's observations. "But let's go through the others you got first."

Instead of thinking we're getting somewhere, I'm getting more frustrated. "They could be squatting. They might not have rented a place legally."

"We know that, Road. But for now, this is all we've got. We could sit here playing with our dicks, ride around aimlessly not having a clue where we're going, or get out searching possible locations." Snatcher doesn't look happy.

I stare at him for a moment, then have to admit he's got a point. I suppose doing something is better than nothing.

"Next location," Pip instructs.

That's a bust, the next is a possible. After viewing them all, we end up with four where, if, and it's a big if, if, they've actually rented a place where they might be holding Swift. Out of them all, I tend to think the Haven's farmhouse is the most likely. It seems I'm not the only one.

"Let's take a drone and get it sent up to see what's going on at that farmhouse. Stormy, Preacher and Thor will go."

"I'd rather go alone," Stormy complains, at the same time as I raise my hand.

"I want in on this."

"No, to you both!" Pip thunders. "Stormy, you'll need back up. If she's there, you can provide sniper cover and Preacher and Thor will approach. Outside look only." He glares at Stormy and ignores me. "I want Snatcher and Piston at the second location, Rascal and Cowboy at the third. The fourth needs checking, but we've all agreed it's unlikely. It's also further away. Road and Bolt you can ride out there. You all look, listen and learn. If any of you think you've seen something, make contact damn fast, and we," he indicates himself, Duty and Honor, "will be ready to ride. I'll also get Grinch, Goofy and Mystic on standby. They won't want to miss out on this."

I think the one I'm supposed to head for is an absolute waste of time. The fact that Pip is sending me there suggests he too thinks there'll be damn all to find. I get the feeling he doesn't want me to be the one finding Swift.

"It's an Airbnb, Prez," I complain. "Look at it, it's a cute country house by a lake. It's got to be in high demand with vacation types. I'm certain we're not going to find kidnappers there."

"And you know this, how?" Pip challenges. "Look, Road, it has to be excluded. It was rented in the right time span. Just ride out, check it and see. That's all we can do now. I'm not ready to dismiss it without giving it a look."

Bolt's meeting my eyes with a sympathetic look. Like me, he doesn't seem hopeful.

"Until we've got a location, we'll stay back in case of further communications with the kidnappers. Preach, everyone goes out without their cuts, but with Kevlar vests and full communication. You know the drill."

"Right, Prez," the sergeant-at-arms agrees.

"Surveillance only right now. If you find evidence of where Swift's being held, you wait, observe, but don't engage, not until you have backup. We're up against at least four men," Pip reminds us, his eyes scanning each man in turn. "The important thing is to bring her home safe. Any rescue has got to be coordinated carefully." He levels his stare at Stormy. "Which means no one's to go rogue."

I check the details again. The vacation rental I'm being sent to is fifty miles away. The farmhouse Thor, Preacher and Stormy are heading to is much closer, and it's likely Swift will be rescued, or, *fuck I hope not,* killed, before I can get there.

My eyes glare daggers at Pip, but he turns away, and starts having a few private words with Snatcher. Everyone else gets up to leave.

I can't keep silent. I stand and approach him. He sees me, turns away from his VP and raises an eyebrow.

"It's fuckin' obvious you want me out of the way," I rasp out. "What, you don't trust me? I know you probably work as a team, but I can fight. I want to be there if we find Swift. Pip, reconsider, please."

25

Road...

"I don't want you out of the fuckin' way," Pip snarls, standing so fast I take a step back. I notice Snatcher takes the opportunity to leave as Pip's finger begins to poke at my chest. "You're the fastest fuckin' rider I've got along with Bolt and have the fastest bikes if you take that ZX14R. You can be there and back fast. I use the skills my team has got, Road, and riding happens to be yours. I'm trusting you with this. I'm sending you and Bolt out as I know you've both got fuckin' brains and aren't afraid to use them. If you find trouble, you'll assess it, and won't engage. I know you don't expect to find anything, but eliminating possibilities is just as important, and this place is interesting enough for me to want to check it out."

"It's only a two-week rental," I remind him. "Which ends the day after tomorrow."

"So? They could plan for this to be over by then. The timescale's not impossible." When I roll my eyes, he continues, "They're not going to let her go, Road. I've been in this business long enough to know that. We're up against time."

"You reckon they might move her, sell her or something before we find her?"

"It's a risk, Road." When his eyes meet mine, it's clear to see how much he's worrying.

I'd assumed Swift would be held until the kidnappers had gotten what they wanted, which seems to be Pip. I turn away, forcing my mind away from the possibility they might have already harmed her again, making more videos to release in the future.

I walk away from Pip, snatch the piece of paper which Duty had written the location of the address I'm being sent to check out up off the table, and walk out.

"Road. C'mere." Preacher's voice calls and summons me to a room I hadn't entered before. He opens a closet and pulls out some body armour, holding it out so I can try it on. As before, it fits. He then opens a locked drawer and tells me to select one of the array of handguns I see there. I choose a Glock, a model I'm used to, and weigh it in my hands.

Giving a nod of approval at my selection, he then hands me the right ammunition. "Your leg going to hold up, okay?"

I hadn't actually given my damaged limb much thought today, finding Swift had been more important than worrying about myself. "Yeah, I'll strap it up before I go." My tone is offhand. Now he's mentioned it, it's aching, but I haven't got time to worry about that.

"Pip's right." His sharp eyes sum up my mood. "We've got to check everything out. Go to the old clubhouse—Bolt will show you the way in case you can't remember—pick up the Kawasaki. Mystic will already have fixed it up with a place to store the Glock and ammo." At my unenthusiastic nod, he pushes at my arm. "Sooner you go, sooner you'll be back and hopefully one of us will have found Swift." He purses his lips. "If you want my opinion, I doubt we'll find them at any of the rentals, but we still got to check them out."

"I just—"

"You got a thing for her." His words are accompanied by an expression of sympathy. "Look, Swift doesn't hook up with members of the team, just to warn you. She's a different type of woman, more like one of us than I thought possible. Not saying you can't try your hand when we get her back, just warning you she'll be a tough nut to crack. And it might be your nuts that crack before she does."

I know all that.

He's right in everything he's said, not the least that I'll have no chance with Swift. A man like me would only ever be able to dream of someone like her. He's also right that the faster we get going, the sooner we can return. This is a wild goose chase, I can feel it in my gut. If she's being held in any of the premises we've identified so far, I just know the farmhouse is the most likely. It even looks the part for fuck's sake. It hadn't escaped me that's where Pip's sending the enforcer and the sergeant-at-arms. But Pip's also correct, on that ZX14R I can outrun anything on the road, and I'll be twisting that throttle to get to this place and back again. Bolt, I've already seen, has a Ninja which I presume he knows how to ride.

Having detoured back to my room to leave my cut and strap my leg, I waste no time returning downstairs. Then, alongside Bolt, I ride my own bike to the old clubhouse where I find Mystic crouching beside the bike I'm hoping to ride.

"Problem?" My brow creases as I ask him.

"Nah." Mystic stands, rubbing grease off his hands with an already dirty rag which he then places in his back pocket. "Just checking. You'll find her good, Brother."

Casting a fond eye back toward my parked-up Harley, I take the key for the Kawasaki and carefully balance as I swing my leg over the saddle. I start the engine. While the sound isn't throaty, nor has the deep throbbing unique and distinctive pop-pop-pause of a Harley as the pistons fire, it sounds powerful, and the engine vibrates between my thighs like a horse raring to be let loose on the gallops. Despite my disheartening feelings about my mission and my concerns about Swift, part of me is eager to have a chance to ride this machine.

"Good luck, Brother." Mystic slaps my Kevlar-covered back, then steps away.

Feeling naked without my cut, but agreeing if we're breaking speed limits I want no identifying insignia on me, I raise my chin at Bolt, then kick down into first, gently let out the clutch, giving the throttle just a light squeeze. The bike moves off smoothly, screaming its power with a snarling shriek.

I allow myself a few minutes as I drive through the city to get used to the handling, finding the bike stable and easy to ride. Keeping an eye on me, Bolt matches my speed. By the time I've hit open country, I'm already at one with the bike. It's now I open the throttle. Like that horse it had resembled before, the acceleration as it kicks up the pace almost takes my breath away. *Speed.* It's what I live for. Bends in the road? Well, I can lay that thing down almost horizontally.

Oh fuck. There's a bang like a gunshot. Bolt, on the inside, has swerved onto the shoulder struggling with his bike, but managing to stay shiny side up. I slam on the brakes and stop a few yards ahead. Running back to him, I notice the problem immediately....

"Blowout?"

"Fuck it. Yes. I'm fuckin' sorry, Road." Bolt's kicked the stand down and kicks at the remnants of his tyre on the road.

"It can't be helped. You stay and get help. I'll go on my own."

"I'll call Mystic and Grinch. One of them can go with you, Brother, and the other can bring the crash truck and get me home."

I eye the road that lies ahead of me. "You know how I ride, Bolt. I'll get there and back before they even arrive. She won't be there. I'll be fine on my own."

He grimaces and doesn't look happy, but it takes him only a second before he nods. "I agree with you. This place isn't worth the time. Go on, then, but take fuckin' care."

I clasp his arm, thinking again how real it feels, while he uses his other to slap my back. Then, I'm back on the ZX14R.

I'm not going to waste time. Riding even faster than I had done with Bolt, I twist that throttle hard, laughing when I catch the attention of a patrol car, passing it at one hundred and twenty miles an hour. My right hand pulls down. The bike screams like a Formula One racing car, and the cops are left in my dust. I grin.

Shit. This bike lives up to its reputation. It approaches the road like a surgeon would use a scalpel, with one hundred percent precision, nicely stable, well-balanced at any speed. The only thing I'm taking some getting used to is the forward leaning riding position, whereas on my trials bike and on my Harley I'm used to sitting straighter. Still, this way, I'm streamlined with my machine as though I'm in tune with it.

The remainder of the fifty miles fly by. Nearing my destination, I pull off the road, tap my GPS map, then set off again, following the instructions the voice speaks through my earpiece. It's not long until I come to where the vacation rental is located. Pausing before getting close, I stop to peruse the area, raising my shades to take a better look. The building must be set back amongst the trees as it's impossible to see the cabin from here. From the picture I saw, it was set back against the hillside, almost built into the rock. To my left is a lake that looks great for fishing. It's picturesque, and nothing to resemble a setting where a kidnapped victim would be held.

There's a practical looking SUV parked close to the lake,

and shading my eyes with my hand, I notice a lone fisherman casting a line. *He could be from the house.* Or, maybe a local. At the least, he gives me an excuse to draw close.

I ride on, parking next to the other vehicle, noting it's as ancient looking as, I find, is the fisherman himself when I approach.

He turns at my footsteps and narrows his eyes.

"Fishing good here?" I nod toward the lake, staring out across it, shading my eyes with my hand.

"Not today," he grumbles, pointing to his empty net.

I give him a glance of commiseration. "You from around here?"

"Yeah. You?"

"Just moved to Utah." It's a truthful reply. "I'm checking out the area."

"You fish?"

"Always wanted to give it a try." I shift on my leg, exaggerating my limp. "Can't do active sports anymore, so need to slow things down."

He nods, then turns back to his rod. I step back, giving him plenty of room as he casts again.

"Heard there was a vacation rental near here. Wanted to check the location out before I booked it. Places advertised on Airbnb sometimes turn out not to live up to what they're supposed to be."

"Hmm. Only rental up here is old Pete's place. Been done up well, but then, they spent a fortune on it. Pricy to rent though, I expect. I doubt it would disappoint."

I shrug, indicating the price is no problem for me. "Anyone there now?"

As I suspected, a local would keep their eye on comings and goings. "Yes. Strange folks."

"Strange?" I draw in a breath and try not to show my heightened interest.

"Never seen them at the lake. You'd think coming to this spot, they'd be down for a bit of fishing."

"Maybe they're into hiking?" I jerk my head at the foothills behind us.

It's his turn to lift his shoulders and lower them. "Up to them what they get up to, I suppose. Pete's family just wants the money from renting it out."

"Have you seen them at all?"

"Why?" He turns and his eyes view me sharply.

Thinking fast, I come up with an excuse. "Just wanted to know if they seemed approachable. I wondered if they'd mind me checking the place out."

"Fella seemed okay. Bit on the quiet side. I've not seen her."

It's a couple. But Swift hadn't mentioned a woman. Sounds like it will be a bust, and the lack of fishing might mean they're a couple on their honeymoon with better things to do than hang around by a lake. Still, I'll take a ride up there and check it out.

I notice the fisherman is looking at me strangely, his rheumy eyes narrowed. "What you wearing under your shirt?"

"Riding body armour," I think fast, giving him an acceptable solution. "Did my leg in coming off my bike. Makes a man more careful."

His quizzical eyes glance at my head. Yeah, if my story was true, I'd be wearing a helmet. But I'm saved from having to come up with an answer as to why I'm so stupid when at that moment, his rod jerks in his hands and his eyes sparkle with excitement. Clearly losing all interest in me, he focuses his attention on the lake in front of him.

Limping back to my bike, I decide I'll ride up to the property, check it out, then head back to base. Should be there in less than an hour. I wonder about calling to check progress on the other locations, but decide to do that when I can confirm I've had no success here. If I'm right, they'll all be focused on the farmhouse. I'm still upset I'm not there with them, but I don't want my call to distract them if they're in the process of extracting Swift.

While it's not a particularly normal thing to do, as the fisherman hadn't seemed to question my desire to view a property I was thinking of staying in for a vacation, I decide that the same excuse would probably suffice if I'm stopped on the property, or could maybe work if, as a last resort and necessary for the process of elimination, I knock on the front door.

Starting my engine, I continue up the paved track, soon breaking out of the trees and into a more open area. I pull over and park, then continue cautiously on foot. Instead of approaching directly, I keep to the circle of trees, following the tree line. The ground is littered with twigs and fallen logs, and I pick my steps with care. Deliberately dislocating my knee had weakened it. The bandage helps, but it's still fragile, and I can't afford to have it pop out now. I could have done with my stick, but hadn't thought to bring it with me, and the Kawasaki's not equipped to carry it anyway.

I stop every so often, casting a glance toward the picturesque property innocently sitting in the midst of a clearing. It's an attractive place and must have cost a fortune to restore as the fisherman had said. It has big glass windows which surely aren't original, and a wrap-around porch that looks new and sturdy. A swing seat gently swings to-and-fro in the breeze. If I were really in the market for somewhere to spend a vacation, there'd be worse places to choose. If it were anywhere close to my price range, which is doubtful.

I concentrate on my feet once more, tossing up whether to make the full circuit or to just say *fuck it* and walk up and bang on the front door. I turn for another furtive look—

Fuck! I'm on the ground. My ribs feel like I've been kicked by a horse. I try to breathe, then try once more. *Christ, my chest is burning.*

While I'm still attempting to get air into my lungs, I feel someone turning me over. "Fuck, Saul. He's wearing body armour. Want me to finish him off with a head shot?"

Opening my eyes fast, I see I'm staring down the barrel of a gun fitted with a silencer and feel hands divesting me of my own weapon.

For an inane moment I want to laugh hysterically, if I was capable of moving at all. I'm in the right place, but instead of rescuing Swift, I'll be meeting Satan much sooner than I expected.

"No." I receive a vicious kick to my side. "Get to your fuckin' feet."

I try. I honestly try. I roll over, get to my hands and knees and then try to push myself up. It's not easy. While the Kevlar had protected me, it hadn't stopped the rib cage over my heart feeling like it's been smashed to smithereens.

Impatient, Saul—at least the dropping of his name confirms Pip had been right in who had taken Swift—indicates to the other man who takes the hint and pulls me roughly the rest of the way to my feet.

"Take off your shirt." The terse instruction is accompanied by the jerk of a second gun that's appeared in the speaker's hand.

"Look, I was interested in this property, was just looking at it to see whether it was going to suit me for a vacation." My words tumble out one after the other. If I take off my shirt and the armour I wear under it, there'll be no hiding who I am. Like all my brothers, I sport a full Satan's Devils back-patch tattoo.

"Wearing body armour?" If anything, my words have only served to make him more impatient.

"I ride a bike, man. It's in case I crash."

But he's not so easy to fool as the fisherman. Another jerk of his head and I lose my choice. My shirt is easily ripped away from my body, the material proving traitorous in its lack of resistance.

"Man, I—"

"Take it fuckin' off."

A knife flashes, and for some reason I don't want them to touch me. I straighten my back and pull down the zipper on the Kevlar vest to which I owe this probably short extension of my life. Glancing down as I do, I see a deep red mark spreading across my chest. I don't pause to examine it, instead, I slip off the vest.

The man who shot me turns me roughly, and I hear boss man draw in a sharp breath.

"As I fuckin' thought. A fuckin' Devil. Who's with you?"

"No one."

"Want me to check that out?" the man who had shot me asks.

"Yeah. Take West with you. And this time, make sure you fuckin' shoot them in the head."

His words make me relieved Bolt isn't with me.

"And this one?"

Saul's brow creases and he's quiet for a moment, then he raises his eyes to mine. "Guess you already dodged a bullet, maybe it's your lucky day." His expression doesn't suggest my luck is going to last long as to his companion he says, "Search him."

With a gun in my face and bare chested, I can do no more than hold out my arms. My phone is removed from the pocket of my jeans. When his fingers try to probe deeper, I shift my body. "Careful of my junk, for fuck's sake."

The man's hand moves as though he doesn't want to be accused of fondling my cock. I suppress any sign of pleasure, then wait as my knife is taken from its ankle sheath. Then, wearing only my jeans and boots, my shredded t-shirt left lying where it was discarded, I'm frogmarched up to the house. Well, frog-limped in my case.

"West?" Saul calls out.

The biggest man I've ever seen in my life approaches. Oh, I've seen bigger, but their bulk was fat, not muscle. Even if I wasn't still winded, I doubt whether I'd be able to take him on, or not without knowing the techniques Swift uses. He'd beat me to a pulp in seconds.

"Take our *guest* down to the cellar and make sure he's secured. Then go with Dean and check out the perimeter, see if we've got other visitors. Find this asshole's bike and bring it here."

Well, at least I now know the name of the man who shot me. *Dean.* I file it away in case I ever get out of here. Chances are not looking good at the moment. They look even worse when West, from behind, takes hold of both my arms and effortlessly lifts me, half carrying, half pushing me toward a doorway beneath the stairs. He kicks it open then unceremoniously pushes me down a flight of bare stone steps.

Unable to prevent myself falling, I tuck and roll as I make an awkward landing at the bottom, banging hard against a door. Somehow my luck lasts and my knee doesn't dislocate. Which is good, as seconds later, with his boot heavily on my back, West keeps me immobile as he shoots a bolt and turns the key in a padlock, dragging me into a cellar without caring about any additional injuries. His foot is replaced by his knee on my spine keeping me prone as he expertly zip ties my hands behind me. He then proceeds to restrain my ankles in the same manner, then, rendering me completely helpless, he hog-ties me.

I'm unable to move.

Heavy steps thumping up the wooden stairs tell me he's leaving. It's then I hear a voice ask tentatively, as though disbelieving, "Road?"

26

───────

Swift...

How long have I been here?

I have no idea how many hours have gone by or if it's day or night. That light bulb keeps burning, giving me no indication whether the sun's setting or rising. I presume at least one night has passed, maybe two, but part of my torture appears to consist of them giving me no way of knowing.

If they switched the light off, I might be able to close my eyes and get some sleep, as it turning back on would wake me. But I haven't had that luxury. So, for what I suspect is getting on for forty-eight hours, I've only catnapped, keeping both eyes open.

I need sleep.

Sleep deprivation was part of my training, a way of trying to get me to break. I hadn't then, and I won't now.

I can survive.

I'm already missing a finger. As time passes, I know it won't be long before they come back for me, probably to chop off more body parts to persuade Pip to give himself up in exchange, or using other methods I'd find equally unsavoury. I couldn't risk missing them approach, as the next time, I'll go down fighting, and hopefully take at least one of them with me.

Pip won't give himself up for me. He knows as well as I do, now that I've seen their faces, they can't leave me alive. Instead, he'll be concentrating on finding out who took me and instigating a rescue. I've just got to be patient until the Satan's Devils come. Just as when I was part of a squad in the army, the Devils will never leave a man behind. Or, a woman in my case. One thing I've learned since riding with them, once the brothers got over the surprise, they accepted me, judging me only on my ability to fight and ride, and to live their life. I became one of them. They'll be coming for me.

Partly to keep myself awake, partly from needing to do anything that might see me get out of here alive, I keep working at that ring attached to the wall. While neither kicks nor tugs seem to shift it, I can't give up, remaining optimistic that eventually it will loosen. I have to remain positive.

Without being able to hear footsteps overhead, means I don't have any forewarning that someone is approaching. It feeds a growing fear that they've already gone and have forgotten all about me. Now Pip's been given the message, I might be of no more use. I'll die here, my body simply left to rot chained to this wall. That hadn't been the end I'd ever envisaged. Die in battle, yes, a shot to the head by an insurgent who'd snuck up on me, even having something go wrong with a parachute or abseil line. Never had I dreamed I'd die tied up like a dog.

I'd give anything, sell my soul, to be able to hear and know what's going on. I redouble my efforts, trying to get loose. *If they've already gone...*

When did they last feed me? The rumbling of my stomach suggests it was long ago.

They might have left the house.

I've gotten into a routine. Pull, kick, tug, then jerk and waggle the chain to see if it's loosened at all, then glance at the door. Pull, kick, tug, jerk, waggle, glance. Rinse and repeat. Ten times, a hundred, a thousand perhaps. My muscles are screaming and sore. Pull, kick, tug, jerk, waggle, glance....

There's nothing I can hear to alert me something is going to happen, but this time I glance, I see the door shudder as though something heavy has landed against it. *Is it now? Have the Devils arrived?*

While every fibre of my being hopes that it is, I suppress my delight just in case I'm to be disappointed. When the door opens, I find I'm half right and half wrong. The Devils, or at least one of them, has at least found me, but as a rescuer, he's clearly failed. When Tiny, as I call the large man in my head, has finished with him, Road is trussed like a Christmas turkey, and the way he looks is as though the stuffing has already been beaten out of him. Tiny then leaves without a backward glance.

"Road?" I tentatively ask in case my eyes are deceiving me.

Hog-tied, Road rolls onto his side, and it's only then his eyes find me. A half-smile appears on his face, then he grimaces, and if I could hear, I would suspect he's let out a groan. *He's hurt.*

It's not hard to see why. There's an enormous bruise on his naked sternum, one I've seen before, one I've had occasion to feel and so know how much it bloody well hurts. While body armour can save you from being killed, the punch of the bullet is a son of a bitch.

"Are the others here?" I ask eagerly. "Are they hurt, injured..." I can't bring myself to voice the last option. *Or dead.* "Is Pip here?"

Road's shaking his head. *But to which question?* I backtrack and ask again slowly.

"Is the team with you?"

A shake.

There must be someone. Pip wouldn't have sent him out on his own. "One person, or two?" I add hopefully, knowing Tiny's probably a two-man job on his own.

Again Road's head moves side to side. *Did Road follow a clue and stupidly not let anyone else know?*

Road's moving nearer, flopping like a landed fish on the floor. It would be comical were the situation not so dire. He's close enough for me to touch him now, and he's mouthing something at me, using exaggerated movements.

Yet again berating myself that I never learned to lip read, I shake my head. He starts thrusting his hips up toward me.

Oh God. Typical man. Well, if he thinks I'm in any mood for... *Road wouldn't.* Despite our last conversation, Road wouldn't be asking me to give him a hand job, not in the situation he's in, and not with that look of desperation on his face as though he's trying to get through to me. Chained as I am, I can't get my head close enough to him so I can hear him speak, and something tells me he wouldn't want to shout anyway.

He mouths the words again, this time jerking his head at his groin area. My eyes look down. His zipper is up, his button buttoned, his pockets... I try out the word, "Poc-ket," feeling my lips form the same shape as his had done. "Pocket? Something in your pocket?" A handcuff key would be great about now.

I indicate his right, he shakes his head, and nods to the other side. I'm conscious my hand's getting very close to the part of his body I've been thinking far too much about when I feel something that I didn't expect.

My eyes go wide. I don't dare breathe as I slide them out, feeling something totally unexpected and amazingly wonderful as well. *My precious hearing aids.* They must have searched him. How the fuck did he manage to keep them from finding them? Sloppy, not a mistake I would make, but I'm not going to complain at being kidnapped by amateurs.

I don't hesitate to put them in and turn them on.

But Road's not yet done with his surprises. "My left boot," he states, then rolls onto his stomach and flip flops closer until he can get his boot in reach of my hands. "No, not the boot itself, the heel. See that pin head? Pull it out."

I do. My eyes growing even wider as what emerges from his boot is a long, thin stiletto. I waste no time cutting through the zip tie holding his feet to his hands, then freeing his feet. He changes to a sitting position, stretching his legs in front of him with a groan, then manages to offer me his hands. When I release them from their ties, he stretches his arms, flexing his muscles.

As soon as he's shaken life back into his hands, he meets my eyes and says the words which come as music to my ears. "Let's get you free."

I jangle the chain and pull at the iron ring in the wall. "Believe me, I've tried." But maybe between the two of us we could succeed.

But he grins and shakes his head. Instead of helping me tug, he sits beside me, taking my hand and placing it in his lap. It draws my eyes to his fly, and I try to concentrate on the cuff around my wrist, realising his intention.

"Can you pick it?"

"Let's find out." His brow creases and his eyes narrow in concentration as he places the tip of the stiletto into the lock. I sit stock still, already knowing the weapon is sharp.

Hardly daring to breathe, I watch. It's only a second until there's a snick, and the cuff opens. Immediately I rub my wrist, then, realising I'm free, I fling my arms around my rescuer.

"I love you right now," I declare, immediately wanting to

snatch my words back. *I don't hug or make emotional declarations.*

"Only right now?" His voice is full of amusement, and he smiles.

Taking my arms back fast, I let them drop by my sides and redden, remembering all the hours I spent thinking about him. "Well, at the moment you've made me feel pretty good."

His eyes sharpen, and his mirth fades, but still his tone is light as he leans in. "When we're out of here, I could make you feel even better."

As if moving all by itself with my brain incapable of getting it to follow a more sensible instruction, my now free hand touches the side of his face, noting how his skin feels soft and warm to the touch. My breath comes unevenly. "That would be a huge mistake, Road. I'm not looking for a relationship."

His larger hand covers mine, holding it to his cheek. "What makes you think I am? Fuck, Swift, you make me horny as hell, and I may be being overly optimistic, but I think you feel the same way. What's worse? Partners who dance around each other, getting distracted because we're turned on, or partners who've fucked and got it out of their system?"

That's one way of looking at it. But would we ever be able to work together again? The last thing I want is a man who thinks he has to put my needs first. Who labels me as a little woman needing to be protected.

When I fuck, I'm in charge. I dictate the when and how of any liaison. With Road, we'd come together as friends, as equals. Would he cede his control, or would he expect me to give up mine? Unlike my other sexual encounters, I don't think it would all be on one side. It would change us irrevocably.

He's staring at me as though awaiting an answer that I don't know how to provide. Hell, I don't even know which one to give. His closeness, that he was the one to find me, let alone his bared torso which in this situation I find more distracting than I should, makes me want to throw caution to the wind and reply in the affirmative. *Yes, Road, make me yours.* But years of caution, of avoiding the risk of any commitment, makes this a subject I want to discourage.

"We've got to get out of here first," I remind him. "Can you pick that lock?" I point to the door.

He squeezes my hand, and then removes it from where I'd left it, resting against his warm skin. I miss the contact immediately.

"No. It's not a lock, it's bolted and padlocked on the other side. We need to plan. Weston is going to be the one that will be the hardest to take down." He speaks quietly, as though worried someone might be listening. "Is this room bugged?"

"No," I reply thoughtfully. "If it were, they'd be here by now. They were geared up to imprison one person, and unless they thought I was going to talk to myself..." which is a laugh as I couldn't hear myself replying. I smile, then frown again as I dismiss my private joke. "It wouldn't have been worth the bother. But who's Weston?" I think I know but would appreciate the confirmation.

"The big fucker. He's an ex-heavyweight boxer."

That figures, but also verifies he'll know how to fight. "Leave him to me." I know how to take a man of his size down. During my training, they'd thrown everything at me, and I've no doubt now my hands and legs are free, Tiny would be no obstacle. I've got speed. I know the weak points of a man's body. Were I to get into a fistfight with the man, it's probably me who'd go down. So I'll fight dirty, strike when he least expects it, using the techniques I've perfected. I've lost count of the number of males who thought they could better me and who usually lost, particularly when the element of surprise was on my side.

I expect Road to argue, to insist it should be him that takes Tiny on. When he doesn't, and simply nods, he scores another point in his favour.

Road's been staring at me. Now he touches my arm, the one with the injured hand. He eyes the bandage, dark with dried blood. "Fuck, Swift, this—"

"Is fine," I tell him. "Ignore it."

"I hate—"

"I do too," I tell him fast. "But it's done now. Nothing to do but get on with it. Sure, it hurts, but I'll be alright. It's only… a finger."

His eyes meet mine again, then he chuckles softly. "You know, they have no idea who you are. They think you're a club whore."

"I sort of got that impression." It's good to have it validated. I've the element of surprise on my side. It's far from the first time I've been underestimated. But I remind him, more concerned for him than for me, "It's still four against two, Road. And they're armed."

"They expect me to be hog-tied and you to be chained. We'll have seconds when they won't be on their guard. We need to use them wisely."

I like the way he thinks. "They usually come down in pairs. The main man—"

"Saul Kincaid. He's the twin brother of a man Pip dispatched."

Kincaid? I remember something about the case when I'd been a prospect, but not having my patch, hadn't known details. But at least I now know the reason why they're so anxious to get their hands on Prez. I file the information away.

"One of the men who entered your house is Christian McGregor." He pauses, but I've never heard that name before.

When I look mystified, he adds, "He could be the other man here now."

"How did you find that out?" As far as I knew, all the cameras would have stopped working.

"Honor got the DNA in his blood examined."

Idly I rub the graze on my arm. "Blood?" I frown. "I don't remember."

Road grins. "Though you have no recollection, I bet you lashed out when they were chloroforming you. You probably got in a lucky shot."

I hope I broke his fucking nose, but none of the men I've seen looked like they'd had one broken recently. Hopefully, at least, I'd bloodied it.

"Don't know a last name, but the man who shot me is called Dean."

Again, another name which means nothing to me.

Road stands, rubs his leg, then stretches. "It's your play, tell me where you want me."

Again he goes up in my estimation as he asks my advice, acknowledging that I've been trained in combat, and know more about these types of situations than he does. My brothers in the MC would act the same way, but they learned to trust my skills during my prospecting time. Road's going just on what he's seen to date, and what I've told him. It saves time not having to convince him.

I frown, then suggest a few ways this could play out, looking at outcomes and adjustments. If this happens, I'd do this, Road that, if that happens, then we'll work it another way. By the time we finally hear footsteps approaching, I'm pretty certain we both are word perfect in our parts.

Road is lying huddled in a heap, and I'm on the bed, with my hand again appearing restrained in its cuff.

I'd discounted waiting by the door. As soon as it was opened a crack, they'd see I wasn't on the bed which is in direct line of sight and that would be sufficient warning for them to slam that door, and lock it again, leaving us both trapped. Like counters sliding down a snake, we'd be back at square one. What we've got planned should see us on a ladder instead.

Glancing over at Road, I realise now he's here and has freed me, I have a real chance of getting out of here alive.

I owe Road my life. While we wait, my heart beating fast in anticipation, I know there's one way I'd like to thank him.

But can I let myself make that mistake?

27

———

*R*oad...

Awkwardly, I lie on my back as that's the only way I can disguise I'm no longer tied. In my head, I go over Swift's plan once again. It goes against everything I am to let a woman do my fighting for me, and if Weston appears, then my gut tells me it should be me who tries to take him down, keeping Swift out of harm's way. Then I remember how quickly she took out Stormy and know I have to trust her confidence in herself.

When I hear the bolt shoot in the door, I prime my muscles, ready to push myself up.

Three men enter, Weston, a man I haven't seen before who I suspect might be Christian, and Saul Kincaid, twin to his rapist dead brother. It's his eyes that land on me, his mocking grin showing he suspects nothing from the way I'm lying, accepting I could have turned to keep my eye on the door.

"You're a stupid fucker. There's no one with you." He comes over and kicks me hard in the side.

I let out an oomph and will myself to stay still as though I really am incapacitated, knowing I've got to let Swift make her move first. She's only got one chance at taking Weston, lunging for him when he least expects it.

Apart from the narrowing of my eyes, I say nothing. Swift, I notice, doesn't react. *As far as they know, she's still deaf.*

"If Pip knows about this place and you've disappeared, it's time we moved this on." Kincaid's tone is sneering. "Thanks to you I've had an idea. Something to show Pip we're not messing around. And I'll be relying on you to give Pip that message."

When Weston takes a step forward, I start to get an idea of what type of missive he's talking about, one which will leave me in a heap of hurt and pain. But I play dumb, and spit out, "I've told you before, I've no fuckin' idea who this Pip is you're talking about. I only came to check out this house—"

"You're a fuckin' Satan's Devil—"

"From Tucson. My club's in Arizona. I was here looking for a vacation spot just as I told you." It's worth a try, and it keeps his focus on me.

He rolls his eyes. "It's not worth you lying to me. Though, actually, whether you're telling the truth or not, doesn't matter one fuck. Pip will see what I'm capable of when he finds your body in pieces. And you, my dear…" As he turns to Swift, her eyes meet his, but she gives no indication she's heard his words and stays completely passive as he adds, "Can't be bothered to remove your cuff, easier to cut off your hand and send him that."

"What the hell are you talking about?" I have ears and prove there's nothing wrong with my hearing. "Whatever your beef is with this Pip you keep mentioning, why mutilate an innocent girl?"

He gives an evil laugh. "Because I can. Because Pip took something valuable to me. Because he took my other fuckin' half. You got a twin, Road?"

"No." I shake my head as though I have no idea what he's

talking about. "Only family I've got are my brothers back in Tucson."

Kincaid looks unconcerned. "Well, I'm sure Pip will make sure you get back to them. When he's found all the pieces of your body." His cheeks stretch as he grins evilly at the largest of his companions. "Weston here has a beast that needs feeding inside him and chopping off your limbs one by one will soothe him. Shame the girl won't be able to hear you screaming, but bitches do tend to get squeamish about blood. It should teach her a lesson that I'm not one to be messed with."

Chills go through me. *Our plan has to work.* The alternative really doesn't sound attractive.

"Which do you want me to start with?" Weston asks, sounding bored.

Swift may be acting as though she can't understand, but I notice she's showing she's reading the tension, *and danger*, in the room, as she draws up her legs so she's crouching on the bed. The chain jangles, but the men pay her no attention.

"Him," Kincaid decides. "She'll be pissing herself seeing him chopped to bits, wondering whether we're going to be doing the same to her. It'll fuckin' break her."

"I'll break her for you, boss." Tiny—the name Swift coined for him helps me diminish him in my mind—places his meaty paw over his groin, making sure he's in Swift's line of sight. He pumps himself through his pants a couple of times. Even someone who's deaf couldn't fail to get the gist of what he's suggesting. The chain rattles again as though Swift is trying to back away from him.

Kincaid laughs, putting his hand on Tiny's back. "Now hurry up and move this along. We don't know how much time we've got before Pip comes looking for him."

As though I'm still tied, terrified of what Tiny's going to

do, without taking my eyes off Kincaid or the giant standing by his side, I rock and roll my way closer to Swift.

Tiny approaches menacingly and raises a cleaver that's held in his hand. I wonder what he's going to do. *My hands are tied behind me,* or so he thinks, *my legs too. The only thing he can chop off is my head, or through my thigh.* Neither of which I prefer.

As if in slow motion, the cleaver starts to fall…

And sails harmlessly to the floor when Swift karate kicks him in the kidneys, then uses the stiletto to pierce him in the jugular. Tiny's dead, he just doesn't quite know it yet, but with his blood pumping all he can do is drop to the floor with a disbelieving roar, his hands trying to stem the flow.

I roll, grab the cleaver and swing it wildly, catching the third man as he steps forward to tackle Swift. That I'm free takes him by surprise, as does his arm dropping to the floor.

In an urgent tone I hear, "Road, watch out."

Throwing myself to the side, I feel a burn in my arm, and know I've been shot, but it doesn't slow me down.

From the corner of my eye, I see Swift has Kincaid unarmed. *There's another man, and he'll have heard the shot.* I need to stop the one-armed man from being a distraction, so I raise the cleaver again, telling myself he was prepared to watch me be chopped like liver, and putting all my momentum behind it, slash his neck. It's effective. His head is all but severed from his body. It's safe to say he's dead.

"You alright, Saul?" a voice shouts. "What's going on down there?"

"Tell him you're fine," Swift growls, painfully twisting Kincaid's neck.

"Bastards got the jump on—."

Swift applies some sort of pressure hold that cuts his words off, and Kincaid drops to the ground.

"Watch him," she instructs, then goes to the doorway.

I do, my gaze flicking between the unconscious man at my feet and the doorway. *It's an amateur,* I notice, as a gun appears first. Swift has that out of his hand with one chop, but it's fast replaced by a knife.

He parries. She jumps back, her eyes fixed on his face. He feints left, she protects her opposite side.

They dance like that for a few steps, then Swift announces, "Fuck this." One punch and the man who had shot me, Dean, is out like a light, and she's shaking her hand out.

"You alright?"

"Bloody hell. My finger's bleeding again."

Well it's not her finger, but her bloody stump. The sight of it and the reminder of what she's lost has me throat punching Kincaid as he starts to come around. This time, he's out like a light.

"Search Tiny. See if he's got more zip ties," Swift instructs me.

Once again, I have no problem following her lead. Nor when I do find said items and she issues her next commands. "Hog-tie Kincaid and chuck me over some ties." I do, and we soon have them both trussed. I search Kincaid, removing the knife from his ankle sheath and his phone and wallet. For good measure, I remove his boots. Swift copies my actions with the other man.

"What now?" I ask.

"We leave them here. I suspect Pip might appreciate us leaving him something to deal with."

Still in professional mode, she ushers me out of the room. I close and lock the door behind me, then follow her up the stairs. The bruises I obtained on the way down throb to remind me exactly how I descended. That I'm limping heavily doesn't surprise me. My breathing is coming fast, and I feel sweaty, and if I'm honest, a tiny bit dizzy.

When we reach the top, Swift looks around, inspecting the

rooms, then starts opening doors and drawers.

"What are you after?"

"Something to use as a bandage for you."

"Shouldn't we call Pip?" That, to me, seems more urgent. While I'm certain the men are secured, there could be a snowball's chance in hell they'd free themselves.

She rolls her eyes, and points. I notice with surprise that my arm has blood running down it in rivulets. I clamp my hand over the wound to try to stem it. "It just winged me. I'm all right. Call Pip."

Another glance at the ceiling and back down, but she's Swift. A quick assessment tells her I'm not in immediate danger of dying, so she's not going to fuss. She picks up one of the phones we'd appropriated downstairs, and keys in a number. While I'm waiting for Pip to pick up, I realise my arm's now starting to smart and throb. In the adrenaline rush, I'd forgotten all about it until Swift had pointed it out. Lifting my hand, I eye it. Nah, it doesn't need stitches, just needs a bandage to stop the blood flowing. In a way, that pain's a distraction from the ache in my leg and the tenderness on my chest. I'm a fucking mess.

When the phone is at last answered, she puts it on speaker.

"Yeah?" Pip sounds cautious. Well, it is an unknown number.

"Prez, it's—"

"Swift? Fuck. You alright? How the fuck are you talking to me? I thought you were taken without your hearing aids."

"I was. But Road brought them with him."

"Road? *Fuckin'* Road? Road brought them... You were there? At the vacation house?"

As her eyes widen, I realise she's not got a clue where she is, but she recovers fast. "Not much of a vacation house. Got four rats in the basement. Two we managed to kill, two trapped." Swift grins in my direction.

"They're contained?"

"Yeah. Could do with an exterminator though."

"I'll get it arranged. Will be there as soon as possible. Both of you okay? Neither got bit I hope?" Pip's voice drips with concern.

"One caught Road's arm. But he'll live."

"We'll be there to make sure your rodent problem is dealt with."

The call ends abruptly. I'm certain Pip's going to waste no time making arrangements.

Spying a first aid box up on the kitchen wall, I make my way over to it, taking out a roll of bandage and proceeding to try to wrap it around my arm in an effort to stem the blood. Swift bats my hand away and takes over for herself, making a much better job than I could do one handed. Moments later and with not a little gnashing of teeth on my part, my arm is wrapped tight enough to slow, if not stop, the bleeding.

"Have you seen my phone?" I ask, in part to take my mind off my various hurts. When I start looking around, hoping to find it, Swift does the same. It doesn't appear to be in the house, so I go outside, wondering if they dropped it where they found me. Breathing in deeply, I pause once I'm outside, taking the chance to fill my chest with fresh air. I bend, placing my hands on my knees, coming down hard now that the fighting is done.

"Here. Is this it? It was in the kitchen. I think this is your wallet too. Hey, are you alright?"

I glance up, nodding as I recognise the device I was looking for. Taking it from her, I slide both it and my wallet into my pocket. "Sure. I just—"

"You did good, Brother."

Her praise doesn't affect me, her moniker does. I don't want to be relegated to some damn team member.

I straighten again, and approach her, wishing I could make

a better impression than limping toward her. "Swift," I growl. "I've not forgotten our conversation."

She doesn't pretend to misunderstand. "Road, it wouldn't work…"

I'm just about to contradict her, when my phone vibrates in my pocket.

Taking my phone out, I see it's my prez.

"Drummer," I acknowledge, cautiously.

"Road, what the fuck's going on?"

He's called at the worst possible moment, with adrenaline still coursing through me from the fight for our lives only moments before. My various injuries are making themselves known, making rational thought impossible. I want him off the line fast, so I try to reassure him. "Nothing, Prez."

"Nothing? You're telling me everything's as it should be in Utah?" I know from his tone that my voice won't be sounding quite like normal and I'm not surprised he picked up on it.

He's caught me off balance. I've been shot, I'm just about to persuade Swift that us fucking is the best possible idea despite her objections, but he's expecting me to come up with some fiction about the Utah club. "Nothing out of the ordinary," I say again, knowing I'll be out bad if I'm caught in a lie to Drummer, but right now unable to summon a better response. I've got Swift back, and my gut tells me I don't want to lose her. To buy some time, I have to be careful what I say about this chapter. I've got to throw him off the scent.

But it seems Drummer's intent on knowing more. "How do they make their money?"

"The usual stuff." Well, it's quite unusual, actually.

There's a pause. It stretches out. "Seems like you've done what I asked and found out what our brothers in Utah get up to. So, you're getting ready to come back? Marvel's getting fed up staring at pussy all night."

If he is, I suspect it's more because he's found managing

the strip club is not all staring at naked bodies, he's actually had to do some work. "Yeah, thinking about it, Drummer." I'm also thinking seriously about transferring to Utah. Swift's here, for a start. She wouldn't be able to transfer to Tucson, and I couldn't ask her to give up her patch.

He goes quiet again, then his voice blasts down the phone. "You're thinking about it?" adding, so loudly I have to move the phone to one side, "You're fuckin' thinking about it? Don't you think you ought to give me a heads-up if you're staying away for an extended time? Or are you thinking of transferring? You'd have to ask me if you were. What's Snatcher been saying to you? Is he pressuring you to stay?"

"It's not like that, Prez." My eyes land on Swift, and suddenly I know what to say that he would accept as a valid excuse. "There's a woman."

Another silence followed shortly by a strangled laugh. "You as well? Well why not bring her back with you?"

"It's early days, Prez. I don't know where, if anywhere, this is going to go."

"Tell me how Utah makes their money," he suddenly throws in, trying to catch me out.

"I gotta run, Prez. Speak later."

I end the call, then look up to see Swift is half grinning, half looking concerned. "Was that wise?"

I shrug. "What can I say? He wasn't going to let it drop." I run back over the call in my mind. "He's suspicious as hell, so I had to come up with something to throw him off the scent."

"And this woman?" Now there's a challenge in her eyes. "Now who would she be, this woman of yours?"

"Not yet mine," I hold her gaze with mine, "but give it time."

She returns my stare for a few beats, then tosses her head. "In your dreams," she scoffs.

28

*S*wift...

I'm playing with Road. I know exactly who the woman is that he just told his prez about. The problem is, that woman is me, and while I guessed he was struggling for something to say to Drummer to get him off the line, I could also see from the softening of Road's eyes, that in his offhand statement there was an element of truth.

I can't be the reason Road stays here and doesn't return to his Tucson brothers. It's not fair to lead him on.

Road might say he's good with a quick fuck so we can get our sexual frustrations dealt with and then both move on, but telling his prez he's met a woman he might make his isn't just a different ballgame, it's not even in the same ballpark. The signs are there that Road's words are at odds with what's in his heart. He doesn't want a one-night stand, he's starting to view me as someone to whom he could make a commitment.

Trouble is, I've a sneaking suspicion I might feel the same way, and that scares me, far worse than the prospect of taking a man like Tiny on. The more Road and I are together and the more I see of him, the more I discover things I like. Unfortunately, so far, he hasn't put a foot wrong.

He hadn't once indicated as I was a woman, I should therefore follow his masculine lead. Instead, he'd followed every instruction I'd given, deferring to me as I've more knowledge and experience than him. He's in pain but doesn't complain about it and doesn't try to make it all about him. His chest must be sore, his arm too, and that's not even considering the pain from his leg. Yet, he's not moaned once nor played on my sympathy.

Neither has he been making allowances for my injured hand or being overprotective. He's given me exactly what I need, an acknowledgement it's happened, acceptance there's nothing that can be done to fix it, leaving any provision I need to make to me.

His quick smile, his deep laugh, his handsome looks, his hands that can kill but also be so gentle and which I want all over me are other positive factors. Everything about him leads me to suspect if we fucked, it might be me who wanted more.

While we're waiting for the cavalry, I need to turn this unsettling conversation away from him and me. "I didn't have time to ask earlier, but why the fuck are you here all alone?" That that's not Pip's way of operating has been playing on my mind.

"Duty came up with a number of places which had recently been rented." He raises and lowers his shoulders. "One looked a probable, but I wasn't included on the team to check it out. This one seemed a loser from the start, but Pip wanted it looked at anyway. It's fifty miles from the clubhouse, you know that?"

I was unconscious when I'd been brought here. "I didn't. They chloroformed me, remember."

He raises his chin. "I could be here in under an hour on

that ZX14R, and Bolt's bike is almost as fast. He sent both of us to check this place out." He grimaces and looks pained. "I thought he was getting me out of the way and fully expected the others would rescue you."

"Bolt? But he's not here." I frown and quickly check. "Is he okay?"

"He had a blowout about ten miles out of town. He's embarrassed but fine."

Thank fuck for that. "How did they get you?"

Road's eyes settle on me, and one side of his mouth turns up. He knows exactly what I'm doing by asking questions—I'm avoiding a discussion I don't want to have. Then, he sighs, and touches at the bruise on his chest. It brings my attention to those pecs and abs I find so fascinating. Quickly I raise my eyes to his face, focusing instead on his lips, which is another mistake.

"I was careless, angry, frustrated at not being on the team going to the most likely place. I met a fisherman at the lake. He seemed to think there was a couple here. I didn't fuckin' think of security cameras or that there'd be people looking out." An abrupt shake of his head. "I was so certain this place was a bust."

"But there were."

"Yeah. So it was my stupidity that I got caught. It's thanks to Preacher that I was wearing Kevlar. Fuckin' saved my life. When the bullet didn't kill me, Kincaid decided he'd question me instead. Luckily their first thought was that I hadn't come alone, so they secured me, as you know, and then went out to search."

He's not making excuses or justifying his actions. He'd been stupid, but at the end of the day, he found me and rescued me.

"It worked out," I tell him sincerely, my hand somehow finding its way onto his arm. "And I can't thank you enough for bringing my hearing aids" There are no words to express how grateful I am, how lost I felt when all my nightmares came true. I'd been stolen away because I'd had no warning anyone was coming, and held captive without being able to hear the threats or anything else being said. I had had to stay alert and awake and unable to relax. I'm tired and crashing fast now. With Road, I feel safe enough to admit. "I-I was scared." I bite my lip even though I'm not known for doing such actions. Somehow with him, I feel like I can let down my guard. "I couldn't hear what Kincaid was saying. I had no warning when they took my finger. I tried to get free, but it didn't work. And I didn't know what else they had planned. I felt *weak*." I spit out the last word.

He raises my injured hand and gently rubs his fingers across the back of it over the top of the bandage. "Never weak. You kept it together, you're so fuckin' brave, Swift."

Just then, in that moment, I don't feel brave at all. Without thinking what I'm doing, I lean into him, resting my face against the warm skin of his chest. His arms come around me and he holds me loosely.

"It wasn't what they did, Road. Though it hurt like the son of a fuckin' bitch. I'll survive without a finger. It was not knowing what else they'd do."

"So fuckin' brave," Road repeats. Then his hands move, and he applies a little pressure. In a moment, he's holding me at arm's length, his eyes fixing on mine. "That would be terrifying for anyone, Swift. You know that, don't you?"

"It hurts, Road. It throbs. And it's not even bloody well there." I don't have to tell him I'm talking about the lack of my finger.

They'd stolen something from me which I'll never get back. The stump will heal. I'm not even particularly concerned about it looking ugly. It's that it will be a constant reminder of how I'm no longer complete. I pretend to be normal, as though losing my hearing is just a mild inconvenience. Instead, it's a big fucking deal as the last couple of days had proved. They'd never have gotten the drop on me if I'd been able to hear. That's going to have more lasting effects than the loss of my finger. Right now, I'm not sure where I'll find the strength to pick up and carry on. Fear, I think, will be my constant companion. I can no longer pretend. I've experienced the worst of what can happen when silence descends.

He pulls me back into his chest, one hand smoothing my hair. I'm not ashamed to admit I'm taking comfort from him.

What would it be like to have him to lean on forever? Why is it with him I don't need to insist I'm okay? Why do I let him see my weakness? *Because he doesn't mock me for it.* He doesn't act as if it's unexpected, as though, me being Swift, he expects more.

"You're so fuckin' strong," he reassures me, as though able to read my mind. "You'll come back from this, Swift. Honor and Duty will already be thinking of ways to power proof your house, or cope with the lack of it. This has been a wakeup call, but you came out relatively unscathed. It's all too raw now, but you'll come through stronger than before. I know it."

I wish I had his confidence.

"Christ." His free hand squeezes between my back his front, and he rubs his chest. "I still feel I've been kicked by a horse." His reminder makes me smile, then I'm actually giggling as he starts to chuckle. "We're a right pair, aren't we?"

I need to concentrate on the positives. "We're free." We'd worked well as a team. I'd released him, he'd freed me, and together we'd taken the bad guys out. "I count that as a success."

"Swift?" Road's voice has become serious and slightly strained. I raise my eyes. "I'd like to kiss you."

That's all the warning I get. Before I can think to push him away, his hands cup my face, and turns it up. I'm about to say *No, that's a crazy idea,* when his lips find mine. At first, it's just a brush of our mouths meeting. Then, he applies a little more pressure, and I open, allowing his tongue to slip inside.

We'd kissed before in California. Despite my indignation at the time, I have to admit I enjoyed it. But that hadn't prepared me for what happens when Road takes control of my mouth, and I start to melt beneath his onslaught.

The sound of multiple motorbikes approaching makes us both jump guiltily apart. I wipe my mouth with the back of my hand, knowing my eyes are wide. Road's lips were soft, as was his beard against my face. Thank fuck Pip's arrival has stopped me from making a mistake. Even that brief melding of our mouths was an error of judgement I shouldn't have made.

I enjoyed it too much.

I'm not averse to exchanging kisses in the throes of passion, but don't seek them out. If mouths are involved, then there's another place where a man can use his tongue which is much more satisfying. Why waste time when sex organs aren't involved? That's the whole point of the encounter, isn't it? I suppose I must have kissed back in my school days but can't remember having an interaction involving just lips with a man before.

Why do my knees feel weak?

Because, I answer myself firmly, *I've just come through an ordeal where I had to fight off PTSD with everything I have.* Because the sound of those bikes tells me I can stand down and relax.

While I've been standing, shaken because of the kiss we just shared, Road's pulled himself together faster. He's walking toward the approaching bikes.

"Road."

I hear Pip's voice, put on my game face just in time to see

Road getting slapped firmly on his back. Then Pip spies me and gives me the same brotherly hug.

"Fuck, Swift." His eyes roam from my head to my toes. "You really okay?"

Why, I have no fucking idea, but my traitorous body makes my eyes water. *Maybe the pollen is high today?* Or, maybe it's because now, I know I'm really safe. I hold up my hand which will never be the same as it was before, and simply reply, "Apart from this, I'm fine."

In my SAS training, I was treated as an enemy captive. I was sleep deprived, I'd been left hungry and thirsty and subjected to interrogation using methods the Geneva convention would frown upon. I survived and came through with flying colours. I didn't want to curl into a ball and pray that someone would rescue me. I endured whatever was thrown at me with strength and resolve.

This is the first time I've been challenged since losing my hearing, and that's what floored me. I'm not weak, I'm strong. But my confidence has taken a knock.

Pip's eyeing me carefully. "Who's left alive?"

"Kincaid and Dean someone or other. Weston and the man who could be Christian McGregor are dead." I clear my throat and say again more firmly. "They're restrained in the basement. Follow me—"

"No, you've done enough." Pip moves his gaze from me to Road. "As have you. I want you both to get back to the compound. Doc will be there and waiting."

"I don't need a medic."

Road protests at the same time as I tell Pip, "I'll stay here. I want to be in on this."

"No. That's an order," Pip says firmly. "Your hand needs looking at Swift. Can't reattach the finger, it's been too fuckin' long, but you'll need antibiotics. Same goes for you, Road."

Pip's eyes linger on the bandage on Road's arm which is reddening, showing his wound hasn't closed up.

Road lets out a deep sigh. "Okay. Did you see my bike? They might have moved it."

Pip rolls his eyes. "Gears is here with the truck. You're not fuckin' going back on the bike."

Part of me is pleased he said that as I haven't got mine, and the only option would be to ride up behind Road. It's not the principle, it's the thought of having to be so close to him, to have my arms around him for each one of the fifty miles he said we'd need to traverse.

"I can ride." Road's face darkens with displeasure.

Pip snorts. "You're shirtless and have a bloody bandage wrapped around your arm. Swift is wearing sleep shorts and a tank top and has an injured fuckin' hand. You don't think the cops might think that strange?"

Put that way, Pip might have a good point. Knowing he's won the argument, Pip turns and signals, and the truck approaches. When it pulls up beside us with Gears behind the wheel, Igor jumps out.

"Hey, Road, you got the key for the ZX14R?" Igor looks excited, so I expect he'll be riding it back.

Sparing a moment to glare at Pip, Road pats the pockets of his jeans. "Nah, they must have taken it." He looks disgusted.

"Find the bike, it might be with it. Or, I'll get where it is out of them." Pip's eyes flare with anticipation.

"Grinch will probably have a spare."

As Pip acknowledges my comment, Road's already walking toward the truck. He doesn't look happy, he's favouring his leg hard, and his shoulders are hunched. Prez is right to stop him riding. I watch as he pulls himself into the passenger side. He winces as the action pulls on his chest.

I follow, sliding into the back seat. I refrain from making any observation.

Taking the driver's side, Gears wastes no time getting moving. I'll be happy when there's distance between me and this house where nightmares become real.

As the truck proceeds down the drive, it's the first proper time I've seen the outside of the house and the position it's in. I'm not surprised that this pretty location had been thought unlikely to hide a kidnap victim within its walls. Well, however pretty it is, it's not somewhere I'll ever want to spend a vacation.

As we exit the driveway, in the distance I see the lake where Road must have spoken to the fisherman. Then, when we get out on the freeway, having no interest in looking at anything more, I lean back, closing my eyes for the first time since I'd been taken. Feeling safe, I quickly drop off to sleep and just as fast startle awake again. In my dream, I'd been whimpering. When I open my eyes to find Road looking over his shoulder at me, his eyes softened with concern, I suspect it wasn't only in my sleep I'd been making sounds of distress.

"You're safe," he tells me, his voice dark and deep, washing over me like velvet. "And you're fuckin' exhausted. Get some rest. You'll soon be safe back in your own bed."

Safe in my own bed. That's where they got me.

I'm tired, I've had no sleep for thirty-six hours. That must be why I'm shaking, that must be the reason all my training has escaped me and my weakness taunts me. *Will I ever feel safe again?*

Now worried if I drop off to sleep I'll start dreaming again, I don't allow myself to give in to my tiredness. Instead, I let everything play through my head, an internal debrief of my mission. *What had I done right? What had I done wrong? What could I do to prevent this happening again?*

I should sell my house, turn my back on my piece of independence. Question Pip as to whether there are any more skeletons in his cupboard that could rise from their graves and take me. I grow angry thinking I was targeted just because I don't happen to have a dick, and that Kincaid had assumed I was a whore because I lived at the club. Pip would have gone to the ends of the earth to rescue any of the brothers, just as Kincaid had wanted revenge for the loss of one of his blood. Yet I was taken as I was thought a weak female.

I'm not angry at Pip, it's not his fault I'm returning minus a finger. It will be inconvenient—typing will be hard as unlike most of my brothers who only use two fingers, I use ten. But I'll live, albeit with the everlasting reminder I haven't a 'P' finger anymore. I hadn't been raped, though that was only because Road had appeared in time.

I hate that after everything I've done, getting a place in the SAS and proving I was good enough to join an MC, I was taken because I was female.

I wish I was there to question Kincaid, yet trust Prez to get the answers I'm seeking, as he'll want to know the same ones as well. How did they know how to get into my security? And, how did they find Pip in the first place? Have we got a breach?

As the truck covers the miles, I notice Road turning occasionally. Each time he sees I'm still awake, a little frown plays at his lips. The prospect drives carefully, not risking being pulled up by the cops, not with two injured people as passengers—one with their finger chopped off, and one with an obvious bullet wound.

I hug my arms around myself, suppressing a shiver. Road leans forward, turning the heat on his side up. Gears has the air conditioning running full blast, no wonder I'm cold. Road's top half is naked, and my sleep attire is flimsy.

As we drive on, I realise I've never felt as vulnerable as I now am, and I really dislike the feeling.

29

———

*R*oad…

I'm worried about Swift. She hadn't expressly told me, but it was clear she's had no rest since she was taken. She'd have been unable to relax in case someone crept up on her and would have forced herself to stay alert. But even now she can't turn off, even with her hearing aids and in the safety of the truck with me and the prospect to keep watch over her.

It's knocked her for a loop. Probably the only reason I was able to take advantage and steal a kiss. Wow, I turn to look out of the window to hide my grin. What a kiss, short though it was. She had fitted into my arms as though she was made to be there. The memory of her taste, the feeling of her soft lips against mine, that brief gliding dance of our tongues, has my cock swelling. I've kissed women, sure I have, they seem to expect it. But before now, I've wanted to get it over with fast so I could get down to the real business. I can't remember enjoying it for anything other than a prelude to sinking my dick into whatever orifice the woman was happy for me to use. I wasn't fussy, their cunt, mouth, or on an exceptional occasion, their ass.

I've had more women than I can remember, would probably be unable to identify who exactly I'd fucked and who I'd not were a number of them lined up. Anonymous faces of which I hadn't taken much notice. Even if I could pick them out, it wouldn't be any kiss I'd remember.

But Swift? I think our brief intimacy is now ingrained on my psyche. Her, I'll never forget. It makes me more determined to repeat the experience, and who knows, take it further if she'll let me.

Fuck her to get her out of my system? I don't think that will work. Make her mine? What a joke, you don't tame someone like her. The most I could hope for is that she'd make me hers.

Now I'm a selfish bastard thinking just of myself. Swift's got more issues than a potential relationship with me to worry about.

Will she ever feel safe in her home again? Somehow, I doubt it. Even if we set up a secondary system to kick in were the first to be taken out, she'll have difficulty turning off and sleeping. How can I make it so Swift feels safe at night?

My first thought is that I could stay with her, hold her in my arms and act as her ears. My cock again perks up at the thought of being so close to her.

But no. Pip might think I fucked up by getting caught, decide I was less resourceful than he had thought. I certainly hadn't demonstrated common sense or intelligence. As a result, he may rescind his invitation to join the Utah chapter, and I'll be returning to Tucson. Or if Drummer discovers the truth about Utah and knew I withheld that information from him, he could send me out bad from the club as I lied by omission. I groan inaudibly as I remember that last conversation with my prez, wishing he hadn't called right then. I was hurting, still fired up and unprepared.

If Drummer discovers Pip doesn't ride, it's unlikely he

could retain control of the Utah club. If by some chance, he wasn't removed, if I was out in bad standing, he'd lose the Satan's Devils charter were he to give me a place in it. I'm no fool. I'm a grunt with nothing particular to offer. I wouldn't be the reason Pip blew his operation apart. So, even if I wanted to stay every night with her, and she permitted that liberty, I might not be able to fulfil that promise to her.

There must be an answer.

I don't have to hear it from her lips, I already know she'll never trust any system again.

At least she can stay at the clubhouse. There'll always be someone around who can watch out for her. But who'll comfort her when she has flashbacks and nightmares? Or when she's trembling when the PTSD takes hold?

Gears is driving competently and safely, so I lean my head against the headrest and close my eyes. It might be because I'm letting my mind drift, but an idea suddenly appears. I start to get excited, wondering if my thought has legs, or if Swift would ever go for it. It wouldn't hurt for me to check it out.

I doze. It's only when Gears cuts the engine that I awake, wipe my eyes, and roll my shoulders. I hear the door behind me open and know Swift's already getting out. I do the same and breathe in deeply as soon as I'm outside the truck and immediately regret doing so as a sudden pain shoots through my bruised chest.

It might only have taken ninety minutes or so to get back, but I've stiffened up. Maybe because I'm back at my temporary home, and I'm no longer on high alert, but I realise I hurt. My arm stings like fuck, and my leg from having twisted when I was pushed down the stairs, I suspect I'll find my hip is bruised when I get out of my pants. My neck too feels like I've got whiplash, and now it's stiffened up.

I'm no stranger to pain. My last crash was the worst, but I've come off my trials bike too many times to count, so am used to bruises and sprains, or pulled muscles and the occasional, but luckily rare, broken bone. Now I realise my body's been pushed to its limits and I'd like nothing more than to collapse into a bed.

I glance at Swift in time to see her mouth wide open in a yawn. Sheepishly, she covers it with her hand when she sees I'm looking. "Best get this over with. When Prez says the doc's waiting, well, he'll be here now."

"Where?" I eye the clubhouse wondering where we'll be heading. While I'd prefer to just sit somewhere and rest, I doubt there's any point in arguing.

"Medical room," she replies.

They've got a medical room? In Tucson, we use one of the crash rooms if necessary. Of course, cleanliness can't be guaranteed, but hey, if your arm's falling off, you'll take anything in an emergency. Anyway, nowadays it's normally one of the kids has fallen off their bikes, and they just get a Band-Aid and kisses from Mom which seem to make it better.

"Lead the way," I request, stepping forward and holding the door open for her.

Brute's on reception duty. He raises his chin and wordlessly presses the button to open the inner door. Swift walks down the hallway leading to the gym, but peels off before getting there, entering a smallish room with stocked shelves along one wall, and the type of bed you find in your doctor's office in the middle of the room.

There's a man propped against a table, an open magazine in his hands. He closes it and puts it down as we enter.

"Who's the patient and what am I dealing with?" he immediately asks, stepping forward, expert eyes examining us. "Ah," he pronounces, as his eyes land on my still bare chest. "I take it you were wearing body armour?" I nod, looking down myself at the blossoming red and purple blaze across my skin.

"It will be painful, but I doubt anything's broken. Lie down," he points to the bed, "and let me take a look."

"It's nothing." I send a pointed glance toward Swift. "She needs attention first." Which she's clearly trying to avoid, as she's holding her bandaged hand behind her back.

"Swift?" His brow creases. "What's wrong with you, Swift? You're normally the one causing trouble, not the one I need to stitch up." I grin at his comment. Though seeing the state Stormy was in after their time in the ring, I can believe that.

Swift hesitates, then turns to me. "You want to wait outside?"

"Not unless you need me to." She's hurt. I'd like to know how bad it is, and know what to do to help her look after herself.

Her lips press together, but she turns back to doc, reluctantly raising her bandaged hand. "I lost my finger," she explains.

"Lost? That was careless." The doctor's words sound casual, but he gives her a cautious look as he bends his head and starts unwrapping the bandage.

Seeing Swift's face turn away, I move closer to her, not touching, but allowing her to feel my warmth at her back.

I hadn't spent much time staring at her hand, if any at all. Now I notice it's small and elegant, with long fingers like that of a concert piano player. Her nails are unvarnished and cut short. The side opposite to her thumb though is red and swollen, and the tiny stump, all that remains of her fifth digit, is swollen and angry looking and still oozing blood.

Swift's other hand fists and she places it to her mouth and refuses to look at her hand. I grit my teeth. She might not have been raped, but they'd taken something from her without her consent. Not a serious injury in itself, inconvenient and painful but with no particularly difficult long-term disadvantages, except that stump will forever remind her of how she was unable to protect herself.

The doctor is professional, asks no questions and confines himself to his medical opinion. "It's a clean cut, but it's been left too long for any surgeon to put the finger back, even if you have it. I'll prescribe painkillers, and you need antibiotics. One needs to be applied directly to the skin and some for you to take. There's already some infection setting in, and that's what we need to stop. Dressings will have to be regularly changed."

"Can I shower?"

"Yes. Keeping it clean is best, but make sure you apply the ointment and bandage it again after."

She shudders, and I know I'm going to offer to help with that.

"Any other injuries?" When Swift shakes her head, the doctor's attention turns to me, his eyes landing on my bandaged arm. "Now, you. Please, lie on the bed."

This time I do, sucking in air as the doctor feels around my bruised chest. He pronounces, as expected, he doubts I've got broken ribs, though I wish he hadn't prodded and poked so hard to prove it. He then unwraps the bandage Swift had applied in the house. My arm starts bleeding profusely, and he keeps dabbing gauze to mop it up.

"Bullet wound?"

Dismissively I tell him, "Just a scrape."

"Yeah, lucky for you there's no bullet in it. It does need a few stitches, and I'll prescribe antibiotics for you too."

A local anaesthetic, a needle prodding my skin, then a few minutes later he pronounces me good to go.

The doctor washes his hands a final time as I sit up. He hands us both prescriptions, telling us to go get them filled, then comments about sending his bill in. *He's obviously a fairly regular visitor*, I muse, as I watch him go.

"I'll get Gears to go and get these filled," Swift tells me. "Then, I want a shower, put on some clothes, then get some food. I'm starving."

When she walks toward the reception desk, I hang back and wait. Shower then food sounds pretty good to me too. I'm looking forward to putting a shirt back on, as I'm getting pretty bored with walking around displaying my chest, although I've noticed it does attract Swift's eyes, so maybe I should do a rethink. But it's not overly warm in the clubhouse and I've no further excuse to go around with bared skin. I'm loathed to change her view though. Sometimes there's shared pain in her eyes as they land on the purple skin over my heart, sometimes they become heated as they settle lower, looking at my taut stomach and the definition of my muscles. Or that could be wishful thinking on my part.

As we walk toward the elevator, the mention of her hunger worries me. "They feed you?"

"Not much."

She's exhausted as hell, that's plain to see. In the elevator she leans her shoulders back against the wall, her head drooping. We reach the third floor. I stop outside the room that had been allocated to me, while Swift's is obviously further along.

"Meet you downstairs?"

With those parting words, she walks off. I show the key card to the lock. When the light flashes green, I go inside.

Fresher after my awkward shower following the doc's instructions to keep the bandage on my arm dry, which I sort of was fairly successful at and it only ended up a little damp, I brush the tangles out of my hair, then delve into the dwindling selection of clothes I'd brought with me on my bike. Even putting them through the laundry means I'm changing out just two pairs of jeans and four t-shirts, one of which has now been ruined. Buy new? Or return to Tucson and collect more of my own. But that would mean facing the music, and maybe Drummer wouldn't want me to return to Utah again.

As I put on my cut, the thought hits me, I'm not ready to leave. The time is approaching when I need to make a decision, if it's in within my power to make. Apart from Swift, Utah offers new opportunities for me. As far as Swift's concerned, there's unfinished business between us, and one way or another, I'd like to see where it goes. What she'd have to say about it is anyone's guess. I suspect she'll try and keep me at arm's length, though I'll do what I can to get under her guard.

My stomach growls, reminding me I could do with some food myself. I don't think I've taken long, but when I take the return journey down in the elevator, I hear Swift already washed and changed telling Gears to go to a twenty-four-hour pharmacy. Knowing I've completely lost track of time, I take my phone out of my cut I'd been pleased to put back on after my shower, surprised to see it's already late in the evening.

Once again, I find myself following in her wake as she goes into the cafeteria. Cowboy is missing, he'll have gone with Pip and the others to the vacation house, and the lack of voices means they've not yet returned.

But Swift isn't fazed, she just walks straight around the counter. She pauses at the entrance to the kitchen, her uninjured hand holding onto the doorjamb. When I notice her trembling, I think she's forgotten I'm behind her, until she speaks.

"It's all so normal, Road. But I feel changed. I know if I walk in, there'll be leftovers put away in the fridge. Cowboy always makes extra for times when some of the team gets called away and miss mealtimes. I should just walk over, find what I want and put it in the microwave to heat. Everything's the same, but it's not somehow."

I place my hands on her shoulders and gently squeeze. "You're still the same, Swift." I know she's not talking about the pain in her hand nor that she's missing a finger.

"I'm not," she says softly. "I could do anything, go anywhere. Fuck, Road, I've abseiled out of a helicopter though I had a phobia of heights. I've conquered all my fears. I thought nothing could ever break me."

"You're not broken."

"I am," she insists. "I've been kidding myself. I thought I hadn't changed when I lost my hearing, not when I could hear with hearing aids. But being kidnapped without them showed how helpless I am."

"You're not broken or helpless," I tell her again. "Swift, you're kick ass. What Kincaid did hasn't diminished that."

"Thank you." She turns suddenly and looks up into my face. "Thank you for thinking to bring my hearing aids with you. I was going crazy without them."

"I should have given them to one of the others," I admit, my lips thinning. "No one expected you to be where I found you. Pip should have had them—"

"They didn't think. They've known me far longer than you have, yet you were the one who realised what I'd need most." Her eyes regard me wonderingly.

"That's because you're so kick ass, they forget you're deaf." I come up with an acceptable explanation.

"I try to hide it. I try to go on as if I'm normal. I try my best to act as if there's nothing different about me so no one makes allowances." She grimaces slightly. "I think I may have been too successful. Whereas you, you seem to be able to read me like a book. You knew I'd need them."

"They don't make allowances because they don't have to. You are normal, Swift." I try to think of comparisons. "You think Bolt's not normal because of his prosthetic hand?"

A small smile plays about her lips. "Bolt's *not* normal, but it's got nothing to do with him being an amputee."

Chuckling, I nod my head, tending to agree. Then my brow creases. "Okay, Swift. Here's how I see it. You're not normal." As her mouth drops open, I move my head to one side then to the other. "I can't begin to imagine what it's like to wake up deaf. To be told you'd never hear again. Hell, I was broken when I was told I couldn't ride in my chosen sport. Yet you've really got a life-changing injury, but has it stopped you? Fuck no. You've gotten into an MC. Your prez twisted the rules and made you a fully patched member. All your life as a woman you've had to work twice as hard to prove yourself and get respect. And that's what you've fuckin' done. Look what you achieved? Getting accepted into the SAS and then, even though you're deaf, becoming a Satan's Devil. You're not normal, Swift. You're fuckin' amazing."

"Kincaid—"

"Kincaid showed up where you're vulnerable. So you do what you did the first time around, you work on your weaknesses and see where you can build strength."

Her head tilts slightly as though I've caught her interest. "Just like that?"

"Just like that." She's looked away. I place my hand gently under her chin and turn her face back. "I might have an idea."

Her eyes narrow. "What?"

"Not being secretive, just want to check a few things out first. But we'll get there, okay? We'll get you your confidence and independence back. We'll see what changes we can make and then make them."

"We?"

I realise how presumptuous I must have sounded. I feel my cheeks burn and hell, I'm someone I never thought even knew how to blush.

"We." She tries out the word again. Then, without giving

me a clue as to what's in her head, she turns away from me and takes a step into the room. "Now, shall *we* find what Cowboy's left for us to eat?"

That sounds like a fucking good idea. Even if she has left me hanging about whether she'll accept my assistance.

There's some cold chicken in the fridge. Opening a cupboard, I find there's a packet of tortillas and a spice mix for fajitas.

"You know how to put that together?" she asks, looking dubious.

I snort. It's easy enough.

She might have given the orders when we were taking down the four men, but now I'm the one issuing instructions. Side by side we work until we at last sit loading the soft unleavened bread with chicken and salsa, adding dollops of sour cream and guacamole. It's good, even if I say so myself, and we're silent as we stuff our faces. When we've finished, we clear everything away, placing our used plates in the dish-washer. I take out my phone and see it's already eleven pm. Once again, I notice Swift yawning.

So I offer the solution, "Bed. Come on, you're dead on your feet."

30

———

Swift…

Making fajitas alongside Road had been relaxing. A mind-numbing task that didn't require much thinking —me just following what he said as we gathered together what we needed. Then, filling my stomach which was crying out for food had consumed all my attention. Road hadn't made small talk, hadn't gone back to the subject we'd addressed when entering the kitchen, that is, that my self-confidence had taken a beating.

I'd needed him to suggest I was bruised but not broken. Right now, I'm at a total loss how I can move forward or how I can ever feel safe again, but Road's confident reassurance that there was a way ahead had settled something inside me. Not healed me, not given me answers, but posed the idea that there were resolutions that could be found. A way of beating not my daytime reliance on hearing aids, I'll have that for the rest of my life, but something to make me able to sleep at night without either suffering discomfort or rendering me vulnerable.

A problem without solution is an insurmountable weight.

If ways around it were possible, then it's one more thing to fight. And fighting is what I'm made for.

The food filling my empty belly and the comforting presence of Road have left me feeling easier than at any time over the past two days. Until he went and brought my issues to the fore.

"Bed. Come on, you're dead on your feet."

Immediately, panic floods through me. Last time I laid down and closed my eyes, I thought I was safe. I'd had confidence in all the technology surrounding me. Nothing could get me when I was wrapped up in my cocoon. *I'd been wrong, so dreadfully, horribly wrong.* Now I'm missing a finger to prove it.

But I'm not in my house. I'm safe here on the compound. My impending panic attack doesn't agree.

I'm not alone, I tell myself firmly. Road will be sleeping along the corridor, if the electricity fails, he'll awake, *won't he?*

What if he's a deep sleeper and doesn't hear? What if the painkillers the doctor suggested he take render him to sleep so soundly, he doesn't hear anyone coming to take me away? My PTSD is in full flow.

Pip will have dealt with Kincaid. There's no one coming after me.

But there might be.

I can't go to bed.

I try to compose the expression on my face and to suppress yet another yawn I feel coming. I know there's a tremble in my voice as I offer an excuse. "Pip and the others aren't back yet. They'll want a debrief when they are." It's a good reason to put off going to bed a little longer. I sway a little. Even with the meal I've just eaten, I feel lightheaded. I see Road's face tighten, and he opens his mouth, probably to point out the obvious that I'm dead on my feet, but luckily, we're interrupted.

"Road, Swift. Got these. Sorry about the wait."

I turn to take the paper sacks from the pharmacy off of the prospect, who, having completed his task, walks away.

At that moment my phone pings with a text. It's from Pip. I read it, "Cleanup is going to take a while. We'll be back late. Church in the morning." Damn.

Well, nothing for it, but to go and get my head down. *I can do this.* But instead of getting my feet moving, I start trembling.

It's an electronic system. The locks are failsafe. They'll unlock if there's a fire alarm and someone could get in.

Road's sharp eyes miss nothing. I could lie to him, but I find that I can't, so I answer his questioning look by wrapping my arms around myself and telling him the truth. "I'm scared, Road. Even here," I indicate the clubhouse around me, "I don't feel safe."

He heaves a deep sigh. "I'm aching and sore, Swift. I just want to get a good night's sleep and you need one too."

I'm keeping him from his rest. But there could be a solution, though I hesitate to suggest it. "Will you, will you sleep with me, Road?" The question comes out of my mouth without me thinking about implications or what he'll think I'm offering. Part of me wants to snatch the words back, but if I'm going to get any rest tonight, maybe fucking Road won't be too high of a price to pay. At least it will relax me, and we can deal with any fallout when we're refreshed.

"Swift, it kills me to think of you all alone, unable to switch off and relax, when it's clear you need sleep. I'll stay in your room. I was going to suggest it."

We make the upward trip in the elevator again. When the doors open, he does something totally unexpected. He holds out his hand.

It's big, calloused, showing not only does he do the job of a manager, but he must also work on his bike. For a moment, I simply stare at it. *How long has it been since I took a man's hand?* Apart from that of my father, I'm not sure I ever have. I've always been a tomboy, the girl who gave off a self-sufficient vibe. But here, now, it seems more natural to take it, to walk with him by my side instead of striding out in the lead.

He's patient, just waiting. There's no rush, no hurry, no persuasion. He doesn't awkwardly withdraw the gesture, doesn't push it either, letting me know any decision made will be mine.

Gingerly, I place my smaller palm in his, feeling the warmth of his skin gently cradling mine. He doesn't squeeze, doesn't trap me.

When I start moving, our paces match. We reach my room, he drops a step back, allowing me to open the door, then follows me inside. He looks around, and I know he's noticing the room is as basic as his. Sure, there are a few more of my belongings around, but no ornaments, no pictures. Everything personal I keep in my house. *If I sell it, where would I store all my shit?* It's too much to keep here.

"You're tidy."

I wince at his observation. "Habit. I'm just going to use the bathroom."

"Ah, I'll pop back and use mine."

"Road, you can take a piss here. I don't care."

He grins. "Forgot my toothbrush, so I'll use it while I'm there."

I pass over the key to my room so he can let himself back in, then proceed to do what I was going to, multi-tasking by sitting on the loo and cleaning my teeth at the same time. I'm back, dressed in a fresh pyjama set and under the sheets when Road returns. He climbs onto the bed fully clothed.

"You can't sleep like that. Take your clothes off, Road."

Grimacing, he shakes his head. "If I strip down to my

boxers, you'll see just how much I want you, Swift. And that's not what tonight is about."

I want him too, why deny it? An orgasm might help me switch off. "Why not? A fuck will help us both sleep."

"Uh-uh." Again his head moves side to side. "When I give you my cock, you're not going to be half dead to the world or…" he breaks off and his eyes narrow. "Have you taken your painkiller, Swift?"

I swallow, and tentatively ask, "Have you?"

"Nah. I want to be fully alert, and the pain's nothing I can't deal with."

"Same here."

But he gets up, walks to my bedside table and empties the paper bag I left by the bed. He nods when he checks there's an antibiotic missing, then reads the other packet, and pushes out two tablets into his hand. He passes them to me with the bottle of water I'd left there.

"Road—"

"Take them. I'm here, Swift. You're hurting and tired as fuck. You haven't slept for forty-eight hours. You need to switch off and let your mind and body heal. It doesn't make you weak, Swift, it makes sense."

Maybe it's because I'm so bloody tired, but I don't have the strength to argue. A painless deep sleep sounds pretty good right now. "You promise you'll stay?"

His hand makes the sign of a cross over his chest, then he gives a quick boyish grin. "Devil's honour."

"Then take off your clothes." Some illogical part of me thinks he's less likely to leave if he has to get dressed again, while really I know that I'll have better dreams if the last thing I see before going to sleep is him naked.

When he gets up to obey me, I know I should turn away, but I don't, instead I shamelessly watch. Noticing, he makes a show of removing his cut and then his shirt, pumping his hips and rotating them.

I chuckle. "I see you've learned some shit from those strippers."

"You better believe it, babe." He winks. Then slowly, he pops the button at the top of his jeans, and circling his hips once again, slides that zipper down. I put my hand over my mouth and laugh when he turns his back, then glances at me over his shoulder as again he offers an exaggerated wink, drops his pants and boxers to reveal his ass, and pulls them up again. Then he does a repeat. I wish I wasn't so tired as he taunts me with his firm glutes.

Finally, he pushes his jeans all the way down, having returned to my room barefoot, there's nothing in the way to impede them. His boxers though, well, they remain. I see his back tighten, as he presumably takes a breath, then he turns around. His jeans and t-shirt lie where they've fallen, while I've tidily put my discarded clothes away.

Sitting up, I beckon with my hand. When he steps closer to the bed, brazenly I hook my finger through the elastic of his boxers which tent in the front impressively. But he steps back, waggling a digit at me. "Sleep," he commands.

My eyelids feel heavy, but my lady parts have come alive during his striptease. I pout, but his expression warns me, I won't be getting my way. As another yawn overtakes me, I know he's right. I turn over onto my side.

"Goodnight, Road."

"Hey, you can take your aids out. I'm here, babe." His hand rests on my shoulder. "You need sleep."

Again, he's right. But I'm reluctant. As soon as I remove my hearing aids, the room will go quiet and anyone could sneak up on me.

Road moves closer. I feel his warmth at my back, then I feel his skin against mine, and one meaty arm pulling me close. "Take them out. Tonight, lean on me. I'm going nowhere. I promise I'll be right here when you awake."

He releases me so I can put the hearing aids by the side of the bed, and then I'm back with his arm draped over me. *I feel safe.*

"Will you fuck me tomorrow?" My voice sounds groggy.

But, of course, I hear no reply, just feel the slight tightening of his muscles and his body vibrate, suggesting he's chuckling.

I wake with the light of the sun streaming in through my windows. By its position, I know day has only just dawned. No need to rush, if the others got in late last night, they'll still be sleeping.

I stretch, throwing up my arm, inadvertently elbowing a body sleeping beside me.

"Oh, bloody hell, I'm sorry." I go to reach for my hearing aids so I can have a proper conversation, but Road's arm stops me.

I turn back, looking into his face, swallowing hard at the heated look in his eyes. His pupils are dilated, and his breathing has sped up.

Without removing his eyes from mine, he takes hold of my hand and places it on a very hard, and respectably thick cock which I can feel through the material of his boxers. Then he loosens his grip, and I know he's leaving the decision to me.

I close my eyes. *Do I want this?*

Several outcomes go through my mind. One, that Road doesn't fulfil his body's promise, we won't be compatible at all, that it would be a pleasant experience but one neither of us will want to repeat. *Quite likely.* Two, that I find it only tolerable, and Road thinks it's fantastic, then I'll have a clingy man to get off my back. *Very possible.* Three, it could be the other way around, that he'd think me mediocre, and I'll be the one desperate to have him inside me again. *Unthinkable.* I don't cling, that's not me. Or, the fourth option, that we both want more. *Impossible and unworkable.*

Road might go back to Tucson. Or, I'm not blind to the Satan's Devils ways, Drummer might not forgive him for hiding the truth and send him out in bad standing, which would mean we'd have to part ways. Even if he stayed, how could it work? How could I be in a relationship with a brother? Wouldn't all the brothers look at me with fresh eyes, thoughts I suspected could always be rumbling beneath the surface appearing, *she's just a weak woman who needs a man to complete her.* They'd slap Road on the back and congratulate him for going where no one else had dared. Road would lap it up.

No, he wouldn't. He'd have my back, and I'd have his. Together we'd take no crap.

I realise all the time I've been thinking, my hand has stayed on Road's dick, and automatically my fingers have been squeezing, feeling it growing if that's even possible. I should pull it away. There are too many risks, one, or both, of us will end up hurting. I can't start anything.

31

———

$\mathcal{S}$wift…

Shit. I'm used to going after something if I want it, and right now, every fibre of my being screams that I want Road. Despite all the reasons why it's a bad idea, my body's overruling my head, and I know I want him inside me now.

It need only be this once, then I can move on with my curiosity satisfied. I should look at it that saying yes would do us both a favour. We've been dancing around our mutual attraction almost since he arrived at the club. Getting it out of our system would mean we could put the inconvenience behind us.

Giving his cock one last pump, I sit up and pull my tank top over my head. Road's eyes go wide as his eyes land on my breasts. I'm not large, thank goodness, carrying bazookas on my front with a fifty-five pound weight on my back would be a bit too much, but I hope he's satisfied with what I've got. They're perky, kept that way by the amount of exercise I do to stay fit.

The gratified smile curving his lips suggests he's in no way disappointed, nor in how his hands reach for me. He seems

326

fixated on my dark pink nipples, which harden just from the attention paid to them by his eyes. When his fingertips graze them, I breathe in a gasp of air, as tingles shoot down my spine, and make my clit come to life.

Shamelessly, I push my breasts further into his hands. He plumps them, then grins up at me. I realise I don't need to hear words, his upward curved mouth and sparkling eyes show his appreciation, and oh yeah, he likes.

Rising to my knees, making him pout as I remove his new playthings, I inch down the bed, and hook my fingers like I had last night into the waistband of his boxers. This time he makes no move to prevent me, doing the opposite instead, lifting his hips to help me take them off.

I don't normally give head. I'm in charge in bed, men serve me. They get off in my cunt when I'm ready. But Road? I want to please him, and that cock, well, it's mouthwatering. Lowering my face, I sweep my tongue over the head where pre-cum is already leaking. His hips jerk, and I notice his hands, now lying at his sides, are fisting.

In for a penny, in for a pound, as they say back home. Encouraged by his reaction, I take more of him into my mouth. He's too big for me to take his whole length, but the tension in his loins, together with little jerks of his hips suggests even this is pleasing him as I suck and lick those delicious veins, lapping up further pre-cum that leaks from the tip.

Suddenly I'm lifted by Road's strong arms and I'm flat on my back, and he's sweeping my own sleep shorts down. I raise one knee, then the other, and finally help by toeing them off.

I've no embarrassment being naked in front of him. My stomach is flat, my pubic hair neat and well maintained. I keep myself in good shape. While I might not win a beauty pageant, I'm confident in my looks. Though I rarely bother to use makeup, only if the occasion calls for it, I'm certain I could rival most of the strippers he comes across, well the less curvy ones anyway. If I entertained any doubts he didn't like what he sees, that fire in his eyes would have erased them.

Slowly, tortuously slowly, he parts my thighs, staring at my cunt for a moment. Then, with a quick grin my way, he lowers his face and starts his administrations.

Somehow I had known Road wouldn't disappoint. Unlike some men I've been with, he needs no instructions. He tries one thing, and depending on my reaction, either does it again, or tries something different. His mouth works, sucking, then his tongue licks and his teeth tighten.

My hips trap his head, my strong muscles holding him to me. He broadens his shoulders and uses his own strength to push them apart, giving himself more room to work, and finds my slit and laps my cream. His tongue delves deep inside me, then rises back to my clit, as he swaps it for first one finger, and then adds another. Again, no instruction is required, and he finds my g-spot unerringly. I gasp…

He retreats. *The bastard is teasing me.* One glare down toward his face and he stares back cockily, unrepentant at leaving me on the edge.

Then he resumes his work, ramping up my desires so I'm again teetering on the brink, when once more he ceases.

I could scream with frustration. My body bows, my mouth begs though I can't hear my words.

I'm almost at the point of pushing him away and finishing myself off, when he lowers his head, and once again, begins to assault me. This time, *thank fuck*, he doesn't stop.

It's hard to get air into my lungs as my body completely freezes. I know it's coming, but to the point, I don't know whether I'll survive and live to come down the other side. *The little death?* I think he really might have killed me. I swear I start to see all the stars in the universe, I feel dizzy and then the explosion hits me. Every nerve stretched taut, the freshly released endorphins flooding through every part of my body.

I'm shaking. My body jerking as further minor detonations continue to hit. My eyes are squeezed tightly shut. Never, ever, have I come so hard in my whole life.

As I feel Road move, I make an effort to open my eyes to see him looming over me. Somehow, while I was in outer space, he's prepared his cock with a condom. As our eyes lock, I feel him positioning himself at my entrance.

If he speaks from that position, I wouldn't be able to hear him. If he questions my consent, I won't know what he's asking. But Road turns out to be the master of non-verbal communication. He pushes against me slightly, then cocks his head, his eyes do the talking for him. I give a shy nod, *shy?* and open my hips giving him room to move.

I'm wet, Road's earlier administrations had made certain I'd be able to take him. There's a slight burn because of his size, but it's not painful, more of a delicious feeling as he stretches me. He fits, so well. As if he'd been made for me.

He advances, retreats, then regains his ground and advances again. He takes my leg, raising it up and over my shoulder, so I'm even more open to him, and he's able to thrust all the way. His eyes question, *You okay?* I smile back, wriggling at the same time. *I'm fine. What's taking so long?*

He starts moving, *thank fuck,* gentle glides in and out, ramping up my arousal all over again. My body shudders with delight as he finds that spot inside me that drives me wild. He knows and proves it by finding it again. And again. Then, feeling my body tighten, he speeds up, his thrusts become more forceful, hammering into me time after time. I jerk, my stomach muscles ripple. *I need more.* I start to move my hand down to my clit.

Lifting it away, he shakes his head and grins a knowing smile, *No you don't.* As if he knows me better than I know myself. Road keeps to the pace he wants to, and Jesus, though I would have said it was impossible without external stimulation, I can feel another orgasm building, the symptoms multiplying and merging so it's hard to know one from the other. I go up, up and up again. Squeezing my eyes tightly shut, I reach the edge of a cliff, teeter for a moment then let myself go and soar up into the sky, only just conscious of Road's heavy breathing. I can feel sharp exhaled breaths on my cheeks.

I've never had sex in silence before, never given up so much control. I've never trusted anyone enough to leave myself vulnerable. I never felt so much emotion as I got off.

I've never made love.

Made love?

Road rests his forehead against mine. After a few seconds, he moves his mouth down, placing gentle kisses in a line from my brow to my mouth. He pauses, then puts his lips to mine. Putting my arms around him, I pull him close. Our tongues meet and dance. It's sensual and slow, not hurried and urgent, something to be enjoyed for itself, and not as a prelude which needs to be over and done with. We kiss for a long time though I don't measure it, until, reluctantly, Road pushes himself up first on his elbows, then up onto his hands. Balancing on one arm, he reaches out the other and picks up something. Seconds later, I have my hearing aids in my hands.

It doesn't escape me, he knew where they were all the time, could have handed them to me at any stage of the proceedings. If he'd spoken directly into my ear, I would have heard him, and he knows that as well. *Had he been making a point?* Or just showing me my lack of hearing doesn't detract from our coming together, in more ways than one. There had been something magical about sex in silence, our bodies talking without needing words.

But now I have them, I waste no time putting them in and switching them on.

"Good morning." Road rolls to his side, props himself up on one elbow, and adorably huffs a puff of air to blow away hair that's fallen over his face.

It just tumbles back, so using my uninjured hand, I reach up and tuck it behind his ear. It's as intimate gesture as anything else we've shared.

"I've dreamed of wrapping my hand in your hair while you were going down on me," I tell him, with a smirk. I'd forgotten earlier, as he'd needed no direction, but could rectify that now.

"Be my guest," he replies, with a shrug and a grin. "But not now."

"No?" I frown.

"Had a text from Pip while you were still sleeping."

I try to sit up, he pushes me back. "We've got plenty of time to get dressed and ready, but just not enough to go another round."

To be honest, I'm still sated and I shouldn't be greedy.

Road stares at me, his smile fading, and lines appearing on his brow. He sits up, his brow creasing, his playfulness gone. What he says next shocks me. "So, have we gotten it out of our systems? Is this it, Swift? We part and go our separate ways now?"

Is that what he thinks? Or wants? My breathing stops. He might have gotten it out of his, but he's only woken a new appetite in mine.

"I'm giving you the option, Swift." His hair flops over his face again. This time he brushes it back himself. "I know how you like to play things, and hey, so did I up to now. If you still think that way and want to call a stop to this seeing as we've fucked, I won't make any waves. I'll sleep with you while you need someone to reassure you, you're safe, and I'll keep my hands to myself."

"You could do that?" I'm curious. He might be sure of himself, but I don't think I could. As for getting him out of my system, I think it's the opposite. I just want him more. I worry I could even become addicted. But if that's not what he wants, I'll step away. I'm not going to make a fool of myself.

"It would be hard." He glances down at his cock, having slipped out of my body, it's swelling again. "But we'll just ignore him."

Not responding to his playful remark, I focus on what's important. "Is that what you want, Road?" It would be tidier. No messy relationship to deal with, no working out how we could have a sexual liaison and keep it all quiet.

"I…" He winces slightly, sliding the condom off and tying it "I want what you want, Swift." But his eyes won't meet mine. I wonder why not, and what they'd reveal if he looked at me. His posture is rigid, and it hits me—while the right words are coming out of his mouth, they don't reflect how he's really thinking.

What do I want? Suddenly it's blindingly obvious, and to hell with any complications. We'll just have to deal with it. Yesterday we got free, killed two men, incapacitated two more. We worked as a team and well together. We can handle whatever lies ahead. After a moment, I respond, "You can't have what I want," I tell him, in a serious tone.

He glances at me. It's enough to show me his face has twisted and the corners of his mouth have turned down. He thinks I'm rejecting him. I don't leave him hanging.

"You can't have it because you've already got it. What I want is you, Road." His brows draw down as he tries to understand my statement. So I clarify myself. "I'm not ready to give you up. I want you back in my bed, and everything that goes along with it."

"My cock?" His eyebrows rise, his expression a little wary.

Damn men. I was also thinking about sleeping cocooned in his arms. But I give him what he's waiting for with a roll of my eyes. "Your cock."

The tension leaving him is obvious, he wants this too. He breathes out, then pinches the bridge of his nose. He speaks after a moment has passed. "How do you want to play this?" He jerks his head toward the world outside my room.

That's the complicated bit. There's no saying where this will be going, whether it would last long enough to make waves. "Let's keep things between us for now. Out there we act as normal. There's no reason for anyone to know what goes on in our bed."

If anything, he seems relieved. Neither of us went looking for or wanted to find a relationship. If anyone else knew, there would be teasing, awkwardness, discomfort, which would be a hundred times worse if we didn't work out and it ended. He knows that as well as I. I don't have to teach him anything about the Satan's Devils brotherhood.

"Better get ready for that meeting with Pip." He winks and starts to push himself up. "I'll get my clothes on and do the walk of shame back to my room."

I snort. Then reach out my hand, my fingers curling around his arm. "Come 'ere first." I pucker my lips. *I pucker my damn lips. What the fuck has gotten into me?*

But Road's eyes just gleam, and his mouth comes down on mine.

Again it hits me how strangely satisfying a kiss can be. I'm sure we've both got morning breath, but as it's two sided, neither of us cares. Eventually, he pulls away, then comes back for one last peck, which has my arms anchoring him to me again.

The next time we break apart, he reminds me, "Pip's waiting. Remember him? Your prez? We're going to be late if we don't get a move on."

"Damn, Road. Why the bloody hell didn't you say?"

He easily evades my playful punch and slides off the bed laughing.

As he throws on his clothes, I feast my eyes on his disappearing skin. When he bends to pull up his jeans, I admire his rather nice ass. Then, with a final wink in my direction, he opens the door cautiously, makes sure the coast is clear, and leaves.

I roll over and stretch. It's been a good start to my day. I feel refreshed, I must have had a good rest. I'd slept soundly, trusting Road to watch out for me. Then, when I'd awoken, he'd taken care of me in another and very pleasurable way.

It wouldn't be hard to get used to this.

32

——————

*R*oad...

Sexually, Swift is everything I've ever wanted in a woman yet never have found. She's an active partner, not afraid to ask for what she wants, even though I purposefully hadn't used words. I'd wanted to show her there were some things she could enjoy even while embracing that she's deaf.

Sex, particularly with a new partner, is often punctuated with 'right theres' and 'move pleases', or 'a little bit to the left or right', but when two bodies are in such harmony as ours had been, directions hadn't been necessary. I'd enjoyed watching her responses and interpreting them, as she had certainly understood mine. We'd used a language as old as time.

Last night the clubhouse was quiet, apart from Brute and Igor, we were the only ones here. Today there's movement and sound coming from all directions. Brothers stirring in their rooms, toilets flushing, showers running, and voices coming along the hall. Quickly, I open my door and slip inside before anyone spots me.

I respect and support Swift's desire to keep what's between us quiet for now. Who wants to stir up shit when we've no idea where this will go? The destination could be far off, years into our future, or just a few more nights might show the magic we thought was between us, doesn't exist.

Most importantly, before I take an old lady, there are matters I have to resolve. I have to decide what I want out of life, starting with in which state I'm going to live. Disregarding the mess I'm in, that I'll either have to keep lying to Drummer, or expose Pip for what he is, my stars now seem more aligned with Utah now that I'm with Swift. I just don't know how to get out of the hole I've dug for myself.

Tossing my clothes on the bed—both the jeans and shirt were clean last night, and I'd worn them for such a short time, they'll do for today—I walk naked into the shower. There, I let the water run over my back, cascading down my body. Balancing myself on my stitched-up arm to keep it out of the stream, I rest my forehead against the tiles.

A few months back, I had my future mapped out and there was no woman in it, or none I wanted around for more than a few hours. If I wanted a woman to talk to, there were my brothers' old ladies. Kids? Well there were enough of those getting under my feet, and none of them mine. I had no yearning to take a woman and certainly none to start a family.

Could it have been that the blow to my head had not only given me a concussion but also screwed with my brain and changed what I want out of life? Or was it simpler, that having had the opportunity to achieve what I'd worked for so long taken away, I needed something else to look forward to? Was Swift a substitute for what I'd lost?

I don't believe so but shouldn't dismiss it.

If I'd ever thought of my ideal woman, it would have been someone who wasn't afraid to speak her own mind. I didn't want to be the one always leaned on, I wanted my perfect old lady to have more strength than that. Someone like Sam, Drummer's woman, I suppose. Drummer might have grown men cowering before him, but she stands up for herself. There's a lot to admire about Sam, and she can't even hold a candle to Swift. If anything, I'd be the one running to keep up in this relationship.

And that, I don't have a problem with. I've an inkling Swift would make me a better man. I'd always strive to be worthy of her. More than anything, though, I love to make her smile. Which reminds me, when I get a moment later, I need to call Beef, the Tucson member who transferred out and who's now the Colorado VP. There's that idea I want to discuss with him. Out of anyone, he should be able to help.

The cafeteria is busy by the time I get down to the first floor. Noticing Swift is encircled by concerned brothers wanting to check she's okay after her ordeal, I keep my distance, though I do keep one eye on her. They're all treating her as one of them. Had it been an old lady or club girl, then she'd have been hugged or coddled. But she's being treated with respect, and no more touching than they'd allow for each other. A hearty backslap from Stormy that puts her off balance makes my temperature rise, but my ire's quickly replaced by mirth as she quickly deals with that herself, having the asshole's armed twisted up behind his back. If I'm not wrong, he's currently begging for mercy.

I'm secretly smiling at how the woman who's caught my attention needs no one to look after her, when Bolt comes up alongside me.

"Fuckin' sorry, Brother," he starts.

His words need no explanation, and I shrug off his apology. "Don't sweat it, man. It couldn't be helped. I was the idiot who rode on without waiting."

"Still can't believe she was there. Fuckin' good job finding her. She really okay?" His eyes narrow.

While half of me wants to defend her and let everyone know she's come through her ordeal unscathed, it's not the whole truth. As brothers, we protect each other, and no one can help if they're in the dark. "She'll get there. Being taken like that brought home her vulnerability."

Igor approaches me with a cup of coffee in his hand. He passes it over, and I give him a nod, then return my attention to my companion.

Bolt glances down at his hand which looks so real but is not. "This has become part of me, Road. If I were in danger and I didn't have my right hand, well, I'd be worried as fuck. And, probably scared. There's not much I can do with my stump." His expression oozes sympathy. He glances quickly over to Swift. "She won't want a big thing made of it."

"Try having no legs." Pip's overheard and joined in the conversation. He jerks his head toward Bolt, who takes the hint.

"Want me to grab you a plate?"

"Thanks." I raise my chin thankfully toward Bolt who goes off to join the short queue at the counter.

My brain's focused on the delicious smells coming from the heaping serving bowls. This morning's activities have made me hungry as fuck. It takes a few moments for words I just heard to filter through my head. Suddenly my eyes swing to Pip, glancing down at his legs encased in jeans.

"What the fuck, Pip? Who's got no legs?" I glance around the room at the rest of the brothers but come up, pardon the pun, stumped.

He chuckles softly. "It's the reason I don't ride. I left both of mine in Iraq, back in the days of Desert Storm."

I choke while swallowing my coffee. Pip slaps my back. Once I can speak again, I feel my brow crease. "So that's the fuckin' reason you don't ride a bike?"

He raises his chin. "Sure is. Like Bolt, I've got the best

prosthetics money can buy, but I don't want to risk damaging them by giving riding a try. If I damaged them, not only would they be expensive to replace, but I'd be fuckin' vulnerable." His head turns slightly so his gaze lands on Swift before coming back to mine.

"You know how she feels," I state, not needing it confirmed. Like her, Pip hides his disability well. Why should I have known he was a double amputee, except that it explains things, and why the MC is okay having a prez who doesn't ride.

Pip's eyes meet mine again. "I take my legs off at night but keep them close by. I've practiced getting them back on so I can do it in a blink of an eye. But like Bolt said, you feel you have a weakness when you haven't got your own working parts. Maybe in normal life it's different but given how we live, it's a liability. Not being able to hear an alarm or intruder must be scary as fuck, just like if I was kidnapped without my legs and unable to escape. You know if she managed to get any rest last night?"

That final slipped in question was a loaded one. I've got a feeling Pip doesn't miss much. That Swift's bright and breezy and clearly well rested won't have escaped his attention. He also understands how she probably wouldn't be that way had she been left all alone. I could deny it, but I'm already hiding shit from Drummer. If I'm moving to Utah, I don't want to get off on the wrong foot with my new prez.

"I stayed in her room so she felt safe," I admit.

A smirk comes and goes, and this time the slap to my back isn't to stop me from choking. "Appreciate that, Brother. What you and Swift do is your personal business, and I'm not going to mention anything about her in church. Not unless she thinks we need to know how vulnerable being kidnapped made her feel. But I'm glad you're looking out for her. Anyone who's gone through what she has needs support. Me and Bolt know that better than any of the others."

"I had an idea, Pip." It's his clubhouse and will be his decision whether I can bring any changes to it. "I don't know whether it would work, and probably need your permission to look further into it."

I take a moment to explain what my idea is. Listening, his eyes widen and for the third time the palm of his hand meets the leather on my back. "That's fuckin' great, Brother. Let me know if you need help sorting it out. And I'll make sure there are no objections from anyone."

"I need to check shit out first," I warn him. "Keep it quiet until I know it's even possible."

As he nods and turns away, Bolt returns and places a plate loaded with every breakfast item imaginable into my hands. My stomach growls in appreciation, and I pull out a seat at a table and start tucking in.

"So you're the fuckin' hero of the hour."

Someone slams a plate on the table, sits down opposite without permission and proceeds to glare at me. Ignoring Stormy, I lift my fork and start shovelling food into my mouth, musing that Cowboy really does know his shit.

"Nothing to say?"

Starting to feel replete, I swallow and raise my narrowed eyes. "What *is* your problem, Stormy?"

"You got yourself caught."

Yeah. I should have been more cautious. I don't have any excuse. Shouldn't have gone in on my own. Should have waited with Bolt for backup before proceeding. Should have, could have and a whole lot of ifs. Apart from the bullet graze on my arm, and the nice bruise on my chest, in retrospect it all worked out. Swift might have suffered more had I not arrived when I had. I don't explain that to the man staring daggers at me.

As the silence stretches on, Stormy's expression changes and he gives what for him passes for a grin. It seems he appreciated me not defending my actions. "Though from what Swift says, you weren't entirely helpless. That stiletto in your sole is an idea I think we should copy."

I give credit where it's due. "That's thanks to Blade, the enforcer in Tucson. He's besotted with knives."

"Next time, take one of these with you." Stormy places a gadget on the table. Curious, I pick it up, finding it sits comfortably in the palm of my hand.

"What is it?"

"Drone." He takes it back and shows me how to open it up.

I hadn't realised they came this small. It would be easy to take in my saddlebags, if not in a pocket at a stretch. "What size is the controller?" I ask him.

"You can install the app on your phone. If you're interested, I'll show you how it works."

I am. If I'd been able to view the surroundings, I'd have seen people were patrolling the grounds, or that they had cameras set up. There could have been something that would have warned me. I start to thank Stormy, full of surprise he'd given me one of his toys, but he waves aside anything I was going to say, and instead, distaste covers his face.

"Oh fuck, got to go waste time chewing the fat again." Stormy glowers as people around us are moving. "Fuckin' hate all these meetings."

"You don't like church?" I ask, as he's being his version of friendly.

"I don't like people," he responds succinctly, and then stands. "And I don't trust anyone either."

As I hastily finish off the last piece of bacon, I stare after the man who's just left me. The chip on his shoulder is a mile wide, and there must be a story of what happened to put it there. Such dislike and distrust don't come naturally, or not in my experience. Could he have been born that way? Not likely.

Drummer had sent me to Utah as my accident had taken all my patience away. I'd been angry at everyone, even though they hadn't done anything. Stormy's me to the extreme. *What had happened to him?* Pip called him back to the club and stripped him of his nomad status because he'd all but gone rogue, but Stormy's actions had been fuelled by his distrust, his return to the club hadn't caused them.

Having realised how insightful the Utah prez is, I wonder now whether there was more to Stormy's recall, and that by forcing him back into the fold, there was perhaps a route for his redemption.

Pushing my thoughts aside, I take my dirty plate and place it with the others, noticing Brute is on kitchen duty clearing stuff away, then, following the example of the others walk along the hallway and enter church.

Pip, Snatcher, Thor and Preacher are already seated. Swift's taking her chair. Seeing me entering, she kicks out the one beside her. Sitting, I simply raise my chin to thank her, while breathing in deeply through my nose, finding her scent intoxicating, immediately pulling my seat in closer to the table so I don't betray myself.

The room fills up fairly fast, and as previously, I notice the jokes and conversations I'd expect in Tucson are missing. But today I don't mind, now better understanding the vibe here. Rather than updates about the money the strip club and tattoo parlour are bringing in, a meeting like this could be a matter of life or death. From my discussions with Grinch and Goofy, meetings I'm more used to happen as well, with the additional three members present. That's when matters like dues and pay packets are discussed.

Pip bangs the gavel once everyone's taken a seat. His stare focuses on Swift. "Fuckin' glad to have you back, Swift."

She raises her chin but follows it up with the words, "Fuckin' glad to be here, Prez." A murmur of lighthearted laughter goes around.

"Debrief. We've yet to hear your side." Pip's eyes are still levelled on her.

I almost feel the deep intake of breath by my side. "They must have cut the electric." She shudders. "I hadn't a clue anyone was there. First thing I knew was someone putting a chloroform drenched rag over my face. Woke up chained in that basement."

Honor points across the table at her. "They disabled your backup generator first. I'm looking into alert systems running on lithium batteries." He brushes a hand over his head. "We looked at fail safes for normal occurrences, not for you being deliberately targeted."

Pip makes a gesture that gets our attention. "Kincaid admitted he'd been watching me and the club. He focused on Swift as she was the only woman he saw going in and out of this building. Seems he learned a lot in the pen, like being careful and not moving without knowing exactly what was going on. McGregor, apparently, had studied electrical engineering inside." He pauses, then remarks with disgust, "Fuck knows why we teach them such skills. Anyway, he checked out your house and noticed your security system, Swift, and the generator as well. Disabled that, then cut the electricity. Somehow got inside and left a bug and camera there. But seeing no one visited you, he hadn't known you were deaf. That was a bonus according to him." Pip's eyes narrow. "He enjoyed fuckin' with your mind."

"He still alive?" Swift asks, her own eyes becoming slits.

"Nah. But he suffered before I ended him." It's Pip's delivery rather than the actual words that make me believe death had probably come as a welcome release for Kincaid.

"Any loose ends?" Swift asks.

"We sorted it," Thor tells her. "Bodies taking to the crematorium, a few dollars passed over and they'll be gone by now. Honor supervised the cleanup. If anyone comes looking or the owner of the Airbnb checks in, they'll find nothing amiss."

I suppose Honor being an ex-cop should know how to hide shit from forensic experts. I wonder what happened to make both him and Duty turn their backs on a career in law enforcement. Seems I'm becoming interested in more than one backstory of the members who, if everything works out, will be my brothers.

"We could have a problem. The Airbnb was rented by a woman." Snatcher looks around, knowing his words will be unwelcome. "The agent thought a couple was staying."

"That's what the fisherman told me," I interrupt. "Though he hadn't seen the woman around."

"So there could still be someone out there?"

Pip's eyes gentle when they land on Swift. "That's what we need to find out. I want you staying in the clubhouse until we find out if this woman exists, who she is, and whether she's got resources behind her to carry this fight on."

"Or," Swift sits up straighter and looks straight toward Pip, "I act as bait to draw her out."

My gut screams I want her to keep her head down, to let others take on this fight. My mouth opens and shuts as I realise were Swift any other woman, I'd be telling her to let me protect her and keep her safe.

But she's Swift. She's going to run headfirst into danger if that's what the job calls for. She's not going to hide. The only decision I've got to make is whether I'm man enough to accept it.

"Okay. Let's get going. I need Kincaid's past gone through with a fine-tooth comb. Any girlfriends, ex-wives, fuck, any female he could be associated with. We need to know whether this is ended, or whether we've still got a fight on our hands."

Pip moves his expression to the man seated opposite me, "Oh, and Bolt, get yourself a new set of tyres. Mystic said there was barely any fuckin' tread left." That Bolt should have checked his bike first goes unsaid.

Bolt's sheepish eyes meet mine, showing he hadn't needed the verbal dressing down.

"I should have checked everything. Sorry, Prez, but we headed out so quickly." Piston, the road captain looks contrite.

"Man should have checked his own fuckin' ride." Stormy doesn't hold back.

Now Bolt looks like he wants to slide under the table and disappear from sight.

"Prez?" Again it's Piston who speaks. "I'm getting involved in so much other shit nowadays, I don't always have time to keep my eyes on the rides. I'm not sure I was ever the right man for the job. If we can convince Road to transfer, he'd be ideal."

Pip looks at him carefully. "You'd be alright with that?"

Piston shrugs. "Would take a load off of me."

I wonder whether I'm being set up, but if I am, it means I haven't fucked up, and they're making a place for me in the Utah club. More than that, they're dangling an attractive carrot in front of me. Road captain? Okay, so not quite up there with the officers at the head of the table, but a responsibility and a title I hadn't dreamed of. "Not sure I'd be the right person, P... Pip." I'd almost called him Prez, but for now, for me, Drummer's still that. "I'm also not certain I'll be able to transfer to Utah."

"No?" Pip raises an eyebrow.

I want to look at Swift, wanting her opinion and needing to know if me agreeing to move and taking an official position, is her idea of taking things slowly and seeing how things naturally progress between us, but I don't want to draw attention to there being anything particular between us. Guess I'm on my own with this one.

Pip grins, he's, of course, noticed the position he's put me in. "You know bikes? You've got a head on your shoulders? I reckon Piston's right, you'd do it well for us. In my view, you're right for this chapter, and I suspect it would be a good move for you."

"You're asking me to make the decision now?" I don't relish being put on the spot, but it's warming to know he, at least, wants me. I frown. "I'll need to make things square with Drummer, and it's still up in the air as to how I do that."

Pip stares and actually grimaces, knowing that were I to accept, I'll need to lie and continue the cover-up. He gives me a chin lift acknowledging the uncomfortable spot that I'm in. "No reason we can't take a hypothetical vote, just so Road knows what lies ahead. Saying he transfers, who'd vote on offering him the position of road captain?"

"About fuckin' time we had someone to focus on us riding safe," Preacher observes. "No disrespect, Piston, but you get easily distracted now you've discovered your IT skills."

"No objection here." Honor's head jerk toward Duty makes it look like he speaks for both of them.

"Er, I can't object." Bolt's face has gone red.

Others just raise their hands and say, "Aye."

"Stormy?" Pip asks, when he's the only person who's not endorsed me.

"I keep my own fuckin' bike in order," he growls. "But if the rest of you assholes need instruction, Road would do just as well as anyone. 'Bout all he knows anyway."

Well, damned with faint praise from that corner, I half smile, now not expecting anything else.

"Right." Pip bangs the gavel. "Position's yours if you want it, Road."

And I think my decision has been made. Perhaps if anyone

had spoken against me, I'd think twice about it, but I do get a warm glow inside that they all seem to want me. I give a chin lift to Pip. "I'll work out something with Drummer."

My statement hangs in the air, the question still remaining, how the fuck do I do that?

33

Swift...

I hadn't been sure how Road would treat me this morning, whether he could actually be circumspect, or whether he wouldn't be able to suppress his possessive nature.

It had only been after he'd snuck back to his room that I began to have regrets. Not that I'd fucked him—how could I resent a man who'd given me the best orgasms of my life? No, it was the thought that I'd broken my rules and gone with a potential team member.

Should I hope that he'd go back to Tucson as he'd originally planned? But that would mean little time for repeats, and heaven help me, I want at least one. If only to show me the first time had been an exception, both of us fuelled by the remnants of the adrenaline from our escape. Maybe next time I'd find sex with him boring, though I suspect that thought is more aspiring than realistic. There's no doubting Road and I had clicked and had shown in bed we were more than compatible.

What I'm afraid of is that we won't be such a good match when we're out of it. Now we've fucked, would he treat me differently? If we'd done the deed before yesterday, would he have been so inclined to follow my lead, or tried to push me behind him?

I'd gone through my morning rituals far quicker than he had and reached the cafeteria before him. I was immediately surrounded by brothers who, not surprisingly, wanted to ask me questions, me making them laugh by my worry that I wouldn't be able to P anymore, referencing how I use a keyboard.

Really, I'm beyond angry something so simple, yet still life-changing, had been taken from me, but then, I'm alive to live another day so any complaining isn't really worth it. I'd tried to make light of it.

For me, at least, the air had become charged when Road had entered the room. I must already be attuned to him as I sensed his presence before I saw him. I carried on talking while crossing my fingers on my unbandaged hand, hoping that he wasn't going to come over. Various scenarios flicked through my mind—Road coming over and hugging me, marking me as his territory, Road unable to resist joining the group that had congregated around me, and giving himself away by soft looks in my direction. But I needn't have worried. He'd got talking to Bolt, and I think I was the only one to see him tensing when Stormy slapped my back just a little too firmly, and I hadn't missed his smirk when I gave the asshole what he deserved.

In church, Road had sat in his normal seat which placed him next to me. No affectionate words, glances or touches. Half of me bristled as I wondered how little I meant to him, before slapping myself mentally and accepting this was exactly what I wanted.

Not having to worry about him betraying me, I was able to give my full attention to the meeting. That an unknown woman was involved was concerning. No one likes loose ends which could need tying.

When Piston both offered to step down and suggested Road should become road captain, after Pip had put it to a hypothetical vote, well I felt a sense of pride. Which was strange, why should anything which was essentially praising the man mean anything to me? Instead I should be worried, it's given him a reason for staying. What if a relationship between us doesn't work out? Will it make our necessary interactions awkward? What if it does? How the fuck would that work? Would we be able to keep it a secret, or would it be best to admit to it, and what would that do for the dynamics of the club, or for us?

Church over, Road hangs back, indicating to Piston he wants to talk to him. No mystery there, he'll be wanting to know more about the position he'd all but officially accepted. Knowing keeping our distance is for the best, I head on into the comms room, wasting no time booting up my laptop.

"Where are we at?" I ask Honor, who's doing the same.

"Duty and I will dig into Kincaid's background and contacts in prison. You want to look into his family tree?"

I nod, I'll do that. In effect, they'll start at the back end and work forward, while I'll start with what I can find out about Kincaid and who he had contact with in the present, then if I find nothing recent, track back to his family living and dead.

It's not long before Piston joins us. He's right, nowadays he'd rather be sat at a desk than getting his hands greasy as a mechanic. He's shown an aptitude for tracking shit down.

"What d'ya want me to do?" he asks as he enters.

Honor glances up. "Get back to the agent for the Airbnb owner. See how the booking was made. He seemed insistent it was a female, but we need to check that, see if there's any chance he was mistaken."

"What's my cover story?"

"I told him we were chasing up a non-payment on a previous rental. The details are in the folder." Honor slides a file across the desk, and Piston pulls it closer.

"On it," Piston says, reaching simultaneously for a keyboard and his cell, and putting on headphones.

I crack on with my own task, calling up Kincaid's last known address, his rental records, contacts, and bank account to see if anyone else had a card on it. It's taking me longer than usual. I can't hit P, or the return on the right side, and the rest of my fingers on my right hand are still bound by the bandage, stiff and not cooperating. The more I work, the more I find I miss that finger. If Kincaid was buried and not incinerated, I reckon I'd dig him up just to kill him again.

How will I hold a cup of tea if I can't hold my pinky out? I snort at my own English joke. Not that I was ever particularly ladylike.

Unable to use my right hand properly, I hunt and peck at the keys, getting increasingly exasperated.

"Use speech to text," Duty, eyeing my slow progress, suggests.

"I've got it," I snap, knowing this is my new normal and I'm just going to have to get used to it.

Immediately I feel guilty, not being known for having a short fuse. I notice three heads are studying me, and my face goes red. But no one says anything, and only a few seconds have passed before fingers start tapping keyboards again. I consider Duty's option of using text to speak and decide it could work if I'm typing long passages and not just search terms, and decide to tell him how useful his suggestion would be later.

Just as I've landed on a plan to make things right with the brothers, the door to the comms room opens. That's not unusual of course, but who's entering uninvited is. It's Igor.

"What the fuck?" Honor asks, his eyes narrowing as he

lowers the lid on his laptop. Prospects don't come into the comms room other than by specific invitation, and after we've had time to close what we're working on or cover monitors up. Except for Gears, of course, who gets a little more leeway as he draws closer to getting his patch.

"We've got visitors," Igor explains, but from the set look to his features, they're neither expected nor wanted. Having delivered his message he disappears again without having disclosed who it is.

Having a bad feeling about whoever's come calling, I check my gun is loaded then slide it into my shoulder holster where it's ready at hand, noticing my companions do the same. Then, as one, Honor, Duty, Piston and I are moving, and heading out to the reception area.

The first thing I notice is that there's a number of bikes pulled into the visitors' parking lot. We hadn't heard them arrive in the soundproofed comms room. Men are getting off wearing cuts, but as luck would have it, as they're facing the building, it means I can't see what's on their back patches. I certainly don't recognise any of the faces as men who've I've met before. I'm so focused on trying to make them out, I don't notice not all of the unknown bikers are outside.

"What the actual fuck?" A loud bark which all but causes the windows to rattle makes me jump.

Swinging around, it's to find a man with salt and pepper hair and beard glaring at me with piercing grey eyes in such a glacial way I immediately want to drop to my knees and beg for forgiveness for a crime I didn't commit. I resist the impulse, of course, and instead stare steadily back, while keeping my hand firmly at my side in case I inadvertently snap to attention and salute.

"Snatcher!" the man roars, looking around as if hoping the man that he named would magically appear. "Where the fuck are you, Snatcher?" He turns to the prospect standing behind the reception desk, thumping a heavy hand on the wooden top. "Go get your prez, now!" Poor Gears looks totally lost.

When his attention is turned to someone else, the spell holding me fixated seems to be broken, and now I move my eyes away from his and down to his cut. *Satan's Devils Tucson Chapter* read the top and bottom patches, the middle one is identical to the one I wear on my back, and which I gave blood, sweat and tears to earn. The man swings back around, his eyes catching mine once again. Now I take the opportunity to read the patches on the front. *President,* says one, and another under that, *Drummer.*

Oh, fuck.

Snatcher appears almost at a run, followed by Pip. Drummer sees them immediately. Ignoring the man behind, he addresses himself to the one he assumes is still the prez of our MC.

"Snatcher. What the fuck's going on? Where's Road, and what the fuck is *this*?" This, as indicated by a wave of his hand, appears to refer to me.

"Road's in the meeting room." Snatcher wipes a tired hand over his face. "This way, Drummer."

"Need us, Drum?"

"Yeah, Wraith. Peg and Blade, you come too."

When Snatcher indicates the way, Drummer and his three men follow them down the corridor. Most of them ignore me, though as he passes, the final one sneers at me and mimes cutting his throat.

"You want me in there?" I ask Pip quietly as he goes by. If anyone has any explaining to do, I'd rather be there to present the case for myself.

"Nah. But don't go too far. Wait in the clubroom."

The disrespect shown in our clubhouse has already made my hackles rise. But I suppress my anger, as I watch them all disappear, wondering how this is going to play out. While I squeeze into the elevator along with the brothers, my mind's going through all the scenarios I can imagine. Drummer had seen my patch denoting I'm a full member. Pip had twisted the regulations when he gave it to me, and it's more than clear the president of the mother chapter, nor any of his men with him, liked the knowledge a woman has been brought into their ranks.

Will Pip give in? Could it be tonight, I'm no longer a member of the Satan's Devils? Then I look at the faces of the men surrounding me and realise we've got worries deeper than how Drummer's visit affects me personally. It's possible in a short time, this chapter won't be comprised of any Devils at all, once Drummer finds out he's been lied to for the past ten years, and Snatcher's not even the president. By tonight, our club may not exist.

I don't think any of us know what to do while we wait to find out our fate. I pace. Honor sits with his head in his hands, Duty hovering near him. Bolt fidgets and can't keep still. Piston and Cowboy get shot glasses filled but seem unsure whether to drink them or not.

"We should be fuckin' in there!" Stormy's face looks black as he arrives, obviously having come straight from the gym as he has a towel around his neck.

"You really think that would help?" Preacher cuffs him around his head. "You may get your chance. If Pip tells Drummer everything, you'll have some explaining to do."

"Yeah?" Stormy goes chest to chest with the sergeant-at-arms. "You think I'm afraid of Drummer?"

"I think you'd be a fool not to show some respect for the man who holds our fate in his hands," Thor advises, his foot resting on a chair as he leans his weight over his knee.

"We can take them. They'll never get back to Tucson alive."

"Kind of your answer for everything," I observe.

"Yeah? Well, what if Pip gives in and you're out, Swift?

Seems you've got the most to lose." Stormy points out what I already know.

"Pip won't give in." Unable to resist taunting him, I add, "If he throws anyone to the lions, it's more likely to be you for fuckin' things up."

Stormy sweeps the towel off his shoulders and tosses it down. "Yeah?" He adopts a fighting stance. "Come on then, little girl."

"Christ." Preacher grabs him and pulls him back. "Don't you ever give up? And Swift's got one fuckin' hand out of action."

"I could still take him." The look I shoot him is full of derision.

"Swift?" Brute steps into the clubroom, his eyes warily eyeing Stormy, keeping well out of his reach. "Pip says you're to go to the meeting room now."

Just me? Fuck.

"Good luck," Thor offers as I walk past, but the way his jaw is set suggests I'm right to be worried.

Fuck it. I like living this life, I don't want to lose my patch. And definitely not because I lack the right tackle between my legs.

My shoulders held up, my back ramrod straight, I waste no time taking the elevator down, march along the hallway, then opening the door, step inside the meeting room.

Drummer doesn't look any more mollified than he'd done earlier. I notice he's taken Pip's place at the head of the table. I presume he thinks he's got that right as the mother chapter prez. Snatcher's sitting on his right, Pip to his left. The three men who came in with him also grouped at the top, along with Road, who's the only one giving me an encouraging look.

I don't feel comfortable enough to take a seat for myself. I might not be here long. I stand with legs apart and my hands clasped behind my back.

The effect of those steel-grey eyes hasn't diminished. I remind myself I've stared down much harder men than the mother chapter prez, men whose sole purpose was to break me. Then, I realise, it's much the same. Like the officers challenging me whether I was good enough to join the SAS, I've now got to prove I've got what it takes to be a Satan's Devil.

The silence stretches out, but I hold Drummer's gaze, resisting the urge to look down or anywhere other than straight into his face. I half expect him to bark, name, rank and number.

"You're ex-SAS," Drummer voice booms at last.

"No," I contradict, noticing Drummer raises his eyebrows at Pip as if asking whether this is another lie he's been told. Wanting to take the heat off my prez, I expand, "I qualified, but was invalided out before I could take my place."

"Fuckin' hard for a woman to get into that arm of the services. Like getting into Delta Force if I'm right."

I respond as I would to a superior officer. "Yes, Sir." I respect the hell out of Pip, always have done, always will do, but there's something about the prez who's learned his trade through street smarts and not having the benefit of training from the CIA that makes him both even more of a threat, and someone you'd want to have your back.

"And you want to be a Satan's Devil?"

I bite my tongue holding back the fact I already am, knowing the best response to someone in command, "Yes, Sir."

I still haven't looked away. Our gazes are locked. Drummer continues to rest his steely eyes on mine, and I stare steadily back.

"Oh, for fuck's sake, at ease soldier." Drummer's the one to break first. "Sit the fuck down."

He waves at a chair opposite Road. I pull it out and do as

instructed. Road's half smirking, *the bastard.* I wish I knew what conversations have already gone down.

Drummer waves at the men I haven't met yet and introduces them in turn. "Wraith, my VP, Peg, sergeant-at-arms, Blade, our enforcer." I give them nods, summing them up quickly. Blade's still glowering at me, Peg might be a man hard to take down, but I'm certain I'd be a match for the Tucson prez, or his VP and enforcer.

Introductions made, Drummer tugs at his beard. "Looks like we've got a fuck of a mess to sort out, and you, Swift, are right in the midst of it." He looks uncomfortable for a moment. "The spirit of the regulations is that only men can be patched members of the Satan's Devils MC. It's implied, but not clearly stated, that no women can join." He glances at Road for a moment, then at Wraith. "My old lady's thinking of forming a Satan's Devils MC Ladies Riding Club. Maybe even have a patch made to show they're affiliated to us. Wouldn't turn anyone's head if you were to start the same thing here."

"Permission to speak?" I ask politely on the surface, but there's no doubting my tone is snarky. "With no disrespect to your woman, she hasn't prospected to join the club." Or maybe she has, but on her back. That observation I keep to myself.

"She's an ace mechanic." Road throws me a warning glance. "Rebuilt a Vincent Black Shadow and rode it three thousand miles, not many men could have done that. She did a lot of the tuning on my race bikes. Heart's woman, another of our old ladies, well she built her own rat bike from spare parts. No one can fuckin' keep up with her when she rides that thing."

"Fuckin' rat bike," their sergeant-at-arms grumbles, causing the enforcer sitting beside him to stop frowning and smirk.

I shrug. "I prospected for a year which would have earned

me the right to ride with your chapter. Then I prospected a further year learning what this chapter needs." I wonder if I've said too much about how Utah is different, so change track. "I passed every test set for me. As a woman, I'm used to proving myself not only as good as any man, but better. The fact I've not got a dick shouldn't come into account. I can ride and fight just as well as any of the brothers."

I notice Drummer's VP leans over and says something into his ear. Even if I could lip read, I wouldn't be able to know what he's saying as his hand is hiding his mouth. Drummer reacts by giving a thoughtful nod.

"I knew us coming to Utah was going to open a whole can of worms. Just didn't know how many of them I'd find wriggling. Gonna ask you to leave us now, Swift."

"Am I still a member?" I ignore Road's warning glance.

"That's for us to discuss," Drummer replies, his expression so unreadable I note never to play poker against him.

34

———

$\mathcal{R}$oad…

Drummer stares at the closed door for a moment after Swift departs. To be honest, I feel sorry for him. During the conversation today, his face resembled what mine probably looked like when I'd first arrived, a mixture of *what the fuck* and *you've got to be kidding me*.

Everyone lets Drummer have his moment of contemplation, knowing there's a lot for him to take in. It might be true he inherited the role of prez of the mother chapter, but in all the years he's been in that chair, no one's wanted to take it from him. Except for Snake in San Diego, but he was a twisted egocentric man. Drummer views his position as a privilege, not a right, and is driven by his desire to run the club in the best possible way and treat all members fairly, which up to now, has only included men.

He sits, shaking his head, then taps his fingers against the tabletop. "Let me get this right. Snatcher isn't prez, Pip is. A man I have never met nor know the first fuckin' thing about. I, and the other prezes have been lied to for ten fuckin' years.

On top of that, you've patched in a woman, something that goes against the spirit, if not the wording of our rules."

Pip sighs. "There's more. I think you ought to hear it." He glances at me and momentarily his eyes soften.

"More?" Drummer's incredulous eyes land on him. He drops his head into his hands for a moment, then massages his temples and looks up. "Go on."

Now Pip shrugs. "You haven't asked why we deceived you, so I'll pre-empt that now. I can't ride a bike and will never be able to. That's why Snatcher takes the lead when the club rides out."

Drummer looks like he's about to fall off his chair. "You don't fuckin' ride." He snorts loudly. "*You don't fuckin' ride?* You call yourself Prez, but that's right up there as one of the main requirements of being a member of this club."

"Why don't you ride?" Peg's sharp, and he's caught something Drummer's missed. "You didn't say you didn't want to but inferred that you can't."

"Lost both my legs," Pip informs him without missing a beat.

"Fuckin' sorry about that," Drummer says fast, his sharp eyes assessing him. "You served?" At Pip's nod, Drummer breathes in deeply and holds it. When he lets his breath out, it's with the words, "But that doesn't change things. Rules are rules."

"Pip's the right man to lead this club." Snatcher leaps to his prez's defence.

"Prez?" I get Drummer's glare turned my way. "There are things you don't know."

"I'm beginning to wonder if I know my own fuckin' name right now, Road. But I do know you've been keeping things from me. It's time you spill."

"Drummer, I—"

"Shut the fuck up, Pip. You too, Snatcher. I don't know

who I trust to tell me the truth right now, but I trust myself to know when Road is lying. He's got tells which I know only too well. So it's him I'm going to listen to."

I've got tells, have I? No wonder I've lost so much money to him playing cards. But I put that thought behind me, too much else is at stake to dwell on that now. I clear my throat. "I was as shocked as you when I walked in here, Drummer." I notice Snatcher raising his eyebrows and smirking but ignore him. "Pip here is a disavowed CIA agent. His expertise is in negotiation and hostage extraction. He's in deep with Devil." I see Drummer's eyes widen. "And it was Devil's suggestion that he came to the club. Pip couldn't work officially anymore but didn't want his expertise to go to waste. Utah doesn't run a tattoo parlour or a restaurant. A couple of the older members keep an auto-shop going as a front, but Utah's main business is in preventing kidnappings or slave trafficking, or, if they take place, stepping in and getting the victim out." I pause, then tell them with a hint of pride in my voice, "I went along with them to Santa Barbara where we rescued a little girl. Got her back home to her parents."

Drummer lets that sink in for a moment. Then he turns to Pip. "And you do that under the umbrella of the Satan's Devils MC?"

Pip shakes his head. "We don't wear our cuts, and normally we go in masked. There's nothing to connect our operation to the Satan's Devils."

"You're using the club as a front?" Wraith asks.

"No." Snatcher sounds firm. "We are Satan's Devils, but this is our line of work."

"There's more," I tell Drummer, getting a roll of his eyes as though he's wondering when the blows will stop. "This whole chapter is based on intelligence. We always thought Utah didn't have a man like Mouse. In fact, a number here could give him a run for his money. They really can," I take a breath, then pronounce the words which are likely to get an explosion, "get into Fort Knox, well, the equivalent of that information-wise, anyway."

Drummer's face goes blank as he computes what I've said. Then he stands so fast his chair falls over backwards. "San fuckin' Diego? You were the fuckers leading Lost around by his dick?"

Pip grimaces, throws a look my way that's impossible to interpret, and nods. "Yeah."

Knowing Drummer needs to know everything, I continue to throw my new chapter to the wolves. "And Demon."

"Major?" Drummer roars. He leans over the table, then drops back down in his seat so hard I wouldn't be surprised to hear the chair break. His head drops into his hands. While he thinks, it would be possible to hear a pin drop. Then, without raising his head, he says, "Snatcher, Pip, Road. Out."

I stand. I'm being banished by my prez, and I don't know what to make of that. Because I'm not an officer, perhaps? Nah, that's wishful thinking. It's because I've wronged my club. I should have been honest with him from the start.

Out in the corridor, Pip's hand lands on my shoulder. "I'll explain I was the one texting him when you first got here, Road. It wasn't you that misled him."

"You gave me back my phone," I remind him. "I still didn't clue him in."

His hand slips to my back, and he pushes me in the direction of the elevator. "Let's join the others. They'll be wanting news."

Sure. But what exactly can we tell them? I could enlighten them I've never seen my prez so angry, but somehow, I don't think that would help.

As the elevator dings and the door opens, I feel much like a celebrity entering a party as all eyes turn our way. Pip steps to the fore and moves toward the bar, which seems like a good idea. If ever there was a time I needed a drink, it's now.

Thor and Preacher are first to approach. Pip nods, takes a beer which Brute has put into his hand, then turns to the prospect.

"Go join Igor and Gears downstairs. Keep an eye on the meeting room. If our visitors come out, see if they need anything, and if they want me, you know what to do."

"Sure, Prez."

"Is Swift still a Devil?" Stormy shouts from the back of the room.

I notice Swift, standing by the bar, straightens at that question. My eyes linger on her a second too long, trying to signal no one's yet made a decision.

"Are any of us?" Pip responds enigmatically. "Fuck knows."

"They know the truth?" Preacher asks.

Wondering whether he's going to drop me in it, I glance to the elevator seeing the doors are closed and recall Brute's in it heading down to the first floor. Without knowing where the stairwell is located, my immediate escape route is blocked off now.

"Yeah, and then some. We came completely clean."

Inwardly I sigh with relief as Pip shoulders the blame.

"What happens if we lose the charter?" Piston asks. "Is that possible?"

"More than possible, likely," Snatcher states, raising a shot glass and downing it in one. Having wiped the back of his hand across his mouth, he continues, "We've bent the rules so far away from true, I'm not sure how Drummer can condone it."

"Could he strip our patches and send us out in bad standing?"

"Unlikely, I'd say," Pip responds. "We might no longer be

Satan's Devils, but that doesn't mean we can't stay together. Form our own club."

"Unless he thinks we've wronged the Satan's Devils' patch," Thor observes, pinching his nose between his finger and thumb.

"How the fuck could we have wronged them?" Swift's eyes widen with her indignation. "We rescue people, that's not wrong. Or is it because I'm a member?"

Pip's eyes land on one man, and when heads turn, they all point in the same direction.

"What? Oh, hell, yeah. Blame me." Stormy throws up his hands. "I get the job done—"

"While pissing people off in the process."

I've not seen Pip show much emotion before, but it's clear he's making a concerted effort to bring himself under control. His knuckles are white as he holds his empty bottle, his jaw is clenched, and twin spots of red adorn his cheeks.

I'm clearly not the only person to notice.

Preacher, throwing a glower Stormy's way, his eyes signalling a threat that he's to keep his mouth closed, he nods to Piston who goes behind the bar and gets Pip a fresh beer.

"What are our options?" the sergeant-at-arms asks, once Pip's hand relaxes as it moves the drink to his mouth.

Pip breathes out, and some of his tension goes with it. I might not know the man well, but well enough that finding solutions to problems is what he's best at.

"Do we want to keep the charter enough to throw Swift out?" His challenge rings out around the clubroom.

"Fuck no." Thor's response is loud and firm. "Swift's one of our best fuckin' operatives, and a true brother in every sense of the word but one."

"We stand with her." This time it's Duty speaking for him and Honor.

Swift steps closer, receiving a few slaps on her back, non-verbal declarations of support for her. She acknowledges the comments, but still makes the offer. "I could turn in my patch."

"You're not fuckin' doing that," Pip growls.

"Hear me out, please?" Swift waits for him to raise his chin at her. "Doesn't mean I have to stop doing what I do. I can still work for the club, just without wearing a cut on my back."

"Wouldn't work." Thor looks disgusted at the thought. "You fuckin' proved you were worthy when you prospected and have shown your loyalty to the club. Each one of us," he waves his hand incorporating everyone, "knows how this shit works. You fuckin' earned that patch, Swift. Not one of us would give that up, not while we've got air in our lungs."

"You're all forgetting me." Pip drains his second bottle, and I really don't blame him. "If Swift hasn't got the expected apparatus, I haven't either. The lack of flesh and blood legs is a big fuckin' drawback."

"Said it before, Prez. We could attach a side car to a bike to give it balance, or hell, get you a trike."

Pip looks at Piston. "What would that look like? A fuckin' prez on a kiddie cart."

My ears catch the sound of the elevator in motion, but intent on the conversation, I don't pay it much attention.

"Who the fuck cares what it looks like?" Thor's eyes widen. "I don't give a fuckin' damn. Our club, our rules."

"Satan's Devils regulations," Pip reminds them.

"Then let's break off and start our own fuckin' club." Preacher rolls his eyes. "What do we get from being Satan's Devils?"

"What do you fuckin' get?" a voice roars, making us all spin around. It's no surprise to see Drummer exiting the elevator, it's only him who can command the attention of a room like he can. "What do you fuckin' get? You get our name, our reputation. You get our history, though it sounds like you want to toss that to the wind. You get the right to exist from the dominant club. You go it alone? You reckon the Wretched Soulz will let you set up your own club, if you've been expelled from the Devils?" Drummer's face is red. He's even angrier than he was in the meeting room. "The time for breaking away without retribution is long gone. You have to know that."

Pip starts to speak, but Drummer holds up his hand to stop him. "I've decided this is too big for me to make the decision on my own. I've put in a call to the prezes of the other chapters. Red, Demon and Lost will be here tomorrow."

Fuck, that's serious. All the prezes coming together can't be good. For me, or the Utah brothers. For the Vegas prez, the Colorado prez and Lost from San Diego to ride or fly up for an emergency meeting means it's not just a case of Drummer accepting he's got a chapter who runs things differently from the rest.

My eyes catch those of Swift, who's staring into space, looking like a soldier about to face a firing squad. Then I move my gaze to Stormy, who, for once, hasn't that cocky expression on his face. Finally I look at Pip, who's looking resigned, as though he's readying himself to be disavowed once again. This time by the Satan's Devils MC.

I'd thought Preacher's suggestion might have been the answer but setting up as a new MC doesn't sound like it would work. Not if Drummer refused to back up such a request with the dominant club.

I might just be a lowly member, but I know the Wretched Soulz are *the* club that operates in all the states where we have chapters. Any MC wanting to form has to get their backing and permission first. Anyone flying colours in their territory without their permission risks a severe beatdown, or death. If Utah loses Drummer's respect and endorsement, if all members here, and me, are sent out bad, there's a chance none of us will be able to live the MC life again.

Christ, this is bad.

"We're staying tonight," Drummer pronounces. "Have you got space for us here?"

No one wants to get further on the wrong side of Drummer. Offers come from all sides of brothers giving up their rooms to accommodate the prez of the mother chapter and his three officers.

Stormy, Preacher and Rascal are the first to offer up their rooms. I jump in as well, hoping Swift will need me tonight just like yesterday and I assume I'll be in hers. The decisions made, they're followed by a flurry of activity, the three brothers hurrying to tidy their rooms, prospects enlisted to change the sheets on the beds.

Cowboy stirs himself to go and make a meal for our visitors, and anyone else who's still got an appetite after the news we've received that all our futures will be discussed and decided tomorrow.

I'm given an insight of how much it's going to affect me when Blade passes me, and murmurs, "You gone and fucked up good this time, Road."

I don't fail to note, the *brother* he's always called me, is missing.

35

———

$\mathcal{S}$wift…

It's going to happen again.

Something else I've worked hard for, fought for, given my all for, is going to be taken away.

I'm a soldier. While my training included survival skills for being on my own, I was, even then, part of a team. That's why joining the MC had been so appealing to me. I was again part of something and had brothers at my back. I'd proved myself, just as I'd done when I qualified to join the SAS, and now that appears to count for nothing again.

I don't resent being born as a woman; I don't want to be a man. All I want is the chance to be me. I don't much care for feminine things. I'm able to fight in hand-to-hand combat, am a sharpshooter with any gun handed to me and can kill several ways with a knife, let alone being an expert in a variety of other weapons, including those improvised when nothing else is at hand. But that doesn't make me masculine. I eschew wearing dresses as for me jeans or fatigues are far more practical. I don't bother with makeup as there's normally no need, but that doesn't mean I can't play dress up, or that there aren't times I want to.

I just want to be accepted as me. I've earned my place in the MC, but because of their, to my mind, outdated rules, now I may be asked to leave. It's not fair. It's the twenty-first century, but women are still not regarded as equals. We have to fight harder than men for everything, and even then, we might not win.

As I stand in the clubroom, hearing the conversation around me, I zone out. It's not fair, but if the survival of the club depends on me turning in my patch, I would take the fall for the team. The question is, would I really want to stay, still do my part, but under a civilian title? Wouldn't that just prove how unequal being female was?

If I left, where would I go? What would I do? Here is where I've got everything I love.

Suddenly I tune back into the conversation, realising it's not just me who may have decisions to make. We all know why Pip doesn't officially carry the title of prez, and why Snatcher's the outward face of the club. Maybe Pip will have to move on? Not being able to ride is the same disadvantage as me not having a dick.

Start our own club? One where we make all the rules? Yes, that sounded like the best solution all around. I'm just getting excited about the idea, when Drummer appeared, throwing a bucket of ice-cold water on it.

Out bad? When all we do is good? The Wretched Soulz unlikely to give a new club a charter? Which would leave all of us discarded and left out in the cold.

What would Rascal do, Piston? Or Grinch, Goofy and Mystic, or any of us come to that? We all live for the club. Surely Drummer had to see that wasn't right.

From the wide-eyed looks exchanged when Drummer

pronounces this is too big a decision for him to make on his own, it's clear I'm not the only one dreading a future that might be ours from the next day. As for Stormy, well, he might not have to worry about much at all for much longer. He's fucked up too many times and will now face the prezes he wronged.

The shoes I'm wearing are bad enough. No way would I want to wear his.

Like everyone, I want to keep on the right side of Drummer. It's on the tip of my tongue to offer up my room, when Road offers his and no more are needed. Which brings me to another issue.

It's clear Road expects to share mine.

There are selfish reasons why that's a good idea. One, I'd get a chance to see whether those orgasms could be repeated, and two, I wouldn't have to be alone in the quiet of the night.

But what if it hadn't been a fluke with Road? What if I find he can do a repeat and I enjoy it just as much, or now we're starting to learn each other's bodies, possibly even more? What if I lost my patch and he stayed with the club, or Drummer let him go back to Tucson, but disbanded Utah? I wouldn't be welcome in Arizona, I know that. Could I let him walk out of my life when I've found a man who gives me such sexual pleasure? I almost want it to fail to meet expectations again. That way I wouldn't be faced with disappointment.

There's also the problem that I can't live my life depending on someone else. It's not fair to expect Road to give his life up just because I need him. If there's no Utah club and he has the chance to go back to Tucson, I can't keep him. I've got to bite the bullet sometime and get my PTSD under control. Find ways to cope with being deaf, as had been suggested, having battery-powered adaptations which don't rely on electricity. *As long as I keep them charged.* Thinking it is the easy part, but it will look different when panic creeps in when the night falls silent.

I lower my head in my hands and rub at my temples.

It's only a week since Road walked into my life, and now, when circumstances may dictate our next move, I know I don't want to lose him. He keeps me safe when I'm unable to protect myself. I need him, but does he need me?

I can't rely on Road. I might end up using him as a sexual toy and for company.

What's wrong with that? the devil on my shoulder asks.

Because that's not who I am., the sensible angel on my other replies.

"I'm assuming I'll be in your room."

I startle. My hearing aids might be switched on, but so lost in my thoughts, his approach takes me by surprise. And Road's assumption and the way he asserts it, makes me snap. "There are perfectly good couches here."

He stares at me, then shakes his head. "I thought you'd appreciate the excuse to have company."

I shrug. "Yeah? I've managed alone up to now. The clubhouse is full Road, if something happens, they'll warn me." Why I'm pushing him away, I don't know. What has changed since this morning? *Only everything.* I'd wanted time to explore whether we had something going, now I've got to cope with not having what I wanted. Using Road isn't the answer. Relying on myself, as I've always done, the only sensible way forward.

"Swift, please." His voice softens, then he frowns, and examines my face. He sighs deeply, and his shoulders slump. "Okay. Of course I'll sleep out here. Christ, Swift. I wish we were back to this morning."

That he doesn't argue, that he, too, realises everything is changing, makes me feel guilty, and I rethink. "Your leg, you won't get comfortable."

"I'll be okay."

It's not just that I don't think the couches are long or wide enough for him to get a good night's sleep, it's that I know I'll toss and turn all night, not just because I no longer trust technology to keep me safe, but I'll be berating myself for not allowing myself the pleasure I'd find had I given in to the man sleeping one floor down. That's not all. I'll hate myself for disappointing both me and him. I enjoyed having him lying holding me, and not just because of his cock.

"We need to talk." I glance up at him through my eyelashes.

Once again, Road proves he's not just a pretty face. "Laying ground rules?"

I raise my chin. "Foundations, perhaps. Which could be for nothing. Who knows where any of us will be tomorrow?"

Road glances around. Some brothers have disappeared, either to get food which I don't think I'd be able to digest, some to show our visitors to their beds, or give them a guided tour as there's not much point hiding anything here now. The rest are huddled around Pip, deep in conversation about how the club can survive, I expect. But until the meeting tomorrow, who knows? Anything decided tonight will only be hypothetical and dependent on too many variables to know if they are viable options.

"Come," I say, once I've decided no one will miss us.

Road follows me out. He lets me use my key card to summon the elevator, then follows me along the hall until we reach my room. I open the door, he enters after me, shuts it, then leans back against it.

With my back turned toward him, I hug my arms around my waist. "I don't need a man."

"I don't need a woman," he retorts. "But I think I'd like being able to call one particular woman mine. I think she'd complete me."

"Are you still looking, or have you found her?" I ask, just to make sure. Because if he's decided on something permanent involving him and me, he'll be sleeping on that couch. Especially not now, I'm not ready, nor in a position to make a long-term commitment.

"I've found her. And she's you." His voice sounds closer now. "I know you don't think this will work. It's probably the worst possible time to think about our future, but whatever happens, wherever we go and whoever we are, I want us to be together. Maybe today has focused my mind, but I'm asking you to give us a chance, Swift."

"Of course it won't work," I scoff. "I'm not going to be anyone's ol' lady. You'll be calling me property next—"

"Property works both ways, doesn't it? I'll be yours, same as you'll be mine."

"I think you've got me wrong," I object, haughtily. "I'm not going to be subservient to anyone."

"That's not how partnerships work. Fuck, Swift. I don't want a submissive woman. You walk out of my life, then I don't think I'll ever find anyone else. I never have so far. Never found a woman I want to commit to, but hell, I do to you. If you'll have me that is."

"I don't want anyone to dominate me. Not even in bed." Part of me is lying, I might want him to do that, but I'm not going to admit it.

"Babe." His voice is right by my ear, so close I can feel the heat of his breath. "You can dominate me, I don't mind. You can tie me up, hell, flog me, gag me, take all my senses and choices away."

"You're submissive?"

"Not a fuckin' chance, but maybe there'll be times I want to let go, leave you in total charge."

There's an image in my head, but it's not of him tied to my bed, it's of me, restrained and under his control. Heaven help me, but fuck, the thought gets me wet. Surrendering control to someone you trust, someone you know would do the same for you, could be freeing.

Oh fuck. Road's everything I would go looking for if I was in the market for a man. I may not have been looking for a relationship, it might not have come to me on my terms, nor in the timeframe I thought was still to come, but he's here now, and why am I fighting it? Is it because, with me, everything's a battle and one more thing I have to overcome? Perhaps it's time to admit I have feelings for him. I'm lying to myself if I believe I could watch him walk out of my life without giving a relationship between us a try. Men like Road are few and far between. I've never yet found a man his equal and am not sure I ever would.

So, rather than concentrating on reasons why it wouldn't, I ask the opposite. "How could it work?"

"Babe, I know you best me in almost everything you can do."

"In everything," I correct him with a smirk.

"Nah." He chuckles. "My bike riding skills are the best, and, I apparently have common sense. Oh, and while I don't cook much, I haven't poisoned anyone as yet."

"I don't have common sense?" I turn and find that puts me within reach of his held-up arms. Against my better judgement, I walk into them.

He grins. "No, you don't. You're too damn prickly trying to justify yourself that you can't see what a good fit we are. Relax, let's take this one step at a time. We have tonight. Tomorrow can look after itself."

"One more night, Road, and I may not want to lose you."

After holding my eyes for a moment, he sighs. "Back atcha, babe. Back atcha."

He lowers his head, his lips hovering above mine, giving me a chance to walk away, the option to say this isn't what I want. The problem is, there's nothing at this moment I want more. I don't just want him here so I can relax and sleep, I want Road, the man, in my bed.

"What have you done to me, Road?"

"I don't know," his lips lower more, "but you've got me tied in knots too, if that's any help."

This morning we'd come together without the need for words. Now, once his mouth completes its descent and we start to devour each other's mouths, we go silent again.

His scent fills my nostrils, his taste mingles with mine on my tongue. The surprising softness of his lips is the touch I'm starting to cherish. I close my eyes and just feel.

The kiss is sweet, gentle at first, then we both up the pace and it becomes more demanding until we break apart, both breathing fast.

No words are needed. My hands move to his cut and his go to mine. In unison, we slide off our leathers, then turn and reverently lay them neatly down. Turning back, mutual smirks adorn our faces.

We undress each other in silence, his actions matching mine. We both fold to remove our boots as if performing a chorcographed dance. It's not long before we're standing in front of each other completely naked. I take a moment to feast my eyes on all the perfection which is Road. From his varied tats to the way his impressive cock juts from his neat pubic hair, it reminds me there are definite benefits to being female and straight.

I take hold of his cock, my hand clasping and stroking it firmly, making him hiss and toss back his head in appreciation.

There's power in my touch, and in the word I speak, "Mine."

He acknowledges the control I have. "Yours."

Another hiss, then his head rolls forward again. "And that pussy is mine."

"Then I think you ought to fill it."

A slight tug on his cock has him moving with me to the

bed. I lose my grip when we tumble onto it. I'm torn, wanting him in my mouth, but also wanting pleasure myself. A conundrum rapidly solved when I push him onto his back, then turn around, my pussy hovering above his lips, and my face descending to his throbbing appendage.

Placing his hands around my hips, he pulls me down to him.

Oh God. For a moment I forget what I'm doing, then I'm sucking, licking, nibbling, trying to take him as far down as I can, my actions spurred by the reciprocal movements of his lips and tongue on my clit. Then his tongue probes inside me, and I rock, trying to ride his mouth.

It doesn't take long before I'm close to coming, and his dick is thickening in preparation to blow.

Rolling off, I lie on my back, instructing, "I want to come with you inside me."

"I'll get a—"

"You clean?"

"Yup."

"I'm on the shot."

It's a sign of how much we trust each other that he doesn't hesitate, but instead of taking what I'm offering, he rolls me again and pulls me up on my knees.

Oh fuck, yeah.

My thought repeated as he enters into me in one long slide. It's just what I needed as it forces the air to leave my lungs.

There's nowhere for me to go. His hand is wrapped around my stomach, and all I can do is balance on my hands and take what he's giving me as he sets up a punishing rhythm. Of course I know ways of getting loose, but there's nowhere I'd rather be. I love being fucked this way, feeling him so deep inside of me, and somehow managing to reach that spot which has me tightening and feeling out of control.

"Yes, Road. Yes," I encourage him.

"You feel so fuckin' good."

So does he. My legs are quivering as I admire his stamina, my stomach clenches, and then, with a scream I try to swallow down, I'm coming. But he hasn't, not yet. He picks up his pace, thrusting and hammering in. *Jesus H Christ, I'm coming again.*

This time, when I clench around him, he grunts deliciously, and I feel him emptying himself inside me, then leaning his chest over my body as though reluctant to let go.

"First time I've ever gone bare."

"Me too." Well, let a man bare inside me, but it seems he knows what I mean. "Which means I need to—"

"You stay here."

"Road, I'm going to get a mess all over the bed."

"Hold your legs up in the air or something." He laughs, pulling out and cupping his hand to my pussy as though trying to keep the cum in there as I roll onto my back.

I'm laughing as he leaves the bed, goes to the bathroom them comes back with a washcloth. I'm exhausted, so allow him to clean me up.

"I think I need a shower else I'll leak all over the bed."

"Romantic, aren't you?" But he holds out his hand in invitation. I take it, using it to help me pull myself up straight.

"My legs are still shaking," I admit, following him into the bathroom.

It's a squeeze in my small shower, but we make it work. He washes my short bob, I shampoo his long locks. Then, when we've dried off, I use the blow dryer I normally ignore for myself and comb the tangles out of his hair.

"And this," I tell him, when he winces as I pull at a knot, "is why I keep my hair short."

"Preference or habit? Because you were in the military?"

"Preference. I could never be bothered with all the grooming."

"Do you mind mine?"

"Your hair? You're joking right? I love it."

There isn't a lot about Road I dislike. In fact, I can think of nothing at all, I muse, as we get into bed, him pulling my back against his front as though we've been doing it for years.

"Tomorrow—" I start.

"Can look after itself. Swift, whatever happens, I'll be there for you, okay?"

"Do you think you'll still be a member?"

"It partly depends on how badly I've fucked things up with Drummer. And it depends on you."

"On me?"

"Yeah." He pauses as though to gather his thoughts. "It was odd coming to this chapter and seeing a woman sitting at the table. At first, I thought you were some sort of PA or something like that. Didn't dream you were a member. Then I saw you take down Stormy and then was partnered with you. And fuck it, Swift, if anyone deserves their place around that table, that's you. Doesn't matter what sexual organs you have, you're an equal to any of us. Superior to me, that's for sure."

"No, I'm—"

"Let me finish? I've got this speech composed." When I shut my mouth with a smirk he can't see, he picks up where he left off. "If the decision is that you have to leave this club without acknowledging how you proved yourself, then I don't want to be part of the Satan's Devils anymore. If the choice is down to me, I'll leave too."

"I couldn't ask you to turn in your patch."

"You wouldn't be asking. It's something I'd do."

I digest that for a moment, part of me elated that he'd stay. "What about Pip?"

"Pip?" Road hugs me closer as though I'm his own personal

teddy bear. Strangely, I like that he does. "Pip," he murmurs again, "I'm not sure. I haven't been here long enough to get the measure of him as prez. But he can't fuckin' ride, Swift. That's a deal breaker for sure."

What Road has said is completely true. But I owe being in this club to Pip. If he was kicked out, would I want to stay?

I reach up and take my hearing aids out, preparing to go silent for the night. I've a lot of thinking to do. Tonight I take them out without trepidation, knowing Road's in my bed and he's not going anywhere.

Maybe I'll keep him forever.

While a week ago I'd have said I never wanted a man in my life, that I was a loner, much the same way as Stormy, already I see a future with Road at my side, and one on my own without him is no longer attractive.

36

*R*oad...

Being so tied up in trying to persuade Swift to let me spend the night, I forgot to grab the saddlebags out of my room. That's how this morning I end up doing the walk of shame again, wearing last night's clothes, and knocking at my own door, without using the key card.

It's opened by Wraith.

"What do you want?" His face is tight as though he expects me to plead my case.

"My clothes." I back up my words by pointing to my things.

The Tucson VP leans back against the dresser as I go to pick them up. "Should have fuckin' warned us, Brother."

"I know," I tell him. "But I was getting the lay of the land. Knew it would stir shit up."

Wraith holds up his hands. "Forget I spoke. You'll have a chance to have your say later."

There's no point asking him what Drummer is likely to do. The VP and prez are tight, and Wraith won't let anything drop to give me a prewarning about what's coming. I grab my bags and, giving him a respectful chin lift, exit the room.

I meet no one as I pass the next few doors, then quietly tap for Swift to let me back in. When she does, she queries me with raised eyebrows, but I just shake my head, and going into the bathroom, dress in my other pair of jeans, and put on my last clean t-shirt. I feel like a man getting ready for his execution.

When I come out and reach for my cut, I slide my arms into it, noticing Swift's deep in thought by the window, staring out. She turns as she hears me.

"The future can't be faced with more lies," she starts. "There's been enough of those."

I wonder where she's going with this. Is she preparing to tell me something about her past, or thinks there's something hidden in mine? There's not. With me, what you see is what you get.

She holds out her uninjured hand. I step nearer, accepting the invitation, and enclosing it in mine. "Breakfast?" she asks, looking down where are fingers are entwined.

I hardly dare breathe. "Like this?"

"If we're together. If you meant we're together whatever comes, then, I don't think we should hide that."

"You didn't want anyone to know yesterday," I remind her.

"Yesterday I hadn't felt we'd made a commitment. Last night, I think we did. If there's going to be issues with us being together, then I think those should be addressed now. There's been too many things brushed under the carpet as it is." She glances up at me, almost shyly. "Do you mind?"

"No." I offer a half-smile. "We can make anything work, Swift. There are two brothers, Joker and Lady back in Tucson. They're together. They both sit around the table. Don't see any difference in that we're both members, just as they are."

"At the moment."

I didn't need that reminder. But the day will bring whatever it brings. "Ready to face the music?" I ask her.

"Give me your lips, first?" She tilts her head up, and I close the distance. We make the most of what is probably our last moment of peace for the next few hours.

"You know?" I ask rhetorically when we pull apart. "I'm falling hard for you, Karen."

She starts. "I *hate* my name," she warns me.

"Do you only hate it because of the memes and the connotations?"

She grimaces and that gives me the answer.

"Then reclaim it. If you prefer, I'll only use it when we're here together."

She thinks for a moment. "I'd like that. I'm Karen, but not *a* Karen. But when others hear it—"

"Brothers will be brothers," I remind her. "They make the most of any perceived weakness."

"It's women too. Stupid that the name my mum thought was pretty thirty-three years ago now stands for something objectionable. I feel every time I admit my name, people see a privileged white woman and examine my every word and action, searching to find me wanting in some way."

"That's stupid," I tell her. But from what I've seen of human nature, understandable. "They've just got to get to know you, that's all."

She sighs. "Even then, if I say something which comes out wrong, I get 'Karen' thrown at me." Not when I'm around, she won't. "But you can call me Karen, if I get to call you Lucas."

"Luc," I correct her. "That's what my friends called me." Then I bend my head and am kissing her again, telling her softly as I raise my lips, "And if you ask me, Karen is a very pretty name." I straighten, and roll my shoulders. "Come on. We didn't eat much yesterday. Let us condemned go have a hearty breakfast."

She offers a quick grin and nudges my arm. "I don't think we're going to be hung, drawn and quartered, do you?"

I let my eyes narrow. "I'd put nothing past Blade, so please do not suggest that."

She gives a short bark of a laugh, but her merriment fades when she sees I'm still looking serious. Then deciding I must be joking after all, and keeping hold of my hand, leads me out of her room.

The cafeteria is fairly full, but apart from the clanking of plates and utensils, it's quiet, with people sitting in one of two camps. The larger headed by Pip and the Utah members sits on one side of the room. They've pushed tables together so they can have whispered conversations unheard by the men sitting along the other wall, Drummer and his brothers from Tucson. *His brothers*, I realise had immediately come into my head. They're not likely to be mine anymore. So engrossed in thoughts about where my future might lie, that I've entered with my fingers still wrapped around Swift's is something that feels so natural, I've totally forgotten the stir it would be likely to cause.

"Fuckin' hell." Preacher's eyes have gone wide. "Road, er, hate to tell you this, man, but you're about to lose your fuckin' hand."

Oh fuck. Here it comes. I don't have to wait long before finding out what Swift is going to do. She drops my hand, but instead of taking a step away from me, she puts her arm possessively around my waist to show I'm in no danger and sending another signal that causes my heart to miss a beat, a sure sign that I'm hers.

Piston pretends to look behind me and points. "Where's Swift? You left her upstairs?"

Like lightning, Swift leaves my side, takes hold of Piston's index finger and twists it back, applying pressure as she does, making him drop to his knees and howl.

"I think you've found her," Bolt calls out, laughing his ass off.

Swift lets the stricken man go, who rolls onto his back cradling his finger. "You've broken it."

"If she has it's no less than you deserve," Thor observes. "Talking of fingers, how's yours now?" He eyes the bandage wrapped around Swift's hand that the two of us try to ignore.

"I think Pip threw it in the garbage." Swift makes the joke that's on herself.

Thor looks down, probably realising how his question was poorly worded, but takes the hint about how Swift wants to play this. It's gone, time to move on.

A loud whistle gets my attention from the other side of the room, where Drummer, Wraith, Peg and Blade are seated. Turning I see Drummer beckoning me over.

Swift holds me back but only to tell me, "I'll fix you a plate."

Knowing I'd rather extend my time with her, I reluctantly nod. "I'll come find you." Then I straighten my shoulders and go to see what my prez wants.

Drummer wastes no time getting to the point. "So that's her?" He jerks his head behind me. "The woman who's got you tied in knots?"

"Yes." My shoulders straighten imperceptibly.

"Christ, it gets worse." Peg's shaking his head but giving nothing away.

All four men sitting in front of me have old ladies themselves, so Peg's reaction has annoyed me. "I don't see the fuck how?" I snarl.

Drummer takes a breath and narrows his eyes at me. "If, and it's a big fuckin' if, if she stays a member, how are we going to have two members fuckin' each other?"

"You mean like Joker and Lady?" My comeback is fast and is answered by eyes going wide. It seems they've gotten so used to Joker and Lady that the thought didn't occur to them that it was an example how two members could be together without it causing trouble.

Drummer eyes me wearily. "I'd have the same worry I had with them, when they admitted the truth and came out. Like when the bullets are flying, they'd protect each other first."

I snort. "That's never happened, has it? And if the bullets are flying, I'll be the one waiting for Swift to protect me."

Blade simply stares.

"You okay, Road?" Pip's walked over, and he gives the four at the table a nod. When he places a hand on my back, it feels like he's sending a message, that he's now the one looking out for me.

"You knew about Road and your lady member?" Drummer asks him, leaning back on his chair so it balances on two legs.

Pip shrugs. "Saw which way the wind was blowing. Well, saw Road was interested, but wasn't sure about Swift reciprocating."

"Christ, man." Blade still won't address me as brother. "It's only been a few days."

"Escaping death together probably accelerates the feelings," Pip offers, his eyes gentling as he turns to me. "You'd either end up hating or loving each other. You make a good team. Now why don't you go join Swift?"

Drummer's eyes narrow as Pip makes the suggestion, but jerks his head, dismissing me. He continues talking to Pip but doesn't invite him to sit at their table.

I cross the room, moving toward the woman who's drawing me to her like a magnet, the woman who so quickly has become important to me. Yeah, it's fast, but apparently the heart knows what it wants. I'm just fucking pleased that my feelings for her weren't one-sided. How the fuck did I get to be so lucky as to attract the interest of her?

She had been right. If the Utah brothers are going to have

a problem with us giving a relationship a try, getting it out in the open is better than keeping it hidden. As she said, there have been too many lies, if only by omission. But apart from derisive comments coming from Stormy which are ignored, most brothers seem amused rather than upset at the change in our relationship, Duty going so far as to say that they, meaning he and Honor, had seen it coming. Of course, I get warnings that I'd have to be the one to tread carefully, that if I upset Swift, no one would find my body. The observation only makes me grin.

They might not know me, but they've ridden beside Swift long enough not to think she'll let us being together affect her role in the club. Should the club continue to exist, that is.

I can't help but think that maybe if we were going to out our fledgling relationship, now was probably the best time to do it. It's just one more change, and in the scheme of things, probably not the biggest.

I've cleared my plate when Pip finally steps away from Drummer. He looks around the room, then approaches the pushed together tables where the Utah members are sitting.

"Drummer's asked for two prospects and two trucks to go to the airport. They," he jerks his head toward the table he's just left, "are going to meet the other prezes. I think they're intending on having a pre-meet before bringing them here to meet us."

"Drummer taking the chance to get his view across out of our hearing?" Snatcher frowns.

I have to stand up for my prez. "More likely he'll be giving them the facts as he's found them, saving us going back over everything twice."

Pip raises his chin at me, then continues to address everybody, his eyes moving along the table as he does. "Drummer wants the whole club, including Grinch, Goofy and Mystic in church. I'll get Gears to sort out extra space at the table, but I warn you, there's going to be standing room only for some."

"Do we draw lots?" Piston grins, reaching for the ketchup to dress his second plate of the morning, stress clearly not diminishing his appetite. He's a thin, lithe man, and I have to wonder where he's putting all his breakfast fare.

"Nah. The key players will get chairs. Road will be seated, and so will Swift and Stormy. Our officers too. The rest of you will have to sort yourselves out."

His hand rests on my shoulder and squeezes, then he moves it and does the same to Swift. He leaves to pass on the message to the next table.

Swift leans in closer. "Want to make a run for it?"

I bend my head to hers. "I'm tempted. Very tempted." I nod across the room, where Blade has got out one of his famous knives. Sure, at the moment he's only cleaning his fingernails with it, but when he raises his head and catches my eye, he smiles, and it's not a friendly one. I hide my mouth behind my hand and whisper to Swift, "You don't need to be as worried as I am."

"Why's that?" she whispers back.

"Because you don't have a dick Blade can slice off."

"Oh but I do," she contradicts, moving her hand slightly under the table so that it covers my cock. "This is mine, as I believe we ascertained last night. I don't think you wearing a strap on would be quite the same."

I choke, my head dropping onto the table as she slaps my back, but I wave her off as my coughing fit turns into laughter.

"What's so funny?"

At Duty's question, Swift and I just crack up again.

"And that's why there should be no relationships around the table," Bolt states, looking a combination of amused and disgusted.

I do notice while others look like they're in agreement with the one-handed man, Duty and Honor do not. There's something there, I'm certain of it. I couldn't give a damn unless they're hiding something because they don't think they can bring it out into the open. I frown, thinking it would be good for Joker and Lady to come for a visit, to show them they'd be accepted as Satan's Devils whatever they are.

After Drummer and his officers set off for the airport, having hours to kill, gradually people meander from the cafeteria and congregate in the clubroom. Grinch, Goofy and Mystic appear, looking uncomfortable in this environment. It's obvious they feel more relaxed and at home with nicotine-stained walls and ceilings. I notice Snatcher and Thor do their best to get them to relax, Thor rolling a joint and sharing it.

He's not the only one to get out his gear. After a short while I start to feel homesick for Tucson as the room begins to smell like Mouse's office. Neither Swift nor I partake, and I notice neither does Stormy nor Snatcher. While weed can help you relax, the four of us need to keep sharp and our heads straight. One careless slip of the tongue and Drummer would be all over it.

Pip's absent, I notice, as the time rolls on.

Swift and I play a few games of pool, but our hearts aren't in it. No one's talking much. Mystic tries to start a discussion about bikes, but for once no one's interested. Not when our futures are up in the air and serious decisions will be made on the chapter's very existence.

At last, when nerves have been stretched almost to breaking point, Brute exits the elevator and steps out into the clubroom. While the prospects don't have a clue what's going on, they're not stupid, and have picked up something significant is happening.

That's clear by the sombre expression on Brute's face as he announces, "They're back. Everyone is required in church."

37

Swift...

There were twelve seats around this table until Road arrived. Adding him made it an unlucky thirteen. Maybe he brought bad luck with him. We were doing well minding our own business until he came to Utah. Now I, Pip or the club itself could lose everything we've worked so hard to build.

Maybe we should have done what Stormy suggested, taken Road out so Drummer never learned anything. But now, just as then, the thought of ending a man just because his appearance was inconvenient didn't settle well with me, and that was even before I began to get to know him. Now, of course, the idea of Road not breathing is unthinkable. I wouldn't change a thing or go back and do things differently. Except, a throb of my missing digit reminds me, maybe that night he'd asked me, if I could have dusted off my crystal ball and known what was going to happen, I'd have taken him to bed and have let him have his drunken way with me. Maybe then I'd still have ten fingers.

When we have full church with the additional members,

this table can just about comfortably seat fifteen, with Road joining us we could squeeze in one more seat. Today though, seventeen is pushing it, and we're seated shoulder to shoulder with not much elbow room.

Drummer's again taken Pip's chair at the head, with his VP and sergeant-at-arms seated either side of him. Next comes Blade, then Red, a big man with an untamed mane of red hair sitting beside him, and next to him the man who has just introduced himself as the Vegas VP, Crash. Opposite them sit the prez and VP from Colorado, Demon and Beef. Beef, I notice, had exchanged chin lifts with Road, suggesting at one time at least, they'd been friendly. Our final two visitors are Lost and his VP Dart from San Diego. Dart being another man who seems to know Road.

The other six seats grouped at the bottom of the table are occupied by myself, Road, Snatcher, Preacher, Thor and Stormy, and sitting in the direct line of sight to Drummer is my prez, Pip.

The room is crowded. Leaning against the walls, most looking intimidating with arms folded over their chests, stand the rest of our members. Mystic and Grinch in particular are fidgeting, looking like they'd rather be fixing up engines or being anywhere but here. Goofy, well, he's unreadable, but then, despite his name, he takes everything seriously.

Once all have shuffled in and assumed positions, Drummer wastes no time picking up the gavel and banging it.

There's no preamble, if someone hadn't already picked up on a newcomer's name and position, then Drummer isn't going to repeat it. He just dives straight in.

"Never in my years leading the Satan's Devils have I ever come across a situation such as what I've found at Utah." His steely eyes glare at everybody, singling no one out in particular. "Well, a whole bunch of issues come to think of it. Today's agenda will be heavy going, so we'll get straight on with it.

First item, there's a woman sitting around this table who to my mind shouldn't be here. We'll start with that. If there is a general concurrence with that observation, she shouldn't be present for the rest of the discussions."

They're beginning with me, not Pip? But I suppose there's justification for it. Feeling like I've been summoned to a court martial, I sit, back ramrod straight and fix my eyes ahead of me. *Don't speak unless spoken to.* That adage has always served me well. From Drummer's wording and the fact they're dealing with me right at the start strongly suggest they've already made the decision. Women aren't welcome in the Satan's Devils MC. There will be no right of appeal, no one is higher than the mother chapter prez.

Demon taps the table as an indication he wishes to speak. Drummer nods at him. Demon sits forward and starts to speak. "Our regulations don't disqualify women, but the unwritten rule is that Devils are men only. We risk every old lady wanting to take up arms and ride with us if we allow a chapter to have a female member."

"Exactly," Blade confirms. I wince when he slams the tip of a knife into the hitherto unmarked tabletop and leaves it there quivering.

Drummer shakes his head at his enforcer's action, before remarking, "It's a can of worms certainly, and one we may be best to keep the lid firmly on."

Stormy opens his mouth but shuts it when Thor puts his fist in his stomach, effectively silencing him. As he doubles over, I'm left wondering whether what he was going to say was in support of Drummer's assertion. Stormy hates everyone, but me, it would seem, in particular.

The red-headed man with the appropriate name waggles his fingers. "Most women wouldn't get through the prospecting stage. I haven't got an old lady, so I've no iron in this fire. But those of you who have, can you really see them going through our probation and surviving?"

"Tash would help me bury a dead body." Blade grins widely.

"Darcy would dig the fuckin' hole," Peg observes, winking at Blade.

Making a concerted effort, I stop my eyes from rolling. *But would they create the corpse, killing without blinking?* Only this week I took out two men and while I may have since lost sleep, it wasn't as a result of killing them. No, my lack of sleep had been down to Road and I fucking. Even at that thought, I keep my face impassive.

Red raises his chin, acknowledging their contributions, but he holds the floor. "Swift, can you remind us of your qualifications?"

I start at the direct question, and answer succinctly, "British Army trained. Served eight years, made the rank of corporal. Accepted into the SAS but invalided out before I could take up any assignment."

Red nods, then his gaze moves to Drummer. "Swift's background is exceptional. If a man came to us with those credentials, we'd bite off his hand to recruit him. I understand Pip was instrumental in her joining, and that that was his reasoning."

"Pip?" Drummer queries.

"Red's right," my prez confirms. "When I met her, she got me out of a tight spot, and I recognised her potential."

"How do your members feel about having a woman around the table?" This question is from Beef.

Stormy's not going to be silenced again. He leans back out of reach of Thor and jumps in without asking permission. "Swift is as good, if not better, than any fuckin' man around this table. Me fuckin' included. I have no problem riding beside her. Hell, half the time I forget she's any different to anyone else." His unexpected support takes me by surprise, as do the murmurs of agreement from the brothers standing.

Drummer narrows his eyes, wanting confirmation. "Utah members. Show of hands if you're happy to have a woman member in your club. If you've got doubts about her, no one's going to hold it against you."

I don't look, I can't. It had taken me time to earn the trust of everyone normally seated around this table, but perhaps now they're asked a direct question, it's possible someone will show a previously hidden grievance.

"Anyone uncomfortable with Swift being a member?"

"It's unanimous," Red observes. He sits back and folds his arms. "Two questions come to my mind. First, is it right that men who haven't ridden with her, judge her? Second, if we let her stay on, what does that mean for other chapters?"

"Not having women members in Colorado," Demon pronounces, his face set.

"Can't see it in San Diego," Lost offers, then qualifies, "Unless they served with Delta Force."

"Are there women in Delta?" Dart enquires.

"Support roles only, I believe," Peg offers.

Drummer raps his knuckles on the table taking back control. "If I read you right, then if a woman with Swift's background or similar wanted to become a member, then you wouldn't have a problem with her joining?"

Red raises his chin. "Prospecting is fuckin' hard. As long as we make no allowances, that should weed them out pretty damn fast. I suspect Utah made it even harder on Swift."

They had done, I know it.

Lost indicates he has something to say, and Drummer lets him. "We've been through our regulations in the same way as Pip probably did and found there's no exclusion for females. So why change anything? I'm with Red. A potential prospect has to impress us as a hangaround even before getting their prospect patch. If a woman did impress, then I can't see a problem with giving them a chance. But I wouldn't actively encourage it. With no disrespect, or maybe it's the opposite, with respect to Swift, this life isn't for the fainthearted. Swift must have proved she'd give her life for the men she rides beside."

Again I hear murmurs of agreement from behind me.

"We've got a lot to discuss today, so maybe we can draw a line under it." Drummer bangs the gavel to show he's going to announce his decision. "No changes necessary to our regulations. If a woman wants to join, our customs would discourage it unless she was exceptional like Swift." He nods toward me. "For now, while the Utah chapter exists, you, Swift, have the sanction of the Satan's Devils to stay a full member."

He stares at me while that sinks in. I don't think until that moment I realised how much I'd expected the opposite. When the breath I'd been holding leaves me, he turns his attention to Pip.

"If you'd come to me earlier, we could have avoided having to debate her membership in public. The argument that her credentials override her lack of a dick would have been just as persuasive then as now. Which brings us to the reason why I, and my fellow prezes are so irate about this situation. You're too fuckin' secretive."

I'd always looked to Pip as the leader, like a general leading his army. He makes the final decision, and nobody questions it. But today, faced down by Drummer, he shifts uneasily in his seat.

"Point well made, Drummer." Pip raises his chin.

"Now we discuss your future, Pip." Drummer tugs his beard as he moves on to the next item on the agenda. "The regs might be grey when it comes to Swift, but in your case, they're fuckin' black and white. You don't ride, you can't be a member. That follows, you can't be the prez of this, or any chapter."

"We've discussed a trike—"

Thor's suggestion is cut off and met with disdain. The suggestion clearly comes ten years too late.

"You mentioned secrecy, Drummer. I'd like to discuss what the fuck the Utah chapter does."

Drummer acknowledges Red's comment with a raise of his chin and then stares down to the opposite end of the table.

"We deal in information," Pip says. "Primarily we deal with preventing, and if that fails, interceding in kidnapping operations. We also find out about people trafficking, and either step in if there's anything we can do, or let the authorities have the information. In addition, we aid pipelines helping people escape abusive situations."

Demon starts to open his mouth, but Drummer forestalls him. "Before we get into specifics, let's keep to the general issues." He waits until Demon sits back again, and then accuses Pip, "You're using the club as a front."

"Yes, and no," Pip starts. "Devil, Jason Deville, suggested I step in when Utah was in a fuckin' mess and needed direction. Yes, it's a cover where I can do shit and stay undetected, but information *is* the business of this club, in the same way as you run your tattoo parlours and strip clubs."

"And our security operation," Red inputs.

"Ours too," Demon offers.

Crash raises his hand. When Drummer nods at him, he asks, "On these missions of yours, is there anything to connect you back to the Satan's Devils?"

"Nothing," Pip reassures him. "We don't wear cuts and go in incognito, usually masked."

Drummer's tapping against the table again. "On the face of it, we could say Utah is just in a different business to ours."

"They think they're better than us," Blade interrupts. "They take us for fuckin' fools, them and their fuckin' secrecy." He extracts the knife from where it's stilled lodged in the table and now points the blade straight at Stormy.

"Blade." Drummer's warning growl gets a huff from his enforcer, but he does stand down. "Pip, again, why the secrecy?"

Pip blows out air and shakes his head. "I'm ex-CIA. It's ingrained in me to play things close to my chest, and to treat everyone with suspicion. It's my fault, not anyone else's, though some of my instincts may have rubbed off." I don't miss his side-eyed glance toward Stormy.

"I don't have a problem with Utah being in a different business," Red notes. "But we," he indicates Crash sitting silent beside him, "do have a problem with being played for fools. I can't count the times Snatcher's come cap in hand begging Keys to get them some information, because 'they don't have a computer guy.'" He puts the last phrase in air quotes.

"Or Cad," Demon growls.

"Token too," Lost agrees.

"And fuckin' Mouse." Blade looks furious on his brother's behalf.

The men standing against the walls shift, and some exchange sneaky smiles. Drummer of course, notices. "It's no fuckin' laughing matter. You've been wasting our time."

"Helping you too," Pip inputs. "When Devil was helping Mouse find Mariana, some of that information came from us. We work with Devil's team quite a lot."

"How you help us is a matter we'll get to in a moment. But for now, this is about you, Pip." If Drummer's tone was directed toward me, I'd want to slide under the table, despite my experiences facing down commanding officers. But Pip stares back firmly.

"We've already decided Pip. You can't ride for a start which disqualifies you, and you've been lying to the Satan's

Devils for years. A chapter can't appoint a prez without agreement from the mother chapter, and such permission was never sought. I can't rescind what I never allowed, but seeing as you stepped into the prez seat, I'm telling you to step back out."

Pip's eyes shutter.

"Now wait a minute, Drummer." Snatcher jumps to Pip's defence. "We need Pip to lead us. We need him in this club. We do good fuckin' work, and that will stop if we don't have Pip's contacts, or his ability to direct us. Have you any idea how many little girls sleep safe in their beds at night because we've prevented a kidnapping or gotten traffickers locked up? Our business isn't like deciding whether to open or close a tattoo parlour. You shut us down, then there'd be ramifications, and not of the kind anyone would like."

Drummer's eyes become slits as he stares at our VP. "Don't think I don't see you as a liar too, Snatch. For ten years you've pulled the wool over my eyes."

Snatcher goes red, but he can't argue with that. By acting as the figurehead prez, he had indeed perpetuated a lie.

"We," Drummer pointedly lets his gaze fall on Red, Demon and Lost in turn, as though emphasising he speaks for them all, "agree that the work you do is too important to bring to a halt if we can avoid it. But there are conditions to Utah continuing to hold a Satan's Devils charter." Both Pip and Snatcher sit forward, their eyes staring intently. "First, you will be under a probationary period of six months. The Utah prez will report to me and keep me updated. Weekly at least, more often if necessary. You don't so much as breathe without my fuckin' permission."

Pip gives a quick up and down jerk of his head. I think at this moment he'd agree to almost anything.

Red catches Drummer's attention. "After six months, if Utah is still in existence, the communication doesn't stop."

Again Pip nods. "Now everything's out in the open, there's no reason to be secretive."

Personally I think that's a weight off all our shoulders.

Drummer eyes the other prezes, then his stare goes to the man sitting at the other end of the table. "There's another condition to Utah retaining the charter. You, Pip, will step aside. Snatcher, though fuck me he doesn't deserve it, takes back the top seat." Now his stern gaze moves to the man seated at Pip's side. If anything, his eyes harden. "One fuck up, Snatcher, just one, and it won't be the patch you lose, it will be your fuckin' life."

Snatcher glances toward Pip, who shrugs. It looks like mentally he's already packing his bags. "I can't do this without Pip," Snatcher states. "Utah won't be able to—"

"Let me fuckin' finish," Drummer requests, and not too gently. "I'm persuaded Pip's contribution is vital to Utah. He stays at the club. For all intents and purposes he'll continue doing what he's done up to now, but as an advisor, not as the prez."

Lost looks at the man under the spotlight with sympathy in his eyes. "You can't ride, man, per se, you can't wear a Satan's Devils cut."

Pip seems like he's computing Drummer's words. "You're saying I live at the club. I keep my office. I retain my contacts and direct the chapter in what needs doing and send them out?" A bit of life has come back into Pip's eyes.

Drummer raises his gaze, regarding the men standing. "Any of you have a problem with that?"

"Fuck no," is echoed around.

"Snatch?"

Snatcher looks like a weight has been lifted from his mind. "If that's okay with prez… Pip."

Pip raises his chin at the man at his side. "Division of labour won't be much different to what it is now."

"You'll come to church as an advisor?"

Pip does a chin lift again. "Whenever I'm invited… Prez." The title directed toward Snatcher sounds odd coming from Pip's mouth, but I suppose we'll get used to it.

Drummer heaves a loud sigh. "Fuck it. We're only halfway through the agenda. Someone get the prospects to bring some beers in. My throat is fuckin' dry."

38

———

*R*oad...

I've stayed quiet, not wanting to draw atten-tion to myself, but from where I'm sitting, so far, the meeting is going well. Swift's our first official female Satan's Devil, her position now ratified. On her behalf, I'm pleased. As for Pip, well, he had that coming. Unless he gets a bike, which his lack of flesh and blood legs makes improbable and seeing he's no inclination to even ride a trike being prez is an anomaly. But apart from taking away his leather, there won't be much difference. He'll still guide the club, with Snatcher doing the day-to-day MC business, so nothing has materially changed.

Quiet conversations start around me in this informal break. When the prospects appear with trays full of bottles and start handing them out, I think we all need a moment to step back from the intensity of this meeting. It's not over by a long shot. It doesn't escape me there are still the matters of myself and Stormy still be up for discussion.

Men stand, stretch, and in at least one case, farts audibly. Swift's head swings around in the direction of the sounds, but if I was expecting a ladylike admonishment, that doesn't come. Instead she places her hand against her chest and gives a loud belch.

I notice the sound catches Blade's attention. His eyes shoot to her and narrow as a thoughtful expression appears on his face. None of the Utah crew seem surprised. Not that they should be, here Swift is just one of the guys.

It amuses me. I'm still softly chuckling when she leans into me. "You okay?"

"Fuckin' relieved so far."

"I thought I was out." Her features are more relaxed than they were earlier. Worry lines have smoothed out.

"Nah. Drummer was always going to let you stay."

She regards me curiously. "It didn't seem that way."

I nod toward the man I'm talking about. "Drummer does that. Says something to get people thinking, then circles back to what he wanted all along. Makes him a good fuckin' leader. When all's said and done, everyone thinks they came to the decision by themselves."

"I'm sorry for Pip."

"I'm not." I brush back my hair. "Devil and Pip were playing a game, using this chapter for their own purposes. Now Pip works for the club rather than the club working for him. Won't make much difference in practice, but it's a solution to get everything above board. Pip's lucky he's so fuckin' valuable. Blade wanted him kicked out or dead."

Her eyes go wide. "He told you that?"

I snort. "Nah, I know Blade, I could see it in his eyes."

"Will everyone accept that compromise?"

"Compromise was already decided on in the pre-meet, that's why there wasn't too much discussion. So yeah, it's been accepted."

The gavel bangs, and silence descends. "Who's your secretary?" Drummer enquires.

"That's me. I'm treasurer and double as notetaker." Rascal waves his hand.

"I've just been reminded that while Utah cannot put Pip back in the prez's seat, you do need to vote on the man to replace him. Put that top of the agenda for your next church, and note Snatcher is the strong suggestion of the mother chapter prez."

"Can we get that out of the way now?" Thor asks.

"I vote Snatcher prez and Thor VP," Preacher suggests. "All those in favour?"

There's a chorus of ayes.

"We need an enforcer." Surprisingly it's Grinch who points that out.

"I vote Swift," comes from Bolt.

The eyes of the woman at my side open wide. *"Fuck yeah,"* I hear her say under her breath, making me grin wide.

Drummer has gone still as a statue, then suddenly he barks an incredulous laugh. "Just when I didn't think things could get fuckin' worse." His head moves from side to side, and he bangs the gavel. "I'll ratify Snatcher as prez and Thor as VP for now, but you can discuss how this flows down later. That's Utah business."

Blade's eyeing Swift carefully, his head tilted slightly to the side. Suddenly he grins wide, points his knife toward her, and raises his chin.

"You want that job?" I ask Swift quietly out of the side of my mouth, seeing she's got a mark of respect from the Tucson enforcer.

"Yes," she replies, just as softly, with no hesitation at all.

I have no problem envisaging her as a female equivalent to Blade. A smile plays at my lips. Like him, she'd take no prisoners, or if she did, she'd have no hesitation in making them hurt, and they'd think as a woman she'd be squeamish. That she's not makes me so fucking proud of her.

"Moving on. Now we come to Stormy." Drummer's eyes narrow as he glares down the table at the man he's just named. "You made two hits that weren't yours. Two men died clean deaths which they didn't deserve. You robbed Demon and Lost of the chance to question Major and Alder, respectively. In Lost's case, there are answers he and his old lady needed, not in the least to know for certain that business is ended."

"It is," Stormy speaks, sounding unrepentant. "We checked, there are no trails, no contacts waiting to take on unfinished shit. Both chapters are closed."

Demon and Lost both sit forward, their faces carrying identical expressions of rage. It's Lost, the normally mild-mannered prez who speaks first. "Your excuse, as I understand it, is that you didn't fuckin' trust us to interrogate our captives. You fuckin' thought both Demon and I would see the lure of lucrative deals instead. What the hell do you fuckin' take us for?"

Stormy just can't help himself. His hand crashes down onto the table. "I don't know you," he yells. "Yeah, it was unlikely, but Major and Alder were experts at twisting things to suit themselves. If enough money was on the table, you might have been tempted. I had the shots, so I took them. Problem solved."

"You took the shots because it was a fuckin' challenge." Drummer's correction thunders down the table. "I don't buy your suspicions for a fuckin' moment. You were showing off. What the fuck is your problem, Stormy?"

"I ain't got a problem."

"From where I'm sitting, you have," Drummer snarls.

"I'll get the answers out of him, Prez." Blade looks gleeful as he offers his assistance. Knowing my brother, it's Stormy I feel sorry for, especially when Blade adds, pointing at the woman beside me, "And she can help. Could be useful for her to pick up some pointers."

Drummer looks like he's seriously considering it for a second, then shakes his head. "No, he deserves to have his patch taken and sent out in bad standing."

I watch as the blood drains from Stormy's face. "You... you're sending me out bad?"

I don't know the man's issues, other than he has them, but now it's been put into words, it's plain stripping him of his patch is the worst thing that could happen to him. His mouth opens and shuts, but he doesn't say another word. His Adam's apple bulges as he swallows hard.

Snatcher raises his hand. "I'll rein him in, Drummer. He's already been called back from being nomad. I'll keep him close so he can't cause more trouble."

"You think you can control him?"

"Yeah, Drum." But Snatcher's expression suggests he's not so sure.

"Send him out bad," Demon growls. "He's no Satan's Devil. What's our motto? We fuckin' ride together. Ride. Together. Yet he's a loose cannon and does what he wants and doesn't trust the other chapters. We can't afford to have someone like him as a member."

"I agree," Lost says, looking disgusted.

Red grimaces and says, "I'm afraid I do too."

"This club is all I've got." Stormy tries to put his case forward. Seeing how he's acted since I've been here, I'm surprised he wants to stay part of it.

Swift fidgets beside me, then tentatively raises her hand. When Drummer nods at her, she speaks.

"Stormy's got issues, fuck knows what they are, but though he doesn't always show it, he lives for the club. He needs us, but I think he's forgotten how much. You say he shouldn't be a member, well, I agree with that." Stormy's full on glaring at her by this point. "Why not bounce him back down to prospect? Give him six months. Let him reprove his loyalty to the brotherhood. Let him remember what it's like to be one for all and not all for one. If he can't do it and fails to regain our trust, then he's out."

"Out bad," Lost grumbles.

"Swift's made a good suggestion. I for one, could live with that." Red looks at her admiringly.

A slow grin spreads across Drummer's face. "Knew there was a reason we allowed women members," he starts, pausing for the laughter that follows. "Demon and Lost were the ones wronged. If they're happy with that suggestion, then I'll go along with it."

Stormy's mouth drops open. I can't see why he's upset. Sure, six months being at everyone's beck and call isn't anything anyone would volunteer for, but it's better than being sent out bad, or losing your life.

"I could go for that on the condition he gets a beatdown," Demon suggests after giving it some thought.

Drummer eyes the men standing, and slowly a smirk appears on his face. "I've got a feeling we can leave that to the Utah members. And if anyone's thinking of holding their punches, Stormy came close to losing you your charter."

From the sounds around me, Stormy is in for a world of hurt. To my mind, he deserves the lesson he's going to receive.

"Right. Prospect." Drummer jerks his chin toward, and then pointedly to the door. "Leave us. Prospects are not allowed in church." Drummer's smirk broadens as he reminds him. Stormy, taken by surprise, opens his mouth as if he's going to say something, then he snaps it back shut. While multiple pairs of narrowed eyes stare at him, slowly he places his palms on the tabletop and pushes himself to his feet. He throws a glare toward Swift, then goes to the door and opens it. It slams loudly behind him.

Drummer brushes his hand down his beard. "You sure you can control him, Snatcher?" But it seems he's not expecting an answer, as he moves on. "Now we come to Road."

Momentarily, Swift's hand lands on my thigh and squeezes it.

"Road lied by omission." Drummer's eyes hold mine. "I sent Road to Utah as I sensed something was wrong in this chapter. As soon as Road arrived, he should have told me everything."

"Er, I had his phone. I was the one texting you, Drummer."

"I know that, Pip. I'm not fuckin' stupid. But you gave him his phone back, and he still kept quiet." He lets that sink in for a moment. "What have you got to say for yourself, Road?"

I lean forward, placing my clasped hands on the table. "My initial reaction was to clue you in, Drummer. But Pip asked me to give Utah a chance, to see what happens here. Once I knew Stormy had been responsible for those hits, I knew there'd be a fuckin' shitstorm. Then I went out on a hostage rescue and knew I couldn't be responsible for that type of good work having to stop. I was caught between a rock and a hard place. I didn't know what your reaction would be, or what would happen if you split the chapter up."

"In other words, you didn't trust me. You didn't come to me and talk it out."

I huff. "To be honest, I got a little tied up."

"Quite literally," Bolt puts in, which starts a few chuckling, adding under his breath, "Hog-tied," making Honor and Duty snort.

Even Drummer can't stop his mouth quirking, but he recovers fast. "As an aside," he purses his lips, "is that business done and dusted or are there any loose ends?"

The question is directed at me, so I tell him what I know. "There could have been a woman involved." Drummer looks up then back down. "But the guys here are trying to find out whether there is, and if so, who she is."

"No progress yet," Duty confirms, while Honor nods. "But we'll keep digging. Anyone involved in kidnapping Swift will wish they'd never been born."

Blade raises his chin toward the pair, for once in total agreement with the Utah members.

After staring at them for a moment, Drummer turns back to me. "I'm not happy with you, Road. Not happy that you didn't contact me the first chance you could. But in your place, I might not have done different. You took the decision to wait and see what was what, and what would be the implications of dropping Utah in it with me. Just one question, Road. Would you have ever told me the truth?"

I try to be as honest as I can. "I think I would, but I was trying to get my head around what was going on. I wasn't happy that Pip wasn't qualified to be a member, let alone, prez, but I did, do, respect him, and understand what he was about. I worried you might disband the chapter, and though there's a bunch of assholes here, some of them are alright."

There are snorts from the men standing and Piston calls out, "Takes one to know one, Brother."

I give a quick grin, and show him my middle finger, then my face tightens again. "Yeah, I'm not good with secrets. I'd have come clean, but I wanted to work out the best way of telling you."

Drummer's head moves slowly side to side. "Knew I had a fuckin' problem when you said there was a woman involved."

"Didn't expect you to fall for a ball-breaker." Wraith softens his comment with a wink at Swift.

Swift's not bothered, she just tosses me a grin full of evil promise.

"You coming back to Tucson, Brother?"

Those five words along with the title of *brother* fill me with warmth. I hadn't expected to hear them. To be certain I heard right, I ask for clarification. "You'd have me back?"

"I voted to take your patch," Blade states cheerily.

Peg threatens loudly to gut him with his own knife.

It's good to see the camaraderie of my brothers again, the men I've ridden and fought alongside. I've missed them. But then I turn my head, taking in Bolt, followed by the mystery that is Honor and Duty. I eye Preacher, remembering how I hoped never to have to fly again, but admit that trip to Santa Barbara had been both thrilling and rewarding, and I know I'd regret it if I never had the chance to go on such a mission again. Piston's a joker, Rascal seems a good sort. Cowboy, well, his food is to die for and that's certainly a plus. Thor and Snatcher, I can both respect. Even Grinch, Goofy and Mystic have already become friends. As for Swift, I don't want to leave her, and know she'd find Tucson too frustrating for a woman of her skills. If I stay, I'd be road captain. A position I never thought I'd have, and one which suits me down to the ground. And here there are fewer reminders of the sport in which I can no longer take part. Also here, is that Kawasaki ZX14R.

"What are you thinking?" Swift leans into me, asking quietly.

"About staying because of the Kawasaki," I tell her with a wink.

Her punch to my arm has me reeling but grinning all the same. The real reason I'd stay is her.

I raise my chin at my Tucson brothers. "I think Utah is far enough out of Blade's range, so if the offer's still open, I'd like to request a transfer."

"Be fuckin' glad to have you, Brother." Now I throw chin at Snatcher.

Blade won't let my comment drop, "Oh, oh, he's too scared

of the big bad enforcer to come home. Little baby going to stay here with his mommy." He's smirking.

I feel Swift bristle, and grin. If those two get into it, my money would be on her.

"Nah," I fix my eyes on Blade, "I just prefer my enforcers with balls, even if they don't have a dick."

Blade snorts and points his knife at me. "Later, *Brother*," he promises.

Ignoring the to-and-fros of the lighthearted insults, Drummer's eyeing me carefully, then his eyes go to the woman at my side, and again he shakes his head. "Fuckin' women. Always at the heart of everything. Wraith, what d'you reckon, transfer request agreed or denied?"

Wraith, the bastard, keeps me hanging, giving me a careful look of his own. "You sure about this, Brother?"

I glance at Swift, wink, then tell them seriously, purposefully widening my eyes, "They've given me a ZX14R."

Peg looks completely disgusted, but the other three bellow laughs.

"Transfer request agreed," Drummer states. "Tucson clearly is no longer up to Road's speed. Snatcher, we'll do the paperwork later." He wipes a hand over his face, then picks up the gavel. "On that note, church is fuckin' over."

"You alright?" Swift asks as I continue to sit while everyone else starts to walk out.

"What? Yeah." Truthfully, I'm dealing with a surprisingly sharp pang of regret. Tucson had been my home for a third of my life, and I've made friends there. Utah is a very different club. Apart from Swift, there are no women to bring out the brothers' softer sides and certainly no children. Of course saying goodbye to my past is going to be hard.

I notice Drummer walking toward me. "If you want my opinion, I think you've made a good choice, Road. You need a new challenge in your life, and Utah will provide you with that. As will your woman, I suspect." He raises his chin at Swift. "And as for your man," he comments to her, "go easy on him."

She grins at my now ex-prez. "You're leaving him in safe hands."

"As for hands," he nods down at her right, "fuckin' shame losing a finger. I was sorry to hear about that."

She grimaces and raises her chin. There's not really anything more to be added about that.

"How's the leg, Brother? I see you're not using the stick."

Seeing Peg frown, I try and put his mind at rest. "I'm taking it carefully, Peg. Probably done a bit too much with it the last few days, but I've strapped it up."

"I'll get him working in the gym," Swift promises.

"Want me to share the exercises he should be doing?"

"Hey, *he's* here," I remind them both. "One thing, Peg, she'll be prettier than you to look at when I'm doing leg presses."

Peg stares at Swift, then barks a loud laugh. "Can't argue with that. Why don't you both come on down to Tucson soon? You'll be wanting to pick your stuff up. I reckon Darcy and Sam would like to meet Swift."

"I'll fly you down if you want?" Preacher, who's just walking out, overhears and shouts.

Drummer shakes his head and rolls his eyes. Then his gaze sharpens. "That a Satan's Devils' plane, Brother?"

Preacher, put on the spot, can't do anything but nod. Drummer just gives a knowing smile. "Well, that's fuckin' good to know."

"Are you hanging around?" I'd appreciate a catch up without being in fear of losing my patch or my life.

But I'm to be disappointed. "Nah. We'll see the others head off to the airport and then get on our bikes and head home. Christ knows what Eli and Zane are getting up to. Sam will appreciate having me there to take some of the load."

"Olivia and Zoey will be running rings around Sophie as well." Wraith's loving parental smile reminds me how much his daughters have him wrapped around their little fingers.

"Noah will be good, but Lisa's teething, so Darcy will be glad to see me back." Peg's voice brims with pride.

"Mason and Sabrina will be behaving themselves if they know what's good for them."

"Blade, we all know your kids get away with murder," Peg scoffs.

"Yeah, so? I've taught them well."

The enforcer's retort makes me snort.

A new voice joins in. Another I know well. "Might not have kids, but I've a woman and a dog who'll be missing me. Road, I'm off too, but before I go, I got some info for you." Beef glances at Swift, then winks at me. "Reckon it's exactly what you need."

Taking the piece of paper from the Colorado VP, I thank him and pocket it.

The next few minutes are back slaps, hellos to Swift and goodbyes to me. Dart and Lost come over for a couple of minutes as well.

"Don't worry, we'll take good care of him." Snatcher, having left at the end of the meeting with Pip, has now returned. His words remind me that I'm not losing brothers, but gaining new ones.

Then, finally, the visiting prezes and assorted officers leave, and the clubhouse seems strangely quiet and empty.

39

*S*wift...

Despite our misgivings this time yesterday, we'd all survived. Well, all of us except Stormy. When we exited the meeting, it had been to find Stormy had taken off on his bike, leaving his cut behind. I can't say I was surprised. He'll have some decisions to make about turning his life back around. If he really wants to continue as a member, he'll need to return and take his punishment like a man.

It won't be the beatdown he'll be afraid of, Stormy's made of stronger stuff than that. It will be whether he can hack it as a prospect for six months. He'll know he'll have to prove himself all over again, and that includes jumping to every reasonable or unreasonable request made of him, while being respectful to the members at all times. In order to do that he'll need a personality transplant. It makes me wonder how he got through his time as a prospect when he first patched in.

I think we'll see him again, but none of us are entirely certain. If he doesn't return, well, he'll be out bad for certain.

Yesterday's meeting had been mentally exhausting. The outcomes, I believe, were positive and well decided by the mother chapter prez. I may previously have only known him by name, now having met him, I've a lot of respect for him. We're certainly all breathing easier now everything's out in the open, not least myself.

Pip doesn't seem unhappy with his loss of status, but then Snatcher always did run the day-to-day shit of the club.

After our visitors had left the clubhouse, Cowboy had thrown burgers and brats on a barbeque as no one really wanted to sit down and eat. We were all processing how the changes would affect us. I, for one, was happy we no longer had to hide what we did at the club, and I knew we'd have a much better relationship with the other chapters, and maybe get involved with them more. I'm looking forward to going to Tucson when we eventually go down to collect Road's stuff, riding alongside him as an equal, not having to pretend I'm an old lady. I'm not at all certain whether I could have pulled that off.

First thing this morning, Road had headed out. His excuse was that he needed to hit a store to replenish his clothing supply, intending to stock up on some new t-shirts, jeans and other essentials. His reasoning had made sense, but I thought he might also have wanted to have some time to himself. It's a big deal leaving brothers behind who clearly mean so much to him. Understanding on occasion we all need space, I'd refrained from commenting.

The meeting yesterday had cemented Road and my roles in the club. Of course, it will need an official vote, but from the comments I've picked up, no one here would object to my taking on the role as enforcer. The only one who might have voted no, is not currently a member. It might seem strange for a woman to want such a job, but I know I could do it well. I'm familiar with every torture and interrogation technique known to mankind and then some, and have had many of those methods turned on myself.

Which means I know their effectiveness and when to apply them. Though I hope it's not too often, if my skills are called for, I'll have no hesitation in using them, not when the goal is protecting my club. I'm also a disciplinarian and will have no hesitation in enforcing the Satan's Devils' rules.

I pour myself another cup of tea while I'm waiting for Road to return, a smile coming to my lips as I remember how tender he'd been while making love last night. Making love had been the only way to describe it. It transcended sex. Afterwards, we'd talked, discussing tentative plans about our future. I suggested his moving into my house. After just a week, it might seem too soon to other people, but both of us agreed it felt right. We've gone through so much together, there's little I don't know about him, and so far, I've found nothing I don't like. If we're going to give us a try, then living together seems a logical step.

Children? Our far-ranging topics for discussion covered that, and even there, both of us seem to be on the same page. Maybe, but not yet, and if it's never, then we'll be fine with that. For now, we're just enjoying being a couple, something neither of us have ever had.

As though I sense him returning, I swing around as the elevator reaches the clubroom level, seeing the doors open, and out steps my man. My sharp eyes notice he's not carrying anything.

"Didn't you find anything?" I query once he nears me.

"Dropped the bags off in your room. Hey, come 'ere woman. I've missed you." He pulls me to him, and his mouth descends to mine.

"You two make me sick. Can't you limit the PDAs to when you're on your own."

Road and I both raise our middle fingers and point them toward Bolt. After taking all the time he wanted, Road pulls his head away from mine, and addresses the man who'd interrupted us. "You're just jealous."

"Jealous? Huh. Me, I like being single."

"You better watch it," Thor, who's rolling a joint, yells out. "You know what they say about Tucson, don't you?"

Bolt falls for it. "What?"

"That they've caught something from the Arizona water and got a rash of old ladies and kids."

"So?" Bolt's brow creases.

"Paladin and Beef went to Colorado and boom, an old lady and kiddie explosion was the result in that club."

Bolt's gaze settles on Road and me again, then he starts backing away, and making the sign of the cross over his chest.

Thor snorts with laughter. "That's to ward off evil spirits, don't think it works if Road's already infected us."

"Nah, never. No fuckin' way. I'm not getting caught in any old lady trap."

Road speaks quietly into my ear. "Think we ought to start looking for a woman to push Bolt's way."

I thump him on the shoulder. "Stop it. No matchmaking, Road. You'll only perpetuate that rumour about the Arizona club."

He chuckles. "Hey, you busy today?"

"Nah, it's quiet and Honor and Duty have it covered in the comms room. What do you want?" I waggle my eyebrows suggestively.

"Not that. Well, not right now," he corrects. "That's something we'll save for later. Now, I want you to come somewhere with me."

"You going to tell me where?" He's caught my interest.

"I'd rather not."

He'd rather I don't ask, that's obvious. My eyes narrow. "Not the courthouse."

"What?" His eyes go wide in shock. "No. What? Hell no."

I pretend to be upset. "You don't want to marry me then?"

"What?" He's gone red and flustered. "No, yes. Wait. That's it. We should wait."

I can't hold my laughter in anymore. "I was kidding with you."

He looks upward for a moment. "Thank you, God." Then his twinkling eyes come back to mine. "So, you coming?"

While I don't much care for being kept in the dark, it seems Road's got something planned as a surprise, something I think he's excited about. So, for once, and trusting him, I don't ask questions, just take the elevator down with him, and once outside, start heading for my bike.

Road grabs my hand and gives a little tug. "I'd prefer to take the truck."

I stare at him for a moment but see no point in objecting. Climbing into the passenger seat, I settle in for the mystery drive.

We head out of the city and take I-15 heading north. After we've been driving for an hour, having expected a short journey, I can't stop myself asking, "Where the fuck are we going, Road?"

"Er, Salt Lake City," he tells me.

"But that's three hours away."

"So, you said you weren't busy?"

"I thought you meant into town or somewhere, not halfway across the state. Why are we going there, Road?"

"Would you believe me if I said there was a bike I wanted to look at?" His glance toward me is shifty.

There isn't, and there's a good reason why. "No, because you'd have just told me. I'm a biker, Road, I'd be just as curious if there was a bargain to be had. So no, it's not that."

He reaches over and grasps my hand. "I want this to be a surprise." His next glance at me is pleading.

I kind of already got that. "Salt Lake City, huh?"

"Uh-huh."

Road won't do anything to hurt me. Pushing my curiosity back down and knowing we've got another couple of hours of driving time, I stare out at the scenery for a while, then rest my head back and doze. Yes, it had been a stressful day yesterday, and afterward, Road had worn me out until late into the night.

I must drift off completely, as the jolting of the truck jerks me awake with a start. I see we haven't come to the city proper, in fact we seem to be pulling into a farm. No, not a farm. *Are those kennels?*

The barking of numerous dogs tells me I'm right on the money. I just can't think what we've come here for.

As Road parks and I open the door, the scent of the country—and dogs—assails me. I look around, always wary of any new situation, but there doesn't appear to be any threat here, only a middle-aged woman approaching. Despite her non-threatening appearance, my training makes me examine her carefully, noting her hair's tied up in a messy bun and her t-shirt is awry, as though she's just been roughhousing with some of the pets she seems to have.

The mystery deepens as to why we're here. *Is she a friend of Road's?* He's got no relatives, so she can't be an eccentric aunt, which is exactly what she resembles.

"Mr Winchester?"

Road holds out his hand. "Luc, please. And you must be Muriel? This is my partner, Karen."

She doesn't laugh, doesn't smirk, just gives me a welcoming smile, so I forgive Road's use of my first name.

"Well, come on back, and you can meet him."

Meet who? Seems I don't know Road as well as I thought as I still don't have a clue what we're doing here. Even less so when she leads us to a kennel where a beautiful black cocker spaniel with gleaming fur is lying on his side, soaking up some sunshine that's found its way into the kennel. At our approach, he bounds up and is immediately up on his hind legs pawing at the wire door and emitting little whines. His tail is beating back and forth so fast the movement blurs.

"This is him. Apollo."

Does Road want to get a dog? I frown. Surely this is something that partners should discuss, especially as he's moving into my house.

"Apollo, sit. Show your manners," Muriel instructs.

As the dog's bottom hits the floor fast, I note he's well trained. I'll give him that.

"Can he come out?" Road asks.

No, no. Don't let him out. In my line of work I never thought about getting a dog and taking on the responsibility that goes along with being a doggy mum. He looks so cute there's a risk I might get attached to him and consider a canine in my life. I notice he also looks well bred, and not one I'd expect to find in need of adoption. Not a pup, nor an old dog. In his prime I expect.

But the door's opened, and, ignoring Road, Apollo comes straight to me. He sits at my feet and tilts his head. I can't resist. Sinking to my haunches, I make a fuss of him.

"He's two years old," Muriel speaks to Road over my head. I'm only half listening as I have to admit to already having my heart stolen. *Perhaps Road did right bringing me here if he wants to adopt him.* If he'd spoken about it, I'd have said I wouldn't countenance a dog, but now that I've met him...

"The other person?" Road prompts.

"Found she was allergic to dog hair. She tried antihistamines, but the longer she had him, the worse it got." I sense Muriel tut-tutting.

"And how long was he with her?" Road asks.

"About four months."

"He's cute." I feel I ought to say something. But cute is not a good enough word to describe him. If he's in need of a loving home, I might just have one.

I stand, surprised at the direction of my thoughts. This isn't me. I don't make snap decisions, well, only those necessary in the heat of a battle. In my everyday life, I'm normally cautious. I try to resist petting the spaniel any more than I already have. *I need to be sensible.* I won't dismiss the possibility, but Road and I need to consider the implications carefully, if indeed that's the reason he's brought me.

My eyes narrow as Road takes out his phone, and rudely, to my mind, places a call right in front of Muriel. My phone rings in my pocket. I frown, wondering who's calling me right now. Both of us on the phone at once would be the height of impoliteness.

Apollo cocks his head and immediately puts his paw on my leg. My phone stops ringing. The dog takes his paw away.

Then it rings for a second time, and again doggy toes rest on my shin.

Muriel laughs at my look of confusion. "Your man here wanted to keep him as a surprise. He's a hearing dog, my dear. Phones, alarms, intruders. He'll alert you to anything."

A hearing dog? *A fucking hearing dog?*

"Road?" My eyes widen and I shake my head.

"He's not run on electricity, he doesn't have batteries." Road can't keep the satisfied grin off his face as he explains. "Feed him, care for him, that's all he needs. And in return, he'll be your ears when you can't hear yourself."

Could I sleep, knowing Apollo would warn me?

"Road?" I say his name questioningly again.

"He's a service dog, Swift. Properly trained. What do you say?"

What do I say? I'm lost for words. I haven't cried since I was a child, nothing's been able to break me. But Road bringing me here and clearly having arranged to get a service dog for me? Well, it takes me a moment to realise the wetness on my cheeks is from the tears leaking from my eyes.

But there must be a hitch. People don't get service dogs that easily. "Do I have to go onto a waiting list?" I ask warily, not wanting to get my hopes up.

"Normally, yes," Muriel explains. "But as I told Luc, his enquiry yesterday came just after Apollo was handed back, and I immediately saw he's not going to do well in the kennels. He needs to be in a home. Lucas explained your circumstances, and that you needed to feel safe at night. I said come and meet Apollo and see how you get on with him, and of course, it gives me a chance to meet you too."

I'm still having difficulty processing all this. *A hearing dog?* I never considered that could be an answer for me. I mean, more than half the time I live at the club.

But Road's anticipated that too. As if I'd spoken aloud, he answers the question in my head. "I cleared it with Pip and Snatcher. No problems about you having him at the club." It's Road's turn to sink to his knees, reaching out his hand to ruffle the dog's head, and Apollo laps up the attention.

I force myself to think about the commitment, about the exercise needed... *but he'll keep me safe. I won't have to worry about sleeping through alarms, or having my electricity cut off.* Sure, he'll take work, but the benefits outweigh the drawbacks. It means I won't be reliant on Road, or terrified during the times when I'm home, and he's away on a mission.

"Apollo, in." She holds the door of the kennel, and gestures to the spaniel. He doesn't look happy about it but does as he's told. "Let's go into the office and discuss it." As we walk away the dog whimpers. Muriel looks back with a worried glance. "I really would like to place him as soon as possible."

"I want him," I tell her suddenly. In fact, I'll drain my bank account if necessary to have him.

Road chuckles and puts his arm around me, pulling me

close. Most of me is back there in the kennel with the dog we'd just left, so when Road and Muriel talk about vaccinations, microchips and other information, it washes over my head.

"Can I take him today?"

"I wish you could." She opens a diary. "Oh, look. I'm free the day after next. I can bring him down to your house. We'll let him sniff around and see what sounds he'll need to learn to warn you of. The sound of your alarm system might be new to him. He'll stay with you for a couple of days so you can see how you get on together. Then, if all goes well, he'll come back to complete his training which will be specific to the sounds in your environment. Once that's done, you will come here and stay for a few days, train together, then we can have the final handover."

I bite my lip. I, Swift, bite my fucking lip. Glancing at Road, I see the bastard is grinning, understanding I'm like a child who's been told they have to wait until Christmas to play with a toy they know they're going to receive.

What's she's said though does make sense. Apollo will have to learn the particular sounds in my life if this is going to work.

I waited patiently for my chance to join the SAS, did my two years prospecting for the club. I can wait for my dog.

I just wish I didn't have to.

40

$\mathcal{R}$oad...

The sight of Swift's face when she knew she was going to get a hearing dog will forever be etched on my mind.

Being taken unawares and kidnapped had really fucked with this strong woman's head. Worse, I knew it was going to be hard for her to fully recover when she had a permanent reminder in the healing scar that's now on her right hand where her little finger should be.

Swift needs to be in control of her world one hundred percent of the time. Knowing that soon she'd have a loyal companion to be her ears for those times when she's vulnerable would restore her confidence in being able to live her life just how she wants to.

She's in a daze as we walk back out to the truck. Eyeing the truck, she asks, "Did you think we'd be bringing him home?"

"Yeah. I didn't think it through. I didn't realise how much was involved, but him having specific training makes sense."

She glances over her shoulder, then at me. "I hate leaving

him there, but just as I was trained, he needs to be the best he can. This process will allow me to have confidence in him, you know?"

Placing my hand under her chin, I turn her face up to me. "In the meantime, you'll have me." She'll always have me if I have any say in it, so I hope she understands what I mean.

A twinkle appears in her eyes. "So you'll be my dog, allow me to pet you and groom you, get some practise in for when I bring him home?"

I smirk. "I've never been into puppy play before, but I'll give it a try for you."

She snorts, then tilts her head, half closing her eyes as though considering it.

I bark a laugh. "Come on, let's get back."

With one last longing look thrown over her shoulder, Swift swings herself up into the truck. As I go to start the engine, her hand rests on my arm.

"I didn't think I needed anyone, Road. Thought having somcone in my life would steal my energy, would stop me being able to concentrate one hundred percent on the things I have to do. What I never dreamed of was meeting someone like you. You don't take, you don't consume me. You just make things easier. With you I feel I could be more, not less."

If that's my role for the rest of my life, I'm not going to complain. This works two ways. "Swift, babe, I told you before, you complete me. You make me want to be better."

This time, when she leans back her head and closes her eyes, a small smile plays on her lips. As I drive, I spare a look her way, noticing some of the worry lines on her face have eased.

I put that smile there.

I vow that's what I'll spend the rest of my days doing, if she'll let me.

"So?" Pip's in reception when we arrive back at the clubhouse and breaks off from his conversation with Gears. I notice the ex-prez looks somehow right without his cut, as if the leather was wrong on him. He certainly hasn't appeared to resent the change.

Swift looks from me to him, her eyes narrowing as she realises Pip knows exactly where we've been, but then shrugs and fills Pip in. "I'm getting him. Well, so I hope." Animatedly she explains what the process will be.

Pip listens and nods in all the right places, sparing a few amused glances my way.

Men start to pass us, heading for the cafeteria. I wait until Swift finishes talking to Pip, then suggest we too should get some food.

Every black cloud has a silver lining, they say. Well, that's true today. The delicious aromas had alerted me Cowboy was having a bad day, and I'm not surprised to find there's a fucking three-course gourmet meal on offer.

"I wish there was something we could do for him," I murmur into Swift's ear.

She glances over to the counter where Cowboy's plating up amazing looking and smelling food. "I don't think there's anything that will take his hurt away."

As I tuck into my beef wellington, cooked to perfection, a mushroom duxelles sitting atop of a prime filet steak, encased in light and buttery puff pastry, I muse Cowboy should be running his own restaurant, not here, cooking for the likes of me.

"It hits Cowboy harder some days," Swift confides. "I think hearing the Tucson members talking about their kids and old ladies brought home to him what he's missing."

Knowing Cowboy's story, I wish there was some way we could bring him peace. Of course, it might just be that I'm in that sickening place where I want everyone to be as happy as me. So, I'll never raise the champion's cup, but that no longer matters to me. How can that compare to saving people's lives and doing that with Swift beside me?

"Let's go back to your house tonight." I know I'm challenging her, that she's wary of returning, even with me. We'd slept in her room at the clubhouse the last couple of nights, but her home is something she needs to face.

"Something may come up. I'd rather be here." That she won't meet my eyes shows she's grasping for excuses.

"I'll be with you." I signal with my eyes my place is by her side, and I'll never leave.

Thoughtfully, she puts food into her mouth, chews and swallows. After a moment, she turns to face me, and a hesitant word comes out of her mouth. "Okay."

An hour or so later, stomachs filled and feeling completely replete, we ride side by side through the streets of the city, turning into the driveway to the single-storey house on the outskirts of town. I take a moment to breathe in the fresh air, then turn to the house as though I've not seen it before.

Of course I've been here, but I wasn't in the state of mind at that point to take it in, more intent on searching for clues as to who had taken Swift and where she could be. I try to push that out of my mind now and instead concentrate on the house which I hope will become my permanent home too.

"You did well. It's a great place," I tell her.

She aims a remote and the double garage door starts to rise, then we turn our bikes and paddle walk them inside, drawing up alongside her jeep.

With my arm around her, we walk to the door that leads to the kitchen, and I can feel her shaking.

"Nothing's going to happen, Swift," I say firmly, taking off my cut and finding a hook to hang it on. Then I kick off my boots. There's just something about this place that immediately relaxes me.

She's heard my words but doesn't acknowledge them.

I give her space to process her thoughts and look around. Swift's room at the clubhouse is bare, utilitarian. Here, there are photos dotted around. I point to one. "Your folks?"

"Yeah. That's my mum and dad. And my Uncle Bob. He was the one who encouraged me to follow my dreams."

I take a closer look. Uncle Bob looks like a soldier himself, I notice. Her mom is petite and fair, and her dad is clearly where she got her looks from. She's got the same shaped nose and dark colouring.

"I'll need to go visit them soon. Would... would you come with me?"

I'd like nothing more than to meet her folks and be introduced to them as her man. "They going to be happy that you're with someone like me?"

"Mum will love you." She grins. "She's got a thing for men with long hair."

I lean into her. "She's going to be disappointed. I'm already with the only woman who interests me."

She chuckles and bats my arm. "Dad will be okay, and my uncle will question you about your intentions."

"All evil," I tell her. "Right now my intention is to get you into bed."

She shudders, a perfectly normal reaction when she eyes the room where she'd been abducted from.

I turn her around to face me. "When you've got your ears, you can take on anything, Swift. When you haven't," I shrug, "you've got me. And in time, you'll have Apollo. No one's going to sneak up on you ever again."

"Have I really got you, Road?"

"For as long as you'll have me."

"That woman's still out there. That's what worries me. That this isn't over."

I grasp her chin, forcing her to look at me. "You can take on anything, Swift. You've been knocked off balance, but

Duty and Honor were here while we were out today and have already installed failsafe devices on your security systems. Between what they set up, with me and eventually Apollo, you'll have nothing to worry about, whoever this woman is, and whether she's got unfinished business with Pip."

"I hate this. Hate feeling unbalanced."

Placing my arm around her, I guide her into the room she's trying to avoid entering. Holding her to my front, I let my hands find her breasts, small and perky, and one hundred percent right for me. As I dip my fingers into the neckline of her t-shirt and from there move them inside her bra and tease her nipples with my fingers, some of her tension begins to recede.

I nuzzle her neck, sucking that point that drives her wild, loving the moans that come from her mouth.

Putting my hands to the hem of her shirt, I soon have her top half naked for me.

"Too many clothes, Road. You're wearing too many clothes." Her voice is breathy.

I rectify that in moments, and while I do, she removes her jeans. Soon we're falling naked onto her bed, and not long after, I have her screaming my name.

It's only then I slide with ease into her wet warm depths.

Never in my life have I taken a woman bare, not until Swift. It's a whole new, forgive the pun, ball game. Each time I take her like this, I have to fight to hold off until I know she's coming with me.

When I do let go, I have nothing to compare with that moment of ecstasy I achieve with her. It's not just a release, it's an outpouring of emotion from her to me, which I recip-rocate in spades.

She's sleepy when I finally fold her into my arms, pulling her to me.

Then, my beautiful Swift looks up into my eyes. "I think I love you, Luc."

"Babe, Karen. I love you, too. You stole my heart from the moment I saw you sitting in church."

She sits up, pauses, then takes her hearing aids out. When she says goodnight, I know she can't hear me repeat it, but I tell her anyway.

I've done my best to relax her, but it doesn't work. She twists, turns, rolls this way and that. When she finally falls asleep, she drops into an uneasy dream.

I hate this. Hate that her security has been taken away and know I'll do everything possible to make her feel safe again.

I come awake fast. Alarms are screaming and lights are flashing and the bed's vibrating. I'm off the bed and in my jeans as fast as Swift. Guns appear in both our hands, and Swift has her hearing aids in. But we don't speak, and still those alarms sound. It's like waking to a nightmare.

Opening the door, I sidle around it, Swift right behind me. Together we search the house, checking windows and points of entry.

I waggle my hand, showing nothing here, seeing Swift doing the same.

The alarms don't stop until Swift hits a panel by the side of the door.

"Clear," I tell her, now I don't need to shout as I look into the guest room.

"Clear here," she says from the living area.

The backyard is floodlit, lights coming on with the alarms. Swift indicates the back door, I'm right by her side as she opens it...

"Guess you're going to have to do something about your fencing before we get Apollo," I tell her, as my adrenaline starts to fade.

"Will you just look at that? A fuckin' coyote."

We watch as the animal easily jumps the fence and disappears into the night.

As we stand in the doorway, I pull her close, feeling how hard she's breathing, and know her heart's beating fast like mine.

It's then we hear motorbikes racing up the street.

"Your neighbours are going to love you," I tell her, noting the time on my phone says four am.

"So are they." She jerks her head toward the front of the house.

As I accompany her to the front door, I stop her forward progress to tell her, "Everything worked, babe." As it would, even if her electricity was cut. Honor and Duty had modified her system so it switched to a battery-powered backup system now.

"False alarm," Swift calls out after she opens the door. "There was a coyote in the yard."

Snatcher and Thor look relieved, Bolt murmurs about being dragged out of bed by a fuckin' wild dog. Honor and Duty give her a salute as they turn their bikes around and leave.

When the sound of the motorcycles fades into the night, I give a massive yawn.

"Let's try to get some sleep."

"No, I'm awake now. I'm going for a run. When I get back, we'll both go to the club and hit the gym. You've got to work on that leg, Road."

I cock my head toward her, my eyes signalling, *Really?*

The mention of the gym doesn't bother me, I work out when I can. I think Swift will be even harder on me than Peg, she's as invested as I am in my leg mending. But if I ever had pictured myself with an old lady, it wouldn't have been one who thought a six-mile run at dawn was fun.

I suppose when I saw my brothers settling down, it was

into the bliss of domestic harmony, and that's what I didn't see as being right for me. I never envisaged there could be a woman like Swift, and instead of her being my old lady, I'm her old man.

I belong to her. She doesn't belong to me.

"See you later," she calls out, with a wave of her hand.

As she sets off, the sound of her footsteps pounding the ground rapidly fading, I calculate I can get in another hour's sleep, then cook her breakfast while she's showering. And you know what? That makes me content and happy.

I'd set out with one simple task, to make a trip to Utah and check out the chapter. Instead, I feel like I tripped into an alternate universe, and one that's perfect for me.

Grumbler

I've given this club more years of my life than I care to remember, serving as sergeant-at-arms under three presidents now. My life is settled and just the way I like it. I'm too old to change now.

I've never had a woman to call my own, nor fathered kids, and never felt I missed out. My brothers sometimes joke my motorcycle is my old lady, and I can't argue.

So when a photographer wants to feature my baby, I can't resist showing her off. It should have been simple, instead it brought complications that I never dreamed off.

Mary

I'm a frazzled single mom of a seventeen-year-old girl. Her life seems to revolve around trying to challenge me. She's not quite adult, but doesn't see herself as a child, constantly pushing at boundaries.

I spend my time trying to keep one step ahead of her, but if

I give an inch, she takes a mile. Her latest endeavour? To model for a perfect stranger. Oh, the battles we had when I said she wasn't going without me as chaperone.

I was right, something was off about the situation, but what it was took a while to emerge. I can't imagine how I'd have coped if it hadn't been for Grumbler.

OTHER WORKS BY MANDA MELLETT

Blood Brothers – A series about sexy dominant sheikhs and their bodyguards

Stolen Lives (#1) Nijad and Cara

Close Protection (#2) Jon and Mia

Second Chances (#3) Kadar and Zoe

Identity Crisis (#4) Sean and Vanessa

Dark Horses (#5) Jasim and Janna

Hard Choices (#6) Aiza

Satan's Devils MC - Arizona Chapter

Turning Wheels (Blood Brothers #3.5, Satan's Devils #1) Wraith and Sophie

Drummer's Beat (#2) Drummer and Sam

Slick Running (#3) Slick and Ella

Targeting Dart (#4) Dart and Alex

Heart Broken (#5) Heart and Marc

Peg's Stand (#6) Peg and Darcy

Rock Bottom (#7) Rock and Becca

Joker's Fool (#8) Joker and Lady

Mouse Trapped (#9) Mouse and Mariana

Blade's Edge (#10) Blade and Tash

Heart Mended: A Satan's Devils MC Novella

Truck Stopped (#11) Truck & Allie

Satan's Devils MC Boxset 1 Books 1-5

Satan's Devils MC Boxset 2 Books 6-8

Satan's Devils MC Boxset 3 Books 9-11

Satan's Devils MC - Colorado Chapter

Paladin's Hell (#1) Paladin and Jayden

Demon's Angel (#2) Demon and Violet

Devil's Due (#3) Beef and Steph

Devil's Dilemma (#4) Pyro and Mel

Ink's Devil (#5) Ink and Beth

Devil's Spawn (#6)

Satan's Devils MC - Next Generation

Amy's Santa (#1) Wizard and Amy

Hawk's Cry (#2) Hawk and Olivia

Satan's Devils MC - San Diego Chapter

Being Lost (#1)

ACKNOWLEDGMENTS

Acknowledgements and Author's Note

I'd referred to Road transferring out from the Tucson chapter of the Satan's Devils a few books back, but never said where he'd gone to. For months I've known the answer but didn't let on. I knew he'd gone to Utah, and that Utah was a very different club.

If you've read Devil's Spawn and Being Lost, you'll know I've been setting up the groundwork for this story, and I hope you've been wondering just who the mysterious Pip and Stormy were. Well, now you've got your answers.

The reactions of the beta readers and those who received advanced reader copies put a huge smile on my face as I realised I'd achieved what I'd set out to do, which was to bring surprises and twists and turns your way. Do authors like toying with readers' minds? You bet we do. If you've had a few *what the hell?* moments while you've been reading Road Tripped, then I've done my job.

I hope you've enjoyed reading about a different club and have questions you want answered about some of the characters. Does Stormy ever return and take the punishment he's deserved? What is there between Honor and Duty? Does Cowboy get his happy ending, and does Bolt succumb to the Tucson disease and end up with an old lady? Oh, there's more than enough material for a few more books in this series, and I'll gradually be bringing them your way.

What I enjoyed most about writing Road's story was introducing the kickass character, Swift. I think we can all admire how she forces herself into the male-dominated world, and now, as enforcer, she'll be taking no prisoners—or when she does, it will be hard for them to resist her methods of getting information. I can't wait to see how she grows into her new role.

With the mention of Swift, I must throw out a huge thank you to the admirable Kelly. Kelly is deaf and advised me on Swift's character and also beta read the book to make sure I portrayed her correctly. I'm immensely grateful to people who help me get the details correct, and I'm also pleased to have her join my beta reading team.

I hate to bring the real world into this note, but have to mention the obvious, Road Tripped was written during the pandemic. With all the distractions, getting words onto the page was sometimes like squeezing blood out of a stone. It wasn't that I didn't have the story in my head, it was getting it out that was difficult. Hence it was written in dribs and drabs and I had inconsistencies all over the place. I have to give a huge shout out to my amazing editor and beta team who helped me get everything straight.

All my beta readers are amazing, but Sheri and Danena deserve special mention. Without their talents at spotting where I've gone wrong, this book wouldn't have come together. Disappearing bikes and cuts come to mind, so thank you both for helping me sort it all out. Thanks also go to Tami, Alex, Nicole, Terra, and Zoe. Your reactions showed me I'd got a storyline which works.

What can I say about my editor, Maggie Kern? I was so cruel to her, showing her the first few chapters then refusing to discuss the rest of the book until I'd finished it. She was left hanging wanting to know how it was going to work out. Her encouragement was invaluable, and when she finally read the book, she worked her editing magic brilliantly.

Thank you to Martin Williams for the proofreading. A great job, thank you.

When I looked for a cover, I had an image of Road in my head wearing a what the fuck expression. Golden Czermak of Furious Fotog had the perfect model in Tyler Bland. Thanks to you both.

Dar of Wicked Smart Designs again brought the cover to life. I think it's perfect.

Finally, last as always, but definitely not least, thanks to all of you, my wonderful readers who've taken a chance on this book. If it wasn't for your encouragement, I wouldn't keep writing. I have recently received messages and emails telling me how much you like my books, and I love reading every one. A positive message inspires me to write more.

If you've enjoyed this book, please consider writing a review. Reviews are essential to us authors, and I appreciate and read them all.

This book may be done, but don't worry. There'll be another Satan's Devil coming along very soon. This time we're heading back to San Diego and to Grumbler.

STAY IN TOUCH

Email: manda@mandamellett.com

Website: www.mandamellett.com

Sign up for my newsletter to hear about new releases in the Satan's Devils and Blood Brothers series.

Facebook reader group: https://www.facebook.com/groups/mandasbadboys/

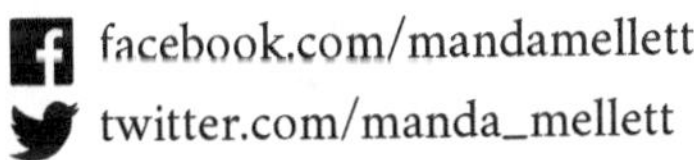

facebook.com/mandamellett

twitter.com/manda_mellett

ABOUT THE AUTHOR

Manda's life's always seemed a bit weird, starting with a child-hood that even today she's still trying to make sense of, then losing her parents in the late teens. Going from the tragic to the bizarre, who else could be unlucky enough to have had two car accidents, neither her fault, one involving a nun, and another involving a police woman?

There isn't enough space to list everything that's happened to Manda, or what she's learned from it. But by using the rich fabric of her personal life, psychology degree, varied work experiences, and amazing characters she's met, Manda is able to populate her books with believable in-depth characters and enjoys pitting them against situations which challenge them. Her books are full of suspense, twists and turns and the unexpected.

Manda lives in the beautiful countryside of Essex in the UK, the area's claim to fame being the Wilkin's Jam Factory at nearby Tiptree. She can usually find jars of jam which remind her of home wherever she goes. As well as writing books and reading, Manda loves walking her dogs and keeping fit. She lives with her husband of over 30 years, who, along with her son, is her greatest fan and supporter.

Manda is thankful that one of the more unusual, and at the time unpleasant, turns her life took, now enables her to spend her time writing. Confirming, in her view, every cloud has a silver lining.

Photo by Carmel Jane Photography